# THE WITNESS

Gently, quietly, Paul tried to make Gila understand. He told her that he could do nothing that would drive God's presence from him.

Gila's clasped hands had been dropped straight down at the side of her lap, the fingers interlaced and tensed in excitement; but when he reached this point in his argument she sprang to her feet and away from him, standing with her shoulders drawn back, her head thrown up, her chin out, her whole lithe body stiff and imperious.

"It is time this stopped," she said. "It is time you put away forever this ridiculous idea of a presence, and of setting yourself up to be better than anyone else. Either you give up this idea and accept Mr. Ramsey Thomas's offer this afternoon, or you and I part. You can choose, now."

He rose to his feet, gone suddenly white and stern, and stood looking at her as if his own heart had turned traitor and slain him. . . .

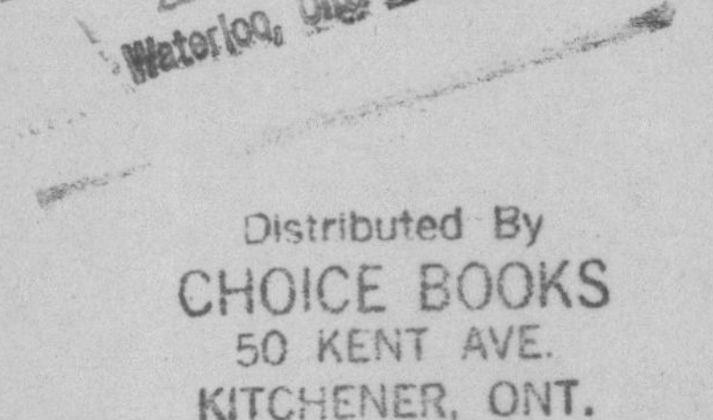

Bantam Books by Grace Livingston Hill
Ask your bookseller for the books you have missed

#65 AN UNWILLING GUEST
#66 THE GIRL FROM MONTANA
#67 A DAILY RATE
#68 THE STORY OF A WHIM
#69 ACCORDING TO THE PATTERN
#70 IN THE WAY
#71 EXIT BETTY
#72 THE WHITE LADY
#73 NOT UNDER THE LAW
#74 LO, MICHAEL
#75 THE WITNESS

# *The Witness*

*

Grace Livingston Hill

BANTAM BOOKS
TORONTO • NEW YORK • LONDON • SYDNEY • AUCKLAND

# THE WITNESS

*A Bantam Book / published by arrangement with Harper & Row, Publishers, Inc.*

*PRINTING HISTORY*

*First published in 1917*

*Bantam edition / September 1986*

Library of Congress Catalog Card Number: 83-11105



ISBN 0-553-25930-X

*Published simultaneously in the United States and Canada*

---

*Bantam Books are published by Bantam Books, Inc. Its trademark, consisting of the words "Bantam Books" and the portrayal of a rooster, is Registered in U.S. Patent and Trademark Office and in other countries. Marca Registrada. Bantam Books, Inc., 666 Fifth Avenue, New York, New York 10103.*

---

PRINTED IN THE UNITED STATES OF AMERICA

KR 0 9 8 7 6 5 4 3 2 1

*"He that believeth on the Son of God hath the witness in himself. . . ."*

I John 5:10

# Chapter 1

❋

Like a sudden cloudburst the dormitory had gone into a frenzy of sound. Doors slammed, feet trampled, hoarse voices reverberated, heavy bodies flung themselves along the corridor, the very electrics trembled with the cataclysm. One moment all was quiet with a contented after-dinner peace before study hours; the next it was as if all the forces of the earth had broken forth.

Paul Courtland stepped to his door and threw it back.

"Come on, Court, see the fun!" called the football half-back, who was slopping along with two dripping fire buckets of water.

"What's doing?"

"Swearing-match! Going to make Little Stevie cuss! Better get in on it. Some fight! Tennelly sent Whisk for a whole basket of superannuated cackleberries"—he motioned back to a freshman bearing a basket of ancient eggs—"we're going to blindfold Steve and put oysters down his back, and then finish up with the fire hose. Oh, the seven plagues of Egypt aren't in it with what we're going to do; and when we get done if Little Stevie don't let out a string of good, honest cusswords like a man then I'll eat my hat. Little Stevie's got good stuff in him if it can only be brought out. We're a-going to bring it out. Then we're going to celebrate by taking him over to the theater and making him see 'The Scarlet Woman.' It'll be a little old miracle, all right, if he has any of his whining puritanical ideas left in him after we get through with him. Come on! Get on the job!"

Drifting along with the surging tide of students, Courtland sauntered down the corridor to the door at the extreme end where roomed the victim.

He rather liked Stephen Marshall. There was good stuff in him; all the fellows recognized that. Only he was woefully unsophisticated, abnormally innocent, frankly religious, and a little too openly white in his life. It seemed a rebuke to the other fellows, unconscious though it might be. He felt with the rest that the fellow needed a lesson. Especially since the bald way in which he had dared to stand up for the old-fashioned view of miracles in biblical lit class that morning. Of course an ignorance like that wouldn't go down, and it was best he should learn it at once and get to be a good fellow without loss of time. A little gentle rubbing off of the "mamma's-good-little-boy" veneering would do him good. He wasn't sure but with such a course Marshall might even be eligible for the frat that year. He sauntered along with his hands in his pockets; a handsome, capable, powerful figure; not taking any part in the preparations, but mildly interested in the plans. His presence lent enthusiasm to the gathering. He was high in authority. A star athlete, an A student, president of his fraternity, having made the Phi Beta Kappa in his junior year, and now in his senior year being chairman of the student exec. There would be no trouble with the authorities of the college if Court was along to give countenance.

Courtland stood opposite the end door when it was unceremoniously thrust open and the hilarious mob rushed in. From his position with his back against the wall he could see Stephen lift his fine head from his book and rise to greet them. There was surprise and a smile of welcome on his face. Courtland thought it almost a pity to reward such openheartedness as they were about to do; but such things were necessary in the making of men. He watched developments with interest.

A couple of belated participants in the fray arrived breathlessly, shedding their mackinaws as they ran, and casting them down at Courtland's feet.

"Look after those, will you, Court? We've got to get in on this," shouted one as he thrust a noisy bit of flannel headgear at Courtland.

Courtland gave the garments a kick behind him and stood watching.

There was a moment's tense silence while they told the victim what they had come for, and while the light of welcome in Stephen Marshall's eyes melted and changed into lightning. A dart of it went with a searching gleam out into the hall, and seemed to recognize Courtland as he stood idly smiling, watching the proceedings. Then the lightning was withheld in the gray eyes, and Marshall seemed to conclude that after all, the affair must be a huge kind of joke, seeing Courtland was out there. Courtland had been friendly. He must not let his temper rise. The kindly light came into the eyes again, and for an instant Marshall almost disarmed the boldest of them with his brilliant smile. He would be game as far as he understood. That was plain. It was equally plain that he did not understand yet what was expected of him.

Pat McCluny, thick of neck, brutal of jaw, low-browed, red of face, blunt of speech, the finest, most unmerciful tackler on the football team, stepped up to Stephen and said a few words in a low tone. Courtland could not hear what they were save that they ended with an oath, the choicest of Pat McCluny's choice collection.

Instantly Stephen Marshall drew himself back, and up to his great height, lightning and thunderclouds in his gray eyes, his powerful arms folded, his fine head crowned with its wealth of beautiful gold hair thrown a trifle back and up, his lips shut in a thin, firm line, his whole attitude that of the fighter; but he did not speak. He only looked from one to another of the wild young mob, searching for a friend; and, finding none, he stood firm, defying them all. There was something splendid in his bearing that sent a thrill of admiration down Courtland's spine as he watched, his habitual half-cynical smile of amusement still lying unconsciously about his lips, while a new respect for the country student was being born in his heart.

Pat, with a half-lowering of his bullet head, and a twisting of his ugly jaw, came a step nearer and spoke again, a low word with a rumble like the menace of a bull or a storm about to break.

With a sudden unexpected movement Stephen's arm shot forth and struck the fellow in the jaw, reeling him half across the room into the crowd.

With a snarl like a stung animal Pat recovered himself and rushed at Stephen, hurling himself with a stream of oaths, and calling curses down upon himself if he did not make Stephen utter worse before he was done with him. Pat was the "man" who was in college for football. It took the united efforts of his classmates, his frat, and the faculty to keep his studies within decent hailing distance of eligibility for playing. He came from a race of bullies whose culture was all in their fists.

Pat went straight for the throat of his victim. His fighting blood was up and he was mad clear down to the bone. Nobody could give him a blow like that in the presence of others and not suffer for it. What had started as a joke had now become real with Pat, and the frenzy of his own madness quickly spread to those daring spirits who were about him and who disliked Stephen for his strength of character.

They clinched, and Stephen, fresh from his father's remote western farm, matched his mighty, untaught strength against the trained bully of a city street.

For a moment there was dead silence while the crowd in breathless astonishment watched and held in check their own eagerness. Then the mob spirit broke forth as someone called out:

"Pray for a miracle, Stevie! Pray for a miracle! You'll need it, old boy!"

The mad spirit which had incited them to the reckless fray broke forth anew and a medley of shouts arose.

"Jump in, boys! Now's the time!"

"Give him a cowardly egg or two—the kind that hits and runs!"

"Teach him that we will be obeyed!"

The latter came as a sort of chant, and was reiterated at intervals through the pandemonium of sound.

The fight raged on for minutes more, and still Stephen stood with his back against the wall, fighting, gasping, struggling, but bravely facing them all; a disheveled object with rotten eggs streaming from his face and hair, his clothes plastered with offensive yolks. Pat had him by the throat, but still he stood and fought as best he could.

Someone seized the bucket of water and deluged both. Someone else shouted, "Get the hose!" and more fellows tore off their coats and threw them down at Courtland's feet; someone tore Pat away, and the great fire hose was turned upon the victim.

Gasping at last, and all but unconscious, he was set upon his feet, and harried back to life again. Overpowered by numbers, he could do nothing, and the petty torments that were applied amid a round of ringing laughter seemed unlimited; but still he stood, a man among them, his lips closed, a firm set about his jaw that showed their labor was in vain so far as making him obey their command was concerned. Not one word had he uttered since they entered his room.

"You can lead a horse to water, but you can't make him drink," shouted one onlooker. "Cut it out, fellows! It's no use! You can't set him cussing. He never learned how. He could easier lead in prayer. You have to teach him how. Better cut it out!"

More tortures were applied, but still the victim was silent. The hose had washed him clean again, and his face shone white from the drenching. Someone suggested it was getting late and the show would begin. Someone else suggested they must dress up Little Stevie for his first play. There was a mad rush for garments. Any garments, no matter whose. A pair of sporty trousers, socks of brilliant colors—not mates, an old football shoe on one foot, a dancing pump on the other, a white vest and a swallowtail put on backward, collar and tie also backward, a large pair of white cotton gloves commonly used by workmen for rough work—Johnson, who earned his way in college by tending furnaces, furnished these. Stephen bore it all, grim, unflinching, until they set him up before his mirror and let him see himself, completing the costume by a high silk hat crammed down upon his wet curls. He looked at the guy he was and suddenly he turned upon them and smiled, his broad, merry smile! *After all that* he could see the joke and smile! He never opened his lips nor spoke—just smiled.

"He's a pretty good guy! He's game, all right!" murmured someone in Courtland's ear. And then, half-shamedly, they caught him high upon their shoulders and bore him down the stairs and out the door.

The theater was some distance off. They bore down upon a trolley car and took a wild possession. They sang their songs and yelled themselves hoarse. People turned and watched and smiled, setting this down as one more prank of those university fellows.

They swarmed into the theater, with Stephen in their midst, and took noisy occupancy. Opera glasses were turned their way, and the girls nudged one another and talked about the man in the middle with the queer garments.

The persecutions had by no means ceased because they had landed their victim in a public place. They made him ridiculous at every breath. They took off his hat, arranged his collar, and smoothed his hair as if he were a baby. They wiped his nose with many a flourishing handkerchief, and pointed out objects of interest about the theater in open derision of his supposed ignorance, to the growing amusement of those of the audience who were their neighbors. And when the curtain rose on the most notoriously flagrant play the city boasted, they added to its flagrance by their whispered explanations and remarks.

Stephen, in his ridiculous garb, sat in their midst, a prisoner, and watched the play he would not have chosen to see; watched it with a face of growing indignation; a face so speaking in its righteous wrath that those about who saw him turned to look again and somehow felt condemned for being there.

Sometimes a wave of anger would sweep over the young man, and he would turn to look about him with an impulse to suddenly break away and attempt to defy them all. But his every movement was anticipated, and he had the whole football team about him! There was no chance to move. He must stay it through, much as he disliked it. He must stand it in spite of the tumult of rage in his heart. He was not smiling now. His face had that set, grim look of the faithful soldier taken prisoner and tortured to give information about his army's plans. Stephen's eyes shone true, and his lips were set firmly together.

"Just one nice little cussword and we'll take you home," whispered a tormentor. "A single little word will do, just to show you are a man."

Stephen's face was gray with determination. His yellow hair shone like a halo about his head. They had taken off his hat and he sat with his arms folded fiercely across the back of Andy Roberts's nifty evening coat.

"Just one little real cuss to show you are a *man*," sneered the freshman.

But suddenly a smothered cry arose. A breath of fear stirred through the house. The smell of smoke swept in from a sudden open door. The actors paused, grew white, and swerved in their places; then one by one fled out of the scene. The audience arose and turned to panic, even as a flame swept up and licked the very curtain while it fell.

All was confusion!

The football team, trained to meet emergencies, forgot their cruel play and scattered, over seats and railing, everywhere, to fire escapes and doorways, taking command of wild, stampeding people, showing their training and their courage.

Stephen, thus suddenly set free, glanced about him, and saw a few feet away an open door, felt the fresh breeze of evening upon his hot forehead, and knew the upper back fire escape was close at hand. By some strange whim of a panic-maddened crowd but few had discovered this exit, high above the seats in the balcony; for all had rushed below and were struggling in a wild, frantic mass, trampling one another underfoot in a mad struggle to reach the doorways. The flames were sweeping over the platform now, licking out into the very pit of the theater, and people were terrified. Stephen saw in an instant that the upper door, being farthest away from the center of the fire, was the place of greatest safety. With one frantic leap he gained the aisle, strode up to the doorway, glanced out into the night to take in the situation; cool, calm, quiet, with the still stars overhead, down below the open iron stairway of the fire escape, and a darkened street with people like tiny puppets moving on their way. Then turning back, he tore off the grotesque coat and vest, the confining collar, and threw them from him. He plunged down the steps of the aisle to the railing of the gallery, and, leaning there in his shirt-sleeves and the queer striped trousers, he put his hands like a megaphone about his lips and shouted:

"Look up! Look up! There is a way to escape up here! Look up!"

Some poor struggling ones heard him and looked up. A little girl was held up by her father to the strong arms reached out from the low front of the balcony. Stephen caught her and swung her up beside him, pointing her up to the door, and shouting to her to go quickly down the fire escape, even while he reached out his other hand to catch a woman whom willing hands below were lifting up. Men climbed upon the seats and vaulted up when they heard the cry and saw the way of safety; and some stayed and worked bravely beside Stephen, wrenching up the seats and piling them for a ladder to help the women up. More just clambered up and fled to the fire escape, out into the night and safety.

But Stephen had no thought of flight. He stayed where he was, with aching back, cracking muscles, sweat-grimed brow, and worked, his breath coming in quick, sharp gasps as he frantically helped man, woman, child, one after another, like sheep huddling over a flood.

Courtland was there.

He had lingered a moment behind the rest in the corner of the dormitory corridor, glancing into the disfigured room; water, eggshells, ruin, disorder everywhere! A little object on the floor, a picture in a cheap oval metal frame, caught his eye. Something told him it was the picture of Stephen Marshall's mother that he had seen upon the student's desk a few days before, when he had sauntered in to look the new man over. Something unexplained made him step in across the water and debris and pick it up. It was the picture, still unscarred, but with a great streak of rotten egg across the plain, placid features. He recalled the tone in which the son had pointed out the picture and said, "That's my mother!" and again he followed an impulse and wiped off the smear, setting the picture high on the shelf, where it looked down upon the depredation like some hallowed saint above a carnage.

Then Courtland sauntered on to his room, completed his toilet, and followed to the theater. He had not wanted to get mixed up too much in the affair. He thought the fellows were going a little too far with a good thing, perhaps. He wanted to see it through, but still he would not quite mix with it. He found a seat where he could watch what was going on without being actually a part of it. If anything should come to the ears of the faculty he wanted to be on the side of conservatism always. That Pat McCluny was not just his sort, though he was good fun. But he always put things on a lower level than college fellows should go. Besides, if things went too far a word from himself would check them.

Courtland was rather bored with the play, and was almost on the point of going back to study when the cry arose and panic followed.

Courtland was no coward. He tore off his handsome overcoat and rushed to meet the emergency. On the opposite side of the gallery, high up by another fire escape he rendered efficient assistance to many.

The fire was gaining in the pit; and still there were people down there, swarms of them, struggling, crying, lifting piteous hands for assistance. Still Stephen Marshall reached from the gallery and pulled up, one after another, poor creatures, and still the helpless thronged and cried for aid.

Dizzy, blinded, his eyes filled with smoke, his muscles trembling with the terrible strain, he stood at his post. The minutes seemed interminable hours, and still he worked, with heart pumping painfully, and mind that seemed to have no thought save to reach down for another and another, and point up to safety.

Then, into the midst of the confusion there arose an instant of great and awful silence. One of those silences that come even into great sound and claim attention from the most absorbed.

Paul Courtland, high in his chosen station, working eagerly, successfully, calmly, looked down to see the cause of this sudden arresting of the universe; and there, below, was the pit full of flame, with people struggling and disappearing into fiery depths below. Just above the pit stood Stephen, lifting aloft a little child with frightened eyes and long streaming curls. He swung him high and turned to stoop again; then with his stooping came the crash; the rending, grinding, groaning, twisting of all that held those great galleries in place, as the fire licked hold of their supports and wrenched them out of position.

One instant Stephen was standing by that crimson-velvet railing, with his lifted hand pointing the way to safety for the child, the flaming fire lighting his face with glory, his hair a halo about his head, and in the next instant, even as his hand was held out to save another, the gallery fell, crashing into the fiery, burning furnace! And Stephen, with his face shining like an angel's, went down and disappeared with the rest, while the consuming fire swept up and covered him.

Paul Courtland closed his eyes on the scene, and caught hold of the door by which he stood. He did not realize that he was standing on a tiny ledge, all that was left him of footing, high, alone, above that burning pit where his fellow student had gone down; nor that he had escaped as by a miracle. There he stood and turned away his face, sick and dizzy with the sight, blinded by the dazzling flames, shut in to that tiny spot by a sudden wall of smoke that swept in about him. Yet in all the danger and the horror the only thought that came was, "God! *That* was a *man*!"

# Chapter 2

*

Paul Courtland never knew how he had been saved from that perilous position high up on a ledge in the top of the theater, with the burning, fiery furnace below him. Whether his senses came back sufficiently to guide him along the narrow footing that was left, to the door of the fire escape, where someone rescued him, or whether a friendly hand risked all and reached out to draw him to safety.

He only knew that back there in that blank daze of suspended time, before he grew to recognize the whiteness of the hospital walls and the rattle of the nurse's starched skirt along the corridor, there was a long period when he was shut in with four high walls of smoke. Smoke that reached to heaven, roofing him away from it, and had its foundations down in the burning fiery pit of hell where he could hear lost souls struggling with smothered cries for help. Smoke that filled his throat, eyes, brain, soul. Terrible, enfolding, imprisoning smoke; thick, yellow, gray, menacing! Smoke that shut his soul away from all the universe, as if he had been suddenly blotted out, and made him feel how stark alone he had been born, and always would be evermore.

He seemed to have lain within those slowly approaching walls of smoke a century or two ere he became aware that he was not alone, after all. There was a Presence there beside him. Light, and a Presence! Blinding light. He reasoned that other men, the men outside of the walls of smoke, the firemen perhaps, and bystanders, might think that light came from the fire down in the pit, but he knew it did not. It radiated from the Presence beside him. And there was a

Voice, calling his name. He seemed to have heard the call years back in his life somewhere. There was something about it, too, that made his heart leap in answer, and brought that strange thrill he used to have as a boy in prep school, when his captain called him into the game, though he was only a substitute.

He could not look up, yet he could see the face of the Presence now. What was there so strangely familiar, as if he had been looking upon that face but a few moments before? He knew. It was that brave spirit come back from the pit. Come, perhaps, to lead him out of this daze of smoke and darkness. He spoke, and his own voice sounded glad and ringing:

"I know you now. You are Stephen Marshall. You were in college. You were down there in the theater just now, saving men."

"Yes, I was in college," the Voice spoke, "and I was down there just now, saving men. But I am not Stephen Marshall. Look again."

And suddenly he understood.

"Then you are Stephen Marshall's Christ! The Christ he spoke of in the class that day!"

"Yes, I am Stephen Marshall's Christ. He let me live in Him. I am the Christ you sneered at and disbelieved!"

He looked and his heart was stricken with shame.

"I did not understand. It was against reason. But I had not seen you then."

"And now?"

"Now? What do You want of me?"

"You shall be shown."

The smoke ebbed low and swung away his consciousness, and even the place grew dim about him, but the Presence was there. Always through suspended space as he was borne along, and after, when the smoke gave way, and air, blessed air, was wafted in, there was the Presence. If it had not been for that he could not have borne the awfulness of nothing that surrounded him. Always there was the Presence!

There was a bandage over his eyes for days; people speaking in whispers; and when the bandage was taken away there were the white hospital walls, so like the walls of smoke at first in the dim light, high above him. When he had grown to understand it was but hospital walls, he looked around for the Presence in alarm, crying out, "Where is He?"

Bill Ward and Tennelly and Pat were there, huddled in a group by the door, hoping he might recognize them.

"He's calling for Steve!" whispered Pat, and turned with a gulp while the tears rolled down his cheeks. "He must have seen him go!"

The nurse laid him down on the pillow again, replacing the bandage. When he closed his eyes the Presence came back, blessed, sweet—and he was at peace.

The days passed; strength crept back into his body, consciousness to his brain. The bandage was taken off once more, and he saw the nurse and other faces. He did not look again for the Presence. He had come to understand he could not see it with his eyes; but always it was there, waiting, something sweet and wonderful. Waiting to show him what to do when he was well.

The memorial services had been held for Stephen Marshall many days, the university had been draped in black, with its flag at half-mast, the proper time, and its mourning folded away, ere Paul Courtland was able to return to his room and his classes.

They welcomed him back with touching eagerness. They tried to hush their voices and temper their noisiness to suit an invalid. They told him all their news, what games had been won, who had made Phi Beta Kappa, and what had happened at the frat meetings. But they spoke not at all of Stephen!

Down the hall Stephen's door stood always open, and Courtland, walking that way one day, found fresh flowers upon his desk and wreathed around his mother's picture. A quaint little photograph of Stephen taken several years back hung on one wall. It had been sent at the class's request by Stephen's mother to honor her son's chosen college.

The room was set in order, Stephen's books were on the shelves, his few college treasures tacked up about the walls; and conspicuous between the windows hung framed the resolutions concerning Stephen the hero-martyr of the class, telling briefly how he had died, and giving him this tribute, "He was a man!"

Below the resolutions, on the little table covered with an old-fashioned crocheted cotton table cover, lay Stephen's Bible, worn, marked, soft with use. His mother had wished it to remain. Only his clothes had been sent back to her who had sent him forth to prepare for his lifework, and received word in her distant home that his lifework had been already swiftly accomplished.

Courtland entered the room and looked around.

There were no traces of the fray that had marred the place when last he saw it. Everything was clean and fine and orderly. The simple saintlike face of the plain farmer's wife-mother looked down upon it all with peace and resignation. This life was not all. There was another. Her eyes said that. Paul Courtland stood a long time gazing into them.

Then he closed the door and knelt by the little table, laying his forehead reverently upon the Bible.

Since he had returned to college and things of life had become more real, Reason had returned to her throne and was crying out against his "fancies." What was that experience in the hospital but the fantasy of a sick brain? What was the Presence but a fevered imagination? He had been growing ashamed of dwelling upon the thought, ashamed of liking to feel that the Presence was near when he was falling asleep at night. Most of all he had felt a shame and a kind of perplexity in the biblical-literature class where he faced "FACTS" as the professor called them, spoken in capitals. SCIENCE was another force which mocked his fancies. PHILOSOPHY cooled his mind and wakened him from his dreams. In this atmosphere he was beginning to think that he had been delirious, and was gradually returning to his normal state, albeit with a restless dissatisfaction he had never known before.

But now in this calm, rose-decked room, with the quiet eyes of the simple mother looking down upon him, the resolutions in their chaplet of palm framing, the age-old Bible thumbed and beloved, he knew he had been wrong. He knew he would never be the same. That Presence, whoever, whatever it was, had entered into his life. He could never forget it; never be convinced that it was not; never be entirely satisfied without it! He believed it was the Christ! Stephen Marshall's Christ!

By and by he lifted up his head and opened the little worn Bible, reverently, curiously, just to touch it and think how the other boy had done. The soft, much-turned leaves fell open of themselves to a heavily marked verse. There were many marked verses all through the book.

Courtland's eyes followed the words:

> He that believeth on the Son of God hath the witness in himself.

Could it be that this strange new sense of the Presence was "the witness" here mentioned? He knew it like his sense of rhythm, or the look of his mother's face, or the joy of a summer morning. It was not anything he could analyze. One might argue that there was no such thing, science might prove there was not, but he *knew* it, had *seen* it, *felt* it! He had the witness in himself. Was that what it meant?

With troubled brow he turned over the leaves again:

> If any man will do his will, he shall know of the doctrine, whether it be of God.

Ah! There was an offer, why not close with it?

He dropped his head on the open book with the old words of self-surrender:

"Lord, what wilt Thou have me to do?"

A moment later Pat McCluny opened the door, cautiously, quietly; then, with a nod to Tennelly back of him, he entered with confidence.

Courtland rose. His face was white, but there was a light of something in his eyes they did not understand.

They went over to him as if he had been a child who had been lost and was found on some perilous height and needing to be coaxed gently away from it.

"Oh, so you're here, Court," said Tennelly, slapping his shoulder with gentle roughness. "Great little old room, isn't it? The fellows' idea to keep flowers here. Kind of a continual memorial."

"Great fellow, that Steve!" said Pat, hoarsely. He could not yet speak lightly of the hero-martyr whom he had helped to send to his fiery grave.

But Courtland stood calmly, almost as if he had not heard them. "Pat, Nelly," he said, turning from one to the other gravely, "I want to tell you fellows that I have met Steve's Christ and after this I stand for Him!"

They looked at him curiously, pityingly. They spoke with soothing words and humored him. They led him away to his room and left him to rest. Then they walked with solemn faces and dejected air into Bill Ward's room and threw themselves down upon his couch.

"Where's Court?" Bill looked up from the theme he was writing.

"We found him in Steve's room," said Tennelly, gloomily, and shook his head.

"It's a deuced shame!" burst forth Pat. (He had cut out swearing for a time.) "He's batty in the bean!"

Tennelly answered the shocked question in the eyes of Bill with a nod. "Yes, the brightest fellow in the class, but he sure is batty in the bean! You ought to have heard him talk. Say! I don't believe it was all the fire. Court's been studying too hard. He's been an awful shark for a fellow that went in for athletics and everything else. He's studied too hard and it's gone to his head!"

Tennelly sat gloomily staring across the room. It was the old cry of the man who cannot understand.

"He needs a little change," said Bill, putting his feet up on the table comfortably and lighting a cigarette. "Pity the frat dance is over. He needs to get him a girl. Be a great stunt if he'd fall for some jolly girl. Say! I'll tell you what. I'll get Gila after him."

"Who's Gila?" asked Tennelly, gloomily. "He won't notice her anymore than a fly on the wall. You know how he is about girls."

"Gila's my cousin. Gila Dare. She's a good sport, and she's a winner every time. We'll put Gila on the job. I've got a date with her tomorrow night and I'll put her wise. She'll just enjoy that kind of thing. He's met her, too, over at the Navy game. Leave it to Gila."

"What style is she?" asked Tennelly, still skeptical.

"Oh, tiny and stylish and striking, with big eyes. A perfect little peach of an actress."

"Court's too keen for acting. He'll see through her in a half a second. She can't put one over on Court."

"She won't try," said the ardent cousin. "She'll just be as innocent. They'll be chums in half an hour, or it'll be the first failure for Gila."

"Well, if any girl can put one over on Court, I'll eat my hat; but it's worth trying, for if Court keeps on like this we'll all be buying prayer books and singing psalms before another semester."

"You'll eat your hat, all right," said Bill Ward, rising in his wrath. "Nelly, my infant, I tell you Gila never fails. If she gets on the job Court'll be dead in love with her before the midwinter exams!"

"I'll believe it when I see it," said Tennelly, rising.

"All right," said Bill. "Remember you're in for a banquet during vacation. Fricasseed hat the *pièce de résistance*!"

# Chapter 3

*

It was a sumptuous library in which Gila Dare awaited the coming of Paul Courtland.

Great, deep, red-leather chairs stood everywhere invitingly, the floor was spread with a magnificent specimen of Royal Bokhara, the rich recesses of the noble walls were lined with books in rare editions, a heavily carved table of dull black wood from some foreign land sprawled in the center of the room and held a great bronze lamp of curious pattern, bearing a ruby light. Ornate bronzes lurked on pedestals in shadows, unexpectedly, and caught the eye alarmingly, like grim ones set to watch. A throbbing fire like the heart of a lit ruby burned in a massive fireplace of grotesque tiles, as though it were the opening into great depths of unquenchable fire to which this room might be but an approach.

Gila herself, slight, dark-eyed, with pearl-white skin and dusky hair, was dressed in crimson velvet, soft and clinging like chiffon, catching the light and shimmering it with strange effect. The dark hair was curiously arranged, and stabbed just above her ears with two daggerlike combs flashing with jewels. A single jewel burned at her throat on an invisible chain, and jewels flashed from the little pointed crimson-satin slippers, setting off the slim ankles in their crimson-silk covering. The whole effect was startling. One wondered why she had chosen so elaborate a costume to waste upon a single college student.

She stood with one dainty foot poised on the brass trappings of the hearth. In her short skirts she seemed almost a child; so sweet the droop of the pretty lips; so innocent the dark eyes as they looked into the fire; so soft the shadows that played in the dark hair! And yet, as she turned to listen for a step in the hall, there was something gleaming, sinister, in those dark eyes, something mocking in the red lips. She might have been a daughter of Satan as she stood, the firelight picking out those jeweled horns and slippers.

"Leave him to me," she had said to her cousin when he told her how the brilliant young athlete and intellectual star of the university had been stung by the religious bug. "Send him to me. I'll take it out of him and he'll never know it's gone."

Paul Courtland entered, unsuspecting. He had met Gila a number of times before, at college dances and the games. He was not exactly flattered, but decidedly pleased that she had sent for him. Her brightness and seeming innocence had attracted him strongly.

The contrast from the hall with its blaze of electrics to the lurid light of the library affected him strangely. He paused on the threshold and passed his hand over his eyes. Gila stood where the ruby light of hearth and lamp would set her vivid dress on fire and light the jewels at her throat and hair. She knew her clear skin, dark hair, and eyes would bear the startling contrast, and how her white shoulders gleamed from the crimson velvet. She knew how to arrange the flaming scarf of gauze deftly about those white shoulders so that it would reveal more than it concealed.

The young man lingered unaccountably. He had a sense of leaving something behind him. Almost he hesitated as she came forward to greet him, and looked back as if to rid himself of some obligation. Then she put her bits of confiding hands out to him and smiled that wistful, engaging smile that would have been worth a fortune on the screen.

He thrilled with wonder over her delicate, dazzling beauty, and felt the luxury of the room about him, responding to its lure.

"So dandy of you to come to me when you are so busy after your long illness." Her voice was soft and confiding, its cadences like soothing music. She motioned him to a chair. "You see, I wanted to have you all to myself for a little while, just to tell you how perfectly fine you were at that awful fire."

She dropped upon the couch drawn out at just the right angle from the fire and settled among the cushions gracefully. The flicker of the firelight played upon the jeweled combs and gleamed at her throat. The little pointed slippers cozily crossed looked innocent enough to have been meant for the golden street. Her eyes looked up into his with that confiding lure that thrills and thrills again.

Her voice dropped softer, and she turned half away and gazed pensively into the fire on the hearth. "I wouldn't let them talk to me about it. It seemed so awful. And you were so strong and great."

"It was nothing!" He did not want to talk about the fire. There was something incongruous, almost unholy, in having it discussed here. It jangled on his nerves. For there in front of him in the fireplace burned a mimic pit like the one into which the martyr Steve had fallen; and there before him on the couch sat the girl! What was there so familiar about her? Ah! now he knew. The Scarlet Woman! Her gown was an exact reproduction of the one the great actress had worn on the stage that night. He was conscious of wishing to sit beside her on that couch and revel in the ravishing color of her. What was there about this room that made all his pulses beat?

Playfully, skilfully, she led him on. They talked of the dances and games, little gossip of the university, with now and then a telling personality, and a sweep of long lashes over pearly cheeks, or a lifting of great, innocent eyes of admiration to his face.

She offered wine in delicate gold-incrusted ruby glasses, but Courtland did not drink. He scarcely noticed her veiled annoyance at his refusal. He was drinking in the wine of her presence. She suggested that he smoke, and would not have hesitated to join him, perhaps, but he told her he was in training, and she cooed softly of his wonderful strength of character in resisting.

By this time he was in the coveted seat beside her on the couch, and the fire burned low and red. They had ceased to talk of games and dances. They were talking of each other, those intimate nothings that mean a breaking down of distance and a rapidly growing familiarity.

The young man was aware of the fascination of the small figure in her crimson robings, sitting so demurely in the firelight, the gauzy scarf dropped away from her white neck and shoulders, the lovely curve of her baby cheek and tempting neck showing against the background of the shadows behind her. He was aware of a distinct longing to take her in his arms and crush her to him, as he would pluck a red berry from a bank, and feel its stain upon his lips. Stain! A stain was a thing that was hard to remove. There were bloodstains sometimes and agonies, and yet men wanted to pluck the berries and feel the stain upon their lips!

He was not under the hallucination that he was suddenly falling in love with this girl. He did not name the passionate outcry in his soul love. He knew she had been a charmer of many, and in yielding himself to her recognized power he was for the moment playing with a force that was new and interesting, with which he had felt altogether strong enough to contend for an evening or he would not have come. That it should thrill along all his senses with this unreasoning rapture was most astonishing. He had never been a fellow to fall for every girl he met, and now he felt himself gradually yielding to the beautiful spell about him with a kind of wonder.

The lights and coloring of the room that had smote his senses unpleasantly when he first entered had thrown him now into a kind of delicious fever. The neglected wine sparkling dimly in the costly glasses seemed a part of it. He felt an impulse to reach out, seize a glass, and drain it. What if he should? What if he flung away his ideas and principles and let the moment sway him as it would, just for once? Why should he not try life as it presented itself?

These fancies fled through his brain like phantoms that did not dare to linger. His was no callow mind, ignorant of the world. He had thought and read and lived his ideas well for so young a man. He had vigorously protested against weakness of every kind; yet here he was feeling the drawing power of things he had always despised; reveling in the wine-red color of the room, in the pitlike glow of the fire;

watching the play of smiles and wistfulness on the lovely face of the girl. He had often wondered what others saw so attractive in her beyond a pretty face. But now he understood. Her childlike speech and pretty little ways fascinated him. Perhaps she was really innocent of her own charms. Perhaps a man might lead her to give up certain of her ways that caused her to be criticized. What a woman she would be then! What a friend to have!

This was the last sop he threw to his conscience before he consciously began to yield to the spell that was upon him.

She had been speaking of palmistry, and she took his hand in hers, innocently, impersonally, with large eyes inquiringly. Her breath was on his face; her touch had stirred his senses with a madness he had never felt nor measured in himself before.

"The lifeline is here," she said, coolly, and traced it delicately along his palm with a seashell-tinted finger. Like cool delicious fire it spread from nerve to nerve and set aside his reason in a frenzy. He would seize the berry and feel its stain upon his lips now no matter what!

"Paul!"

It was as distinct upon his ear as if the word had been spoken; as startling and calming as a cool hand upon his fevered brow; the sudden entrance of a guest. He had seized her hands with sudden fervor, and now, almost in the same moment, flung them from him and stood up, a man in full possession of his senses. "Hark!" he said, and as he spoke a cry broke faintly forth above them, and there was sound of rushing feet. A frightened maid burst into the room unannounced.

"Oh, Miss Gila, I beg pardon, but Master Harry's got his father's razor, an' he's cut hisself something awful."

The maid was weeping and wringing her hands helplessly, but Gila stood frowning angrily. Courtland sprang up the stairs. In the tumult of his mind he would have rejoiced if the house had been on fire, or a cyclone had struck the place—anything so he could fling himself into service. He drew in long, deep breaths. It was like mountain air to get away from that lurid room into the light once more. A sense of lost power returned, was over him. The spell was broken.

He bent over the little boy alertly, grasped the wrist, and stopped the spurt of blood. The frightened child looked up into his face and stopped crying.

"You should have telephoned for the doctor at once and not made all this fuss in the presence of a guest," scolded Gila as she came up the stairs. She looked garish and out of place with her red velvet and jewels in the brilliant light of the white-tiled bathroom. She stood helplessly by the door, making no move to help Courtland. The maid was at the telephone, frantically calling for the family physician.

"Hand me those towels," commanded Courtland, and saw the look of disgust upon Gila's face as she reluctantly picked her way across the bloodstains. It struck him that they were the color of her frock. The stain of the crushed berry. He moistened his dry lips. At least the stain was not upon his lips. He had escaped. Yet by how narrow a margin.

The girl felt the man's changed attitude without in the least understanding it. She thought it had been the cry of the child that made him jump up and fling her hands from him with that sudden "Hark!" in the moment when he had almost yielded. She did not know that an inner voice had called him. She only knew that she had lost him for the time, and her vanity was still panting like a wild thing that has lost its prey.

He gathered the little boy into his arms when he had bound up the cut, and talked to him cheerfully. The boy's curly head rested trustfully against the big shoulder.

"Floor all bluggy!" he remarked, languidly. "Wall all bluggy!" Then his eyes fell on his sister in her scarlet frock. "Gila all bluggy, too!" he laughed, and pointed with his well hand.

"Be still, Harry!" said Gila, sharply, and when Courtland looked up in wonder he saw the delicate brows drawn blackly, and the mouth had lost its innocent sweetness. The child shrank in his arms, and he put a reassuring hand upon the little head that snuggled comfortedly against his coat. It was one of Courtland's strong points, this love of little children. He grew fine and gentle in their presence. It often drew attention on the athletic field when some little fellow strayed his way and Courtland would turn to talk to the child. People would stop their conversation and look his way, and a whole grandstand would come to silence just to see him walk across the diamond with a little golden-haired kid upon his shoulder. There was something inexpressibly beautiful about his attitude toward a child.

Gila saw it now and wondered. What unexpected trait was this that sat upon the young man like a crown? Here, indeed, was a man who was worth cultivating, not merely for the caprice of the moment. There was something in his face and attitude now that commanded her respect and admiration, something that drew her as she had not been drawn before. She would win him now for his own sake, not just to show how she could charm away his morbid fancies.

She continued to stare at the young man with eyes that saw new things in him, while Courtland sat petting the child and telling him a story. He paid no further attention to her.

When Gila set her heart upon a thing she had always had it. This had been her father's method of bringing her up. Her mother was too busy with her clubs and her social functions to see the harm. And now Gila suddenly became aware that she was setting her heart upon this young man. The eternal feminine in her that was almost choked with selfishness was crying out for a man like this one to comfort and pet her the way he was comforting and petting her little brother. That he had not yielded too easily to her charms made him all the more desirable. The interruption had come so suddenly that she couldn't even be sure he had been about to take her hands in his when he flung them from him. He had sprung from the couch almost as if he had been under orders. She could not understand it, only she knew she was drawn by it all.

But he should yield! She had power and she would use it. She had beauty and it should wound him. She would win that gentle deference and attention for her own. In her jealous, spoiled, little heart she hated the little brother for lying there in his arms so, interrupting their evening just when she had him where she had wanted him. Whether she wanted him for more than a plaything she did not know, but her plaything he should be as long as she desired him—and more also if she chose.

When Courtland lifted his head at the sound of the doctor's footsteps on the stairs he saw the challenge in Gila's eyes. Drawn up against the white enamel of the bathroom door, all her brilliant velvet and jewels gleaming in the brightness of the room, her regal little head up, her chin lifted half-haughtily, her innocent mouth pursed softly with determination, her eyes wide with an inscrutable look—something more than challenge—something soft, appealing, alluring, that stirred him and drew him and repelled him all in one.

With a sense of something stronger than he was back of him, he lifted his own chin and hardened his eyes in answering challenge. He did not know it, of course, but he wore the look that he always had when about to meet a foe in a game—a look of strength and concealed power that nearly always made the coming foe quake when he saw it.

He shrank from going back to that red room again, or from being alone with her; and when she would have had him return to the library he declined, urging studies and an examination on the morrow. She received his somewhat brusque reply with a hurt look, her mouth drooped grievedly, and her eyes took on a wide, childlike look of distress that gave an impression of innocence. He went away wondering if, after all, he had not misjudged her. Perhaps she was only an adorable child who had no idea of the effect her artlessness had upon men. She certainly was lovely—wonderful! And yet the last glimpse he had of her had left that impression of jeweled horns and scarlet, pointed toes. He had to get away and think it out calmly before he went again. Oh, yes, he was going *again*. He had promised her at the last moment.

The sense of having escaped something fateful was passing already. The coolness of the night and the quiet of the starlight had calmed him. He thought he had been a fool not to have stayed a little longer when she asked him so prettily; and he must go soon again.

# Chapter 4

*

"I think I'll go to church this morning, Nelly. Do you want to go along?" announced Courtland, the next morning.

Tennelly looked up aghast from the sporting page of the morning paper he was lazily reading.

"Go with him, Nelly, that's a good boy!" put in Bill Ward, agreeably, winking his off eye at Tennelly. "It'll do you good. I'd go with you, only I've got to get that condition made up or they'll fire me off the varsity, and I only need this one more game to get my letter."

"Go to thunder!" growled Tennelly. "What do you think I want to go to church for a morning like this? Court, you're crazy! Let's go and get two saddle horses and ride in the park. It's a peach of a morning for a ride."

"I think I'll go to church," said Courtland, with his old voice of quiet decision. "Do you want to go or not?"

There was something about Courtland's voice, and the way Bill Ward kept up winking his off eye, that subdued Tennelly.

"Sure, I'll go," he growled, reluctantly.

"You old crab, you," chirped Bill, cheerfully, when Courtland had gone out. "Can't you see you've got to humor him? He needs homeopathic treatment. 'Like cures like.' Give him a good dose of religion and he'll get good and tired of it. Church won't hurt him any, just give him a good, pious feeling so he'll feel free to do as he pleases during the week. I had a phone call from Gila this morning. She says he's made another date with her after exams. He fell, all right, so go get your little lid and toddle off to Sunday school. Try to toll him into a big, stylish church. They're safest; but 'most any of 'em are cold enough to freeze the eyeteeth out of a stranger as far as my experience goes."

"Well, this isn't my funeral," sulked Tennelly, going to his closet for suitable raiment. "I s'pose you get your way, but Court's keen intellectually, and if he happens to strike a good preacher he's liable to fall for what he says, in the mood he's in now."

"Well, he won't strike a good preacher. There isn't one nowadays. There are orators in the pulpit, plenty of them, but they're all preaching about politics these days, or raving about uplifting the masses, and that sorta thing won't hurt Court. Most of 'em are dry as punk. If Court keeps awake through the service he won't go again, mark my words."

They chose a church at random, these two who had decided to go up to the house of God. High-arched and Gothic were its massive walls, with intricate carving like lace in the stonework. Softly swung leather doors shut the sanctuary from the outer world. The fretted gold and blue and scarlet ceiling stretched away miles, as it were, in the space above them, and rich carvings in dark, costly wood met the wonderful frescoes at lofty heights. The carpets were soft, and the pews were upholstered in tones to match. A great silence brooded over the place, making itself felt above and beneath the swelling tones of the wonderful organ. People trod the aisles softly, like puppets playing each his part. They bent in form of prayer for a moment and settled into silence. The minister came stiffly into the pulpit, casting a furtive eye about the congregation.

They noticed almost at once that the most unpopular professor in the university was acting as usher on the other side of the church. Tennelly frowned and looked at Courtland, who sat watching the aforesaid usher as he showed people to their seats, wondering if that man had a thing he called religion, and if he was in any way related to Stephen Marshall's Christ. This was a voyage of discovery for Courtland, this visit to a Christian church. He had scarcely been to religious services since he entered the university. He had considered them a waste of time. Now he had come to see if there was really anything in them. It did not occur to him that they had a real connection with those verses he had read in the Bible about "doing the will," or that the going or staying away from them was in any wise obligatory upon one who had allied himself with Christ. The church stood to him as to many other young pagans such as he was, for a man-made institution, to be attended or not as one chose.

The music was not uplifting. It was well done by a paid choir, who had good voices and sang wonderful music, but they had no heart in their singing. The congregation attempted no more than a murmur of the hymns. There was not a large congregation.

The sermon was a dissertation on the Book of Jonah, a sort of résumé of all the argument, on both sides, that has torn the theological world in these latter days. Not a word of Stephen Marshall's Christ, save a sort of side reference to a verse about Jonah being three days and three nights in the whale, and the Son of Man being three days in the heart of the earth. Courtland wasn't even sure that this reference meant the Christ, and it never entered his head that it touched at the heart of the great doctrine of the resurrection of the dead. As far as he could understand the reverend gentleman the arguments he quoted against the Book of Jonah were far stronger and more plausible than those put forth in its defense. What was it all about, anyway? What did it matter whether Jonah was or was not, or whether anybody accepted the book? How could a thing like that affect the life of a man?

Tennelly watched the expressive face beside him and decided that perhaps Bill Ward had been half-right after all.

On their way back to the university they met Gila Dare. Gila all in gray like a dove, gray suit of soft, rich cloth, gray furs of the depth and richness of smoke, gray suede boots laced high to meet her brief gray skirts, silver hat with a single velvet rose on the brim to match the soft rose-bloom on her cheeks. Gila with eyes as wide and innocent as a baby's, cupid mouth curved sweetly in a gracious, shy smile, and dainty little prayer book done in gray suede held devoutly in her little gloved hand.

"Who's that?" growled Tennelly, admiringly, when they had passed a suitable distance.

"Why, that's Bill Ward's cousin, Gila Dare," announced Courtland, graciously. He was still basking in the pleasure of her smile, and thinking how different she looked from last evening in this soft, gray, silvery effect. Yes, he had misjudged her. A girl who could look like that must be sweet and pure and unspoiled. It had been that unfortunate dress last night that had reminded him unpleasantly of the scarlet woman and the awful night of the fire. If he ever got well enough acquainted he would ask her never to wear red again; it made her appear sensual; and even she, delicate and sweet as she was, could not afford to cast a thought like that into the minds of her beholders. It was then he began to idealize Gila.

"Gila Dare!" Tennelly straightened up and took notice. So that was the invincible Gila! That little soft-eyed exquisite thing with the hair like a midnight cloud.

"Some looker!" he commented, approvingly, and wished he were in Courtland's shoes.

"She's got in her work all right," he commented to himself. "Old Court's fallen already. Guess I'll have to buy a straw hat, it'll be more edible."

Courtland was like his gay old self when he got back to the dormitory. He joked a great deal. His eyes were bright and his color better than it had been since he was sick. He said nothing about the morning service, and by and by Bill Ward ventured a question: "What kind of a harangue did you hear this morning?"

"Rotten!" he answered, promptly, and turned away. Somehow that question recalled him to the uneasiness within his soul for which he had sought solace in the church service. He became silent again, and strolling away into Stephen's room and closing the door, sat down.

There was something strange about that room. The Presence seemed always to be there. It hadn't made itself felt in the church at all, as he had half-hoped it would. He had taken Tennelly with him because he wanted something tangible, friendly, sane, from the world he knew, to give him ballast. If the Presence had been in the church, with Tennelly by his side, he would have been sure it was not wholly a hallucination connected with his memory of Stephen.

It was strange, for now that he sat there in that quiet room that had once witnessed the trying-out of a manly soul, and saw the calm eyes of the plain mother on the wall opposite, and the true eyes of the dowdy schoolboy on the other wall, he was feeling the Presence again!

Why hadn't he felt its power in the church? Was it because of the presence of such people in the temple as that little mean-souled professor, whom everybody knew to be insincere from the crown of his head to the soles of his sly little feet? Was it because the people were cold and careless and didn't sing even with their lips, let alone their hearts, but hired it all done for them?

And then there had been that call of his name when he was with Gila Dare, as clear and distinct, like a friend he had left outside who had grown tired of waiting, and worried about him. Why hadn't the sense of the Presence gone with him into the room? Would a Presence like that be afraid of hostile influences? No. If it was real and a Presence at all it would be more powerful than any other influence in the universe. Then why?

Could it be that he had gone deliberately into an influence that would make it impossible for the Presence to guide?

Or was it possible that his own attitude toward that girl had been at fault? He had gone to see her regarding her somewhat lightly. As a gentleman he should regard no woman with disrespect. Her womanhood should be honored by him even if she chose to dishonor it herself. If he had gone to see Gila with a different attitude toward her, expecting high, fine things of her, rather than merely to be amused by one whom he scarcely regarded seriously, perhaps all this strange mental phenomena would not have come to pass.

Finally he locked the door and knelt down with his head upon the worn Bible. He had no idea of praying. Prayer meant to him but a repetition of a form of words. There had been prayers in his childhood, brought about by the maiden aunt who kept house for his father after his mother's death, and assisted in bringing him up until he was old enough to go away to boarding school. They were a good deal of a bore, coming as they did when he was sleepy. There was a long, vague one beginning, "Our Father which art," in which he always had to be prompted. There was, "Now I lay me," and "Matthew, Mark, Luke, and John, bless the bed I lie upon; Wish I may, wish I might, get the wish I wish tonight!" Or *was* that a prayer? He never could remember as he grew older.

He did not know why he was drawn to kneel there with his eyes closed and his cheek upon that Bible. Strange that when he was in that room all doubt about the Presence vanished, all uneasiness about reconciling it with realities, laws, and science fled away.

Later he stood in his own room by the window, watching the great red sun go down in the west and light a ruby fire behind the long line of tall buildings that stretched beyond the campus. The glow in no wise resembled, but yet reminded him, of the fire in the glowing grate of the Dare library. Why had that room affected him so strangely? And Gila, little Gila, how sweet and innocent she had looked when they met her that morning with her prayer book. How wrong he must have been to take the idle talk that people chattered about her and let it influence his thoughts of her. She could not be all that they said, and yet look so sweet and innocent. What had she reminded him of in literature? Ah! he had it. Solveig in *Peer Gynt!*

> How fair! Did ever you see the like?
> Looked down at her shoes and her snow-white apron!—
> And then she held onto her mother's skirtfolds,
> And carried a psalmbook wrapped up in a 'kerchief!—

That ample purple person by her side, with the dark eyes, the double chin, and the hard lines in her painted face, must be Gila's mother! Perhaps people talked about the daughter because of her mother, for *she* looked it fully! But then a girl couldn't help having a foolish mother! She was to be pitied more than blamed if she seemed silly and frivolous now and then.

What a thing for a man to do, to teach her to trust him, and then guide her and help her and uplift her till she had the highest standards formed! She was so young and tiny, and so sweet at times! Yes, she was, she must be, like Solveig.

If a man with a good moral character, a tolerably decent reputation of good taste and respectability, no fool at his studies, no stain on his name, should go with her, help her, get her to give up certain daring things she had the name of doing—if such a fellow should give her the protection of his friendship and let the world see that he considered her respectable—wouldn't it help a lot? Wouldn't it stop people's mouths and make them see that Gila wasn't what they had been saying, after all?

It came to him that this would be a very pleasant mission for his leisure hours during the rest of that winter. All thought of any danger to himself through such intercourse as he was suggesting to his thoughts had departed from his mind.

Half a mile away Gila was pouring tea for two extremely ardent youths who scarcely occupied half of her mind. With the other half she was planning a little note which should bring Courtland to her side early in the week. She had no thoughts of God. She was never troubled with much pondering. She knew exactly what she wanted without thinking any further about it, and she meant to have it.

# Chapter 5

*

It was a great source of question with Courtland afterward, just why it should have been he that happened to carry that telegram over to the west dormitory to Wittemore, instead of any one of a dozen other fellows who were in the office when it arrived and might just as well have gone. Did anything in this world *happen*, he wondered?

He could not tell why he had held out his hand and offered to take the message.

It was not because he was not trying hard, and studying for all he was worth, that "Witless Abner," as Wittemore had come to be called, had won his nickname. He worked night and day, plunged in a maze of things he did not quite understand until long after the rest of the class had passed them. He was majoring in sociology through the advice of a faddist uncle who had never seen him. He had told Abner's mother that sociology was the coming science, and Abner was faithfully carrying out the course of study he suggested. He was floundering through hours of lectures on the theory of the subject, and conscientiously working in the college settlement to get the practical side of things. He had the distressed look of a person with very short legs who is trying to keep up with a procession of six-footers, although there was nothing short about Abner. His legs were long, and his body was long, his arms were long, too long for most of his sleeves. His face was long, his nose and chin were painfully long, and were accompanied by a sensitive mouth that was always on the quiver with apprehension, like a rabbit's, and little light eyes with whitish eyelashes. His hair was like licked hay. There was absolutely nothing attractive about Wittemore except his smile, and he so seldom smiled that few of the boys had ever seen it. He had almost no friends.

He had apparently just entered his room when Courtland reached his door, and was stumbling about in a hurry to turn on the light. He stopped with his lips aquiver and a dart of fear in his eyes when he saw the telegram. Nobody but his mother would send him a telegram, and she would never waste the money for it unless there was something dreadful the matter. He looked at it fearfully, holding it in his hand and glancing up again at Courtland half-helplessly, as if he feared to open it.

Then, with that set, stolid look of plodding ahead that characterized all Abner's movements he clumsily tore open the envelope.

"Your mother is dying. Come at once," were the terse, cruel words that he read, signed with a neighbor's initials.

The young man gave the gasp of a hurt thing and stood gaping up at Courtland.

"Nothing the matter, I hope," said Courtland, kindly, moved by the gray, stricken look that had come over the poor fellow's face.

"It's Mother!" he gasped. "Read!" He thrust the telegram into Courtland's hand and sank down on the side of his bed with his head in his hands.

"Tough luck, old man!" said Courtland, with a kindly hand on the bowed shouder. "But maybe it's only a scare. Sometimes people get better when they're pretty sick, you know."

Wittemore shook his head. "No. We've been expecting this, she and I. She's been sick a long time. I didn't want to come back this year! I thought she was failing! But she wouldn't have it! She'd got her heart so set on my graduating!"

"Well, cheer up!" said Courtland, breezily. "Very likely your coming will help her to rally again! What train do you want to get? Can I help you any?"

Wittemore lifted his head and looked about his room helplessly. It was plain he was dazed.

Courtland looked up the train, phoned for a taxi, went

around the room gathering up what he thought would be necessities for the journey, while Wittemore was inadequately trying to get himself dressed. Suddenly Wittemore stopped short in the midst of his ineffective efforts and drew something out of his pocket with an exclamation of dismay.

"I forgot about this medicine!" he gasped. "I'll have to wait for the next train! Never mind that suitcase. I haven't time to wait for it! I'll go right up to the station as soon as I land this."

He seized his hat and would have gone out the door, but Courtland grabbed him by the arm.

"Hold on, old fellow! What's up? Surely you won't let anything keep you from your mother now."

"I must!" The words came with a moan of agony from the sensitive lips. "It's medicine for a poor old woman down in the settlement district. She's suffering horribly, and the doctor said she ought to have it tonight, but there was no one else to get it for her, so I promised. She's lying there waiting for it now, listening to every sound till I come. Mother wouldn't want me to come to her, leaving a woman suffering like that when I'd promised. I only came up here to get carfare so I could get there sooner than walking. It took all the change I had to get the prescription filled."

"Darn you, Wittemore! What do you think I am? I'll take the medicine to the old lady—ten old ladies if necessary! You get your train! There's your suitcase. Have you got plenty of money?"

A blank look came over the poor fellow's face. "If I could find Dick Folsom I would have about enough. He owes me something. I did some copying for him."

Courtland's hand was in his pocket. He always had plenty of money about him. That had never been one of his troubles. He had been to the bank that day, fortunately. Now he thrust a handful of bills into Wittemore's astonished hands.

"There's fifty! Will that see you through? And I can send you more if you need it. Just wire me how much you want."

Wittemore stood looking down at the bills, and tears began to run down his cheeks and splash upon them. Courtland felt his own eyes filling. What a pitiful, lonely life this had been! And the fellows had let him live that way! To think that a few paltry dollars should bing *tears*!

A few minutes later he stood looking after the whirling taxi as it bore away Wittemore into the darkness of the evening street, his heart pounding with several new emotions. Witless Abner for one! What a surprise he had been! Would everybody you didn't fancy turn out that way if you once got hold of the key of their souls and opened the door?

Then the little wrapped bottle he held in his hand reminded him that he must hasten if he would perform the mission left for him and return in time for supper. There was something in his soul that would not let him wait until after supper. So he plunged forward into the dusk and swung himself on board a downtown car.

He had no small trouble in finding the street, or rather court, in which the old woman lived.

He stumbled up the narrow staircase, lighting matches as he went, for the place was dark as midnight. By the time he had climbed four flights he was wondering what in thunder Wittemore came to places like this for? Just to major in sociology? Didn't the nut know that he would never make a success in a thing like that? What was he doing it for, anyway? Did he expect to teach it? Poor fellow, he would never get a job! His looks were against him.

He knocked, with no result, at several doors for his old woman, but at last a feeble voice answered: "Come in," and he entered a room entirely dark. There didn't even appear to be a window, though he afterward discovered one opening into an air-shaft. He stood hesitating within the room, blinking and trying to see what was about him.

"Be that you, Mr. Widymer?" asked a feeble voice from the opposite corner.

"Wittemore couldn't come. He had a telegram that his mother is dying and he had to get the train. He sent me with the medicine."

"Oh, now ain't that too bad!" said the voice. "His mother dyin'! An' to think he should remember me an' my medicine! Well, now, what d' ye think o' that?"

"If you'll tell me where your gas is located I'll make a light for you," said Courtland, politely.

"Gas!" The old lady laughed aloud. "You won't find no such thing as gas around this part o' town. There's about an inch of candle up on that shelf. The distric' nurse left it there. I was thinkin' mebbe I'd get Mr. Widymer to light it fer me when he come, an' then the night wouldn't seem so long. It's awful, when you're sufferin', to have the nights long."

He groped till he found the shelf and lit the candle. By degrees the flickering light revealed to him a small bare room with no furniture except a bed, a chair, a small stove, and a table. A box in the corner apparently contained a few worn garments. Some dishes and provisions were huddled on the table. The walls and floor were bare. The district nurse had done her level best to clear up, perhaps, but there had been no attempt at good cheer. A desolate place indeed to spend a weary night of suffering, even with an inch of candle sending weird flickerings across the dusky ceiling.

His impulse was to flee, but somehow he couldn't. "Here's this medicine," he said. "Where do you want me to put it?"

The woman motioned with a bony hand toward the table. "There's a cup and spoon over there somewhere," she said, weakly. "If you could go get me a pitcher of water and set it here on a chair I could manage to take it durin' the night."

He could see her better now, for the candle was flaring bravely. She was little and old. Her thin, white hair straggled pitifully about her small, wrinkled face, her eyes looked as if they had been burned almost out by suffering. He saw she was drawn and quivering with pain, even now as she tried to speak cheerfully. A something rebellious in him yielded to the nerve of the little old woman, and he put down his impatience. Sure he would get her the water!

She explained that the hydrant was down on the street. He took the doubtful-looking pitcher and stumbled out upon those narrow, rickety stairs again.

Way down to the street and back in that inky blackness! "Gosh! Thunder! The deuce!" (He didn't allow himself any stronger words these days.) Was this the kind of thing one was up against when one majored in sociology?

"I be'n thinkin'," said the old lady, quaveringly, when he stumbled, blinking, back into the room again with the water, "ef you wouldn't mind jest stirrin' up the fire an' makin' me a sup o' tea it would be real heartenin'. I ain't et nothin' all day 'cause the pain was so bad, but I think it'll ease up when I git a dose of the medicine, and p'r'aps I might eat a bite."

Courtland was appalled, but he went vigorously to work at that fire, although he had never laid eyes on anything so primitive as that stove in all his life. Presently, by using common sense, he had the thing going and a forlorn little kettle steaming away cheerfully.

The old woman cautioned him against using too much tea. There must be at least three drawings left, and it would be a long time, perhaps, before she got any more. Yes, there was a little mite of sugar in a paper on the table.

"There's some bread there, too—half a loaf 'most—but I guess it's pretty dry. You don't know how to make toast I s'pose," she added, wistfully.

Courtland had never made toast in his life. He abominated it. She told him how to hold it up on a fork in front of the coals and he managed to do two very creditable slices. He had forgotten his own supper now. There was something quite fresh and original in the whole experience. It would have been interesting to have told the boys, if there weren't some features about it that were almost sacred. He wondered what the gang would say when he told them about Wittemore! Poor Wittemore! He wasn't as nutty as they had thought! He had good in his heart! Courtland poured the tea, but the sugar paper had proved quite empty when he found it; likewise a plate that had once contained butter.

The toast and tea, however, seemed to be quite acceptable without its usual accessories. "Now," he said, with a long breath, "is there anything else you'd like done before I go?—for I must be getting back to college."

"If you just wouldn't mind makin' a prayer before you go," responded the little old woman, wistfully, her feeble chin trembling with her boldness. "I be'n wantin' a prayer this long while, but I don't seem to have good luck. The distric' nurse, she ain't the prayin' kind; an' Mr. Widymer he says he don't pray no more since he's come to college. He said it so kind of ashamed-like I didn't like to bother him again; and there ain't anybody else come my way for three months back. You seem so kind-spoken and pleasant-like as if you might be related to a preacher, and I thought mebbe you wouldn't mind just makin' a little short prayer 'fore you go. I dunno how long it'll be 'fore I'll get a chancet of one again."

Courtland stood rooted to the floor in dismay. "Why,—I—" he began, growing red enough to be apparent even by the flickering inch of candle.

Suddenly the room which had been so empty seemed to grow hushed and full of breathless spectators, and One, waiting to hear what he would say—whether he would respond to the call. Before his alarmed vision there came the memory of that wall of smoke which had shut him in, and that Voice calling him by name and saying, "You shall be shown." Was this what the Presence asked of him? Was this that mysterious "doing His will" that the Book spoke about, which should presently give the assurance?

He saw the old woman's face glow with eagerness. It was as if the Presence waited through her eyes to see what he would do. Something leaped up in his heart in response and he took a step forward and dropped upon his knees beside the old wooden chair.

"I'm afraid I shall make a worse bungle of it than I did of the toast," he said, as he saw her folding her hands with delight. She smiled with a serene assurance, and he closed his eyes and wondered where were words to use in such a time as this.

"Now I lay me" would not do for the poor creature who had been lying down many days and might never rise again; "Matthew, Mark, Luke, and John" was more appropriate, but there was that uncertainty about it being a prayer at all. "Our Father"—Ah! He caught at the words and spoke them.

"Our Father which art"—but what came next? That was where he had always had to be prompted, and now, in his confusion, all the rest had fled from his mind. But now it seemed that with the words the Presence had drawn near, was standing close by the chair. His mind leaped forth with the consciousness that he might talk with this invisible Presence, unfold his own perplexities and restlessness, and perhaps find out what it all meant. With scarcely a hesitation his clear voice went on eagerly now:

"Our Father, which art in this room, show us how to find and know You." He could not remember afterward what else he said. Something about his own longing, and the old woman's pain and loneliness. He was not sure if it was really a prayer at all, that halting petition.

He got up from his knees greatly embarrassed; but more by the Presence to whom he had dared to speak thus for the first time on his own account, than by the little old woman, whose hands were still clasped in reverence, and down whose withered cheeks the tears were coursing. The smoky walls, the cracked stove, the stack of discouraged dishes, seemed to fade away, and the room was somehow full of glory. He was choking with the oppression of it, and with a kind of sinking at heart lest the prayer had been only an outbreak of his own desire to know what this Force or Presence was that seemed to dominate him so fully these days.

The old woman was blessing him. She held out her hands like a patriarch: "Oh, that was such a beautiful prayer! I'll not forget the words all the night through and for many a night. The Lord Himself bless ye! Are you a preacher's son, perhaps?"

He shook his head; but he had no smile upon his face at the thought, as he might have had five minutes before.

"Well, then, yer surely goin' to be a preacher yerself?"

"No," he said; then added, thoughtfully, "not that I know of." The suggestion struck him curiously as one who hears for the first time that there is a possibility that he may be selected for some important foreign embassy.

"Well, then, yer surely a blessed child o' God Himself, anyhow, and this is a great night fer this poor little room to be honored with a pretty prayer like that!"

Scarcely hearing her, he said good-night and went thoughtfully down the dark stairs, a strange sense of peace upon him. Curiously enough, while he felt that he had left the Presence up in that little dismal room, it yet seemed to be moving beside him, touching his soul, breathing upon him! He was so engrossed with this thought that it never occurred to him that he had given the old woman every cent he had in his pocket. He had forgotten entirely that he had been hungry. A great world-wonder was moving within his spirit. He could not understand himself. He went back with awe over the last few minutes and the strange new world into which he had been so suddenly plunged.

Scarcely noticing how he went, he got himself out of the intricacies of the court into a neighborhood a shade less poverty-stricken, and stood upon the corner of a busy thoroughfare in an utterly unfamiliar district, pausing to look about him and discover his whereabouts.

A little child with long, fair hair rushed suddenly out of a door on the side street, eagerly pulling a ragged sweater about his small shoulders, and stood upon the curbstone, breathlessly watching the coming trolley. The car stopped, and a young girl in shabby clothes got out and came toward him.

"Bonnie! Bonnie! I've got supper all ready!" the child called in a clear, birdlike voice, and darted from the curb across the narrow side street to meet her.

Courtland, standing on the corner in front of the trolley, saw, too late, the swift-coming automobile bearing down upon the child, its headlights flaring on the golden hair. With a cry the young man sprang to the rescue, but the child was already crumpled up like a lily and the relentless car speeding onward, its chauffeur darting frightened, cowardly glances behind him as he plunged his machine forward over the track, almost in the teeth of the up-trolley. When the trolley was passed there was no sign of the car, even if anyone had had time to look for it. There in the road lay a little, broken child, the long hair spilling like gold over the pavement, the little, still, white face looking up like a flower that has suddenly been torn from the plant.

The girl was beside the child almost instantly, dropping all her parcels, gathering him into her slender arms, calling in frightened, tender tones:

"Aleck! Darling! My little darling!"

The child was too heavy for her to lift, and she tottered as she tried to rise, lifting a frightened face to Courtland.

"Let me take him," said the young man, stooping and gathering him gently from her. "Now show me where!"

# Chapter 6

*

Into the narrow brick house from which he had run forth so joyously but a few short minutes before, they carried him, up two flights of steep stairs to a tiny room at the back of the hall.

The gas was burning brightly at one side, and something that sent forth a savory odor was bubbling on a little two-burner gas stove. Courtland was hungry, and it struck his nostrils pleasantly as the door swung open, revealing a tiny table covered with a white cloth, set for two. There was a window curtained with white, and a red geranium on the sill.

The girl entered ahead of him, sweeping back a bright chintz curtain that divided the tiny room, and drew forth a child's cot bed. Courtland gently laid down the little inert figure. The girl was on her knees beside the child at once, a bottle in her hand. She was dropping a few drops in a teaspoon and forcing them between the child's lips.

"Will you please get a doctor, quick," she said, in a strained, quiet voice. "No, I don't know who; I've only been here two weeks. We're strangers! Bring Somebody! Anybody! Quick!"

Courtland was back in a minute with a weary, seedy-looking doctor who just fitted the street. All the way he was seeing the beautiful agony of the girl's face. It was as if her suffering had been his own. Somehow he could not bear to think what might be coming. The little form had lain so limply in his arms!

The girl had undressed the child and put him between

the sheets. He was more like a broken lily than ever. The long dark lashes lay still upon the cheeks.

Courtland stood back in the doorway, looking at the small table set for two, and pushed to the wall now to make room for the cot. There was just barely room to walk around between the things. He could almost hear the echo of that happy, childish voice calling down in the street: "Bonnie! Bonnie! I've got supper all ready!"

He wondered if the girl had heard. And there was the supper! Two blue and white bowls set daintily on two blue and white plates, obviously for the something-hot that was cooking over the flame, two bits of bread-and-butter plates to match; two glasses of milk; a plate of bread, another of butter; and by way of dessert an apple cut in half, the core dug out and the hollow filled with sugar. He took in the details tenderly, as if they had been a word-picture by Wells or Shaw in his contemporary-prose class at college. They seemed to burn themselves into his memory.

"Go over to my house and ask my wife to give you my battery!" commanded the doctor in a low growl.

Courtland was off again, glad of something to do. He carried the memory of the doctor's grizzled face lying on the little bared breast of the child, listening for the heartbeats, and the beautiful girl's anguish as she stood above them. He pushed aside the curious throng that had gathered around the door and were looking up the stairs, whispering dolefully and shaking heads:

"An' he was so purty, and so cheery, bless his heart!" wailed one woman. "He always had his bit of a word an' a smile!"

"Aw! Them ottymobbeels!" he heard another murmur. "Ridin' along in their glory! There'll be a day o' reckonin' fer them rich folks what rides in 'em! They'll hev to walk! They may even have to lie abed an' hev their wages get behind!"

The whole weight of the sorrow of the world seemed suddenly pressing upon Courtland's heart. How had he been thus unexpectedly taken out of the pleasant monotony of the university and whirled into this vortex of anguish! Why had it been? Was it just a coincidence that he should have been the one to have gone to the old woman and made her toast, and then been called upon to pray, instead of Tennelly or Bill Ward or any of the other fellows? And after that was it again just coincidence that he should have happened to stand at that corner at that particular moment and been one to participate in this later tragedy? Oh, the beautiful face of the suffering girl! Fear and sorrow and suffering and death everywhere! Wittemore hurrying to his dying mother! The old woman lying on her bed of pain! But there had been glory in that dark old room when he left it, the glory of a Presence! Ah! Where was the Presence now? How could *He* bear all this? The Christ! And could He not change it if He would—make the world a happy place instead of this dark and dreadful thing it was? For the first time the horror of war surged over his soul in its blackness. Men dying in the trenches! Women weeping at home for them! Others suffering and bleeding to death out in the open, the cold or the storm! How could God let it all be? His wondering soul cried out, "Lord, if Thou hadst been here!"

It was the old question that used to come up in the classroom, yet now, strangely enough, he began to feel there was an answer to it somewhere; an answer wherewith he would be satisfied when he found it.

It seemed an eternity of thought through which he passed as he crossed and recrossed the street and was back in the tiny room where life waited on death. It was another eternity while the doctor worked again over the boy. But at last he stood back, shaking his head and blinking the tears from his kind, tired, blue eyes.

"It's no use," he said, gruffly, turning his head away. "He's gone!"

It was then the girl brushed him aside and sank to her knees beside the little cot.

"Aleck! Aleck! Darling brother! Can't you speak to your Bonnie just once more before you go?" she called, clearly, distinctly, as if to a child who was far on his way hence. And then once again pitifully:

"Oh, darling brother! You're all I had left! Let me hear you call me Bonnie just once more before you go to Mother!"

But the childish lips lay still and white, and the lips of the girl looking down upon the little quiet form grew whiter also as she looked.

"Oh, my darling! You have gone! You will never call me anymore! And you were all I had! Good-bye!" And she stooped and kissed the boy's lips with a finality that wrung the hearts of the onlookers. They knew she had forgotten their presence.

The doctor stepped into the hall. The tears were rolling down his cheeks. "It's tough luck!" he said in an undertone to Courtland.

The young man turned away to hide the sudden convulsion that seemed coming to his own face. Then he heard the girl's voice again, lower, as if she were talking confidentially to One who stood close at hand.

"O Christ, will You go with little Aleck and see that he is not afraid till he gets safe home? And will You help me somehow to bear his leaving me alone?"

The doctor was wiping away the tears with a great, soiled handkerchief. The girl rose calmly, white and controlled, facing them as if she remembered them for the first time.

"I want to thank you for all you've done!" she said. "I'm only a stranger and you've been very kind. But now it's over and I will not hinder you any longer."

She wanted to be alone. They could see that. Yet it wrung their hearts to leave her so.

"You will want to make some arrangements," growled the doctor.

"Oh! I had forgotten!" The girl's hand fluttered to her heart and her breath gave a quick catch. "It will have to be very simple," she said, looking from one to another of them anxiously. "I haven't much money left. Perhaps I could sell something!" She looked desperately around on her little possessions. "This little cot! It is new just two weeks ago and he will not need it anymore. It cost twenty dollars!"

Courtland stepped gravely toward her. "Suppose you leave that to me," he said, gently. "I think I know a place where they would look after the matter for you reasonably and let you pay later or take the cot in exchange, you know, anything you wish. Would you like me to arrange the matter for you?"

"Oh, if you would!" said the girl, wearily. "But it is asking a great deal of a stranger."

"It's nothing. I can look after it on my way home. Just tell me what you wish."

"Oh, the very simplest there is!"—she caught her breath—"white if possible, unless it's more expensive. But it doesn't matter, anyway, now. There'll have to be a *place* somewhere, too. Sometime I will take him back and let him lie by Father and Mother. I can't now. It's two hundred miles away. But there won't need to be but one carriage. There's only me to go."

He looked his compassion, but only asked, "Is there anything else?"

"Any special clergyman?" asked the doctor, kindly.

She shook her head sadly. "We hadn't been to church yet. I was too tired. If you know of a minister who would come."

"It's tough luck," said the doctor again as they went downstairs together, "to see a nice, likely little chap like that taken away so. And I operated this afternoon on a hardened old reprobate around the corner here, that's played the devil to everybody, and he's going to pull through! It does seem strange. It ain't the way I should run the universe, but I'm thundering glad I ain't got the job!"

Courtland walked on through the busy streets, thinking that sentence over. He had a dim current of inner perception that suggested there might be another way of looking at the matter; a possibility that the wicked old reprobate had yet something more to learn of life before he went beyond its choices and opportunities; a conviction that if he were called to go he had rather be the little child in his purity than the old man in his deviltry.

The sudden cutting down of this lovely child had startled and shocked him. The bereavement of the girl cut him to the heart as if she had belonged to him. It brought the other world so close. It made what had hitherto seemed the big worthwhile things of life look so small and petty, so ephemeral! Had he always been giving himself utterly to things that did not count, or was this a perspective all out of proportion, a distorted brain again, through nervous strain and overexertion?

He came presently to a well-known undertaker's and, stepping in, felt more than ever the borderland sense. In this silent house of sadness men stepped quietly, gravely, decorously, and served you with courteous sympathy. What was the name of the man who rowed his boat on the River Styx? Yes! Charon! These wise-eyed grave men who continually plied their oars between two worlds! How did they look on life? Were they hardened to their task? Was their gentle gravity all acting? Did earthly things appeal to them? How could they bear it all, this continual settled sadness about the place! The awful hush! The tear-stained faces! The heavy breath of flowers! Not all the lofty marble arches, and beauty of surroundings, not all the soft music of hidden choirs and distant organ up in one of the halls above where a service was even then in progress, could take away the fact of death; the settled, final fact of death! One moment here upon the curbstone, golden hair afloat, eyes alight with joyous greeting, voice of laughter; the next gone, irrevocably gone, "and the place thereof shall know it no more." Where had he heard those words? Strange, sad house of death! Strange, uncertain life to live. Resurrection! Where had he caught that word in carven letters twined among lilies above the marble staircase? Resurrection! Yes, there would need to be if there was to be any hope ever in this world!

It was a strange duty he had to perform, strange indeed for a college boy to whom death had never come very close since he had been old enough to understand. It came to him to wonder what the fellows would say if they could see him here. He felt half a grudge toward Wittemore for having let him in for all this. Poor Wittemore! By this time tomorrow night Wittemore might be doing this same service for his own mother!

Death! Death! Death! Everywhere! It seemed as if everybody was dying!

He made selections with a memory of the girl's beautiful, refined face. He chose simple things and everything all white. He asked about details and gave directions so that everything would move in an orderly manner, with nothing to annoy. He even thought to order flowers, valley lilies, and some bright rosebuds, not too many to make her feel under obligation. He took out his checkbook and paid for the whole thing, arranging that the girl should not know how much it all really cost, and that a small sum might be paid by her as she was able, to be forwarded by the firm to him; this to make her feel entirely comfortable about it all.

As he went out into the street again a great sense of weariness came over him. He had lived—how many years had he lived!—in experience since he left the university at half past five o'clock? How little his past life looked to him as he surveyed it from the height he had just climbed. Life! Life was not all basketball and football and dances and fellowships and frats and honors! Life was full of sorrow, and bounded on every hand by death! The walk from where he was up to the university looked like an impossibility. There was a store up in the next block where he was known. He could get a check cashed and ride.

He found himself studying the faces of the people in the car in a new light. Were they all acquainted with sorrow? Yes, there were more or less lines of hardship or anxiety or disappointment on all the older faces. And the younger ones! Did all their bright smiles and eagerness have to be frozen on their lips by grief some day? When you came to think of it life was a terrible thing! Take that girl now, Miss Brentwood—Miss R. B. Brentwood the address had been. The name her brother had called her fitted better, "Bonnie." What would life mean to her now?

It occurred to him to wonder if there would be any such sorrow and emptiness of life for anyone if he were gone. The fellows would feel badly, of course. There would be speeches and resolutions, a lot of black drapery, and all that sort of thing in college, but what did that amount to? His father? Oh yes, of course he would feel it some, but he had been separated from his father for years, except for brief visits in vacations. His father had married a young wife and there were three young children. No, his father would not miss him much!

He swung off the car in front of the university and entered the dormitory at last, too engrossed in his strange new thoughts to remember that he had had no supper.

"Hello, Court! Where the deuce have you been? We've looked everywhere for you. You didn't come to the dining hall! What's wrong with you? Come in here!"

It was Tennelly who hauled him into Bill Ward's room and thumped him into a great leather study-chair.

"Why, man, you're all in! Give an account of yourself!" he said, tossing his hat over to Bill Ward and pulling away at his mackinaw.

"P'raps he's in love!" suggested Pat from the couch where he was puffing away at his pipe.

"P'raps he's flunked his Greek exam," suggested Bill Ward, with a grin.

"He looks as if he'd seen a ghost!" said Tennelly, eyeing him critically.

"Cut it out, boys," said Courtland, with a weary smile. "I've seen enough. Wittemore's called home. His mother's dying. I went an errand for him down in some of his slums and on the way back I just saw a little kid get killed. Pretty little kid, too, with long curls!"

"*Good night nurse!*" said Pat from his couch. "Say, that is going some!"

"Ferget it!" ejaculated Bill Ward, coming to his feet. "Had your supper yet, Court?"

Courtland shook his head.

"Well, just you sit still there while I run down to the pie shop and see what I can get."

Bill seized his cap and mackinaw and went roaring off down the hall. Courtland's eyes were closed. He hadn't felt so tired since he left the hospital. His mind was still grappling with the questions that his last two hours had flung at him to be answered.

Pat sat up and put away his pipe. He made silent motions to Tennelly, and the two picked up the unresisting Courtland and laid him on the couch. Pat's face was unusually sober as he gently put a pillow under his friend's head. Courtland opened his eyes and smiled.

"Thanks, old man," he said, and gripped his hand understandingly. There was something in Pat's face he had never noticed there before. As he dropped his eyelids shut he had an odd sense that Pat and Tennelly and the Presence were all taking care of him. A sick fancy of worn-out nerves, of course, but pleasant all the same.

Down the hall a nasal voice twanged at the telephone, shouting each answer as though to make the whole dormitory hear. Then loud steps, a thump on the door as it was flung open:

"Court here? A girl on the phone wants you, Court. Says her name is Miss Gila Dare."

# *Chapter 7*

*

The messenger had imitated Gila Dare's petulant childish accent to perfection. At another time the three young men would have shouted over it. Now they looked at one another in silence.

"Shan't I go and get a message for you, Court?" asked Tennelly. For Courtland's face was ashen gray, and the memory of it lying in the hospital was too recent for him not to feel anxious about his friend. He had only been permitted to return to college so quickly under strict orders not to overdo.

"No, I guess I'll go," said Courtland, indifferently, rising as he spoke.

They listened anxiously to his tones as he conversed over the phone.

"Hello! . . . Yes! . . . Yes! . . . Oh! Good evening! . . . Yes . . . Yes . . . No-o-o—it won't be possible! . . . No, I've just come in and I'm pretty well all in. I have a lot of studying yet to do tonight. This is exam week, you know . . . No, I'm afraid not tomorrow night either . . . No, there wouldn't be a chance till the end of the week, anyway . . . Why, yes, I think I could by that time, perhaps—Friday night? I'll let you know . . . Thank you. Good-bye!"

The listeners looked from one to the other knowingly. This was not the tone of one who had "fallen" very far for a girl. They knew the signs. He had actually been indifferent! Gila Dare had not conquered him so easily as Bill Ward had thought she would. And the strange thing about it was that there was something in the atmosphere that night that made them feel they weren't so very sorry. Somehow Courtland seemed unusually close and dear to them just then. For the moment they seemed to have perceived something fine and high in his mood that held them in awe. They did not "kid" him when he came back to them, as they would ordinarily have done. They received him gravely, talking together about the examination on the morrow, as if they had scarcely noticed his going.

Bill Ward came back presently with his arms laden with bundles. He looked keenly at the tired face on the couch, but whistled a merry tune to let on he had not noticed anything amiss.

"Got a great spread this time," he declared, setting forth his spoils on two chairs alongside the couch. "Hot oyster stew! Sit by, fellows! Cooky wrapped it up in newspapers to keep it from getting cold. There's bowls and spoons in the basket. Nelly, get 'em out! Here, Pat, take that bundle out from under my arm. That's celery and crackers. Here's a pail of hot coffee with cream and sugar all mixed. Look out, Pat! That's jelly roll and chocolate éclairs! Don't mash it, you chump! Why didn't you come with me?"

It was pleasant to lie there in that warm, comfortable room with the familiar sights all around, the pennants, the pictures, the wild arrangements of photographs and trophies, and hear the fellows talking of homely things; to be fed with food that made him begin to feel like himself again; to have their kindly fellowship all about him like a protection.

They were grand fellows, each one of them; full of faults, too, but true at heart. Life friends he knew, for there was a cord binding their four hearts together with a little tenderer tie than bound them to any of the other fellows. They had been together all the four years, and if all went well, and Bill Ward didn't flunk anything more, they would all four go out into the world as men together at the end of that year.

He lay looking at them quietly as they talked, telling little foolish jokes, laughing immoderately, asking one another anxiously about a tough question in the exam that morning, and what the prospects were for good marks for them all. It was all so familiar and beloved! So different from those last three hours amid suffering and sorrow! It was all so natural and happy, as if there were no sorrow in the world. As if this life would never end! But he hadn't yet got over that feeling of the Presence in the room with them, standing somewhere behind Pat and Tennelly. He liked to feel the consciousness of it in the back of his mind. What would the fellows say if he should try to tell them about it? They would think he was crazy. He had a feeling that he would like to be the means of making them understand.

He told them gradually about Wittemore; not as he might have told them directly after seeing him off, nor quite as he had expected to tell them. It was a little more full; it gave them a little kinder, keener insight into a character that they had hitherto almost entirely condemned and ignored. They did not laugh! It was a revelation to them. They listened with respect for the student who had gone to his mother's dying bed. They had all been long enough away from their own mothers to have come to feel the worth of a mother quite touchingly. Moreover, they perceived that Courtland had seen more in Wittemore than they had ever seen. He had a side, it appeared, that was wholly unselfish, almost heroic in a way. They had never suspected him of it before. His long, horselike face, with the little light china-blue eyes always anxious and startled, appeared to their imaginations with a new appeal. When he returned they would be kinder to him.

"Poor old Abner!" said Tennelly, thoughtfully. "Who would have thought it! Carrying medicine to an old bedridden crone! And was going to stick to his job even when his mother was dying! He's got some stuff in him, after all, if he hasn't much sense!"

Courtland was led to go on talking about the old woman, picturing in a few words the room where she lay, the pitifully few comforts, the inch of candle, the tea without sugar or milk, the butterless toast! He told it quite simply, utterly unaware that he had told how he had made the toast. They listened without comment as to one who had been set apart to a duty undesirable but greatly to be admired. They listened as to one who had passed through a great experience like being shut up in a mine for days, or passing unharmed through a polar expedition or a lonely desert wandering.

Afterward he spoke again about the child, telling briefly how he was killed. He barely mentioned the sister, and he told nothing whatever of his own part in it all. They looked at him curiously, as if they would read between the lines, for they saw he was deeply stirred, but they asked nothing. Presently they all fell to studying, Courtland with the rest, for the morrow's work was important.

They made him stay on the couch and swung the light around where he could see. They broke into song or jokes now and then as was their wont, but over it all was a hush and a quiet sympathy that each one felt, and none more deeply than Courtland. There had never been a time during his college life when he had felt so keenly and so finely bound to his companions as this night; when he went at last to his own room across the hall, he looked about on its comforts and luxuries with a kind of wonder that he had been selected for all this, while that poor woman down in the tenement had to live with bare walls and not even a whole candle! His pleasant room seemed so satisfying! And there was that girl alone in her tiny room with so little about her to make life easy, and her beautiful dead brother lying stricken before her eyes! He could not get away from the thought of her when he lay down to rest, and in his dreams her face of sorrow haunted him.

It was not until after the examinations the next afternoon that he realized that he was going to her again; had been going all the time, indeed! Of course he had been but a passing stranger, but she had no one, and he could not let her be in need of a friend. Perhaps— Why, he surely *had* a responsibility for her when he was the only one who had happened by and there was no one else!

She opened the door at his knock and he was startled by the look of her face, so drawn and white, with great dark circles under her eyes. She had not slept nor wept since he saw her, he felt sure. How long could human frame endure like that? The strain was terrible for one so young and frail. He found himself longing to take her away somewhere out of it all. Yet, of course, there was nothing he could do.

She was full of quiet gratitude for what he had done. She said she knew that without his kind intercession she would have had to pay far more. She had been through it too recently before and understood that such things were expensive. He rejoiced that she judged only by the standards of a small country place, and knew not city prices, and therefore little suspected how very much he had done to smooth her way. He told her of the preacher he had secured that afternoon by telephone—a plain, kindly man who had been recommended by the undertaker. She thanked him again, apathetically, as if she had not the heart to feel anything keenly, but was grateful to him as could be.

"Have you had anything to eat today?" he asked, suddenly.

She shook her head. "I could not eat! It would choke me!"

"But you must eat, you know," he said, gently, as if she were a little child. "You cannot bear all this. You will break down."

"Oh, what does that matter now?" she asked, pitifully, with her hand fluttering to her heart again and a wave of anguish passing over her white face.

"But we must live, mustn't we, until we are called to come away?"

He asked the question shyly. He did not understand where the thought or words came from. He was not conscious of evolving them from his own mind.

She looked at him in sad acquiescence. "I know," she said, like a submissive child, "and I'll try, pretty soon. But I can't just yet. It would choke me!"

Even while they were talking a door in the front of the hall opened, and an untidy person with unkempt hair appeared, asking the girl to come into her room and have a bite. When she shook her head the woman said:

"Well, then, child, go out a few minutes and get something. You'll not last the night through at this rate! Go, and I'll stay here until you come back."

Courtland persuaded her at last to come with him down to a little restaurant around the corner and have a cup of tea—just a cup of tea—and with a weary look, as if she thought it was the quickest way to get rid of their kindness, she yielded. He thought he never would forget the look she cast behind her at the little, white, sheet-covered cot as she passed out the door.

It was an odd experience, taking this stranger to supper. He had met all sorts of girls during his young career and had many different experiences, but none like this. Yet he was so filled with sympathy and sorrow for her that it was not embarrassing. She did not seem like an ordinary girl. She was set apart by her sorrow. He ordered the daintiest and most attractive that the plain menu of the little restaurant afforded, but he only succeeded in getting her to eat a few mouthfuls and drink a cup of tea. Nevertheless it did her good. He could see a faint color coming into her cheeks. He spoke of college and his examinations, as if she knew all about him. He thought it might give her a more secure feeling if she knew he was a student at the university. But she took it all as a matter that concerned her not in the least, with that air of aloofness of spirit that showed him he was not touching more than the surface of her being. Her real self was just bearing it to get rid of him and get back to her sorrow alone.

Before he left her he was moved to tell her how he had seen the little child coming out to greet her. He thought perhaps she had not heard those last joyous words of greeting and would want to know.

The light leaped up in her face in a vivid flame for the first time, her eyes shone with the tears that sprang mercifully into them, and her lips trembled. She put out a little cold hand and touched his coat-sleeve:

"Oh, I thank you! That is precious," she said, and, turning aside her head, she wept. It was a relief to see the strained look break and the healing tears flow. He left her then, but he could not get away from the thought of her all night with her sorrow alone. It was as if he had to bear it with her because there was no one else to do so.

When he left her he went and looked up the minister with whom he had made brief arrangements over the telephone the night before. He had to confess to himself that his real object in coming had been to make sure the man was "good enough for the job."

The Reverend John Burns was small, sandy, homely, with kind, twinkling red-brown eyes, a wide mouth, an ugly nose, and freckles; but he had a smile that was cordiality itself, and a great big paw that gripped a real welcome.

Courtland explained that he had come about the funeral. He felt embarrassed because there really wasn't anything to say. He had given all necessary details over the phone, but the kind, attentve eyes were sympathetic, and he found himself telling the story of the tragedy. He liked the way the minister received it. It was the way a minister should be to people in their need.

"You are a relative?" asked Burns as Courtland got up to go.

"No." Then he hesitated. For some reason he could not bear to say he was an utter stranger to the lonely girl. "No, only a friend," he finished. "A—a—kind of neighbor!" he added, lamely, trying to explain the situation to himself.

"A sort of a Christ-friend, perhaps?" The kind, red-brown eyes seemed to search into his soul and understand. The homely, freckled face lit with a rare smile.

Courtland gave the man a keen, hungry look. He felt strangely drawn to him and a quick light of brotherhood darted into his eyes. His fingers answered the friendly grasp of the other as they parted, and he went out feeling that somehow *there* was a man that was different; a man he would like to know better and study carefully. That man must have had some experience! He must know Christ! Had he ever felt the Presence? he wondered. He would like to ask him, but then how would one go about it to talk of a thing like that?

He threw himself into his studies again when he got back to the university, but in spite of himself his mind kept wandering back to strange questions. He wished Wittemore would come back and say his mother was better! It was Wittemore that had started all this queer sidetrack of philanthropy; that had sent him off to make toast for old women and manage funerals for strange young girls. If Wittemore would get back to his classes and plod off to his slums every day, with his long horselike face and his scared little apologetic smile, why, perhaps his own mind would assume its normal bent and let him get at his work. And with that he sat down and wrote a letter to Wittemore, brief, sympathetic, inquiring, offering any help that might be required. When it was finished he felt better and studied half the night.

He knew the next morning as soon as he woke up that he would have to go to that funeral. He hated funerals, and this would be a terrible ordeal, he was sure. Such a pitiful little funeral, and he an utter stranger, too! But the necessity presented itself like a command from an unseen force, and he knew that it was required of him—that he would never feel quite satisfied with himself if he shirked it.

Fortunately his examination began at eight o'clock. If he worked fast he could get done in plenty of time, for the hour of the funeral had been set for eleven o'clock.

Tennelly and Pat stood and gazed after him aghast when, on coming out of the classroom where he had taken his examination, he declined their suggestion that they all go down to the river skating for an hour and try to get their blood up after the strain so they could study better after lunch.

"I can't! I'm going to that kid's funeral!" he said, and strode up the stairs with his arms full of books.

"Good night!" said Pat, in dismay.

"Morbid!" ejaculated Tennelly. "Say, Pat, I don't guess we better let him go. He'll come home all in again."

But when they found Bill Ward and went up to try and stop Courtland he had departed by the other door and was halfway down the campus.

# Chapter 8

*

It was all very neat and beautiful in the little, third-story back room. The gas stove and other things had disappeared behind the chintz curtain. Before it stood the small white coffin, with the beautiful boy lying as if he were asleep, the roses strewn about him, and a mass of valley lilies at his feet. The girl, white and calm, sat beside him, one hand resting across the casket protectingly.

Three or four women from the house had brought in chairs, and some of the neighbors had slipped in shyly, half in sympathy, half in curiosity. The minister was already there, talking in a low tone in the hall with the undertaker.

The girl looked up when Courtland entered and thanked him for the flowers with her eyes. The women huddled in the back of the room watched him curiously and let no flicker of an eyelash pass without notice. They were like hungry birds ready to pounce on any scrap of sentiment or suspicion that might be dropped in their sight. The doctor came stolidly in and went and stood beside the coffin, looking down for a minute as if he were burning remedial incense in his soul, and then turned away with the frank tears running down his tired, honest face. He sat down beside Courtland. The stillness and the strangeness in the bare room were awful. It was only bearable to look toward the peace in the small, white, dead face; for the calm on the face of the sister cut one to the heart.

The minister and the undertaker stepped into the room, and then it seemed to Courtland as if One other entered also. He did not look up to see. He merely had that sense of

Another. It stayed with him and relieved the tension in the room.

Then the voice of the minister, clear, gentle, ringing, triumphant, stole through the room, and out into the hall, even down through the landings, where were huddled some of the neighbors come to listen:

"And I heard a voice from heaven saying unto me: Write—Blessed are the dead which die in the Lord from henceforth . . . But I would not have you to be ignorant, brethren, concerning them which are asleep, that ye sorrow not, even as others which have no hope. For if we believe that Jesus died and rose again, even so them also which sleep in Jesus will God bring with Him. . . . For the Lord Himself shall descend from heaven with a shout, with the voice of the archangel and with the trump of God: and the dead in Christ shall rise first. Then we which are alive and remain shall be caught up together with them in the clouds, to meet the Lord in the air; and so shall we ever be with the Lord. Wherefore comfort one another with these words."

Courtland listened attentively. The words were utterly new to him. If he had heard them before on the few occasions when he had perforce attended funerals, they had never entered into his consciousness. They seemed almost uncannily to answer the desolating question of his heart. He listened with painful attention. Most remarkable statements!

"But now is Christ risen from the dead and become the first fruits of them that slept!"

He glanced instinctively around where it seemed that the Presence had entered. He could not get away from the feeling that He stood just to the left of the minister there, with bowed head, like a great one whose errand and presence there were about to be explained. It was as if He had come to take the little child away with Him. Courtland remembered the girl's prayer the night the child died: "Go with little Aleck and see that he is not afraid till he gets safe home." He glanced up at her calm, tearless face. She was drinking in the words. They seemed to give strength under her pitiless sorrow.

"The last enemy that shall be destroyed is death!"

Courtland heard the words with a shock of relief. Here had he been under the depression of death—death everywhere and always! threatening every life and every project of earth! And now this confident sentence looking toward a time when death should be no more! It came as something utterly new and original that there would be a time when no one should ever fear death again because death would be put out of existence! He had to look at it and face it as something to be recognized and thought out, a thing that was presenting itself for him to believe; as if the Christ Himself were having it read just for him alone to hear; as if those huddled curious women and the tearful doctor, and the calm-faced girl were not there at all, only Christ and the little dead child waiting to walk into another, realer life, and Courtland, there on the threshold of another world to learn a great truth.

"But some will say, How are the dead raised up? And with what body do they come?"

Courtland looked up, startled. The very thought that was dawning in his mind! The child, presently to lie under the ground and return to dust! How could there be a resurrection of that little body after years, perhaps? How could there be hope for that wide-eyed sister with the sorrowful soul?

"Thou fool, that which thou sowest . . . thou sowest not that body that shall be, but bare grain, it may chance of wheat, or of some other grain."

He listened through the wonderful nature-picture, dimly understanding the reasoning; on to the words:

"So also is the resurrection of the dead. It is sown in corruption, it is raised in incorruption; it is sown in dishonor, it is raised in glory; it is sown in weakness, it is raised in power; it is sown a natural body, it is raised a spiritual body."

He looked at the child lying there among the lilies, those spirituelle blossoms so ethereal and perfect that they almost seem to have a soul. Was that the thought, then? The little child laid under the earth like the bulb of the lily, to see corruption and decay, would come forth, even as the spirit of the lilies came up out of the darkness and mold and decay of their tomb underground, and burst into the glory of their beautiful blossoms, the perfection of what the ugly brown bulb was meant to be. All the possibilities come to perfection! No accident or stain of sin to mar the glorified character! A perfect soul in a perfect, glorified body!

The wonder of the thought swelled within him, and sent a thrill through him with the minister's voice as he read:

"So when this corruptible shall have put on incorruption, and this mortal shall have put on immortality, then shall be brought to pass the saying that is written: Death is swallowed up in victory. O death where is thy sting? O grave, where is thy victory? Thanks be to God, which giveth us the victory through our Lord Jesus Christ!"

If Courtland had been asked before he came there whether he believed in a resurrection he might have given a doubtful answer. During the four years of his college life he had passed through various stages of unbelief along with a good many of his fellow students. With them he had made out a sort of philosophy of life which he supposed he believed. It was founded partly upon what he *wanted* to believe and partly upon what he could *not* believe, because he had never been able to reason it out. Up to this time even his experience with the Presence had not touched this philosophy of his which he had constructed like a fancy scaffolding inside of which he expected to fashion his life. The Presence and his partial surrender to its influence had been a matter of the heart, and until now it had not occurred to him that his allegiance to the Christ was incompatible with his former philosophy. The doctrine of the resurrection suddenly stood before him as something that must be accepted along with the Christ, or the Christ was not the Christ! Christ *was* the resurrection if He was at all! Christ *had* to be that, *had* to have conquered death, or He would not have been the Christ; He would not have been God humanized for the understanding of men unless He could do godlike things. He was not God if He could not conquer death. He would not be a man's Christ if He could not come to man in his darkest hour and conquer his greatest enemy; put Himself up against death and come out victorious!

A great fact had been revealed to Courtland: There was a

resurrection of the dead, and Christ was the hope of that resurrection! It was as if he had just met Christ face to face and heard Him say so; had it all explained to him fully and satisfactorily. He doubted if he could tell the professor in the biblical literature class how, because perhaps *he* hadn't seen the Christ that way; but others understood! That white, strained face of the girl was not hopeless. There was the light of a great hope in her eyes; they could see afar off over the loneliness of the years that were to be, up to the time when she should meet the little brother again, glorified, perfected, stainless!

It suddenly came to Courtland to think how Stephen Marshall would look with that glorified body. The last glimpse he had had of him standing above the burning pit of the theater with the halo of flames about his head had given him a vision. A great gladness came up within him that some day he would surely see Stephen Marshall again, grasp his hand, make him know how he repented his own negative part in the persecution that had led him to his death; make him understand how in dying he had left a path of glory behind and given life to Paul Courtland.

In the prayer that followed the minister seemed as though he were talking with dear familiarity to One whom he knew well. The young man, listening, marveled that any dared come so near, and found himself longing for such assurance and comradeship.

They took the casket out to a quiet place beyond the city, where the little body might rest until the sister wished to take it away.

As they stood upon that bleak hillside, dotted over with white tombstones, the looming city in the distance off at the right, Courtland recognized the group of spreading buildings that belonged to his university. He marveled at the closeness of life and death in this world. Out there the busy city, everybody tired and hustling to get, to learn, to enjoy; out here everybody lying quiet, like the corn or wheat in the ground, waiting for the resurrection time, the call of God to come forth in beauty! What a difference it would make in the working, and getting, and hustling, and learning, and enjoying if everybody remembered how near the lying-quiet time might be! How unready some might be to lie down and feel that it was all over! How much difference it must make what one had done with the time over there in the city, when the stopping time came! How much better it would be if one could live remembering the Presence, always being aware of its nearness! To live Christ! What would that mean? Was he ready to surrender to a thought like that?

The minister, it appeared, had a very urgent call in another direction. He must take a trolley that passed the gate of the cemetery and go off at once. It fell to Courtland to look after the girl, for the doctor had not been able to leave his practice to take the long ride to the cemetery. She, it seemed, did not hear what they said, nor care who went with her.

Courtland led her to the carriage and put her in. "I suppose you will want to go directly back to the house?" he said.

She turned to him as if she were coming out of a trance. She caught her breath and gave him one wild, beseeching look, crying out with something like a sob: "Oh, how can I *ever* go back to that room *now*?" And then her breath seemed suddenly to leave her and she fell back against the seat as if she were lifeless.

He sprang in beside her, took her in his arms, resting her head against his shoulder, loosened her coat about her throat, and chafed her cold hands, drawing the robes closely about her slender shoulders, but she lay there white and without a sign of life. He thought he never had seen anything so ghastly white as her face.

The driver came around and offered a bottle of brandy. They forced a few drops between her teeth, and after a moment there came a faint flutter of her eyelids. She came to herself for just an instant, looked about her, realized her sorrow once more, and dropped off into oblivion again.

"She's in a bad way!" murmured the driver, looking worried. "I guess we'd better get her somewheres. I don't want to have no responsibility. My chief's gone back to the city, and the other man's gone across county. I reckon we'd better go on and stop at some hospital if she don't come to pretty soon."

The driver vanished and the carriage started at a rapid pace. Courtland sat supporting his silent charge in growing alarm, alternately chafing her hands and trying to force more brandy between her set lips. He was relieved when at last the carriage stopped again and he recognized the stone buildings of one of the city's great hospitals.

# Chapter 9

*

When Courtland got back to the university the afternoon examination had been in progress about half an hour. With a brief explanation to the professor, he settled to his belated work regardless of Bill Ward's anxious glances from the back of the room and Pat's lifted eyebrows from the other side. He knew he had yet to meet those three beloved antagonists. He seemed to have progressed through eons of experience since he talked with them last night. The intricate questions of the examination on political science over which he was trying faithfully to work seemed paltry beside the great facts of life and death.

He had remained at the hospital until the girl came out of her long semiconsciousness and the doctor said she was better, but the thought of her white face was continually before him. When he closed his eyes for a moment to think how to phrase some answer in his paper he would see that still, beautiful face as it lay on his shoulder in the carriage. It had filled him with awe to think that he, a stranger, was her only friend in that great city, and she might be dying! Somehow he could not cast her off as a common stranger.

He had arranged that she should be placed in a small private room at a moderate cost, and paid for a week in advance. The cost was a mere trifle to Courtland. The new overcoat he had meant to buy this week would more than cover the cost. Besides, if he needed more than his ample allowance his father was always quite ready to advance what he wanted. But the strange thing about all this was that, having paid to put the girl where she would be perfectly comfortable and be well taken care of, he could not cast her off and forget her. His responsibility seemed to be doubled with everything he did for her. Between the problems of deep state perplexities and intrigues was ever the perplexity about that girl and how she was going to live all alone with her tragedy—or tragedies—for it was apparent from the little hints she had dropped that the death of the small brother was only the climax of quite a series of sorrows that had come to her young life. And yet she, with all that sorrow compassing her about, could still believe in the Christ and call upon Him in her trouble! There was a kind of triumphant feeling in his heart when he reached that conclusion.

He lay on the couch in Tennelly's room that night after supper and tried to think it out, while the other three clattered away about their marks and held an indignation meeting over the way Pat was getting blacklisted by all the professors just when he was trying so hard. He didn't know the fellows were keeping it up to get his mind away from the funeral. He was thinking about that girl.

The doctor had told him that she was very much run down. It looked as if the process had been going on for some time. Her heart action was not all it should be, and there were symptoms of lack of nutrition. What she needed was rest, utter rest. Sleep if possible most of the time for at least a week, with careful feeding every two or three hours, and after that a quiet, cheerful place with plenty of fresh air and sunshine and more sleep; no anxiety, and nothing to call on the exhausted energies for action or hurry.

Now how was a state of things like that to be brought about for a person who had no home, no friends, no money, and no time to lie idle? Moreover, how could there be any cheerful spot in the wide world for a little girl who had passed through the fire as she had done?

Presently he went out to the drugstore and telephoned the hospital. They said she had had only one more slight turn of unconsciousness, but had rallied from it quickly and was resting quietly now. They hoped she would have a good night.

Then he went back to his room and thought about her

some more. He had an important English examination the next day, one in which he especially wanted to do well; yet try as he would to concentrate on Wells and Shaw, that girl and what was going to become of her would get in between him and his book.

It was after ten o'clock when he sauntered down the hall and stood in Stephen Marshall's room for a few minutes, as he was getting the habit of doing every night. The peace of it and the uplift that that room always gave him were soothing to his soul. If he had known a little more about the Christ to whose allegiance he had declared himself he might have knelt and asked for guidance; but as yet he had not so much as heard of a promise to the man who "abides," and "asks what he will." Nevertheless, when he entered that room his mind took on the attitude of prayer and he felt that somehow the Presence got close to him, so that questions that had perplexed him were made clear.

As he stood that night looking about the plain walls, his eyes fell upon that picture of Stephen Marshall's mother. A mother! Ah! if there were a mother somewhere to whom that girl could go! Someone who would understand her; be gentle and tender with her; love her, as he should think a real mother would do—what a difference that would make!

He began to think over all the women he knew—all the mothers. There were not so many of them. Some of the professors' wives who had sons and daughters of their own? Well, they might be all well enough for their own sons and daughters, but there wasn't one who seemed likely to want to behave in a very motherly way to a stranger like this waif of a girl. They were nice to the students, polite and kind to the extent of one tea or reception apiece a year, but that was about the limit.

Well, there was Tennelly's mother! Dignified, white-haired, beautiful, dominant in her home and clubs, charming to her guests; but—he could just fancy how she would raise her lorgnette and look Bonnie Brentwood over. There would be no room in that grand house for a girl like Bonnie. Bonnie! How the name suited her! He had a strange protective feeling about that girl, not as if she were like the other girls he knew; perhaps it was a sort of a "Christ-brother" feeling, as the minister had suggested. But to go on with the list of mothers—wasn't there one anywhere to whom he could appeal? Gila's mother? Pah! That painted, purple image of a mother! Her own daughter needed to find a real mother somewhere. She couldn't mother a stranger! Mothers! Why weren't there enough real ones to go around? If he had only had a mother, a real one, himself, who had lived, she would have been one to whom he could have told Bonnie's story, and she would have understood!

He looked into the pictured eyes on the wall and an idea came to him. It was like an answer to prayer. Stephen Marshall's mother! Why hadn't he thought of her before? She was that kind of a mother of course, or Stephen Marshall would not have been the man he was! If the Bonnie girl could only get to her for a little while! But would she take her? Would she understand? Or might she be too overcome with her own loss to have been able to rally to life again? He looked into the strong motherly face and was sure *not*.

He would write to her. He would put it to the test whether there was a mother in the world or not. He went back to his room and wrote her a long letter, red-hot from the depths of his heart; a letter such as he might have written to his own mother if he had ever known her, but such as certainly he had never written to any woman before. He wrote:

Dear Mother of Stephen Marshall:

I know you are a real mother because Stephen was what he was. And now I am going to let you prove it by coming to you with something that needs a mother's help.

There is a little girl—I should think she must be about nineteen or twenty years old—lying in the hospital, worn out with hard work and sorrow. She has recently lost her father and mother, and had brought her little five-year-old brother to the city a couple of weeks ago. They were living in a very small room, boarding themselves, she working all day somewhere downtown. Two days ago, as she was coming home in the trolley, her little brother, crossing the street to meet her, was knocked down and killed by a passing automobile. We buried him today, and the girl fainted dead away on the way back from the cemetery and only recovered consciousness when we got her to the hospital. The doctor says she has exhausted her vitality and needs to sleep for a week and be nurtured; and then she ought to go to some cheerful place where she can just rest for a while and have fresh air and sunshine and good, plain, nourishing food.

Now she hasn't a friend in the city. I know from the few little things she has told me that there isn't anyone in the world she will feel free to turn to. She isn't the kind of girl who will accept charity. She's refined, reserved, independent, and all that, you know. There's another thing, too—she prays to your Stephen's Christ—that's why I dared write to you about it.

You see, I'm an entire stranger to her. I just happened along when the kid was killed and had to stick around and help; that's how I came to know. Of course she hasn't any idea of all this, and I haven't any real business with it, but I can't see leaving her in a hole this way; and there's no one else to do anything.

You wonder why I didn't find a mother nearer by, but I haven't any living of my own, except a stepmother, who wouldn't understand, and all the other mothers I know wouldn't qualify for the job any better. I've been looking at your picture and I think you would.

What I thought of is this (if it doesn't strike you that way maybe you can think of some other way): I'm pretty well fixed for money, and I've got a lump that I've been intending to use for a new automobile; but my old car is plenty good enough for another year, and I'd like to pay this girl's board awhile till she gets rested and strong and sort of cheered up. I thought perhaps you'd see your way clear to write a letter and say you'd like her to visit you—you're lonesome or something. I don't know how a real mother would fix that up, but I guess you do.

Of course the girl mustn't know I have a thing to do

with it except that I told you about her. She'd be up in the air in a minute. She wouldn't stand for me doing anything for her. She's that kind.

I'm sending a check of two hundred dollars right now because I thought, in case you see a way to take up with my suggestion, you might send her money enough for the journey. I don't believe she's got any. We can fix it up about the board any way you say. Don't hesitate to tell me just how much it is worth. I don't need the money for anything. But whatever's done has got to be done mighty quick or she'll go back to work again, and she won't last three days if she does. She looks as if a breath would blow her away. I'm sending this special delivery to hurry things. Her address is Miss R. B. Brentwood, Good Samaritan Hospital. The kid called her Bonnie. I don't know what her whole name is.

So now you have the whole story, and it's up to you to decide. Maybe you think I've got a lot of crust to propose this, and maybe you won't see it this way, but I've had the nerve because Stephen Marshall's life and Stephen Marshall's death have made me believe in Stephen Marshall's Christ and Stephen Marshall's mother.

I am, very respectfully,

PAUL COURTLAND

He mailed the letter that night and then studied hard till three o'clock in the morning.

The next morning's mail brought him a dainty little note from Gila's mother, inviting him to a quiet family dinner with them on Friday evening. He frowned when he read it. He didn't care for the large, painted person, but perhaps there was more good in her than he knew. He would have to go and find out. It might even be that she would be a help in case Stephen Marshall's mother did not pan out.

# Chapter 10

*

Mother Marshall stood by the kitchen window, with her cheek against a boy's old soft felt hat, and she looked out into the gathering dusk for Father. The hat was so old and worn that its original shape and color were scarcely distinguishable, and there was one spot where Mother Marshall's tears had washed some of the grime away into deeper stains about it. It was only on days when Father was off to town on errands that she allowed herself the momentary weakness of tears.

So she had stood in former years looking out into the dusk for her son to come whistling home from school. So she had stood the day the awful news of his fiery death had come, while Father sat in his rush-bottomed chair and groaned. She had laid her cheek against that old felt hat and comforted herself with the thought of her boy, her splendid boy, who had lived his short life so intensely and wonderfully. When she felt that old scratchy felt against her cheek it somehow brought back the memory of his strong young shoulder, where she used to lay her head sometimes when she felt tired and he would fold her in his arms and brush her forehead with his lips and pat her shoulder. The neighbors sometimes wondered why she kept that old felt hat hanging there, just as when Stephen was alive among them, but Mother Marshall never said anything about it; she just kept it there, and it comforted her to feel it; one of those little homely, tangible things that our poor souls have to tether to sometimes when we lose the vision and get fainthearted. Mother Marshall wasn't morbid one bit. She always looked on the bright side of everything; and she had had much joy in her son as he was growing up. She had seen him strong of body, strong of soul, keen of mind. He had won the scholarship of the whole Northwest to the big eastern university. It had been hard to pack him up and have him go away so far, where she couldn't hope to see him soon, where she couldn't listen to his whistle coming home at night, where he couldn't even come back for Sunday and sit in the old pew in church with them. But those things had to come. It was the only way he could grow and fulfill his part of God's plan. And so she put away her tears till he was gone, and kept them for the old felt hat when Father was out about the farm. And then when the news came that Stephen had graduated so soon, gone up higher to God's eternal university to live and work among the great, even then her soul had been big enough to see the glory of it behind the sorrow, and say with trembling, conquering lips: "I shall go to him, but he shall not return to me. The Lord gave, and the Lord hath taken away. Blessed be the name of the Lord!"

That was the kind of nerve that blessed little Mother Marshall was built with, and it was only in such times as these, when Father had gone to town and stayed a little later than usual, that the tears in her heart got the better of her and she laid her face against the old felt hat.

Down the road in the gloom moved a dark speck. It couldn't be Father, for he had gone in the machine—the nice, comfortable little car that Stephen had made them get before he went away to college, because he said that Father needed to have things easier now. Father would be in the machine, and by this time the lights would be lit. Father was very careful always about lighting up when it grew dusk. He had a great horror of accidents to other people. Not that he was afraid for himself, no indeed. Father was a *man*! The kind of man to be the father of a Stephen!

The speck grew larger. It made a chugging noise. It was one of those horrible motorcycles. Mother Marshall hated them, though she had never revealed the fact. Stephen had wanted one, had said he intended to get one with the first money he earned after he came out of college, but she had hoped in her heart they would go out of fashion by that time and there would be something less fiendish-looking to take their place. They always looked to her as if they were headed straight for destruction, and the person on them seemed as if he were going to the devil and didn't care. She secretly hated the idea of Stephen ever sitting upon one of them, flying through space. But now he was gone beyond all such fears. He had wings, and there were no dangers where he was. All danger and fear was over for him. She had never wanted either of her men to know the inward quakings of her soul over each new risk as Stephen began to grow up. She wanted to be worthy to be the mother and wife of noblemen, and fears were not for such; so she hid them and struggled against them in secret.

The motorcycle came on like a comet now, and turned thundering in at the big gate. A sudden alarm filled Mother Marshall's soul. Had something happened to Father? That was the only terrible thing left in life to happen now. An accident! And this boy had come to prepare her for the worst? She had the kitchen door wide open even before the boy had stopped his machine and set it on its mysterious feet.

"Sp'c'l d'liv'ry!" fizzed the boy, handing her a fat envelope, a book, and the stub of a pencil. "Si'n'eer!" indicating a line on the book.

She managed to write her name in cramped characters, but her hand was trembling so she could hardly form the letters. A wild idea that perhaps they had discovered somehow that Stephen had escaped death in some miraculous manner flitted through her brain and out again, controlled by her strong common sense. Such notions always came to people after death had taken their loved ones—frenzied hopes for miracles! Stephen had been dead for four months now. There could be no such possibility, of course.

Just to calm herself she went and opened the slide of the range and shoved the teakettle a little farther on so it would begin to boil, before she opened that fat letter. She lit the lamp, too, put it on the supper table, and changed the position of the bread plate, covering it nicely with a fringed napkin so the bread wouldn't get dry. Everything must be ready when Father got back. Then she went and sat down with her gold spectacles and tore open that envelope.

She was so absorbed in the letter that she failed for the first time since they got the car to hear its pleasant purr as it came down the road, and the big headlights sent their rays out cheerfully without anyone at the kitchen window to see. Father was getting worried that the kitchen door didn't fly open as he drew in beside the big flagstone, when Mother suddenly came flying out with her face all smiles and eagerness. He hadn't seen her look that way since Stephen went away.

She had left a trail of letter all the way from her big chair to the door, and she held the envelope in her hand. She rushed out and buried her face in his rough coat collar:

"Oh, Father! I've been so worried about you!" she declared, joyfully, but she didn't look worried a bit.

Father looked down at her tenderly and patted her plump shoulder. "Had a flat tire and had to stop and get her pumped up," he explained, "and then the man found a place wanted patching. He took a little longer than I expected. I was afraid you would worry."

"Well, hurry in," she said, eagerly. "Supper's all ready and I've got a letter to read to you."

It went without saying that if Mother liked a thing in that home Father would too. His sun rose and set in Mother, and they had lived together so long and harmoniously that the thoughts of one were the reflection of the other. It didn't matter which you asked about a thing, you were sure to get the same opinion as if you had asked the other. It wasn't that one gave way to the other; it was just that they had the same habits of thought and decision, the same principles to go by. So when, after she had passed the hot johnnycake, seen to it that Father had the biggest pork chop and the mealiest potato, and given him his cup of coffee creamed and sugared just right, Mother got out the letter with the university crest and began to read. She had no fears that Father would not agree with her about it. She read eagerly, sure of his sympathy in her pleasure; sure he would think it was nice of Stephen's friend to write to her and pick her out as a real mother, saying all those pleasant things about her; sure he would be proud that she, with all the women they had in the East, should have so brought up a boy that a stranger knew she was a real mother. She had no fear that Father would frown and declare they couldn't be bothered with a stranger around, that it would cost a lot and Mother needed to rest. She knew he would be touched at once with the poor, lonely girl's position, and want to do anything in his power to help her. She knew he would be ready to fall right in with anything she should suggest. And, true to her conviction, Father's eyes lighted with tenderness as she read, watched her proudly and nodded in strong affirmation at the phrases touching her ability as mother.

"That's right, Mother, you'll qualify for a job as mother better'n any woman I ever saw!" said Father, heartily, as he reached for another helping of butter.

His face kindled with interest as the letter went on with its proposition, but he shook his head when it came to the money part, interrupting her:

"I don't like that idea, Mother; we don't keep boarders, and we're plenty able to invite company for as long as we like. Besides, it don't seem just the right thing for that young feller to be paying her board. She wouldn't like it if she knew it. If she was our daughter we wouldn't want her to be put in that position, though it's very kind of him of course—"

"Of course!" said Mother, breathlessly. "He couldn't very well ask us, you know, without saying something like that, especially as he doesn't know us, except by hearsay, at all."

"Of course," agreed Father; "but then equally of course we won't let it stand that way. You can send that young feller back his check, and tell him to get his new ottymobeel. He won't be young but once, and I reckon a young feller of that kind won't get any harm from his ottymobeels, no matter how many he has of 'em. You can see by his letter he ain't spoiled yet, and if he's got hold of Steve's idea of things he'll find plenty of use for his money, doing good where there ain't a young woman about that is bound to object to being took care of by a young man she don't know and don't belong to. However, I guess you can say that, Mother, without offending him. Tell him we'll take care of the money part.

Tell him we're real glad to get a daughter. You're sure, Mother, it won't be hard for you to have a stranger around in Steve's place?"

"No, I like it," said Mother, with a smile, brushing away a bright tear that burst out unawares. "I like it '*hard*,' as Steve used to say! Do you know, Father, what I've been thinking—what I thought right away when I read that letter? I thought, suppose that girl was the one Stephen would have loved and wanted to marry if he had lived. And suppose he had brought her home here, what a fuss we would have made about her, and all! And I'd just have loved to fix up the house and make it look pleasant for her and love her as if she were my own daughter."

Father's eyes were moist, too. "H'm! Yes!" he said, trying to clear his throat. "I guess she'd be com'ny for you, too, Mother, when I have to go to town, and she'd help around with the work some when she got better."

"I've been thinking," said Mother. "I've always thought I'd like to fix up the spare room. I read in my magazine how to fix up a young girl's room when she comes home from college, and I'd like to fix it like that if there's time. You paint the furniture white, and have two sets of curtains, pink and white, and little shelves for her books. Do you think we could do it?"

"Why, sure!" said Father. He was so pleased to see Mother interested like this that he was fairly trembling. She had been so still and quiet and wistful ever since the news came about Stephen. "Why, sure! Get some pretty wall-paper, too, while you're 'bout it. S'posen you and I take a run to town again in the morning and pick it out. Then you can pick your curtains and paint, too, and get Jed Lewis to come in the afternoon and put on the first coat. How about calling him up on the phone right now and asking him about it? I'm real glad we've got that phone. It'll come in handy now."

Mother's eyes glistened. The phone was another thing Stephen insisted upon before he left home. They hadn't used it half a dozen times except when the telegrams came, but they hadn't the heart to have it disconnected, because Stephen had taken so much pride in having it put in. He said he didn't like his mother left alone in the house without a chance to call a neighbor or send for the doctor.

"Come to think of it, hadn't you better send a telegram to that chap tonight? You know we can phone it down to the town office. He'll maybe be worried how you're going to take that letter. Tell him he's struck the right party, all right, and you're on the job writing that little girl a letter tonight that'll make her welcome and no mistake. But tell him we'll finance this operation ourselves, and he can save the ottymobeel for the next case that comes along—words to that effect you know, Mother."

The supper things were shoved back and the telephone brought into requisition. They called up Jed Lewis first before he went to bed, and got his reluctant promise that he would be on hand at two o'clock the next afternoon. They had to tell him they were expecting company or he might not have been there for a week in spite of his promise.

It took nearly an hour to reduce the telegram to ten words, but at last they settled on:

> Bonnie welcome. Am writing you both tonight. No money necessary.
> (Signed) STEPHEN'S MOTHER AND FATHER

The letters were happy achievements of brevity, for it was getting late, and Mother Marshall realized that they must be up early in the morning to get all that shopping done before two o'clock.

First the letter to Bonnie, written in a cramped, laborious hand:

> DEAR LITTLE GIRL:
> You don't know me, but I've heard about you from a sort of neighbor of yours. I'm just a lonely mother whose only son has gone home to heaven. I've heard all about your sorrow and loneliness, and I've taken a notion that maybe you would like to come and visit me for a little while and help cheer me up. Maybe we can comfort each other a little bit, and, anyhow, I want you to come.

Father and I are fixing up your room for you, just as we would if you were our own daughter coming home from college. For you see we've quite made up our minds you will come, and Father wants you just as much as I do. We are sending you mileage, and a check to get any little things you may need for the journey, because, of course, we wouldn't want to put you to expense to come all this long way just to please two lonely old people. It's enough for you that you are willing to come, and we're so glad about it that it almost seems as if the birds must be singing and the spring flowers going to bloom for you, even though it is only the middle of winter.

Don't wait to get any fixings. Just come as you are. We're plain folks.

Father says be sure you get a good, comfortable berth in the sleeper, and have your trunk checked right through. If you've got any other things besides your trunk, have them sent right along by freight. It's better to have your things here where you can look after them than stored away off there.

We're so happy about your coming we can't seem to wait till we hear what time you start, so please send a telegram as soon as you get this, saying when the doctor will let you come, and don't disappoint us for anything.

Lovingly, your friend,
RACHEL MARSHALL

The letter to Courtland was more brief, but just as expressive:

MR. PAUL COURTLAND:

DEAR FRIEND—You're a dear boy and I'm proud that my son had you for a friend.

(When Courtland read that letter he winced at that sentence and saw himself once more standing in the hall in front of Stephen Marshall's room, holding the garments of those who persecuted him.)

I have written Bonnie Brentwood, telling her how much we want her, and I am going to town in the morning to get some things to fix up a pretty room for her. I thank you for thinking I was a good mother. Father and I are both quite proud about it. We are very lonely and are glad to have a daughter for as long as she will stay. But, anyway, if we hadn't wanted her, we could not have said no when you asked for Christ's sake. Father says we are returning the check because we want to do this for Bonnie ourselves; then there won't be anything to cover up. Father says if you have begun this way you will find plenty of ways to spend that money for Christ and let us look after this one little girl. We've sent her mileage and some money, and we're going to try to make her happy. And some day we would be very happy if you would come out and visit us. I should like to know you for my dear Stephen's sake. You are a dear boy, and I want to know you better. I am glad you have found our Christ. Father thinks so too. Thank you for thinking I would understand.

Lovingly,
MOTHER MARSHALL

But after all that excitement Mother Marshall could not sleep. She lay quietly beside Father in the old four-poster and planned all about that room. She must get Sam Carpenter to put in some little shelves each side of the windows, and a wide locker between for a window seat, and she would make some pillows like those in the magazine pictures. She pictured how the girl would look, a dozen times, and what she would say, and once her heart was seized with fear that she had not made her letter cordial enough. She went over the words of the young man's letter as well as she could remember them, and let her heart soar and be glad that Stephen had touched one life and left it better for his being in the university that little time.

Once she stirred restlessly, and Father put out his hand and touched her in alarm:

"What's the matter, Rachel? Aren't you sleeping?"

"Father, I believe we'll have to get a new rug for that room."

"Sure!" said Father, relaxing sleepily.

"Gray, with pink rosebuds, soft and thick," she whispered.

"Sure! pink, with gray rosebuds," murmured Father as he dropped off again.

They made very little of breakfast the next morning; they were both too excited about getting off early; and Mother Marshall forgot to caution Father about going at too high speed. If she suspected that he was running a little faster than usual she winked at it, for she was anxious to get to the stores as soon as possible. She had arisen early to read over the article in the magazine again, and she knew to a nicety just how much pink and white she would need for the curtains and cushions. She had it in the back of her mind that she meant to get little brass handles and keyholes for the bureau also. She was like a child who was getting ready for a new doll.

It was not until they were on their way back home again, with packages all about their feet, and an eager light in their faces, that an idea suddenly came to both of them—an idea so chilling that the eagerness went out of their eyes for a moment, and the old, patient, sweet look of sorrow came back. It was Mother Marshall who put it into words:

"You don't suppose, Seth," she appealed—she always called him Seth in times of crisis—"you don't suppose that perhaps she mightn't *want* to come, after all!"

"Well, I was thinking, Rachel," he said, tenderly, "we'd best not be getting too set on it. But, anyhow, we'd be ready for someone else. You know Stevie always wanted you to have things fixed nice and fancy. But you fix it up. I guess she's coming. I really do think she must be coming! We'll just pray about it and then we'll leave it there!"

And so with peace in their faces they arrived at home, just five minutes before the painter was due, and unloaded their packages. Father lifted out the big roll of soft, velvety carpeting, gray as a cloud, with moss roses scattered over it. He was proud to think he could buy things like this for

Mother. Of course now they had no need to save and scrimp for Stephen the way they had done during the years; so it was well to make the rest of the way as bright for Mother as he could. And this "Bonnie" girl! If she would only come, what a bright, happy thing it would be in their desolated home!

But suppose she shouldn't come?

# Chapter 11

*

The telegram reached Courtland Friday evening, just as he was going to the Dare dinner, and filled him with an almost childish delight. Not for a long time had he had anything as nice as that happen; not even when he made Phi Beta Kappa in his junior year had he been so filled with exultation. It was like having a fairy tale come true. To think there had really been a woman in the world who would respond in that cordial way to a call from the great unknown!

He presented himself in his most sparkling mood at the house where he was to dine. There was nothing at all blue about him. His eyes fairly danced with pleasure and his smile was rare. Gila looked and drooped her eyes demurely. She thought the sparkle was all for her, and her little wicked heart gave a throb of exultant joy.

Mrs. Dare was no longer a large, purple person. She was in full evening dress, explaining that she and her husband had an engagement at the opera after dinner. She resembled the fat dough people that the cook used to fashion for him in his youth. Her pudgy arms so reminded him of those shapeless cookie arms that he found himself fascinated by the thought as he watched her moving her bejeweled hands among the trinkets at her end of the glittering table. Her gown, what there was of it, was of black gauze emblazoned with dartling sequins of deep blue. An aigrette in her hair twinkled knowingly above her coarse, painted face. Courtland, as he studied her more closely, rejoiced that the telegram had arrived before he left the dormitory, for he never could have had the courage to come to this plump-shouldered lady seeking refuge for his refined little Bonnie girl.

The father of the family was a little wisp of a man with a nervous laugh and a high, thin voice. There were kind lines around his mouth and eyes, indulgent lines—not self-indulgent, either, and insomuch they were noble—but there was a weakness about the face that showed he was ruled by others to a large extent. He said, "Yes, my dear!" quite obediently when his wife ordered him affably around. There was a cunning look in his eye that might explain the general impression current that he knew how to turn a dollar to his own account.

It occurred to Courtland to wonder what would happen if he should suddenly ask Mr. Dare what he thought of Christ, or if he believed in the resurrection. He could quite imagine they would look aghast as if he had spoken of something impolite. One couldn't think of Mrs. Dare in a resurrection, she would seem so out of place, so sort of unclothed for the occasion, in those fat, doughy arms with her glittering jet shoulder straps. He realized that all these thoughts that raced through his head were but fantasies occasioned no doubt by his own highly wrought nervous condition, but they kept crowding in and bringing the mirth to his eyes. How, for instance, would Mother Marshall and Mother Dare hit it off if they should happen together in the same heaven?

Gila was all in white, from the tip of her pearly shoulders down to the tip of her pearl-beaded slippers—white and demure. Her skin looked even more pearly than when she wore the brilliant red-velvet gown. It had a pure, dazzling whiteness, different from most skins. It perplexed him. It did not look like flesh, but more like some ethereal substance meant for angels. He drew a breath of satisfaction that there was not even a flush upon it tonight. No painting there at least! He was not master of the rare arts that skins are subject to in these days. He knew artificial whiteness only when it was glaring and floury. This pearly paleness was exquisite, delicious; and in contrast the great dark eyes, lifted pansylike for an instant and then down-drooped beneath those wonderful long curling lashes, were almost startling in their beauty. The hair was simply arranged with a plain narrow band of black velvet around the white temples, and the soft loops of cloudy darkness drawn out on her cheeks in her own fantastic way. There was an attempt at demureness in the gown; soft folds of pure transparent nothing seemed to shelter what they could not hide, and more such folds drooped over the lovely arms to the elbows. Surely, surely, this was loveliness undefiled. The words of Peer Gynt came floating back disconnectedly, more as a puzzled question in his mind than as they stand in the story:

> Is your psalm-book in your 'kerchief?
> Do you glance adown your apron?
> Do you hold your mother's skirt-fold?
> Speak!

But he only looked at her admiringly, and talked on about the college games, making himself agreeable to everyone, and winning more and more the lifted pansy-eyes.

When dinner was over they drifted informally into a large white and gold reception room, with inhospitable chairs and settees whose satin slipperiness offered no inducements to sit down. There were gold-lacquered tables and a curious concert grand piano, also gold inlaid with mother-of-pearl cupids and flowers. Everything was most elaborate. Gila, in her soft transparencies, looked like a wraith amid it all. The young man chose to think she was too rare and fine for a place so ornate.

Presently the fat cookie arms of the mother were enfolded in a gorgeous blue-plush evening cloak beloaded with handsome black fur; and with many bows and kindly words the little husband toddled off beside her, reminding Courtland of a big cinnamon bear and a little black and tan dog he had once seen together in a show.

Gila stood bewitchingly childish in the great gold room, and shyly asked if he would like to go to the library, where it was cozier. The red light glowed across the hall, and he turned from it with a shudder of remembrance. The glow seemed to beat upon his nerves like something striking his eyeballs.

"I'd like to hear you play, if you will," he answered, wondering in his heart if, after all, a dolled-up instrument like that was really meant to be played upon.

Gila pouted. She did not want to play, but she would not seem to refuse the challenge. She went to the piano and rippled off a brilliant waltz or two, just to show him she could do it, played "Humoresque," and a few little catchy melodies that were in the popular ear just then, and then, whirling on the gilded stool, she lifted her big eyes to him:

"I don't like it in here," she said, with a little shiver, as a child might do; "let's go into the library by the fire. It's pleasanter there to talk."

Courtland hesitated. "Look here," said he, frankly. "Wouldn't you just as soon sit somewhere else? I don't like that red light of yours. It gets on my nerves. I don't like to see you in it. It makes you look—well—something different from what I believe you really are. I like a plain, honest white light."

Gila gave him one swift, wondering glance and walked laughingly over to the library door. "Oh, is that all?" she said, and, touching a button, she switched off the big red table lamp and switched on what seemed like a thousand little tapers concealed softly about the ceiling.

"There!" she cried, half-mockingly. "You can have as much light as you like, and when you get tired of that we can cut them all off and sit in the firelight." She touched another button and let him see the room in the soft dim shadows and rich glow of the fire. Then she turned the full light on again and entered the room, dropping into one big leather chair at the side of the fireplace and indicating another big chair on the opposite side. She had no notion of sitting near him or of luring him to her side tonight. She had read him aright. Hers was the demure part to play, the reserved, shy maiden, the innocent, childlike, womanly woman. She would play it, but she would humble him! So she had vowed with her little white teeth set in her red lips as she stood before her dressing table mirror that night when he had fled from her red room and her.

Well pleased, with a sigh of relief he dropped into the chair and sat watching her, talking idly, as one who is feeling his way to a pleasant intimacy of whose nature he is not quite sure. She was very sweet and sympathetic about the examinations, told how she hated them herself and thought they ought to be abolished; said he was a wonder, that her cousin had told her he was a regular shark, and yet he hadn't let himself be spoiled by it, either. She flattered him gently with that deference a girl can pay to a man which makes her appear like an angel of light, and fixes him for any confidence in the world he has to give. She sat so quietly, with big eyes lifted now and then, talking earnestly and appreciatively of fine and noble things, that all his best thoughts about her were confirmed. He watched her, thinking what a lovely, lovable woman she was, what gentle sympathy and keen appreciation of really fine qualities she showed, child even though she seemed to be! He studied her, thinking what a friend she might be to that other poor girl in her loneliness and sorrow if she only would. He didn't know that he was yielding again to the lure that the red light had made the last time he was there. He didn't realize that, red light or white light, he was being led on. He only knew that it was a pleasure to talk to her, to be near her, to feel her sympathy; and that something had unlocked the innermost depths of his heart, the place he usually kept to himself, even away from the fellows. He had never quite opened it to a human being before. Tennelly had come nearer to getting a glimpse than anyone. But now he was really going to open it, for he had at last found another human being who could understand and appreciate.

"May I shut off the bright light and sit in the firelight?" he asked, and Gila acquiesced sweetly. It was just what she had been leading up to, but she did not move from her reticent yet sympathetic position in the retired depths of the great chair, where she knew the shadows and the glow of the fire would play on her face and show her sweet, serious pose.

"I want to tell you about a girl I have met this week."

A chill fell upon Gila, but she did not show it, she never even flickered those long lashes. Another girl! How dared he! The little white teeth set down sharply on the little red tongue out of sight, but the sweet, sympathetic mouth in the glow of the firelight remained placid.

"Yes?" The inflection, the lifted lashes, the whole attitude, was perfect. He plunged ahead.

"You are so very wonderful yourself that I am sure you will appreciate and understand her, and I think you are just the friend she needs."

Gila stiffened in her chair and turned her face nicely to the glow of the fire, so he could just see her lovely profile.

"She is all alone in the city—"

"Oh!" broke forth Gila in almost childish dismay. "Not even a chaperon?"

Courtland stopped, bewildered. Then he laughed indulgently. "She didn't have any use for a chaperon, child," he said, as if he were a great deal older than she. "She came here with her little brother to earn their living."

"Oh, she *had* a brother, then!" sighed Gila with evident relief.

It occurred to Courtland to be a bit pleased that Gila was so particular about the conventionalities. He had heard it rumored more than once that her own conduct overstepped the most lenient of rules. That must have been a mistake. It was a relief to know it from her own lips. But he explained gently:

"The little brother was killed on Monday night," he said gravely. "Just run down in cold blood by a passing automobile."

"How perfectly dreadful!" shuddered Gila, shrinking back into the depths of the chair. "But you know you mustn't believe a story like that! Poor people are always getting up such tales about rich people's automobiles. It isn't true at all. No chauffeur would do a thing like that! The children just run out and get in the way of the cars to tantalize the drivers. I've seen them myself. Why, our chauffeur has been arrested three or four times and charged with running over children and dogs, when it wasn't his fault at all; the people were just trying to get some money out of us! I don't suppose the little child was run over. It was probably his own fault."

"Yes, he was run over," said Courtland gently. "I saw it myself! I was standing on the curbstone when the boy—he was a beautiful little fellow with long golden curls—rushed out to meet his sister, calling out to her, and the automobile came whirring by without a sign of a horn, and crushed him down just like a broken lily. He never lifted his head nor made a motion again, and the automobile never even slowed up to see—just shot ahead and was gone."

Gila was still for a minute. She had no words to meet a situation like this. "Oh, well," she said, "I suppose he is better off, and the girl is, too. How could she take care of a child in the city alone, and do any work? Besides, children are an awful torment, and very likely he would have turned out bad. Boys usually do. What did you want me to do for her? Get her a position as a maid?"

There was something almost flippant in her tone. Strange that Courtland did not recognize it. But the firelight, the white gown, the pure profile, the down-drooped lashes had done for him once more what the red light had done before—taken him out of his normal senses and made him see a Gila that was not really there—soft, sweet, tender, womanly. The words, though they did not satisfy him, merely meant that she had not yet understood what he wanted, and was striving hard to find out.

"No," he said, gently. "I want you to go and see her. She is real sick and in the hospital. She needs a friend, a real girl friend, such as you could be if you would."

Gila answered in her slow, pretty drawl: "Why, I hate hospitals! I wouldn't even go to see Mama when she had an operation on her neck last winter, because I hate the odors they have around. But I'll go if you want me to. Of course I won't promise how much good I'll do. Girls of that stamp don't want to be helped, you know. They think they know it all, and they are usually most insulting. But I'll see what I can do. I don't mind giving her something. I've three evening dresses that I perfectly hate, and one of them I've never had on but once. She might get a position to act somewhere or sing in a café if she had good clothes."

Courtland hastened earnestly to impress her with the fact that Miss Brentwood was a refined girl of good family, and that it would be an insult to offer her secondhand clothing; but when he gave it up and yielded to Gila's plea that he drop these horrid, gloomy subjects and talk about something cheerful, he had a feeling of failure. Perhaps he ought not to have told Gila, after all. She simply couldn't understand the other girl because she had never dreamed of such a situation.

If he could have seen his gentle Gila a couple of hours later, standing before her mirror again and setting those little sharp teeth into her red lip, the ugly frown between her angry eyes; if he could have heard her low-muttered words, and, worse still, guessed her thoughts about himself and that other girl—he certainly would have gone out and gnashed his teeth in despair. If he could have known what was to come of his request to Gila Dare he would have rung up the hospital and had Miss Brentwood moved to another one in hot haste, or, better still, have taken strenuous measures to prevent that visit. But instead of that he read Mother Marshall's telegram over again, and lay down to forget Gila Dare utterly, and think pleasant thoughts about the Marshalls.

# *Chapter 12*

*

Gila Dare, in her very most startling costume, lavishly plastered with costly fur, and high-laced, French-heeled boots, came tripping down her father's steps to the limousine. She carried a dangling little trick of a handbag and a muff big enough for a rug. Her two eyes looked forth from the rim of the low-squashed, bandagelike fur hat like the eyes of a small, sly mouse that was about to nibble somebody else's cheese.

By her side a logy youth, with small, blue, fish eyes fixed adoringly on her, sauntered protectingly. She wore a large bunch of pale yellow orchids, evidently his gift, and was paying for them with her glances. One knew by the excited flush on the young man's face that he had rarely been paid so well. His eyes took on a glint of intelligence, one might almost say of hope, and he smiled egregiously, egotistically. His assurance grew with each step he took. As he opened the door of the luxurious car for her he wore an attitude of one who might possibly be a fiancé. Her little mouse eyes—you wouldn't have dreamed they could ever be large and wistful, nor innocent, either—twinkled pleasurably. She was playing her usual game and playing it well. It was the game for which she was rapidly becoming notorious, young as she was.

"Oh, now, *Chaw*-ley! *Ree*-ally! Why, I never dreamed it was that bad! But you mustn't, you know! I never gave you permission!"

The chauffeur, sitting stolidly in his uniform, awaiting the word to move, wondered idly what she was up to now. He was used to seeing the game played all around him day after day, as if he were a stick or a stone, or one of the metal trappings of the car.

"Chawley" Hathaway looked unutterable things, and the little mouse-eyes looked back unutterable things, with that lingering, just-too-long-for-pardoning glance that a certain kind of men and women employ when they want to loiter near the danger line and toy with vital things. An impressive handclasp, another long, languishing look, just a shade longer this time; then he closed the door, lifted his hat at the mouse-eyed goddess, and the limousine swept away. They had parted as if something momentous had occurred, and both knew in their hearts that neither had meant anything at all except to play with fire for an instant, like children sporting at lighting a border of forest that has a heart of true homes in its keeping.

Gila swept on in her chariot. The young man with whom she had played was well skilled in the game. He understood her perfectly, as she him. If he got burned sometimes it was up to him. She meant to take good care of herself.

Around another corner she spied another acquaintance. A word to the automaton on the front seat and the limousine swept up to the curb where he was passing. Gila leaned out with the sweetest bow. She was the condescending lady now; no mouse eyes in evidence this time; just a beautiful, commanding presence to be obeyed. She would have him ride with her, so he got in.

He was a tall, serious youth with credulous eyes, and she swept his soulful nature as one sweeps the keys of a familiar instrument, drawing forth timeworn melodies that, nevertheless, were new to him. And just because he thrilled under them, and looked in her eyes with startled earnestness, did she like to play upon his soul. It would have been a bore if he had understood, for he was a dull soul, and young—ages young for Gila, though his years numbered two more than hers. She liked to see his eyes kindle and his breath come quick. Someday he would tell her with impassioned words how much he loved her, and she would turn him neatly and comfortably down for awhile, till he learned his place and promised not to be troublesome. Then he might join the procession again as long as he would behave. But at present she knew she could sway him as she would, and she touched the orchids at her belt with tender little caressing movements and melting looks. Even before she reached home she knew he would have a box of something rarer or more costly waiting for her, if the city afforded such.

She set him down at his club, quite well satisfied with her few minutes. She was glad it didn't last longer, for it would have grown tiresome; she had had just enough, carried him just far enough on the wave of emotion, to stimulate her own soul.

Sweeping away from the curb again, bowing graciously to two or three other acquaintances who were going in or out of the club building, she gave an order for the hospital and set her face sternly to the duty before her.

A little breeze of expectation preceded her entrance into the hospital, a stir among the attendants about the door. Passing nurses apprized her furs and orchids; young interns took account of her eyes—the mouse eyes had returned, but they lured with something unspeakable and thrilling in them.

She waited with a nice little superb air that made everybody hurry to serve her, and presently she was shown up to the door of Bonnie Brentwood's room. Her chauffeur had followed, bearing a large pasteboard suitbox which he set down at the door and departed.

"Is this Miss Brentwood's room?" she asked of the nurse who opened the door grudgingly. Her patient had just awakened from a refreshing sleep and she had no notion that this lofty little person had really come to see the quiet, sad-eyed girl who had come there in such shabby little garments. The visitor had made a mistake, of course. The nurse grudgingly admitted that Miss Brentwood roomed there.

"Well, I've brought some things for her," said Gila, indicating the large box at her feet. "You can take it inside and open it."

The nurse opened the door a little wider, looked at the small, imperious personage in fur trappings, and then down at the box. She hesitated a moment in a kind of inward fury, then swung the door a little wider open and stepped back:

"You can set it inside if you wish, or wait till one of the men comes by," she said, coolly, and deliberately walked back in the room and busied herself with the medicine glasses.

Gila stared at her haughtily a moment, but there wasn't much satisfaction in wasting her glares on that white linen back, so she stooped and dragged in the box. She came and stood by the bed, staring down apprizingly at the sick girl.

Bonnie Brentwood turned her head wearily and looked up at her with a puzzled, half-annoyed expression. She had paid no heed to the little altercation at the door. Her apathy toward life was great. She was lying on the borderland, looking over and longing to go where all her dear ones had gone. It wearied her inexpressibly that they all would insist on doing things to call her back.

"Is your name Brentwood?" asked Gila, in the sharp, high key so alien to a hospital.

Bonnie recalled her spirit to this world and focused her gaze on the girl as if to try and recall where she had ever met her. Bonnie's abundant hair was spread out over the pillow, as the nurse had just prepared to brush it. It fell in long, rich waves of brightness and fascinating little rings of gold about her face. Gila stared at it jealously, as if it were something that had been stolen from her. Her own hair, cloudy and dreamy, and made much of with all that skill and care could do, was pitiful besides this wonderful gold mane with red and purple shadows in its depths, and ripples and curls at the ends. Wonderful hair!

The face of the girl on the pillow was perfect in form and feature. Regular, delicate, refined, and lovely! Gila knew it would be counted rarely beautiful, and she was furious! How had that upstart of a college boy dared to send her here to see a beauty! What had he meant by it?

By this time the girl on the bed had summoned her soul back to earth for the moment, and answered in a cool, little tone of distance, as she might have spoken to her employer, perhaps; or, in other circumstances, to the stranger begging for work on her doorsill—Bonnie was a lady anywhere—"Yes, I am Miss Brentwood."

There was no noticeable emphasis on the "Miss," but Gila felt that the pauper had arisen and put herself on the same level with her, and she was furious.

"Well, I've brought you a few things!" declared Gila, in a most offensive tone. "Paul Courtland asked me to come and see what I could do for you." She swung her moleskin trappings about and pointed to the box. "I don't believe in giving money, not often," she declared, with a tilt of her nasty little chin that suddenly seemed to curve out in a hateful, satanic point, "but I don't mind giving a little lift in other ways to persons who are truly worthy, you know. I've brought you a few evening dresses that I'm done with. It may help you to get a position playing for the movies, perhaps; or if you don't know ragtime, perhaps you might act—they'll take almost anybody, I understand, if they have good clothes. Besides, I'm going to give you an introduction to a girls' employment club. They have a hall and hold dances once a week and you get acquainted. It only costs you ten cents a week and it will give you a place to spend your evenings. If you join that you'll need evening dresses for the dances. Of course I understand some of the girls just go in their street suits, but you stand a great deal better chance of having a good time if you are dressed attractively. And then they say men often go in there evenings to look for a stenographer, or an actor, or some kind of a worker, and they always pick out the prettiest. Dress goes a great way if you use it rightly. Now there's a frock in here—" Gila stooped and untied the cord on the box. "This frock cost a hundred and fifty dollars, and I never wore it but once!"

She held up a tattered blue net adorned with straggling, crushed, artificial rosebuds, its sole pretension to a waist being a couple of straps of silver tissue attached to a couple of rags of blue net. It looked for all the world like a draggled butterfly.

"It's torn in one or two places," pursued Gila's ready tongue, "but it's easily mended. I wore it to a dance and somebody stepped on the hem. I suppose you are good at mending. A girl in your position ought to know how to sew.

My maid usually mends things like this with a thread of itself. You can pull one out along the hem, I should think. Then here is a pink satin. It needs cleaning. They don't charge more than two or three dollars—or perhaps you might use cleaning fluid. I had slippers to match, but I couldn't find but one. I brought that along. I thought you might do something with it. They were horribly expensive—made to order, you know. Then this cerise chiffon, all covered with sequins, is really too showy for a girl in your station, but in case you get a chance to act you might need it, and anyhow I never cared for it. It isn't becoming to me. Here's an indigo Charmeuse with silver trimmings. I got horribly tired of it, but you will look stunning in it. It might even help you catch a rich husband; who knows! There's half a dozen pairs of white evening gloves! I might have had them cleaned, but if you can use them I can get new ones. And there's a bundle of old silk stockings! They haven't any toes or heels much, but I suppose you can darn them. And of course you can't afford to buy expensive silk stockings!"

One by one Gila had pulled the things out of the box, rattling on about them as if she were selling corn cure. She was a trifle excited, to be sure, now that she was fairly launched on her philanthropic expedition; also the fact that the two women in the room were absolutely silent and gave no hint of how they were going to take this tide of insults was somewhat disconcerting. However, Gila was not easily disconcerted. She was very angry, and her anger had been growing in force all night. The greatest insult that man could offer her had been heaped upon her by Courtland, and there was no punishment too great to be meted out to the unfortunate innocent who had been the occasion of it. Gila did not care what she said, and she had no fear of any consequences whatever. There had not, so far to her knowledge, lived the man who could not be called back and humbled to her purpose after she had punished him sufficiently for any offense he might knowingly or unknowingly have committed. That she really had begun to admire Courtland, and to desire him in some degree for her own, only added fuel to her fire. This girl whom he had dared to pity should be burned and tortured; she should be insulted and extinguished utterly, so that she would never dare to lift her head again within recognizable distance of Paul Courtland, or she would know the reason why. Paul Courtland was *hers*—if she chose to have him; let no other girl dare to look at him!

The nurse stood, starched and stern, with growing indignation at the audacity of the stranger. Only the petrification of absolute astonishment, and wonder as to what would happen next, took her off her guard for the moment and prevented her from ousting the young lady from the premises instantly. There was also the magic name of the handsome young gentleman that had been used as password, and the very slight possibility that this might be some rich relative of the lovely young patient that she would not like to have put out. The nurse looked from Bonnie to the visitor in growing wrath and perplexity.

Bonnie lay wide-eyed and amazed, startled bewilderment and growing dignity in her face. Two soft, pink spots of color began to bloom out in her cheeks, and her eyes took on a twinkle of amusement. She was watching the visitor as if she were a passing Punch-and-Judy show come in to play for a moment for her entertainment. She lay and regarded her and her tawdry display of finery with a quiet, disinterested aloofness that was beginning to get on Gila's nerves.

"You can have my flowers, too, if you want them," said Gila, excitedly, seeing that her flood of insult had brought forth no answering word from either listener. "They're very handsome, rare ones—orchids, you know. Did you ever see any before? I don't mind leaving them with you because I have a great many flowers, and these were given me by a young man I don't care in the least about."

She unpinned the flowers and held them out to Bonnie, but the sick girl lay still and regarded her with that quiet, half-amused gravity and did not offer to take them.

"I presume you can find a wastebasket down in the office if you want to get rid of them," said Bonnie, suddenly, in a clear, refined voice. "I really shouldn't care for them. Isn't there a wastebasket somewhere about?" she asked, turning toward the nurse.

"Down in the hall by the front entrance," answered the nurse, grimly. She was ready to play up to whatever cue Bonnie gave her.

Gila stood haughtily holding her flowers and looking from one woman to the other, unable to believe that any other woman had the insufferable audacity to meet her on her own ground in this way. Were they actually guying her, or were they innocents who really thought she did not want the flowers, or who did not know enough to think orchids beautiful? Before she could decide Bonnie was speaking again, still in that quiet, superior tone of a lady that gave her the command of the situation:

"I am sorry," she said, quite politely, as if she must let her visitor down gently, "but I'm afriad you have made some mistake. I don't recall ever having met you before. It must be some other Miss Brentwood for whom you are looking."

Gila stared, and her color suddenly began to rise even under the pearly tint of her flesh. Had she possibly made some blunder? This certainly was the voice of a lady. And the girl on the bed had the advantage of absolute self-control. Somehow that angered Gila more than anything else.

"Don't you know Paul Courtland?" she demanded, imperiously.

"I never heard the name before!"

Bonnie's voice was steady, and her eyes looked coolly into the other girl's. The nurse looked at Bonnie and marveled. She knew the name of Paul Courtland well; she telephoned to that name every day. How was it that the girl did not know it? She liked this girl and the man who had brought her here and been so anxious about her. But who on earth was this hussy in fur?

Gila looked at Bonnie madly. Her stare said as plainly as words could have done. "You lie! You *do* know him!" But Gila's lips said, scornfully, "Aren't you the poor girl whose kid brother got killed by an automobile in the street?"

Across Bonnie's stricken face there flashed a spasm of pain and her very lips grew white.

"I thought so!" sneered Gila, rushing on with her insult. "And yet you deny that you ever heard Paul Courtland's name! He picked up the kid and carried it in the house and ran errands for you, but you don't know him! That's gratitude for you! I told him the working class were all like that. I have no doubt he has paid for this very room that you are lying in!"

"Stop!" cried Bonnie, sitting up, her eyes like two stars, her face white to the very lips. "You have no right to come here and talk like that! I cannot understand who could have sent you! Certainly not the courteous stranger who picked up my little brother. I do not know his name, nor anything about him, but I can assure you that I shall not allow him nor anyone else to pay my bills. Now will you take your things and leave my room? I am feeling very—tired!"

The voice suddenly trailed off into silence and Bonnie dropped back limply upon the pillow.

The nurse sprang like an angry bear who has seen somebody troubling her cubs. She touched vigorously a button in the wall as she passed and swooped down upon the tawdry finery, stuffing it unceremoniously into the box; then she turned upon the little fur-trimmed lady, placed a capable arm about her slim waist, and scooped her out of the room. Flinging the bulging box down at her feet, where it gaped widely, gushing forth in pink, blue, cerise, and silver, she shut the door and flew back to her charge.

Down the hall hurried the emergency doctor, formidable in his white linen uniform. When Gila looked up from the confusion at her feet she encountered the gaze of a pair of grave and disapproving eyes behind a pair of fascinating tortoise-shell goggles. She was not accustomed to disapproval in masculine eyes and it infuriated her.

"What does all this mean?" His voice expressed a good many kinds of disapproval.

"It means that I have been insulted, sir, by one of your nurses!" declared Gila, in her most haughty tone, with a tilt of her chin and a flirt of her fur trappings. "I shall make it my business to see that she is removed at once from her position."

The doctor eyed her mildly, as though she were a small bat squeaking at a mighty hawk. "Indeed! I fancy you will find that a rather difficult matter!" he answered, contemptuously. "She is one of our best nurses! James!" to a passing assistant, "escort this person and her—belongings"—looking doubtfully at the mess on the floor—"down to the street!"

Then he swiftly entered Bonnie's room, closing and fastening the door behind him.

The said James, with an ill-concealed grin, stooped to his task; and thus, in mortification, wrath, and ignominy, did Gila descend to her waiting limousine.

There were tears of anger on her cheeks as she sat back against her cushions; more tears fell, which, regardless of her pearly complexion, she wiped away with a cobweb of a handkerchief, while she sat and hated Courtland, and the whole tribe of college men, her cousin Bill Ward included, for getting her into a scrape like this. Defeat was a thing she could not brook. She had never, since she came out of short frocks, been so defeated in her life! But it should not be defeat! She would take her full revenge for all that had happened! Courtland should bite the dust! She would show him that he could not go around picking up stray beauties and sending her after them to pet them for him.

She did not watch for acquaintances during that ride home. She remained behind drawn curtains. Arrived at home, she stormed up to her room, giving orders to her maid not to disturb her, and sat down angrily to indite an epistle to Courtland that should bring him to his knees.

Meantime the doctor and nurse worked silently, skilfully over Bonnie until the weary eyes opened once more, and a long-drawn sigh showed that the girl had come back to the world.

By and by, when the doctor had gone out of the room and the nurse had finished giving her the beef tea that had been ordered, Bonnie raised her eyes. "Would you mind finding out for me just what this room costs?" she asked, wearily.

The nurse had been fixing it all up in her mind what she should say when this question came. "Why, I'm under the impression you won't have to pay anything," she said, pleasantly. "You see, sometimes patients, when they go out, are kind of grateful and leave a sort of endowment of a bed for awhile, or something like that, for cases just like yours, where strangers come in for a few days and need quiet—

real quiet that they can't get in the ward, you know. I believe someone paid something for this room in some kind of a way like that. I guess the doctor thought you would get well quicker if you had it quiet, so he put you in here. You needn't worry a bit about it."

Bonnie smiled. "Would you mind making sure?" she asked. "I'd like to know just what I owe. I have a little money, you know."

The nurse nodded and slipped away to whisper the story to the grave doctor, who grew more indignant and contemptuous than he had been to Gila, and sent her promptly back with an answer.

"You don't have to pay a cent," she said, cheerfully, as she returned. "This bed is endowed temporarily, the doctor says, to be used at his discretion, and he wants to keep you here till someone comes who needs this room more than you do. At present there isn't anyone, so you needn't worry. We are not going to let any more little feather-headed spitfires in to see you, either. The doctor bawled the office out like everything for letting that girl up."

Bonnie tried to smile again, but only ended in a sigh. "Oh, it doesn't matter," she said, and then, after a minute. "You've been very good to me. Sometime I hope I can do something for you. Now I'm going to sleep."

The nurse went out to look after some of her duties. Half an hour later she came back to Bonnie's room and entered softly, not to waken her. She was worried lest she had left the window open too wide and the wind might be blowing on her, for it had turned a good deal colder since the sun went down.

She tiptoed to the bed and bent over in the dim light to see if her patient was all right. Then she drew back sharply.

The bed was empty!

She turned on the light and looked all around. There was no one else in the room! Bonnie was gone!

# Chapter 13

*

Wildly the nurse searched the room, throwing open the wardrobe first! Bonnie's shabby clothes were no longer hanging on the hooks! She rushed to the window and looked helplessly along the fire escape out into the courtyard below, where the ambulance was just bringing in a fresh case. There was no sign of her patient. Turning back, she saw on the table a bit of paper from the daily record-sheet folded up and pinned together with a quaint little circle of old-fashioned gold in which were set tiny garnets and pearls. The note was addressed, "Miss Wright, Nurse." A five-dollar bill fell from the paper. The nurse picked it up and read:

> DEAR NURSE—I am leaving this little pin for you because you have been so good to me. It isn't very valuable, but it is all I have. The five dollars is for the room. I know it is worth more, but I haven't anymore just now. You have all been very kind. Please give the money to the doctor and thank him for me. Don't worry about me; I am all right. I just need to get back to work.
>
> Good-bye, and thank you again,
>
> Sincerely,
>
> ROSE BONNER BRENTWOOD

The nurse rushed down to the office. A search was instituted at once. Everyone in the office and halls was questioned. Only one elevator man remembered a person, dressed in black, going out of the nurses' side door. He had thought it one of the probation nurses.

They searched the streets for several blocks around. It had been only a few minutes, and the girl was weak. She could not have gone far! But no Bonnie was found!

The evening mail came in and a letter with a western postmark arrived for Miss R. B. Brentwood. The nurse looked at it sadly. A letter for the poor child! What hope and friendliness might it not contain! If it had only come a couple of hours sooner!

Later that evening, when it was finally settled that the patient had really escaped, the nurse went to the telephone.

Courtland was in Tennelly's room. They had been discussing women's suffrage, some question that had come up in the political science class that day. Tennelly held that most women were too unbalanced to vote; you never could tell what a woman would do next. She was swayed entirely by her emotions, mainly two—love and hate; sometimes pride and selfishness. *Always* selfishness. Women were all selfish!

Courtland thought of the calm, true eyes of Mother Marshall and the telegram that had come the day before. He held that all women were not selfish. He said he knew *one* woman who was not. All women were not flighty and unbalanced nor swayed by their emotions. He knew two girls whom he thought were not swayed by their emotions. Just then he was called to the telephone.

The nurse's voice broke upon his absorption with a disturbing element: "Mr. Courtland, this is the nurse from Good Samaritan Hospital. I thought you ought to know that Miss Brentwod has disappeared! We have searched everywhere, but can get no clue to her whereabouts. She wasn't fit to go. She had fainted again—was unconscious a long time. She had a very disturbing call from a young woman this afternoon, who mentioned your name and got up to the room somehow without the usual formalities. Of course I didn't know but she had the doctor's permission, and she came right in. She brought a lot of dirty evening gowns and tried to give them to my patient, and called her a working girl; spoke of her little dead brother as 'the kid,' and was very insulting. I thought perhaps you would be able to give us a clue as to where the patient was. She really was too weak to be out alone; and in this bitter cold! Her jacket was very thin. She's just in the condition to get pneumonia. I'm all broken up because I thought she was sound asleep. She left a little note for me, with a pin she wanted me to keep, and five dollars to pay for her room. You see she got the notion from what that girl said that she was on charity in that room and she wouldn't stay. I thought you'd want me to let you know!"

There was almost a sob in the nurse's voice as she ended. Courtland's heart sank.

Poor Gila! She hadn't understood. She had meant well, but hadn't known how! Poor fool he, that had asked her to go! She had never had experience with sorrow and poverty. How could she be expected to understand?

His anger rose as he listened to a few more details concerning Gila's remarks. Of course the nurse was exaggerating, but how crude of Gila! Where were her woman's intuitions? Her finer sensibilities? Where indeed? But, after all, perhaps the nurse had not understood fully. Perhaps she had taken offense and misconstrued Gila's intended kindness! Well, the main thing was that Bonnie was gone and must be hunted up. It wouldn't do to leave her without friends, sick and weak, this cold night. She had, of course, gone home to her room. He could easily find her. He wouldn't mind going out, though he had intended doing other things that evening; but he had undertaken this job and he must see it through. Then there was that telegram from Mother Marshall! And her letter on the way! Too bad! Of course he must make Bonnie go back to the hospital. He would have no trouble in coaxing her back when she knew how she had distressed them all.

"I'll go right down to her old place and see if she's there," he told the nurse. "She has probably gone back to her room. Certainly I will insist that she return to the hospital tonight."

As he hung up the receiver Pat touched his elbow and pointed to a messenger boy waiting for him with a note.

It was Gila's violet-scented missive over which she had wept those angry tears. He signed for the letter with a frown. Somehow the perfume annoyed him. He put the thing in his pocket, having no patience to read it at once, and went hurriedly down the hall.

As he passed the office Courtland found a letter in his box, noting with a sort of comfort that it bore a western postmark. As he waited for his trolley at the corner, he reflected how strange it was that this young woman, whom he had never seen nor heard of before, should suddenly be flung thus upon his horizon and seem, in a measure, his responsibility. He had been shaking free from that sense of accountability since she had been reported getting better; and especially since he had put her upon the hearts of Mother Marshall and Gila. Gila! How the thought of her annoyed just now!

In the trolley he opened Mother Marshall's letter and read, marveling at the revelation of motherhood it contained. Motherhood and fatherhood! How beautiful! A sort of Christ-mother and Christ-father, these two who had been bereft of their own, were willing to be! And Bonnie! How she needed them—and had gone before she knew! He must persuade her to go to Mother Marshall! For, after all, this whole bungle was his fault. If he had never tried to tole Gila into it this wouldn't have happened.

A factory girl, belated, shivered into the car in a thin summer jacket and stood beside a girl in furs and a handsome coat. Courtland thought of Bonnie in her little shabby black suit—a summer suit, of course. He remembered noticing how thin it looked as they stood beside the grave on the bleak hillside, and wondering if she were not cold. But it was mild that day compared to this, and the sun had been shining then. She must have half-frozen in that long, long ride! And had she money enough to buy her something to eat? She had left a five-dollar bill at the hospital. Some instinct taught him that it was the last she had!

He grew more and more nervous and impatient as he neared his destination.

He sprang up the narrow stairs that had grown so familiar to him the past week, watching anxiously the crack under the door to see if there was a light. But it was all dark! He tapped at the door lightly. But of course she would have gone to bed at once after the exertion of the journey! He tapped louder, and held his breath to listen. But no answer came!

Then he tapped again, and called, in half-subdued tones: "Miss Brentwood! Are you there?"

A stir was heard at the other end of the hall, the sound of the scratching of a match. A light appeared under the door of the front room, the door opened a crack, and a frowsy head was thrust out, with a candle held high above it, and eyes that were full of sleep peering into the darkness of the hall.

"Has Miss Brentwood returned? Have you seen her?" he asked.

"Not as I knows of, she 'ain't come," said a woman's voice. "I went to bed early. She might ov and I not hear her, she's so softly like."

"I wonder if we could find out? Would you mind coming and trying?"

The woman looked at him keenly. "Oh, you're the young feller what come to the fun'rul, ain't you? Well, you jest wait a bit an' I'll throw somethin' on an' come an' try." The woman came in an amazing costume of many colors, and called and shook the door. She got her key and unlocked the door, stepping cautiously inside and looking about. She advanced, holding the candle high, Courtland waiting behind. He could see one withered white rosebud on the floor. There was no sign of Bonnie! Her room was just as she had left it on the day of the funeral!

Where was Bonnie Brentwood?

# Chapter 14

*

Suddenly, as Courtland stood in the narrow dark street alone and in uncertainty, he was no longer alone. As clearly as if he felt a touch upon his sleeve he knew that One was there beside him, and that this errand he was upon had the sanction of that Presence which had met him once in the fiery way and promised to show him what to do.

"God, show me where to find her!" he ejaculated, and then, as if one had said, "Come with me!" he turned as certainly as if a passerby had directed him where he had seen her, and walked up the street. That is, *they* walked up the street.

Always in thinking of that walk afterward he thought of it as "they walking up the street"—himself and the Presence.

The first thing he remembered about it was that he had lost that sense of uncertainty and anxiety. How long the route was or where it was to end did not seem to matter. Every step of the way was companioned by One who knew what He was about. It came to him that he would like to go everywhere in such company; that no journey would be too far or arduous, no duty too unpleasant if all could be as this.

He stepped into the telephone office and began calling up hospitals. There were one or two that reported young women brought in, but the description was not at all like the girl of whom he was in search. He jotted them down in his notebook, however, with a feeling that they might be a last resort.

As he turned the pages of the phone book his eye caught the name of the city's morgue, and a sudden horror froze into his mind. What if something had happened to her and she had been taken there? What if she had ended the life which had looked so lonely and impossible to her? No, she would never do that, not with her faith in the Christ! And yet, if her vitality was low, and her heart was taxed with sorrow, she would perhaps scarcely be responsible for what she did.

He rang up the morgue sharply and put tense, eager questions.

Yes, a young woman had been brought in about an hour ago. . . . Yes, dressed in black—had long light hair and was slender. "*Some looker!*" the man who answered the phone said.

Courtland shuddered and hung up. He felt that he must go to the morgue.

When they entered the gruesome place of the unknown dead, although the Presence entered with him, yet he felt that it was there already, standing close among the dead; had been there when they came in!

Courtland's face was white and set as he passed between the silent dead laid out for identification. An inward shudder went through him as he was led to the spot where lay the latest comer, a slim young girl with long golden hair, sodden from the river where she had been found, her pretty face sharpened and coarsened by sin.

He drew a deep breath of relief and turned away quickly from the sight of her poor drowned eyes, rejoicing that they had not been the eyes of Bonnie. It was terrible to think of Bonnie lying so, all drenched and her spirit put out. He was glad he might still think of her alive, and go on searching for her. But a dart of pain went through his heart as he looked again at this little wreck of womanhood, going out of a life that had dealt hardly with her; where she had reached for brightness and pleasure, and had found ashes and bitterness instead. Going into a beyond of darkness, hoping, perhaps, for no kindlier hands to greet her than those that had been withheld from her in this world! What would the resurrection mean to a poor little soul like that? What could it mean? Ah! perhaps it had not all been her fault! Perhaps there were others who had helped push her down, smug in self-righteousness, to whom the resurrection would be more of a horror than to the pretty, ignorant child whose untaught feet had strayed into forbidden paths! Who knew? He was glad to look up and feel the Presence there! Who knew what might have passed between the soul and God? It was safe to leave that little sinful soul with Him who had died to save. It was good to go out from there knowing that the pretty, sinful girl, the hardened, grizzled sot, the poor old toothless crone, the little hunchback newsboy who lay in the same row, were guarded alike and beloved by the same Presence that would go with him.

Around the little newsboy huddled a group of street gamins, counting out their few pennies, and talking excitedly of how they would buy him some flowers. There were tear stains down their grimy cheeks and it was plain they were pitying him, they who had perhaps yet to tread the paths of sin and deprivation and sorrow for many long years. And the Presence there! So near them, with the pitying eyes! The young man knew the eyes were pitying! If the children could only see! He felt an impulse to turn back and tell them as he passed out into the street, yet how could he make them understand—he who understood so feebly and intermittently himself? He felt a great ache in himself to go out and shout to all the world to look up and see the Presence that was in their midst, and they saw Him not!

He was entirely aware that his present mental state would have seemed to him little short of insanity twenty-four hours before; that it might pass again as it had done before; and a kind of mental frenzy seized him lest it would. He did not want to lose this assurance of One guiding through a world that was so full of sorrow as this one had recently revealed itself to him to be. And with the world-old anguished "Give me a sign!" the cry of the soul reaching out to the unknown, he spoke aloud once more: "God, if You are really there, let me find her!"

And yet if any had asked him just then if he ever prayed he would have told them no. Prayer was to him a thing utterly apart from this cry of his soul, this longing for an understanding with God.

He walked on through streets he did not know, passing

men and women with worn and haggard faces, tattered garments, and discouraged mien; and always that cry came in his soul, "Oh, if they only knew!" There was the Presence by his side, and men passed by and saw Him not!

He was walking in the general direction of the Good Samaritan Hospital, just as anyone would walk with a friend through a strange place and accommodate his going to the man who was guiding him. All the way there seemed to be a sort of intercourse between himself and his Companion. His soul was putting forth great questions that he would someday take up in detail and go over little by little, as one will verify a problem that one has worked out. But now he was working it out, becoming satisfied in his soul that this was the only way to solve the great otherwise unanswerable problems of the universe.

They had gone for perhaps three miles or more from the morgue, traveling for the most part through narrow streets crowded full of small dwelling houses interspersed by cheap stores and saloons. The night lowered! the stars were not on duty. A cold wind from the river swept around corners, reminding him of the dripping yellow hair of the girl in the morgue. It cut like a knife through Courtland's heavy overcoat and made him wish he had brought his muffler. He stuffed his gloved hands into his pockets. Even in their fur linings they were stiff and cold. He thought of the girl's little light serge jacket and shivered visibly as they turned into another street where vacant lots on one side left a wide sweep for the wind and sent it tempesting along freighted with dust and stinging bits of sand. The clouds were heavy as with snow, only that it was too cold to snow. One fancied only biting steel could fall from clouds like that on a night so bitter. And any moment he might have turned back, gone a block to one side, and caught the trolley across to the university, where light and warmth and friends were waiting. And what was this one little lost girl to him? A stranger? No, she was no longer a stranger! She had become something infinitely precious to the whole universe. God cared, and that was enough! He could not be a friend of God unless he cared as God cared! He was demonstrating facts that he had never apprehended before.

The lights were out in most of the houses that they passed, for it was growing late. There were not quite so many saloons. The streets loomed wide ahead, the line of houses dark on the left, and the stretch of vacant lots, with the river beyond on the right. Across the river a line of dark buildings with occasional blink of lights blended into the dark of the sky, and the wind merciless over all.

On ahead a couple of blocks the light flung out on the pavement and marked another saloon. Bright doors swung back and forth. The intermittent throb of a piano and twang of a violin, making merry with the misery of the world; voices brokenly above it all came at intervals, loudly as the way drew nearer.

The saloon doors swung again and four or five dark figures jostled noisily out and came haltingly down the street. They walked crazily, like ships without a rudder, veering from one side of the walk to the other, shouting and singing uncouth, ribald songs, hoarse laughter interspersed with scattered oaths.

"O! Jesus Christ!" came distinctly through the quiet night. The young man felt a distinct pain for the Christ by his side, like the pressing of a thorn into the brow. He seemed to know the prick himself. For these were some of those for whom He died!

It occurred to Courtland that he was seeing everything on this walk through the eyes of Christ. He remembered Scrooge and his journey with the Ghost of Christmas Past in Dickens's *Christmas Carol*. It was like that. He was seeing the real soul of everybody! He was with the architect of the universe, noting where the work had gone wrong from the mighty plans. He suddenly knew that these creatures coming giddily toward him were planned to mighty things!

The figures paused before one of the dark houses, pointed and laughed; went nearer to the steps and stooped. He could not hear what they were saying; the voices were hushed in ugly whispers, broken by harsh laughter. Only now and then he caught a syllable.

"Wake up!" floated out into the silence once. And again, "No, you don't, my pretty little chicken!"

Then a girl's scream pierced the night and something

darted out from the darkness of the doorstep, eluding the drunken men, but slipped and fell!

Courtland broke into a noiseless run.

The men had scrambled tipsily after the girl and clutched her. They lifted her unsteadily and surrounded her. She screamed again, and dashed this way and that blindly, but they met her every time and held her.

Courtland knew, as by a flash, that he had been brought here for this crisis. It was as if he had heard the words spoken to him, "Now go!" He, lowering his head and crouching, came swiftly forward, watching carefully where he steered, and coming straight at two of the men with his powerful shoulders. It was an old trick of the football field and it bowled the two assailants on the right straight out into the gutter. The other three made a dash at him, but he sidestepped one and tripped him; a blow on the point of the chin sent another sprawling on the sidewalk; but the last one, who was perhaps the most sober of them all, showed fight and called to his comrades to come on and get this stranger who was trying to steal their girl. The language he used made Courtland's blood boil. He struck the fellow across his foul mouth, and then clenching with him, went down upon the sidewalk. His antagonist was a heavier man than he was, but the steady brain and the trained muscles had the better of it from the first, and in a moment more the drunken man was choking and limp.

Courtland rose and looked about. The two fellows in the gutter were struggling to their feet with loud threats, and the fellow on the sidewalk was staggering toward him. They would be upon the girl again in a moment. He looked toward her, as she stood trembling a few feet away from him, too frightened to try to run, not daring to leave her protector. A street light fell directly upon her white face. It was Bonnie Brentwood!

With a kick at the man on the ground who was trying to rise, and a lurch at the man on the sidewalk who was coming toward him that sent him spinning again, Courtland dived under the clutching hands of the two in the gutter who couldn't quite make it to get upon the curb again. Snatching up the girl like a baby, he fled up the street and around the first corner, and all that cursing, drunken, reeling five came howling after!

# Chapter 15

*

Courtland had run three blocks and turned two corners before he dared stop and set the girl upon her feet again. He looked anxiously at her white face and great, frightened eyes. Her lips were trembling and she was shivering. He tore his overcoat off, wrapped it about her, and before she could protest caught her up again and ran on another block or two.

"Oh, you must not!" she cried. "I can walk perfectly well, and I don't need your coat. Please, please put on your coat and let me walk! You will take a terrible cold!"

"I can run better without it," he explained briefly, "and we can get out of the way of those fellows quicker this way!"

So she lay still in his arms till he put her down again. He looked up and down either way, hoping to see the familiar red and green lights of a drugstore open late; but none greeted him; all the buildings seemed to be residences.

Somewhere in the distance he heard the whir of a late trolley. He glanced at his watch. It was half past one. If only a taxicab would come along. But no taxi was in sight. The girl was begging him to put on his overcoat. She had drawn it from her own shoulders and was holding it out to him insistently. But with the rare smile that Courtland was noted for he took the coat and wrapped it firmly about her shoulders again, this time putting her arms in the sleeves and buttoning it up to the chin.

"Now," said he, "you're not to take that off again until we get where it is warm. You needn't worry about me. I'm quite used to going out in all weathers without my coat as often as with it. Besides, I've been exercising. When did you have something to eat?"

"When I left the hospital this evening. I had some strong beef tea," she answered, airily, as if that had been only a few minutes before.

"How did you happen to be where I found you?" he asked, looking at her keenly.

"Why, I must have missed my way, I think," she explained, "and I felt a little weak from having been in bed so long. I just sat down on a doorstep to rest a minute before I went on, and I'm afraid I must have fallen asleep."

"You were *walking*?" His tone was stern. "Why were you walking?"

A desperate look came into her face. "Well, I hadn't any carfare, if you must know the reason."

They were passing a streetlight as she said it, and he looked down at her fine little white profile in wonder and awe. He felt a sudden choking in his throat and a mist in his eyes. He had it on the tip of his tongue to say, "You poor little girl!" but instead he said, in a tone of intense admiration:

"Well, you certainly are the pluckiest girl I ever saw! You have your nerve with you all right! But you're not going to walk another step tonight!"

And with that he stooped, gathered her up again, and strode forward. He could hear the distant whir of another trolley, and he determined to take it, no matter which way it was going. It would take them somewhere he could telephone for an ambulance. So he sprinted forward, regardless of her protests, and arrived at the next corner just in time to catch the car going cityward.

There was nobody else in the car and he made her keep the coat about her. He couldn't help seeing how worn and thin her little shabby shoes were, and how she shivered now even in the great coat. He saw she was just keeping up her nerve, and he was filled with admiration.

"Why did you run away from the hospital?" he asked, suddenly, looking straight into her sad eyes.

"I couldn't afford to stay any longer."

"You made a big mistake. It wouldn't have cost you a

cent. That room was free. I made sure of that before I secured it for you."

"But that was a private room!"

"Just a little more private than the wards. That room was paid for and put at the disposal of the doctor to use for whoever he thought needed quiet. Now are you satisfied? And you are going straight back there till you are well enough to go out again! You raised a big row in the hospital, running away. They've had the whole force of assistants out hunting you for hours, and your nurse is awfully upset about you. She seems to be crazy over you, anyway. She nearly wept when she telephoned me. And I've been out for hours hunting you, stirred up the old lady on your floor at your home, and a lot of hospitals and other places, and then just came on you in the nick of time. I hope you've learned your lesson, to be a good little girl after this and not run away."

He smiled indulgently, but the girl's eyes were full of tears.

"I didn't mean to make all that trouble for people. Why should you all care about a stranger? But, oh! I'm so thankful you came! Those men were terrible!" She shuddered. "How did you happen to come there? I think God must have led you."

"He did!" said Courtland, with conviction.

When they reached the big city station he stowed his patient into a taxi and sent a messenger up to the restaurant for hot chicken broth, which he administered himself.

She lay back with her eyes closed after the broth was finished. He realized that she had reached the full limit of her endurance. She had forgotten even to protest against wearing his overcoat any longer.

It was a strange ride. The silent girl sat closely wrapped in her corner, fast asleep. The car bounded over obstacles now and then, or swung around corners and threw her about like a ball, but she did not waken; and finally Courtland drew her head down upon his shoulder and put his arm about her to keep her from being thrown out of her seat; and she settled down like a tired child. He could not help thinking of that other girl lying stark and dead in the morgue, and being glad that this one was safe.

Nurse Wright was hovering about the hallway when the taxi drew up to the entrance of the hospital, and Bonnie was tenderly cared for at once.

Courtland began to realize that this great hospital was an evidence of the Presence of Christ in the world! He was not the only one who had felt the Presence. Someone moved as he had been tonight had established this big house of healing. There on the opposite wall was a great stained-glass window representing Christ blessing the little children, and the people bringing the maimed and halt and lame and blind to Him for healing.

The quiet night routine went on about him; the strong, pervasive odor of antiseptics; the padded tap of the nurses' rubber soles as they went softly on their rounds; the occasional click of a glass and a spoon somewhere; the piteous wail of a suffering child in a distant ward; the sharp whir of an electric bell; the homely thud of the elevator on its errands up and down; even the contolled yet ready spring to service of all concerned when the ambulance rolled up and a man on a stretcher, with a ghastly cut in his head and face, was brought in; all made him feel how little and useless his life had been hitherto. How suddenly he had been brought face to face with realities!

He began to wonder if the Presence was everywhere, or if there were places where His power was not manifest. There had been the red library! There had also been that church last Sunday.

The office clock chimed softly out the hour of three o'clock. It was Sunday morning. Should he go to church again and search for the Presence, or make up his mind that the churches were out of it entirely and that it was only in places of need and sorrow and suffering that He came? Still, that was not fair to the churches, perhaps, to judge all by one. What an experience the night had been! Did Wittemore, majoring in philanthropy, ever spend nights like this? If so, there must be depths to Wittemore's nature that were worth sounding.

He drew his handkerchief from his inner pocket, and as

he did so a whiff of violets came remindingly, but he paid no heed. Gila's letter lay in his pocket, still unread. The antiseptics were at work upon his senses and the violets could not reach him.

There were dark circles under his eyes, and his hair was in a tumble, but he looked good to Nurse Wright as she came down the hall at last to give him her report. She almost thought he was good enough for her Bonnie girl now. She wasn't given to romances, but she felt that Bonnie needed one most mightily about now.

"She didn't wake up except to open her eyes and smile once," she reported, reassuringly. "She coughs a little now and then, with a nasty sound in it, but I hope we can ward off pneumonia. It was great of you to put your overcoat around her. That saved her, if anything can, I guess. You look pretty well used up yourself. Wouldn't you like the doctor to give you something before you go home?"

"No, thank you. I'll be all right. I'm hard as nails. I'm only anxious about her. You see, she's had a pretty tough pull of it. She started to walk to the city! Did you know that? I fancy she'd gone about two miles. It was somewhere along near the river I found her. It seems she got all in and sat down on a doorstep to rest. She must have fallen asleep. Some tough fellows came out of a saloon—they were full, of course—and they discovered her. I heard her scream, and we had quite a little scuffle before we got away. She's a nervy little girl. Think of her starting to walk to the city at that time of night, without a cent in her pocket!"

"The poor child!" said Nurse Wright, with tears in her kind, keen eyes, "And she left her last cent here to pay for her room! My! When I think of it I could choke that smart young snob that called on her in the afternoon! You ought to have heard her sneers and her insinuations. Women like that are a blight on womanhood! And she dared to mention your name—said you had sent her!"

The color heightened in Courtland's face. He felt uncomfortable. "Why, I—didn't exactly send her," he began, uneasily. "I don't really know her very well. You see, I'm just a student at the university and of course I don't know a great many girls in the city. I thought it would be nice if some girl would call on Miss Brentwood; she seemed so alone. I thought another girl would understand and be able to comfort her."

"She isn't a *girl*, that's what's the matter with her; she's a little *demon*!" snapped the nurse. "You meant well, and I dare say she never showed *you* the demon side of her. Girls like that don't—to young *men*. But if you take my advice you won't have anything more to do with *her*! She isn't worth it! She may be rich and fashionable and all that, but she can't hold a candle to Miss Brentwood! If you had just heard how she went on, with her nasty little chin in the air and her nasty phrases and insinuations, and her patronage! And then Miss Brentwood's gentle, refined way of answering her! But never mind, I won't go into that! It might take me all night, and I've got to go back to my patient. But you are not to blame yourself one particle. I hope Miss Brentwood's going to get through this all right in a few days, and she'll probably have forgotten all about it, so don't you worry. I think it would be a good thing if you were to come in and see her tomorrow afternoon for a few minutes. It might cheer her up. You really have been fine, you know! No telling where she might have been by this time if you hadn't gone out after her!"

The young man shuddered involuntarily, and thought of the faces of the five young fellows who had surrounded her.

"I saw a little girl in the morgue tonight, drowned!" he said, irrelevantly. "She wasn't any older than Miss Brentwood."

The nurse gave an understanding look. On her way back to her rounds she said to herself: "I believe he's a *real man*! If I hadn't thought so I wouldn't have told him he might come and see her tomorrow!"

Then she went into Bonnie's room, took the letter with the western postmark, and stood it up against a medicine glass on the little table beside the bed, where Bonnie could see it the first thing when she opened her eyes.

# Chapter 16

*

A little after four o'clock, when Courtland came plodding up the hall of the dormitory to his room, a head was stuck out of Tennelly's door, followed by Tennelly's shoulders attired in a bathrobe. The hair on the head was much tumbled and the eyes were full of sleep. Moreover, there was an anxious, relieved frown on the brows.

"Where in thunder've you been, Court? We were thinking of dragging the river for you. I must say you're the limit! Do you know what time it is?"

"Five minutes after four by the library clock as I came up," answered Courtland, affably. "Say, Nelly, go to church with me again this morning? I've found another preacher I want to sample."

"Go to thunder!" growled Tennelly. "Not on your tintype! I'm going to get some sleep. What do you take me for? A night nurse? Go to church when I've been up all night hunting for you?"

"Sorry, Nelly," said Courtland, cheerfully, "but it was an emergency call. Tell you about it on the way to church. Church doesn't begin till somewhere round 'leven. You'll be calm by that time. So long! See you in church!"

Tennelly slammed his door hard, and Courtland went smiling to his room. He knew that Tennelly would go with him to church. For Courtland had seen among the advertisements in the trolley on his way back to the university, the notice of a service to be held in a church away down in the lower part of the city, to be addressed by the Reverend

John Burns, and he wanted to go. It might not be *the* John Burns of course, but he wanted to see.

Worn out with the events of the night, he slept soundly until ten. Then, as if he had been an alarm clock set for a certain moment, he awoke.

He lay there for a moment in the peace of the consciousness of something good that had come to him. Then he knew that it was the Presence. It was there, in his room. It would always be his. There might be laws attending its coming and going—perhaps in some way concerned with his own attitude—but he would learn them. It was enough to know the possibility of that companionship all the days of one's life.

He couldn't reason out why a thing like that should give him so much joy. It didn't seem sensible in the old way of reasoning—and yet, didn't it? If it could be proved to the fellows that there was really a God like that, companionable, reasonable, just, loving, forgiving, ready to give Himself, wouldn't everyone of them jump at the chance of knowing Him personally, provided there was a way for them to know Him? They claimed it had never been proved, never could be. But he knew it could. It had been proved to him! That was the difference. That was the greatness of it! And now he was going to church again to find out if the Presence was ever there!

With a bound he was out of bed, shaved and dressed in an incredibly short space of time, and shouting to Tennelly, who took his feet reluctantly from the window seat, lowered the Sunday paper, and replied, sulkily:

"Thunder and blazes! Who waked you up, you nut! I thought you were good for another two hours!"

But they went to church.

Tennelly sat down on the hard wooden bench and accepted the worn hymnbook that a small urchin presented him, with an amused stare which finally bloomed into a full grin at Courtland.

"What's eating you, you blooming idiot! Where in thunder did you rake up this dump, anyway? If you've got to go to church, why in the name of all that's a bore can't you pick out a place where the congregation takes a bath once a month whether they need it or not?" he whispered, in a loud growl.

But Courtland's eyes were already fixed on the bright, intelligent face and red hair of the man who stood behind the cheap little pulpit. He was the same John Burns! A window just behind the platform, set with crude red and blue and yellow lights of cheap glass, sent its radiance down upon his head, and the yellow bar lay across his hair like a halo; behind him, in the colored lights, there seemed to stand the Presence. It was so vivid to Courtland at first that he drew in his breath and looked sharply at Tennelly, as if he, too, must see, though he knew there was nothing visible, of course, but the lights, the glory, and the little, freckled, earnest man giving out a hymn.

And the singing! If one were looking for discord, well, it was there, every shade of it that the world had ever known! There were quavering old voices, and piping young ones; off the key and on the key, squeaking, grating, screaming, howling, with all their earnest might, but the melody lifted itself in a great voice on high and seemed to bear along the spirit of the congregation.

> I need Thee every hour.
> Stay Thou near by;
> Temptations lose their power
> When Thou art nigh.
> I need Thee, oh, I need Thee,
> Every hour I need Thee;
> O bless me now, my Saviour,
> I come to Thee!

These people, then, knew about the Presence, loved it, longed for it, understood its power! They sang of the Presence and were glad! There were, then, others in the world who knew, besides himself and Stephen and Stephen Marshall's mother! Without knowing what he was doing, Courtland sang. He did not know the words, but he felt the spirit, and he groped along in syllables as he caught them.

Tennelly sat gazing around him, highly amused, not attempting to suppress his mirth. His eyes fairly danced as he observed first one absorbed worshiper, and then another, intent upon the song. He fancied himself taking off the old elder on the other side of the aisle, and the intense young woman with the large mouth and the feather in her hat. Her voice was killing. He could make the fellows die laughing, singing as she did, in a high falsetto.

He looked at Courtland to enjoy it with him, and lo! Courtland was singing with as much earnestness as the rest; and upon his face there sat a high, exalted look that he had never seen there before. Was it true that the fire and the sickness had really affected Court's mind, after all? He had seemed so like his old self lately that they had all hoped he was getting over it.

During the prayer Courtland dropped his head and closed his eyes. Tennelly glanced around and marveled amusedly at the serious attitude of all. Even a row of tough-looking kids on the back seats had at least one eye apiece squinted shut during the prayer, and almost an atmosphere of reverence upon them.

Tennelly prided himself upon being a student of human nature, and before he knew it he was interested in this mass of common people about him. But now and again his gaze went uneasily back to Courtland whose eyes were fixed intently upon the preacher, as if the words he spoke were of real importance to him.

Tennelly sat back in wonder and tried to listen. It was all about a mysterious companionship with God, stuff that sounded like rot to him; uncanny, unreal, mystical, impossible! Could it be true that Court, their peach of a Court, whose sneer and criticism alike had been dreaded by all who came beneath them—could it be that so sensible and scholarly and sane a mind as Court's could take up with a superstition like that? For it was to Tennelly foolishness.

He owned to a certain amount of interest in the emotional side of the sermon. It was true that the little man could sway that uncouth audience mightily. He felt himself swayed in the tenderer side of his nature, but of course his superior mind realized that it was all emotion; interesting as a study, but not to be taken seriously for a moment. It wasn't a healthy thing for Court to see much of this sort of thing. All this talk of a cross, and one dying for all! Mere foolishness and superstition! Very beautiful, and perhaps allegorical, but not at all practical!

The minister was down by the door before they got out, and grasped Courtland's hand as if he were an old friend, and then turned and grasped Tennelly's. There was something so genuine and sincere about his face that Tennelly decided that he must really believe all that junk he had been preaching, after all. He wasn't a fake, he was merely a good, wholesome sort of fanatic. He bowed pleasantly and said a few commonplaces as he passed out.

"Seems to be a good sort," he murmured to Courtland. "Pity he's tied down to that sort of thing!"

Courtland looked at him sharply. "Is that the way you feel about it, Nelly?" There was something half wistful in his tone.

Tennelly looked at him sharply. "Why, sure! I think he's a bigger man than his job, don't you?"

"Then you didn't feel it?"

"Feel what?"

"The Presence of God in that place!"

There was something so simple and majestic about the way Courtland made the extraordinary statement—not as a common fanatic would make it, nor even as one who was testing and feeling around for confirmation of a hope, but as one who knew it to be a fact beyond questioning, which the other merely hadn't been able to see—that Tennelly was almost embarrassed.

"Why—I— Why—no! I can't say that I noticed any particular manifestation. I was entirely too much taken up by the smell to observe the occult. Say, what's eating you, anyway, Court? Such foolishness isn't like you. You ought to cut it out. You know a thing like this can get on your nerves if you let it, just like anything else, and make you a monomaniac. You ought to go in for more athletics and cut out some of your psychology and philosophy. Suppose we go and take a ride in the park this afternoon. It's a great day."

"I don't mind riding in the park for a while after dinner. I've got a date about four o'clock. But I'm not a monomaniac, Nelly, and nothing's getting on my nerves. I never felt better or happier in my life. I feel as if I'd been blind always, been sort of groping my way, and had just got my eyes open to see what a wonderful thing life really is."

"Do you mean you've got what they used to call 'religion,' Court? 'Hit the trail,' as it were?" Tennelly asked as if he were delicately inquiring about some insidious tubercular or cancerous trouble. He seemed half ashamed to connect such a perilous possibility with his honored friend.

Courtland shook his head. "Not that I know of, Nelly. I never attended one of those big evangelistic meetings in my life, and I don't know exactly what 'religion,' as they call it, is, so I can't lay claim to anything of that sort. What I mean is, simply, I've met God face to face and found He's my friend. That's about the size of it, and it makes things all look different. I'd like to tell you about it just as it happened sometime, Tennelly, when you're ready to hear."

"Wait awhile, Court," said Tennelly, half shrinking. "Wait till you've had a little more time to think it over. Then if you like I'll listen."

"Very well," said Courtland, quietly. "But I want you to know it's something real. It's no sick fancies."

"All right!" said Tennelly. "I'll let you know when I'm ready to hear."

Late that afternoon, when Courtland entered the hospital, the sunshine was flooding the great stained-glass window and glorifying the face of the Christ with the outstretched hands. Off in a nearby ward someone was singing to the patients, and the corridors seemed hushed to listen:

The healing of the seamless dress
    Is by our beds of pain.
We touch Him in life's throng and press
    And we are whole again!

All this recognition of the Christ in the world, and somehow it had never come to his consciousness before! He felt abashed at his blindness. And if he had been so long, surely there was hope for Tennelly to see, too. Somehow, he wanted Tennelly to see!

# Chapter 17

*

Bonnie Brentwood was awake and expecting him, the nurse said. She lay propped up by pillows, draped about with a dainty, frilly dressing gown that looked too frivolous for Nurse Wright, yet could surely have come from no other source. The golden hair was lying in two long braids, one over each shoulder, and there was a faint flush of expectancy on her pale cheeks.

"You have been so good to me!" she said. "It has been wonderful for a stranger to go out of his way so much."

"Please don't let's talk about that!" said Courtland. "It's been only a pleasure to be of service. Now I want to know how you are. I've been expecting to hear that you had pneumonia or something dreadful after that awful exposure."

"Oh, I've been through a good deal more than that," said the girl, trying to speak lightly. "Things don't seem to kill me. I've had quite a lot of hard times."

"I'm afraid you have," he said, gravely. "Somehow it doesn't seem fair that you should have had such a rotten time of it, and I be lying around enjoying myself. Shouldn't everybody be treated alike in this world? I confess I don't understand it."

Bonnie smiled feebly. "Oh, it's all right!" she said, with conviction. "'In the world ye shall have tribulation, but fear not, I have overcome the world,' you know. It's our testing time, and this world isn't the only part of life."

"Well, but I don't see how that answers my point," said Courtland, pleasantly. "What's the idea? Don't you think I am worth the testing?"

"Oh, surely, but you may not need the same kind I did."

"You don't appear to me to have needed any testing. So far as I can judge, you've showed the finest kind of nerve on every occasion."

"Oh, but I do," and Bonnie, earnestly. "I've needed it dreadfully! You don't know how hard I was getting—sort of soured on the world! That was the reason I came away from the old home where my father's church was and where all the people I knew were. I couldn't bear to see them. They had been so hard on my dear father that I thought they were the cause of his death. I had begun to feel that there weren't any real Christians left in the world. God had to bring me away off here into trouble again to find out how good people are. He sent you to help me, and Nurse Wright; and now today the most wonderful thing has happened! I've had a letter from an utter stranger, asking me to come and visit. I want you to read it, please."

While Courtland read Mother Marshall's letter Bonnie lay studying him. And truly he was a goodly sight. No girl in her senses could look a man like that over and not know he was a *man* and a fine one. But Bonnie had no romantic thoughts. Life had dealt too hardly with her for her to have any illusions left. She had no idea of her own charms, nor any thought of making much of the situation. That was why Gila's insinuations had cut so terribly deep.

"She's a peach, isn't she?" he said, handing the letter back. "How soon does the doctor think you'll be able to travel?"

"Oh, I couldn't possibly *go*," said the girl, relapsing into sadness; "but I think it was lovely of her."

"Go? Of course you must go!" cried Courtland, springing to his feet, as if he had been accustomed to manage this girl's affairs for years. "Why, Mother Marshall would be just brokenhearted if you didn't!"

"Mother Marshall!" exclaimed Bonnie, sitting up from her pillows in astonishment. "You know her, then?"

Courtland stopped suddenly in his excited march across the room and laughed ruefully. "Well, I've let the cat out of the bag after all, haven't I? Yes, then, I know her! It was I who told her about you. And I had a letter from her two days ago, saying she was crazy to have you come. Why, she's just counting the minutes till she gets your telegram! You *haven't* sent her word you aren't coming, have you?"

"Not yet," said Bonnie. "I was going to ask you what would be the best way to do. You see, I have to send back that money and the mileage. Don't you think it would do to write? It costs a great deal to telegraph, and sounds so abrupt when one has had such a royal invitation. It was lovely of her, but of course you know I couldn't be under obligation like that to entire strangers."

There was a little stiffness in Bonnie's last words, and a cool withdrawal in her eyes that brought Courtland to his senses and made him remember Gila's insinuations.

"Look here!" he said, calming down and taking his chair again. "You don't understand, and I guess I ought to explain. In the first place get it out of your head that I'm acting fresh or anything like that. I'm only a kind of big brother that happened along two or three times when you needed somebody—a—a kind of a Christ-brother, if you want to call it that way," he added, snatching at the minister's phrase. "You believe He sends help when it's needed, don't you?"

Bonnie nodded.

"Well, I hadn't an idea in the world of interfering with your affairs at all, but when I heard you ought to rest, I began to wish I had a mother of my own, or an aunt or something who would know what to advise. Then all of a sudden I thought I'd just put the case up to Mother Marshall. This is the result. Now wait till I tell you what Mother Marshall has been through, and then if you don't decide that God sent that invitation I've nothing else to say."

Courtland had a reputation at college for eloquence. In rushing season his frat always counted on him to bowl over the doubtful and difficult fellows, and he never failed. Neither did he fail now, although he found Bonnie difficult enough. But he had her eyes full of tears of sympathy before he was through with the story of Stephen.

"Oh, I would love to see her and put my arms around her and try to comfort her!" she exclaimed. "I know just how she must feel. But I really couldn't use the money of a stranger, and I couldn't go away with all this debt, the funeral, and everything!"

Then he set carefully to work to plan for her. He read Mother Marshall's letter over again, and asked what things she would need to take if she should go. He wrote out a list of the things she would like to sell and promised to look after them.

"Suppose you just leave that to me," he said, comfortingly. "I'll wager I can get enough out of your furniture to pay all the bills, so you won't leave any behind. Then if I were you I'd just use the check they've sent for your expenses, and trust to getting a position in that neighborhood when you are strong enough. There are always openings in the West, you know."

"Do you really think I could do that?" asked Bonnie, excitedly. "I'm a good stenographer, I've had a really fine musical education, and I could teach a number of other things."

"Oh, sure! You'd get more positions than you could fill at once!" he declared joyously. Somehow it gave him great pleasure to be succeeding so well.

"Then I could soon pay them back," said Bonnie, reflectively.

"Sure! You could pay back in no time after you got strong. That would be a cinch! It might even be that you could help Mother Marshall about something in the house pretty soon. And I'm sure you'll find she just needs you. Now suppose we write up that telegram. There's no need to keep the dear lady waiting any longer."

"He thinks I really ought to go," said Bonnie to the nurse, who had just returned.

"Didn't I tell you so, dear?" said the nurse.

"How soon would the doctor let her travel?" asked Courtland.

"Why, I'll go ask him. You want to put it in your message, don't you?"

"She's a dear!" said Bonnie, with a tender look after her.

"*Isn't* she a peach!" seconded Courtland, enthusiastically.

The nurse was back almost at once, reporting that Bonnie might travel by the middle of the week if all went well.

"But could I get ready to go so soon?" said the girl, a shade of trouble coming into her eyes. "I must go back and pack up my things, you know, and clean the room."

Courtland and the nurse exchanged meaningful glances.

"Now look here!" began Courtland, with an engaging smile. "Why couldn't the nurse and I do all that's necessary? How about tomorrow afternoon? Could you get off awhile, Miss Wright? I don't have any basketball practice till Tuesday, and I could get off right after dinner. Miss Brentwood, you could tell the nurse just what you want done with your things, and I'll warrant she and I have sense enough to pack up one little room."

After some persuasion Bonnie half consented, and then they attended to the telegram.

> Your wonderful invitation accepted with deep gratitude. Will start as soon as able. Probably Wednesday night. Will write.
>
> ROSE BONNER BRENTWOOD

Bonnie had been divided between a desire to save words and a longing to show her appreciation of the kindness.

But the strangest thing of all was that, in his eagerness, the paper Courtland fumbled out from his pocket to write it upon was Gila Dare's unopened letter, reeking with violets. He frowned as he realized it, and stuffed it back in his pocket again.

Courtland enjoyed sending that telegram. He enjoyed it so much that he sent another along with it on his own account, which read:

> Three cheers for the best mother in the United States! She's coming and you ought to see her eyes shine!

It was on the way back to the university that he happened to remember Gila's letter.

# Chapter 18

*

My dear Mr. Courtland:

The very first line translated Courtland into another world from the one in which he had been living during the past three days. Its perfumed breath struck harshly on his soul.

I am writing to report on the case of the poor girl whom you asked me to help. I was very anxious to please you and did my best; but you remember that I warned you that persons of that sort were likely to be most ungrateful—indeed, quite impossible sometimes. And so, perhaps, you will be somewhat prepared for the disappointing report I have to give.

I went to the hospital this afternoon, putting off several engagements to do so. I was quite surprised to find the girl in a private room, but of course your kindness made that possible for her, which makes her utter ingratitude all the more unpardonable.

I took with me several very pretty frocks of my own, quite good, some of them scarcely worn at all, for I know girls of that sort care more for clothes than anything else. But I found her quite sullen and disagreeable. She wouldn't look at the things I had brought, although I suggested several ways in which I intended to help her and make it possible for her to have a few friends of her own class who would make her forget her troubles. She just lay and stared at me and said, quite impertinently, that she didn't remember ever having met me. And when I mentioned your name she denied ever having seen you. She even dared to ask me to leave the room. And the nurse was most insulting.

But don't worry about it in the least, for Papa has promised to have the nurse removed at once from her position, and blacklisted, so that she can't ever get another place in a decent hospital.

I am afraid you will be disappointed in your protégée, and I am awfully sorry, for I would have enjoyed doing her good; but you see how impossible it was.

You are not to feel put out that I was treated that way, for I really enjoyed doing something for you; and you know it is good for one to suffer sometimes. I'll be delighted to go slumming for you any time again that you say, and please don't mind asking me. It's much better for me to look after any girls that need help than it is for you, because girls of that sort are so likely to impose upon a young man's sympathies.

My cousin has been telling me how you have been looking after some of the work of a student who is majoring in sociology, so I'm beginning to understand why you took this girl up. I do hope you'll let me help. Suppose you run over this evening and we can talk it over. I'm giving up two whole engagements to stay at home for you, so I hope you will properly appreciate it, and if anything hinders your coming, would you mind calling up and letting me know?

Hoping to see you this evening.

Your true friend and fellow worker,

GILA DARE

The letter struck a false note in the harmony of the day. It annoyed Courtland beyond expression that he had made such a blunder as to send Gila after Bonnie. He could not understand why Gila had not had better discernment than to think Bonnie an object of charity. His indignation was still burning over the trouble and peril her action had brought to Bonnie. Yet he hated to have his opinion of Gila shaken. He had arranged it in his mind that she was a sweet and lovely girl, one in every way similar to Solveig the innocent, and he did not care to change it. He tried to remember Gila's conventional upbringing, and realize that she had no conception of a girl out of her own social circle other than as a menial to whom to condescend. The vision of her loveliness in rose and silver, with her prayer book in her kerchief was still dimly forcing him to be at least polite and accept her letter of apology for her failure, as he could but suppose it was sincerely meant.

Then all at once a new fact dawned upon him. The invitation had been for Saturday evening! This was Sunday evening! And now what was he to do? He might call her up and apologize, but what could he say? Bill Ward might have told her by this time that he knew the letter had been received. A blunt confession that he had forgotten to read it might offend, yet what else could he do? It was most annoying!

He went to the telephone as soon as he reached the college. The fellows had already gone down to the evening meal. He could hear the clink of china and silver in the distant dining room. It was a good time to phone.

A moment, and Gila's cool contralto answered: "*Hel*lo-*oo*!" There was something about the way that Gila said that word that conveyed a whole lot of things, instantly putting the caller at his distance, but placing the lady on a pedestal before which it became most desirable to bow.

"This is Paul Courtland!"

"Oh! Mr. Courtland!" Her voice was freezing.

But Courtland was not used to being frozen out. "I owe you an apology, Miss Dare," he said, with dignity. He didn't care how blunt he sounded now. It always angered him to be frozen! "Your letter reached me just as I was leaving here last evening on a very important errand. I put it in my pocket, but I have been so occupied that it escaped my mind utterly until just now. I hope I did not cause you much inconvenience."

"Oh, it really didn't *mattah* in the *least*!" answered Gila, indifferently. Nothing could be colder or more distant than her voice, and yet there was something in it this time, a subtle lure, that exasperated. A teasing little something at his spirit demanded to be set right in her eyes—to have her the suppliant rather than himself.

"I really am awfully ashamed," he said, in quite a boyish, humble tone, and then gasped at himself. What was there about Gila that always got a fellow's goat?

After that Gila had the conversation quite where she wanted it, and finally she told him sweetly that he might come over this evening if he chose. She had other engagements, but she would break them all for him.

"Suppose you go to church with me this evening," he temporized. "I've found a minister I'd like to have you hear. He's quite original!"

There was a distinct pause at the other end of the phone, while Gila's little white teeth came cruelly into her red underlip, and her pearly forehead drew the straight, black, penciled brows naughtily. Then she answered, in sweetly honeyed tones:

"Why, that would be lovely! Perhaps I will. What time do we start?"

Something in her tone annoyed him, despite his satisfaction at having induced her to be friends again. Almost it sounded like a false note in the day again. He hadn't expected her to go. Now she was going, he was very sure he didn't want her.

"I warn you that it is among very common people in the lower part of the city," he said, almost severely.

"Oh, that's all right!" she declared, graciously. "I'm sure it will be dandy! I certainly do enjoy new experiences!"

He hung up the phone with far greater misgivings than he had felt when he asked her to call on Bonnie.

Bill Ward was called out of the dining room to the telephone almost as soon as Courtland got down to the table.

It was Gila on the phone: "Is that you, Bill? Well, Bill, this is Gila. Say, what in the name of peace have you let me in for now? I hope to goodness Mamma won't find it out. She'd have a pink fit! Say! Is this a joke, or what? I believe you're putting one over on me!"

"Search me, Gila! I'm all in the dark! Give me a line on it and I'll tell you."

"Well, what do you think that crazy nut has pulled off

now? Wants me to go to church with him! Of all things! And down in some queer slum place, too! If I get into a scrape you'll have to promise to help me out, or Mamma'll never let me free from a chaperon again. And I had to make Artley Guelpin, and Turner Bailey sore, too, by telling them I was sick and they couldn't come and try over those new dance steps tonight as I'd promised. If I get into the papers or anything I'll have a long score to settle with you."

"Oh, cut that out, Gila! You'll not get into any scrape with Court. He's all right. He's only nuts about religion just now, and seems to be set on sampling all kinds of churches. Say! that's a good one, though, for you to go to church with him! I must tell the fellows. Keep it up, Gila, old girl! You'll pull the fat out of the fire yet. You're just the one to go along and counteract the pious line. You should worry about Artley Guelpin and Turner Bailey! You can't keep either of them sore; they haven't got backbone enough to stay so. If it's the same dump Court took Tennelly to this morning you'll get your money's worth, all right. Nelly said it was a scream."

Bill Ward came back, grinning from ear to ear. Every few minutes during the rest of the meal he broke out in a broad grin and looked at Courtland, who was absorbed in his own thoughts; and then he would slap Tennelly on the shoulder and say: "Ho! boy! It's a rare one!" But it was not until Courtland had hurried away after that lady that Bill gave forth his information.

"Oh, Nelly!" he burst forth. "Court's going to take Gila to church! You don't suppose he'll take her to that dump where he led you this morning, do you? I can see her nose go up now. I thought I'd croak when she told me! Wait till you hear her call me up on the phone when she gets home! She'll give me the worst bawling out I ever had! And Aunt Nina would have apoplexy if she knew her darlin' pet was going into that part of town! Oh, boy! Set me on my feet or I'll die laughing!"

Tennelly regarded Bill Ward with solemn consternation. "Do you mean to tell me that Court has asked your cousin to got to that camp meeting hole where he took me this morning? Cut out the kidding and tell me straight! Well, then, Bill, it's serious, and we've got to do something! We can't have a fellow like Court spoiled for life. He's gone stale, that's what's the matter; he's gone stale! He's got to have strenuous measures to pull him up."

"He sure has!" said Bill Ward soberly, getting up from the couch where he had been rolling in his mirth. "What can we do? What about these business ambitions of his? Couldn't we work him that way? For Court's got a great head on him, you know! I thought Gila would do the business, but if he's rung in religion on her it's all up, I'm afraid. But business is a different thing. Not even Court could mix business and religion, for they won't fit together!"

"That's the trouble," said Tennelly, thoughtfully. "If it gets out what's the matter with Court he won't stand half a chance. I was thinking of my Uncle Ramsey, out in Chicago. He has large financial interests in the West; he often wants promising men to take charge of some big thing, and it means a dandy opening; big money and no end of social and political pull to get into one of his berths. He's promised me one when I'm done college, and I was going to talk to him about Court. He's twice the man I am and just what Uncle Ramsey wants. He's coming on East next week, and likely to stop over. I might see what I can do."

"That's just the thing, Nelly. Go to it, old man! Write your uncle a letter tonight. Nothing like giving a lot of dope beforehand."

"That's an idea! I will!" and Tennelly went to his desk and began to write.

Meantime Gila awaited Courtland's coming, attired in a most startling costume of blue velvet and ermine, with high laced white kid boots, and a hat that resembled a fresh, white setting-hen, tied down to her pert little face with a veil whose large-meshed surface was broken by a single design, a large black butterfly anchored just across her dainty little nose. A most astonishing costume in which to appear in the Reverend John Burns's unpretentious little church crowded with the canaille of the city!

It was the first time that Courtland had ever felt that Gila was a little loud in her dress!

# Chapter 19

*

Mother Marshall got strenuously to her feet from the low hassock on which she had been sitting to sew the carpet, and trotted to the head of the stairs.

"Father!" she called, happily. "Oh, Father! It's all done! I just set the last stitch. You can bring your hammer and tacks. Better bring your rubbers, too. You'll need them when you come to stretch it."

Father hurried up so quickly it was clear he had the hammer and rubbers all ready.

"You'll need a saucer to put the tacks in!" and Mother Marshall hustled away to get it. When she came back the carpet was spread out smoothly and Father stood surveying the effect.

"Say, now, it looks real pretty, don't it?" he said, looking up at the walls and down to the floor.

"It certainly does!" declared Mother Marshall. "And I'm real glad the man made us take this plain pink paper. It didn't look much to me when he first brought it out, I must confess. I had set my heart on stripes with pink roses in it. But when he said 'felt,' why that settled it because the article in the magazine said felt papers were the best for general wear and satisfaction. And then when he brought out that roll with the cherry blossoms on it for a stripe around the top, I was just all happy down my spine, it did look so kind of bridey and pretty, like our cherry orchard on a spring evening when the pink is in the sky. And that white molding between 'em is going to be real handy to hang the pictures on. The man gave me some little brass picture hooks. See, they fit right over the molding. Of course, there isn't but one picture, but she'll maybe have some of her own and like it all the better if the wall isn't all cluttered full. You know the magazine said have 'a few good pictures.' I mean to hang it up right now and see how it looks! There! Doesn't that look pretty against the pink? I wasn't sure about the white frame, it was so plain, but I like it. Those apple blossoms against that blue piece of sky look real natural, don't they? You like it, don't you, Father?"

"Well, I should say I did," said Father, as he scuffed a corner of the carpet into place with his rubbered feet. "Say, this carpet is some thick, Mother, as I guess your fingers will testify, having sewed all those long seams. 'Member how Stevie used to sit on the carpet ahead of your seams when he was a baby, and laugh and clap his hands when you couldn't sew any further because he was in the way?"

"Yes, wasn't he the sweetest baby!" said Mother Marshall, with a bright tear glinting suddenly down her cheek. "Why, Father, sometimes I can't really make it seem true that he's all done with this life and gone ahead of us into the next one. It won't be hard dying, for us, because he's there, and we shan't have to think of leaving him behind to go through a lot of trials and things."

"Well, I guess he's pretty happy seeing you chirk up so, Mother. You know what he'd have thought of all this! Why he'd have just rejoiced in it! He hated so to have you left alone all day. Don't you mind how he used to wish he had a sister? Say, Mother, you just stand on the corner there till I get this tack in straight. This edge is so tremenjus thick! I don't know as the tacks are long enough. What was you figuring to do with the bookshelves, put books in, or leave 'em empty for her things?"

"Well, I thought about that, and I made out we'd better put in some books so it wouldn't look so empty. We can take them out again if she has a lot of her own!"

"We could put in some of Stephen's that he set such store by. There's all that set of Scott, and Dickens, and those other fellows that he wanted us to start and read evenings this winter. By the way, Mother, we'd ought to get at that! Perhaps she'll like to read aloud when she comes! That would about suit us. We're rather old to begin loud reading, Steve's always read to us so long. I don't know but I'd buy a few new books, too. She's a girl you know, and you might find something lately written that she'd like. It wouldn't do any harm to get a few. You could ask the bookstore man what to pick out—say a shelf or two."

"Oh, I shouldn't need to do that!" said Mother, hurrying to get her magazine, which was never far away these last two or three days. "There's a whole long list here of books 'your young people will want to have in their library.' Wells and Shaw and Ibsen, and a lot of others I never heard of, but these first three I remembered because Stephen spoke of them in one of his first letters about college. Don't you know he was studying a course with those men's books in it? He said he didn't know as he was always going to agree with all they said, but they were big, broad men, and had some fine thoughts. He thought sometimes they hadn't just got the inner light about God and the Bible and all, but they were the kind of men who were getting there, striving after truth, and would likely find it and hand it out to the world again when they got it; like the wise men hunting everywhere for a Saviour. Don't you remember, Father?"

"I remember!" Father tried to speak cheerily, but his breath ended in a sigh, for the carpet was heavy. Mother looked at him sharply and changed the subject. It wasn't always easy to keep Father cheerful about Stephen's going.

"You don't suppose we could get those curtains up tonight, too, do you?"

"Why, I reckon!" said Father, stopping for a puff of breath and looking up to the white woodwork at the top of the windows. "You got 'em all ready to put up, all sewed and everything? Why, I reckon I could put up those rods after I get across this end, and then you could slip the curtains on while I was doing the rest. You don't want to get too tired, Mother. You know you been sewing a long time today."

"Oh, I'm not tired! I'm just childish enough to want to see how it's all going to look. Say, Father, that wasn't the telephone ringing, was it? You don't think we might get a telegram yet tonight?"

"Not scarcely!" said Father, with his mouth full of tacks.

"You see, it's been bad weather, and like as not your letter got storm-stayed a day or so. You mustn't count on hearing 'fore Monday I guess."

They both knew that that letter ought to have reached the hospital where Bonnie Brentwood was supposed to be about six o'clock that evening, for so they had calculated the time between Stephen's letters to a nicety; but each was engaged in trying to keep the other from getting anxious about the telegram that did not come. For it was now half past eight by the kitchen clock, and both of them were as nervous as fleas listening for that telephone to ring that would decide the fate of the pretty pink room, whether it was to have an occupant or not.

"These white madras curtains look like there's been a frost on a cobweb, don't they?" said Mother Marshall, holding up a pair all arranged upon the brass rod ready to hang. "And just see how pretty this pink stuff looks against it. I declare it reminds me of the sunset light on the snow in the orchard out the kitchen window evenings when I was watching for Steve to come home from school. Say, Father, don't you think those bookshelves look cozy each side of the bay window? And wasn't it clever of Jed Lewis to think of putting hinges to the covers on the window seat? She can keep lots of things in there! Wait till I get those two pink silk cushions you made me buy. My! Father, but you and I are getting extravagant in our old age! And all for a girl that may never even answer our letter!"

There was a kind of sob in the end of Mother Marshall's words that she tried to disguise, but Father caught it and flew to the rescue.

"There now, Mother!" he said, getting laboriously up from the carpet, hammer in hand, and putting his arms tenderly about her. "There now, Mother! Don't you go fretting! You see, like as not she was asleep when the letter got there, and they wouldn't wake her up, or mebbe it would be too much excitement for her at night that way! And then, again, if the mail train was late it wouldn't get into the night deliv'ry. You know that happened once for Steve and he was real worried about us! Then they might not have deliv'ry at the hospital on Sunday, and she couldn't *get* it till Monday morning! See? And there's another thing you got to calc'late on, too! You never thought of that! She might be too sick yet to read a letter, or think what to say to it! So just you be patient, Mother! We'll just have that much more time to fix things; for, so to speak, now we haven't got any limitations on what we think she is. We can just plan for her like she was perfect. When we get her telegram we'll get some idea, and begin to know the real girl, but now we've just got our own notion of her."

"Why, of course!" choked Mother, smiling. "I'm just afraid, Seth, that I'm getting set on her coming, and that isn't right at all, you know, because she mightn't be coming."

"Well, and then again she might. It doesn't matter, we'll have this room fixed up company fine, and if she don't come we'll just come here and camp for a week, you and me, and pretend we're out visiting. How would that do? Say, it's real pretty here, like spring in the orchard, ain't it Mother? Well, now, you figure out what you're going to have for bureau fixings, and I'll get back to my tacking. I want to get done tonight and get that pretty white furniture moved in. You're sure the enamel is perfectly dry on that bed? That was the last piece he worked on. I think Jed made a pretty good job of it, for such quick work. Don't you? Got a clean counterpane, and one of your pink and white patchwork quilts for in here, haven't you, and a posy pincushion? My! but I'd like to know what she says when she sees it first!"

And so the two old dears jollied each other along till far past their bedtime; and when at last they lay quiet for the night Mother raised up in the moonlight that was flooding her side of the room and looked cautiously over to the other side of the bed:

"Father! You awake yet?"

"Yes!" sleepily.

"What'll we do about going to church tomorrow? The telegram might come while we're gone, and then we'd never know what she answered."

"Oh, they'd call up again until they got us. And, anyhow, we'd call them up when we got back and ask if any message had come yet!"

"Oh! Would we?" and Mother Marshall lay down with a sigh of relief, marveling, as she often had, at the superior knowledge in little technical details that men so often displayed. Of course in the real vital things of life women had to be on hand to make things move smoothly, but just a little thing like that, now, that needed a bit of what seemed almost superfluous information, a man always knew; and you wondered how he knew, because nobody ever seemed to have taught him! So at last Mother Marshall slept.

Anxious inquiry of the telephone after church brought forth no telegram. Dinner was a strained and artificial affair, preceded by a wistful but submissive blessing on the meal. Then the couple settled down in their comfortable chairs, one each side of the telephone, and tried to read, but somehow the hours dragged slowly.

"There's that pair of Grandmother Marshall's andirons up in the attic!" said Mother Marshall, looking up suddenly over the top of the *Sunday School Times*.

"I'll bring them down the first thing in the morning!" said Father, with his finger on a promise in the Psalms. Then there was silence for some time.

Mother Marshall's eyes suddenly lighted on an article headed, "My Class of Boys."

"Seth!" she said, with a beautiful light in her eyes. "You don't suppose maybe she'd be willing to take Stephen's class of boys in Sunday school when she gets better? I can't bear to see them begin to stay away, and Deacon Grigsby admits he don't know how to manage them."

"Why sure!" said Father, tenderly. "She'll take it, I've no doubt. She's that kind, I should think. And if she isn't now, Mother, she will be after she's been with you awhile!"

"Oh, now, Father!" said Mother, turning pink with pleasure. "Come, let's go up and see how the room looks at sunset!"

So arm in arm they climbed the front stairs and stood looking about on the glorified rosy background with its wilderness of cherry bloom about the frieze. Such a transformation of the dingy old room in such a little time! Arm in arm they went over to the window seat and sat leaning stiffly against the two pink silk cushions, and looking out across the rosy sunset snow in the orchard, thinking wistfully of the boy that used to come whistling up that way and would never come to them so again. Then, just as Father drew a sigh, and a tear crept out on Mother's cheek (the side next the window), a long-hoped-for, unaccustomed sound burst out belowstairs! The telephone was ringing! It was Sunday evening at sunset, and the telephone was ringing!

Wildly they both sprang to their feet and clutched each other for a moment.

"I'll go, Mother," said Father, in an agitated voice. "You just sit right here and rest till I get back!"

"No! I'll go, too!" declared Mother, trotting after. "You might miss something and we ought to write it down!"

In breathless silence they listened for the magic words, Mother leaning close to catch them and trying to scratch them down on a corner of the telephone book with a stump of a pencil she kept for writing recipes:

"Your wonderful invitation accepted with deep gratitude!"

"What's that, Father? Make him say it over again!" cried Mother, scribbling away. "'Your wonderful invitation—(Oh, she liked it, then!) accepted'—She's coming, Father!"

"Will start as soon as possible!"

("Then she's really coming!")

"Probably Wednesday night."

("Then I'll have time to get some pink velvet and make a cushion for the little rocker. They do have pink velvet, I'm sure!")

"Will write."

("Then we'll really know what she's like if she writes!")

Mother Marshall's happy thoughts were in a tumult, but she had her head about her yet.

"Now, make him say it all over from the beginning again, Father, and see if we've got it right. You speak the words out as he says 'em, and I'll watch the writing."

And so at last the message was verified and the receiver hung up. They read the message over together, and they looked at each other with glad eyes.

"Now let us pray, Rachel!" said Father, with solemn,

shaken voice of joy. And the two lonely old people knelt down by the little table on which stood the telephone and gave thanks to God for the child He was about to send to their empty home.

"Now," said Father Marshall, when they had risen, "I guess we better get a bite to eat. Seems like a long time since dinner. Any of that cold chicken left, Mother? And a few doughnuts and milk? And say, Mother, we better get the chores done up and get to bed early. I don't think you slept much last night, and we've got to get up early. There's a whole lot to do before she comes. We need to chirk up the rest of the house a bit. Somehow we've let things get down since Stephen went away."

Said Mother, as she landed the platter of cold chicken on the table, "How soon do you s'pose she'll write? I'm just aching to get that letter!"

# Chapter 20

*

Gila had counted on an easy victory that evening. She had furnished for the occasion her keenest wit, her sweetest laughter, her finest derision, her most sparkling sarcasm; and as she and her escort joined the motley throng who were patiently making their way into the packed doorway she whetted them forth eagerly.

Even while they took their turn among the crowd she began to make keen little remarks about the company they were keeping, drawing her velvet robes away from contact with the throng.

Courtland, standing head and shoulders above her, his fine profile outlined against the brightness of the lighted doorway, was looking about with keen interest on the faces of the people, and wondering why they had come. Were they in search of the Presence? Had they, too, felt it there within those dingy walls? He glanced down at Gila with a hope that she, too, might see and understand tonight. What friends they might be—how they might talk things over together—if only Gila would understand!

He wished she had had better sense than to array herself in such startling garments. He could see the curious glances turned her way; glances that showed she was misunderstood. He did not like it, and he reached down a protecting hand and took her arm, speaking to her gravely, just to show the bold fellows behind her that she was under capable escort. He did not hear her keen sallies at the expense of their fellow worshipers. He was annoyed and trying by his serious mien to shelter her.

The singing was already going on as they entered. Just plain old gospel songs, sung just as badly, though with even more fervor, than in the morning. Courtland accepted the tattered hymnbook and put Gila into the seat the shabby usher indicated. He was wholly in the spirit of the gathering, and anxious only to feel the spell once more that had been about him in the morning. But Gila was so amused with her surroundings that she could scarcely pay attention to where she was to sit, and almost tripped over the end of the pew. She openly stared and laughed at the people around her, as though that was what Courtland had brought her there for, and kept nudging him and calling his attention to some grotesque figure.

Courtland was singing, joining his fine tenor in with the curious assembly and enjoying it. Gila recalled him each time from a realm of the spirit, and he would earnestly give attention to what she said, bending his ear to listen, then look seriously at the person indicated, try to appreciate her amusement with a nod and absent smile, and go on singing again! He was so absorbed in the gathering that her talk scarcely penetrated to his real soul.

If he had been trying to baffle Gila he could have used no more effective method, for the point of her jokes seemed blunted. She turned her eyes at last to her escort and began to study him, astonishment and chagrin in her countenance. Gradually both gave way to a kind of admiration and curiosity. One could not look at Courtland and not admire. The fine strength in his handsome young face and figure were always noticeable among a company anywhere, and here among these foreigners and wayfarers it was especially so. She was conscious of a thrill of pleasure in his presence that was new to her. Usually her attitude was to make others thrill at her presence! No man before had caught her fancy and held it like this rare one. What secret lay behind that grave strength of his that made him successfully resist those arts of hers that had readily lured other victims?

She watched him while he bowed his head in prayer, and noted how his rich, close-cut hair waved and crept about his temples; noted the curve of his chin and the curl of his lashes on his cheek. More and more she coveted him. And she must set herself to find and break this other power that had him in its clutches. She perfectly recognized the fact that it was entirely possible that she would not care for him after the other power was broken, and that she might have to toss him aside after he was fully hers. But what of that? Had she not so tossed many a hapless soul that had come like a moth to singe his wings in her candle flame, then laughed at him gaily as he lay writhing in his pain; and tossed after him, torn and trampled, his own ideals of womanhood, too; so that all other women might henceforth be blighted in his eyes. Ah! What of that, so that unquenchable flame in her soul, that restlessly pursued and conquered and cast aside, might be satisfied? Was that not what women were made for, to conquer men and toss them away? If they did not would not men conquer them and toss them away? She was but fulfilling her womanhood as she had been taught to look upon it.

But there was something puzzling about Courtland that interested her deeply. She was not sure but it was half his charm. He really seemed to *want* to be good, to *desire* to resist evil. Most of the other men she knew had been all too ready to fall as lightly with as little earnestness as she into whatever doubtful paths her dainty feet had chanced to lead. Many of them would have led further than she would go, for she had her own limitations and conventions, strange as it may seen.

So Gila sat and meditated, with a strange, sweet thrill in the thought of a new experience; for, young as she was, she had found the pleasures of her existence pall upon her many times.

Suddenly her ear was caught by the sermon. The ugly little man in the pulpit, with the strange eyes that seemed to look through you, was telling a story of a garden, with One calling, and a pair of naked souls guilty and in fear before Him. It was as though she had been one of them! What right had he to flaunt such truths before a congregation?

She was not familiar enough with Bible truths to know where he got the story. It did not seem a story. It was just her Eden where she walked and ate what fruit she might desire every day without a thought of any command that might have been issued. She recognized no commands. What right had God to command her? The serpent had whispered early to her, "Thou shalt not surely die." Her only question was ever whether the fruit was pleasant to the eyes and a tree to be desired to make one wise. Till now there had been no Lord God walking in her garden in the cool of the day. Only her mother, and she was easy to evade. She had never been really afraid, nor felt her little soul naked till now, with the ugly little man's bright brown eyes upon her, and his words shivering through her like winds about the unprotected. Hideous things she had forgotten flung into view and challenged her; and somewhere in the room there seemed to be One who dared to call her to account. She looked fiercely back to the speaker, her delicate brows drawn darkly, her great blue-black eyes fierce in their intensity, her whole face and attitude a challenge to the sermon. Courtland, absorbed as he was in what the speaker had to say, thrilling with the message that came to his soul welcomely, became aware of the tense little figure by his side, and, looking down, was pleased that she had forgotten her nonsense and was listening, and somehow missed the defiance in her attitude.

Gila did not smile when service was over. She went out haughtily, impatiently, looking about on the throng contemptuously. When Courtland asked her if she would like to stop a minute and meet the preacher she threw up her chin with a toss and a "No, indeed!" that left no doubt for lingering.

Out in the street, away from the crowd somewhat, she suddenly stopped and stamped her little foot: "I think that man is perfectly *disgusting*!" she cried. "He ought to be *arrested*! I don't know why such a man is allowed at large!"

She was fairly panting in her anger. It was as if he had put her to shame before an assembly.

Courtland turned wonderingly toward her.

"He is outrageous!" she went on. "He has no *right*! I *hate* him!"

Courtland watched her in amazement. "You can't mean the minister!"

"Minister! He's no minister!" declared Gila. "He's a fanatic! One of the worst kind. He's a fake! He's uncanny! The idea of daring to talk about God that way as if He was always around everywhere! I think it's *awful*! I should think he'd have everybody in hysterics!"

Gila's voice sounded as if she were almost there herself. She flung along by his side with a vindictive little click of her high-heeled boots and a prance of her whole elaborate little person that showed she was fairly bristling with wrath.

But Courtland's voice was sad with disappointment. "Then you didn't feel it, after all! I was hoping you did."

"Feel what?" she asked, sharply. "I felt something, yes. What did you mean?" Her voice had softened wonderfully, and she drew near him and slipped her hand again within his arm. There was an eagerness in her voice that Courtland wholly misinterpreted.

"Feel the Presence!" He said it gently, reverently, as if it were a magic word, a password to a mutual understanding.

"Presence?" she said, bewildered. "Yes, I felt a presence, but what presence did you mean?" Her voice was soft with meaning.

"The Presence of God."

She turned upon him and jerked her arm away. "The Presence of God in that place?" she demanded. "No! *Never!* How perfectly dreadful! I think that is irreverent!"

"Irreverent?"

"Yes! Very irreverent!" said Gila, piously. "And a man like that is profaning holy things. If you really care for religious things you ought to come to my church, where everything is quiet and orderly and where there are decent people. Why, those people there tonight looked as if they might all be thieves and murderers! And outlandish! My soul! I never saw anything like it! Some of their things must have come out of the Ark! Did you see that girl with the tight green skirt? Imagine it! A whole year and a half out of date! I think it is immodest to wear things when they get out of style like that! And the idea of that man daring to talk to that kind of people about God coming down to live with them! I think it was the limit! As if God cared anything about people of that sort! I think that man ought to be arrested, putting notions into poor people's heads! It's just such talk as that that makes riots and things. My father says so! Getting common, stupid people all worked up about things they can't understand. I think it's wicked!"

Gila raved all the way home. Courtland, for the most part, let her talk and was silent.

Seated finally in the library, for he could not go away yet, somehow, there was something he must ask her. He turned to her, calling her for the first time by her name:

"But, Gila, you said you felt a Presence. What did you mean?"

Gila was silent. The tumult in her face subsided.

She dropped her lashes and played with the frill on the wrist of the long chiffon sleeve of her blouse. Her eyes beneath their concealing lashes kindled. Her mouth grew sweet and sensitive, her whole attitude became shy and alluring. She sat and drooped before the fire, casting now and then a wide, shy, innocent look up, her face half turned away.

"Does she look adown her apron!" floated the words through his brain. Ah! Here at last was the Gila he had been seeking! The Gila who would understand!

"Tell me, Gila!" he said, in an eager, low appeal.

She stirred softly, drooped a little more toward him, her face turned away till only the charming profile showed against the rich darkness of a crimson curtain. Now at last he was coming to it!

"It was—*you*—I meant!" she breathed softly.

He sat up sharply. There was subtle flattery in her tone. He could not fail to be stirred by it.

"Me!" he said, almost sternly. "I don't understand!" but his voice was gentle, almost tender. She looked so small and scared and "Solveig"-like.

"You meant *me*!" he said, again. "Won't you please explain?"

# Chapter 21

*

Courtland went back to college that night in a tender and exalted mood. He thought he was in love with Gila!

That had been a wonderful little scene before the fire, with the soft, hidden yellow lights above, and Gila with her delicate, fervid little face, great, dark eyes, and shy looks. Gila had risked a tear upon her pearly cheek and another to hang upon her long lashes, and he had had a curious desire to kiss them away; but something held him from it. Instead, he took his clean handkerchief, softly wiping them, and thought that Gila was shy and modest when she shrank from his touch.

He did not take her in his arms. Something held him from that, too. He had a feeling that she was too sacred, and he must not lightly snatch her for himself. Instead, he put her gently in the big chair by his side, and they sat and talked together quietly. He did not realize that he had done the most of the talking. He did not know what they had talked about; only that reluctant whispered confession of hers had somehow entered him into a close intimacy with her that pleased and half awed him. But when he tried to tell her of a wonderful experience he had had she lifted up her little hand and begged: "Please, not tonight! Let us not think of anything but just each other tonight!" And so he had let it pass, knowing she was all wrought up.

He had not asked her to marry him, nor even told her he loved her. They had talked in quiet, wondering ways of feeling drawn to each other; at least *he* had talked, and Gila had sat watching him with deep, dissatisfied eyes. She had sense enough to see that she could not win him with the arts that had won others. His was a nature deeper, stronger. She must bide her time and be coy. But her spirit chafed beneath delay, and dark passions lurked behind and brooded in her eyes. Perhaps it was this that held him in a sort of uncertainty. It was as if he waited permission from some unseen source to take what she was so evidently ready to give. He thought it was the sacredness in which he held her. Almost the sermon and the feeling of the Presence were out of mind as he went home. There played around him now a little phantom joy that hovered over like a will-o'-the-wisp above his heart, and danced, giving him a strange, inexplicable exhilaration. Was this love? Was he in love?

He flung himself down on Tennelly's couch when he got back to the dormitory. Bill Ward was deep in a book under the droplight, and Tennelly was supposed to be finishing a theme for the next day.

"Nelly, what is love?" asked Courtland, suddenly, in the midst of the silence. "How do you know when you are in love?"

Tennelly dropped his fountain pen in his surprise, and had to crawl under the table after it. He and Bill Ward exchanged one lightning glance of relief as he emerged from the table.

"Search me!" said Tennelly, as he sat down again. "Love's an illusion, they say. I never tried it, so I don't know."

There was silence again in Tennelly's room. Presently Courtland got up and said good-night. Over in his own room he stood by the window, looking out into the moonlight. The preacher had said prayer was talking with the Lord face to face. That was a new idea. Courtland dropped upon his knees and talked aloud to God as he had never opened his heart to a living creature before. If prayer was that, why, prayer was good!

Gila, standing bewildered, studying her pretty, discontented little face in the mirror, with all its masks laid aside, would have shivered in fear and been all the more uncertain of her success if she could have known that the man she would have had for a lover was on his knees talking about her to God. Her little naked soul in a garden all alone with the Lord God, and a man who was set to follow Him!

Tennelly looked up and raised his eyebrows as Courtland closed the door. "Guess you needn't have written that letter, after all!" chuckled Bill Ward. "I thought Gila would get in her little old work!"

"Well, it's written and mailed, so that doesn't do any good now. And, anyway, it's always well to have more than one string to your bow!" growled Tennelly. Courtland in love! He wasn't exactly sure he liked it. Courtland and Gila! What kind of a girl was Gila, anyway? Was she good enough for Court? He must look into this.

"Say, Bill, why don't you introduce me to your cousin? I think it's about time I had a chance to judge for myself how things are getting on," growled Tennelly, presently.

"Sure!" said Bill. "Good idea! Why didn't you mention it before? How about going now? It's only half past ten. Court didn't stay very late, did he? No, it isn't too late for Gila. She never goes to bed till midnight, not if there's anything interesting on. Wait. I'll call her up and see. I'm privileged anyway, you know. Cousins can do anything. I'll tell her we're hungry."

So it came about that an hour after Gila had sat in the firelight with Courtland and listened, puzzled, to his reverent talk of a soul-friendship, she ushered into the same room her cousin and Tennelly. She met Tennelly with a challenge in her eye.

Tennelly had one in his. Their glances lingered, sparred and lingered again, and each knew that this was a notable meeting.

For Tennelly was tall and strikingly handsome. He had those deep black eyes that hold a maiden's gaze and dare a devil; yet there was behind his look something strange, dashing, scholarly. Gila saw at once that he was distinguished in his way, and though her thoughts were strangely held by Courtland she could not let one like this go by unchallenged. If Courtland did not prove corrigible, why, there was still as good fish in the sea as ever was caught. It were well to have more than one hook baited. So she received Tennelly graciously, boldly, impressively, and in three minutes was talking with that daring intimacy that young people of her style love to affect; and Tennelly, fascinated by her charms, yet seeing through them and letting her know he saw through them, was fencing with her delightfully. He told himself it was his duty for Courtland's sake. Yet he was interested for his own sake and knew it. But he did not like the idea of Court and this girl! They did not fit. Court was too genuine! Too tenderhearted! Too idealistic about women! With himself, now, it was different. He knew women! Understood this one at a glance. She was a peach in her way, but not the perfect little peach Court ought to have. She would flirt all her life and break old Court's heart if he married her.

So he laughed and joked with Gila, answering her challenging glances with glances just as ardent, while Bill Ward sat and watched them both, chuckling away to himself.

And Courtland, on his knees, talked with God!

The next morning Courtland awoke with a pleasant sensation of eagerness to see what life had in store for him. Was this really the wonderful experience of love into which he had begun to enter? He thought of Gila all in halos now. The questionings and unpleasantnesses were forgotten. He told himself that she would one day see and understand the wonderful experience through which he had been passing. He would tell her just as soon as possible. Not today, for he would be busy, and she had engagements Tuesday evening and all day Wednesday. He had not noticed the subtle withdrawing as she told him, the quick, furtive calculation in her glance. She knew how to make coming to her a privilege. Just because she had let him think he saw a bit of her heart that night, she meant to hold him off. Not too long, for he was not sufficiently bound to her to be safe from forgetting, but just long enough to whet his eagerness. Her former experience in such matters had taught her to expect that he would probably call her up and beg to see her sooner, when she might relent if he was humble enough. And she had not misjudged him. He was looking forward to Thursday as a bright, particular goal, planning what he would say to her, wondering if his heart would bound as it had when she looked at him Sunday night, and if the strange sweetness that seemed about to be settling upon him would last.

Before he left his room that morning he did something he had never done before in college; he locked his door and knelt beside his bed to pray, with a strong, sweet sense of the Presence standing beside him, and breathing power into his soul.

He had not much to ask for himself. He simply craved that Presence, and it had never seemed so close. As he unlocked his door and hurried down the hall to the dining room he marveled that a thing so sweet had been so long neglected from his life. Prayer! How he had sneered at it! Yet it was a reasonable thing, after all, now that he had come believing.

Nurse Wright was on hand promptly at the place appointed. She was armed with a list of written instructions. They went to work at once, setting aside the things to be sold; folding and packing the scanty wardrobe, and putting by themselves the clothes and things that had belonged to little Aleck. One incident brought tears to their eyes. In moving out the trunk a large pasteboard box fell down, and the contents dropped upon the floor. The nurse stooped to pick up the things, some pieces of an old overcoat of fine, dark blue material, cut into small garments, basted, ready to be sewed; a tissue paper pattern in a printed envelope marked "Boy's suit." Courtland lifted up the cover to put it on again, and there they saw, in a child's stiff little printing letters, the inscription, "Aleck's new Sunday suit," and underneath, like a subtitle, in smaller letters, "Made out of Father's best overcoat."

"Poor little kid!" said Courtland. "He never got to wear it!"

"He's wearing something far better!" said the nurse, cheerfully; "and think what he's been spared. He'll never know the lack of a new suit again!"

Courtland looked at her thoughtfully. "You believe in the resurrection, don't you?"

"I certainly do!" said the nurse. "If I didn't I'd get another job. I couldn't see lives go out the way I do, and those left behind, suffering, and not go crazy if I didn't believe in the resurrection. You are a college student. I suppose you've got beyond believing things. It isn't the fashion to believe in God and the Bible anymore, I understand, not if you're supposed to have any brains. But I thank God He's left me the resurrection. And when you come to face the loss of those you love you'll wish you believed in it, too."

"But I do," said Courtland, quietly, making his second confession of faith. "I never thought much about it till lately. It goes along with a Christ, of course. There had to be a resurrection if there was a Christ!"

"Well, I certainly am glad there's one college student that has some sense!" said the nurse, looking at him with admiration. "I guess you had a good mother."

"No," said Courtland, shaking his head. "I never knew my own mother. That'll be one of the things for me to look forward to in the resurrection. I was like all the rest of the fellows—thought I knew it all, and didn't believe anything till something happened! I was in a fire and one of the fellows died! He was a great Christian, and I saw his face when he died! And then, afterward—maybe you'll think I'm nuts when I tell you—but Christ came and stood by me in the smoke and talked with me and I knew Him! He's been with me more or less ever since."

The nurse looked at him curiously, a strange light in her eyes. Then she turned suddenly and looked out of the little window to the vista of gray roofs.

"No! I don't think you're nuts!" she said, brusquely. "I think you're the only sensible man I've met in a long time. It stands to reason if there is a Christ He'd come to people that way sometimes. I never had any vision, or anything that I know of, but I've always known in my heart there was a Christ and He was helping me! I couldn't answer their arguments, those smart aleck young doctors and the nurses that talked so much, but I always felt nobody could upset my belief, even if the whole world turned against Him, for I *knew* there was a Christ! I don't know *how* I know it, but I *know* it and that's enough for me! I don't boast of being much of a Christian myself, but if I didn't know there was a Christ I couldn't stand the life I have to live, nor the disappointments that I've had."

There were tears rolling down her cheeks, but her eyes were shining when she turned around.

"Say, I guess we're sort of relations, aren't we?" laughed Courtland, holding out his hand. "You've described my feelings exactly."

She took the offered hand and gripped it warmly. "I knew you must be different, somehow, when you went out to hunt for my patient so late at night that way," she said.

Courtland went out presently, bringing back a secondhand man with whom he made a quiet bargain that not even the nurse could hear, and the surplus furniture was carted away. It was not long before the little room was dismantled and empty.

They went together to a department store and purchased a charming little bag with a lot of traveling accessories in plain compact form, light enough for an invalid to carry. Courtland begged to be let in on the gift, but the nurse was firm:

"This is my picnic, young man," she said. "You're doing enough! You can't deny it! For pity's sake, wait till you know her better before you try to do any more!"

"Do you think I'll ever know her any better?" laughed Courtland.

"If you have any sense you will!" snapped back the nurse, and waved a grim but pleasant good-bye as she took the trolley back to the hospital.

Wednesday night Courtland was on hand with his car in plenty of time to take Bonnie and the nurse down to the station. He was almost startled at the beauty of the girl as she came slowly down the steps. There were certain little details of her costume that showed the hand of the nurse: a soft white collar; a floating, sheltering veil, gathered up now about the black sailor hat; well-fitting gloves; shoes polished like new. All these things made a difference and set off the girl's lovely face in its white resignation to an almost unearthly beauty. He found himself wanting to turn back often and look again as he drove his car through the crowded evening streets. She looked so frail and sweet he could not help thinking of Mother Marshall and how she would feel when she saw her. Surely she could not help but take her to her heart! He felt a certain pride in her, as if she were his sister. He was half-sorry she was going away. He would like to know her better. The words of the nurse, "until you know her better" floated through his mind. What a strange thing that had been for her to say! It wasn't in the least likely that he would ever see Bonnie again.

They left her in the sleeper, with special instructions to the porter to look after her, and surrounding her with magazines and fruit.

"She looks as if a breath might blow her away!" said Courtland, speaking out of a troubled thought, as he and the nurse stood on the platform watching the train move off. "Do you think she'll get through the journey all right?"

"Sure!" said the nurse, wiping away a wistful tear furtively. "She's got lots of pep. She'll rally and get strong pretty soon. She's had a pretty tough time the last two years. Lost her mother, father, a sister, and this little brother. Her father's heart was broken by being asked to leave his church because he preached temperance too much. The martyrs in this world didn't all die in the dark ages! They're having them yet!"

"But she looks so ethereal!" pursued Courtland. "I wish I'd thought to suggest you going along. We could have trumped up some reason why you had to have a vacation."

"Couldn't do it!" said the nurse, smiling and patting his arm. "I thought of it, but it wouldn't work. I have to be at the hospital tomorrow for a very important operation. There isn't anybody else in the hospital could very well take my place. Besides, she's sharp as a tack, and you needn't think she doesn't see through a lot of the things you've done for her! Mark my words, you'll hear from her someday! She means to know the truth about those bills and pay every cent back! But don't you worry about her. She'll get through all right. She's got more nerve than any dozen girls I know, and she doesn't go alone through this world, either. She's had a vision, too, or you'd never see her wearing that patient face with all she's had to bear!"

"Did it ever seem strange to you that good people have so much trouble in this world?" said Courtland, voicing his same old doubting thought.

"Well, now *why*? What's *trouble* going to be in the resurrection? We won't mind then what we passed through, and this world isn't forever, thank the Lord! If it's serving His plan any for me to get more than what seems my share of trouble, why, I'm willing. Aren't you? The trouble is we can't see the plan, and so we go fretting because it doesn't fit our ideas. If it was our plan now we'd patiently bear everything, I suppose, to make it come out right. We aren't up high enough to get the whole view of the finished plan, so of course lots of things look like mistakes. But if we trust Him at all, we know they aren't. And sometime, I suppose, we'll see the whole and then we'll understand why it was. But I never was one to do much fretting because I didn't understand. I always know what my job is, and that's enough. I'm content to trust the rest to God. It's a God-size job to run the universe, and I know I'm not equal to it."

Her simple logic calmed his restless thoughts, but there was still a strange wistfulness in his heart about Bonnie. She looked so white and resigned and sad! He wished she hadn't gone quite so far out of his life.

Meantime, out in the darkness of the night Bonnie's train whirled along, and sometime during the long hours between midnight and dawning it passed in a rush and a thunder of sound the express that was bearing back to Courtland another menace to his peace of mind.

# Chapter 22

*

Uncle Ramsey was large and imposing, with an effulgent complexion and a prosperous presence. He wore a double-jeweled ring on his arthritic finger, and a scarab scarfpin. His eyes were keen and shifty; his teeth had acquired the habit of clutching his fat black cigar viciously while he snarled his rather loose lips about them in conversation. Uncle Ramsey never looked one in the face when he was talking. He looked off into space, where he appeared to have the topic under discussion in visible form before him. He never took up with the conversation his host offered. He furnished the topics himself and pinned one down to them. It really was of no use whatever to start any subject unless it had been previously announced, because it never got further than the initiative. Uncle Ramsey always went on with whatever he had in mind. Tennelly knew this tendency, realized that in writing the letter he had taken the only possible way of bringing Courtland to his uncle's notice.

After an exceedingly good dinner at the frat house, where Tennelly did not usually dine, and being further reinforced by one of the aforesaid fat black cigars, Uncle Ramsey leaned back in Tennelly's leather chair, and began:

"Now, Thomas!"

Tennelly stirred uneasily. He despised that "Thomas." His full name was Llewellyn Thomas Tennelly. At home they called him "Lew." Nobody but Uncle Ramsey ever dared the hateful Thomas. He liked to air the fact that his nephew was named after himself, the great Ramsey Thomas.

"Suppose you tell me about this man you have for me? What kind of a looking man is he?"

Uncle Ramsey screwed up his eyes, looked to the middle distance where the subject ought to be, and examined him critically.

"Has—ah—he—ah—*personality*? Personality is a great factor in success you know."

Tennelly, in the brief space allowed him, declared that his friend would pass this test.

"Well—ah! And can he—ah!—can he *lead men*? Because that is a very important point. The man I want must be a leader."

"I think he is."

"Um—ah! And does he—?" on down through a long list of questions.

At last, after once more relighting his cigar, which had gone out frequently during the conversation, he turned to his nephew and fixed him sharply with a fat pale blue eye.

"Tell me the worst you know about him, Thomas! What are his faults?" he snapped, and settled back to squint at his imaginary stage again.

"Why—I—Why, I don't think he has any," declared Tennelly, shifting uneasily in his chair. He had a feeling that Uncle Ramsey would get it out of him yet. And he did.

"Yes, I perceive that he has! Out with it!" snapped the keen old bird, flinging his loose lips about restively.

"It's only that he's got a religious twist lately, Uncle. I don't think it'll last. I really think he is getting over it!"

"Religion! Um! Ah! Well, now that might not be so bad—not for my purpose, you know. Religion really gives a confidence sometimes. Religion! Um! Ah! Not a bad trait. Let me see him, Thomas! Let me see him *at once*!"

Tennelly had said nothing to Courtland about the approaching uncle, and therefore it was wholly a surprise to Courtland when Tennelly knocked on his door and dragged him from his books to meet a Chicago uncle.

"He's come East looking for the right man to fill a very important position. It is something along your line, I guess, so I spoke to him about you," whispered Tennelly, hastily, as they crossed the hall together.

Face to face they stood, the financier and the young senior, and studied each other keenly for the fraction of a second, Courtland no less cool and impressive in his way than the older man. For Courtland was not afraid of any man, and his natural attitude toward all men was challenge till he knew them. He stood straight and tall and looked Uncle Ramsey in the eye critically, questioningly, courteously, but with no attempt to propitiate; and not the slightest apparent conception of the awesomeness of the occasion or the condescension of the august personage whom he was thus permitted to meet.

And Uncle Ramsey liked it!

True, he tried to fix the young man much as a cook fixes a roast with a skewer, to be put over the fire; but Courtland didn't skew. He just sat down indifferently and looked the man over; smiled pleasantly now and then, and listened; but he didn't give an inch. Even when the marvelous proposition was made to him which might change the whole course of his future life and cover his name with glory (?) Courtland never flickered an eyelash.

"He took it as calmly as if I'd been offering him toast with his tea when he already had bread and jam, the young whelp!" marveled Uncle Ramsey, delightedly, after Courtland had thanked him, promised to think it over, and gone back to his room. "He's got the personality, all right! He'll do! But what's his idea in being so reluctant? Didn't the offer strike him as big enough, or what's the matter? I must say I don't like to wait. When I find a man I like to nail him. What's the idea, Thomas? Has he got something else up his sleeve?"

"Not that I know of," said Tennelly, looking troubled. "I guess he's just got to think it over. That's Court. He never steps into a position until he knows exactly what he thinks about it."

"M-m-m! Another good trait! You're sure it isn't anything else?"

"I don't know of anything unless some of his religious notions are standing in his way. I'm sure I can't quite make him out lately. He had a shock a few months ago—one of the fellows was killed in a fire—and he can't seem to get over it quite."

"Oh, well, we'll fix him up all right!" said Uncle Ramsey, contentedly. "We'll just send him down to our model factory here in the city and let him see how things are run. Convince him he's doing good, and that'll settle him! All white marble, with vines over the place, and a big rest room and reading room for the hands, gymnasium on the roof, model restaurant, all up to date. Cost a lot of money, too, but it pays! When some whining idiot of a woman, that hasn't enough business of her own to attend to, goes blabbing down there in Washington about the 'conditions' in the factories, and all that rot, we just run a few senators up here for the day and show 'em that model factory. Oh, it pays in the long run. You take your man there and you'll land him all right! By the way, there's a little rat of a preacher down around that factory that I'd like to throttle! He's making us all sorts of trouble, stirring up the folks to ask for all sorts of things! He's putting it in their heads to demand an eight-hour day, and no telling how much more! He's undertaken to tell us how we ought to run our business! Tell us which doors we shall lock and which to leave unlocked, how often we shall let our hands sit down, and what kind of machines we shall get! He's a regular little rat! Know him? His name's Burns. Insignificant little puppy! And he's got a pull down there in Washington, somehow, that's making us a lot of trouble, too! That's one thing I want this new man for. I want to train him to spy on that sort of interference and by and by do some lobbying. We must stop such business as that. What time is it? I guess perhaps I better run down and hunt out that little rat and give him a good scare."

Uncle Ramsey departed "rat-hunting," and Tennelly repaired to Courtland's room. He sat down and began to tell what a wonderful opportunity this was, and how unprecedented in Uncle Ramsey to have offered such a thing to a young man still in college. It showed how wonderfully he had been taken with Courtland. It was most flattering.

Courtland admitted that it was and that he was grateful to his friend for mentioning his name. He said it looked like a very good thing—like the kind of thing he had been hoping would turn up when he got through college, but he couldn't decide it immediately.

Tennelly urged that Uncle Ramsey was insistent; that his business was urgent, and he must know one way or the other immediately. He tried to give Courtland an adequate idea of the greatness of Uncle Ramsey, and the audacity of anybody, especially a little college upstart, attempting to keep him waiting, but Courtland only shook his head and said it wouldn't be possible for him to give his answer at once. If that was the condition of the offer he would have to let it pass.

Tennelly talked and talked, but finally went back to his room baffled. He just couldn't understand what was the matter with Courtland!

When Uncle Ramsey returned from a fruitless search for the "rat" he was enraged to find that Courtland was not awaiting his coming in trembling eagerness to accept his munificent offer.

Another personal interview that evening brought nothing more satisfactory than a promise to look into the matter carefully, and to have another talk the next evening. Uncle Ramsey raged and swore. He blamed the little rat of a preacher, and declared he must leave for Boston that evening; but he finally sent a telegram instead and decided to remain until the next night. There were matters in the city he was intending to look after on his return, and of course he could do it now instead. He felt it was important that that young man should be landed before he had a chance to do too much thinking. Moreover, he was piqued that a youngster like that should presume to consider turning down a job like the one he was offering him.

If Courtland had tried to explain to Tennelly and his uncle just why this offer, which would have delighted him so much three months before, was hanging in the balance of his mind, they would scarcely have understood. He would have to tell them of the Presence which was by his side, which had been very real to him as he stood in Tennelly's room listening to Uncle Ramsey that afternoon, and which had hovered by him since, so close, so strong, with that pervading, commanding nearness that demanded his utmost attention. He would have had to tell them that he was under orders now, being led, and that every step was new and untried; he must look into the face of his Companion and Guide, and find out if this was the way he was to go!

Something, somewhere was holding him back. He did not know why, he did not see for how long. He simply could not make that decision tonight! He must await permission before moving.

Possibly the trip to the factory the next day, which he had promised to take, might give him some light in the matter. Possibly he would find counsel somewhere. But where? He thought of Gila. He took out a lovely photograph of her that she had given him before he left her Sunday night—a charming, airy, idealistic thing of earth and fire that had lain innocently open upon the library table where someone (?) had left it earlier in the day. He stood it up on his desk and studied the spirited will-o'-the wisp face! Then he turned away sadly and shook his head. She would not understand because she had not seen for herself.

Tennelly and his uncle went downtown in the morning and took lunch together. Courtland was to meet them at the factory at three o'clock, but somehow he missed them. Perhaps it was intention. Courtland went early. He wanted to see things for himself; went alone first. Afterward he could go the rounds to satisfy Mr. Thomas, but first he would see it alone.

Then, after all, it was the Reverend Robert Burns who met him at the door and took him through the factory, bent on seeing some parishioner on an errand of love. And there was the strange sense of the Presence having been there before them, walking about among the machinery, looking at the tired face of one, sorrowing over the wrinkles in another forehead, pitying the weary hands that toiled, blessing the faithful! It reminded him of the morgue in that. For a minute he began to think that if the Presence was here in this peculiar sense, then, of course, it was an indication that he was needed here to work for these people, as Uncle Ramsey had tried with strange worldly wisdom to make him understand. But then, suddenly, he caught a glimpse of the face of the little minister, white under its freckles, with a righteous wrath as he fixed his gaze sternly on the door at the end of a long room. He looked up quickly to hear the click of a key in a lock as the foreman passed from one room to another.

He glanced down at the minister and their eyes met.

"They lock them in here like sheep in a pen. If a fire should break out they would all die!" said the minister under his breath. His lips were trembling with the helplessness of himself against the power of a great trust.

"You don't say!" said Courtland, startled. It was his first view of conditions of this sort. He looked about with eyes alive to things he had not seen before. "But I thought this was a model factory! Isn't it absolutely fireproof?"

"Somewhat so, on the *out*side!" shrugged Burns. "It's a whited sepulcher, that's what it is. Beautiful marble and vines, beautiful rest room and library—for the *visitors* to rest and read in—beautiful restaurant where the girls must buy their meals at the company's prices or go without; beautiful outside everywhere; but it's rotten, *absolutely rotten* all through! Look at the width of that staircase! That's the one the employees use. The visitors only see the broad way by which you came up. Look at those machines! All painted and gilded! They are old models and twice as heavy to work as the new ones, but we can't get them to make changes. Look at those seats, put there to impress the visitors! The fact is not one of the hands dare use them, except a minute now and then when the foreman happens to leave the room! They know they will get docked in their pay if they are caught sitting down at their work! And yet it is always flaunted before the visitors that the workmen can sit down when they like. So they can, but they can go home without a pay envelope if they do, when Saturday night comes. Oh, there is enough here to make one's blood boil! You're interested in these things? I wish you'd let me tell you more sometime. And the long hours, the stifling air in some rooms, and the little children working in spite of the law! I wish men like you would come down here and help clean this section out and make conditions different! Why don't you come and help me?"

The minister laid his hand on Courtland's arm, and instantly it seemed as if the Presence came and stood beside him and said: "Here! This is your work!"

With a great conviction in his heart Courtland turned and followed Burns down the broad marble stairs out to the office, where he left word for Tennelly and his uncle that he had been there and had to go, but would see them again that evening, and then down the street to Burns's common little boardinghouse, where they sat down and talked the rest of the afternoon. Burns opened Courtland's eyes to many things that he had not known were in the world. It was as if he laid his hands upon him and said, as of old: "Brother Saul, receive thy sight!"

When Courtland went back to the university his decision was made. He felt that he was under orders, and the Presence would not go with him in any such commission as Uncle Ramsey had proposed. His only regret was that Tennelly would not understand. Dear old Tennelly, who had tried to do his best for him!

The denouement began in Tennelly's room after supper, when Courtland courteously and firmly thanked Uncle Ramsey, but *declined* the offer!

Uncle Ramsey grew apoplectic in the face and glared at the young man, finally bringing out an explosive: "What! You *decline*?"

Uncle Ramsey spluttered and swore. He tore up and down the small confines of the room like an angry bull, bellowing forth anathemas and arguments in a confused jumble. He enlarged on the insult he had been given, and the opportunity that was being lost never to be offered again. He called Courtland a "trifling idiot," and a few other gentle phrases, and demanded reasons for such an unprecedented decision.

Courtland's only answer was: "I am afraid it isn't going to fit in with my views of life, Mr. Thomas. I have thought it over carefully and I cannot accept your offer."

"Why not? Isn't it enough money?" roared the mad financier. "I'll double your salary!"

"Money has nothing to do with it," said Courtland, quietly. "That would make no difference." He was sorry for this scene for Tennelly's sake.

"Well, have you something else in view?"

"No, not definitely."

"Then you're a fool!" said Uncle Ramsey, and further stated what kind of a fool he was, several times, *vigorously*. After which he mopped his beaded brow with trembling, agitated hands, and sat down. The old bull was baffled at last.

Uncle Ramsey blustered all the way to the train with his nephew. "I've got to have that young man, Thomas. There's no two ways about it. A fellow that can stand out the way he did against Ramsey Thomas is just the man I want. He's got personality. Why, a man like that at work for us would be worth millions! He would give confidence to everyone! Why, we could make him a senator in a few years, and there's no telling where he wouldn't stop! He's the kind of a man who could be put in the White House if things shaped themselves right. I've *got* to have him, Thomas, and no mistake! Now, I'm going to put it up to you to find out the secret of this thing. You just get his number and we'll meet him on any reasonable proposition he wants to put up. Say, Thomas, isn't there a girl anywhere that could convince him?"

"Yes, there's a girl!"

"The very thing! You put her wise about it, and when I come back next week I'll stop off again and see what I can do with her! You can take me to call on her, you know. Can you work it, Thomas?"

Tennelly said he'd try, and went around to see Gila on his way back to the university.

Gila listened to the story of Uncle Ramsey's offer with bated breath and averted gaze. She would not show Tennelly how much this meant to her. But in her eyes there grew a determination that was not to be denied.

She planned a campaign with Tennelly, coolly, and with a light kind of glee that fooled him completely. He saw that she was entering into the spirit of the thing and had no idea she had any other interest than to please her cousin and achieve a kind of triumph herself in making Courtland do the thing he had vowed not to do.

But long after Tennelly had gone home she stood before

her mirror, looking with dreamy eyes into the pictures her imagination drew there for her. She saw herself the bride of Courtland after he had succeeded in the big business enterprise to which Uncle Ramsey had opened the door; she saw Washington with its domes and Capitol looming ahead of her ambition; senators and great men bowing before her; even the White House came like a fantasy of possibility. All this and more were hers if she played her cards aright. Never fear! She would play them! Courtland *must* be made to accept Uncle Ramsey's proposition!

# Chapter 23

*

Bonnie's letter reached Mother Marshall Wednesday afternoon while Father was off in the machine arranging for a man to do the spring plowing. She knew it by heart before he got back, and stood at her trysting window with her cheek against the old hat, watching the sunset and thinking it over when the car came chugging contentedly down the road.

Father waved his hand boyishly as he turned in at the big gate, and Mother was out on the side doorstep waiting as he came to a halt.

"Heard anything yet?" he asked eagerly.

"Yes. A nice, dear letter!" Mother held it up. "Hurry up and come in and I'll read it to you."

But Father couldn't wait to put away the machine. He bounded out like a four-year-old and came right in then, regardless of the fact that it was getting dark and he might run into the doorjamb putting away the machine later.

He settled down, overcoat and all, into the big chair in the kitchen to listen; and Mother put on her spectacles in such a hurry that she got them upside down and had to begin over again.

> You Dear Mother Marshall! [the letter began]
> And Dear Father Marshall, too!
>
> I think it is just the most wonderful thing that I ever heard of that you are willing to invite a stranger like me to visit you! At first I thought it wasn't right to accept such great kindness from people I never saw, and who

didn't know whether they could even like me or not. But afterward Mr. Courtland told me about your Stephen and that you had suffered, too! And then I knew that I might take you at your word and come for a little while to get the comfort I need so much! Even then I couldn't have done it if Mr. Courtland and my nurse hadn't told me they were sure I could get something to do and so be able to repay you for all this kindness. If I can really be of any comfort to you in your loneliness I shall be so glad. But I'm afraid I could never even half-fill the place of so fine a son as you must have had. Mr. Courtland has told me how grandly he died. He saw him, you know, at the very last minute, and saw all he did to save others. But if you will let me love you both I shall be so grateful. All that I had on earth are gone home to God now, and the world looks so long and hard and sad to me! I do hope you can love me a little while I stay, and that you will not let me make you any trouble. Please don't go to any work to get ready for me. I will gladly do anything that is necessary when I get there. I am quite able to work now; and if I have a place where I can feel that somebody cares whether I live or die it will not be so hard to face the future. A great, strange city is an awful place for a girl that has a heavy heart!

I am so glad that you know Jesus Christ. It makes me feel at home before I get there. My dear father was a minister.

They wouldn't let me go and pack up, so I had to do the best I could with directing the kind friends who did it for me. I have taken you at your word and had Mother's sewing machine and a box of my little brother's things sent with my trunk. But if they are in the way I can sell them or give them away. And I don't want you to feel that I am going to presume upon your kindness and settle down on you indefinitely. Just as soon as I get a chance to work I must take it, and I shall want to repay you for all you have done for me. You have sent me a great deal more money than I need.

I start Wednesday evening on the through express. I

have marked a timetable and am sending it because we are unable to find out just what time I can make connections from Grant's Junction, where they say I have to change. Perhaps you will know. But don't worry about me; I'll find my way to you as soon as I can get there. I am praying all the time that I shall not disappoint you. And now till I see you,

Sincerely and gratefully,
ROSE BONNER BRENTWOOD

"It couldn't be improved on," declared Mother, beamingly. "It's just what I'd have wanted her to say if I'd been planning it all out, only more so!"

"It's all right!" said Father, excitedly, "but that's one thing we forgot. We'd ought to have sent her word we would meet her at the station, and what time the train left Grant's Junction, and all! Now that's too bad!"

"Now don't you worry, Father. She'll find her way. Like as not the conductor will have a timetable and be able to tell her all about the trains. But I certainly do wish we had let her know we would meet her."

They were still worrying about it that night at nine o'clock while Father wound the kitchen clock and Mother put a mackerel asoak for breakfast. Suddenly the telephone in the next room gave a whir, and both Father and Mother jumped as if they had been shot, looking at each other in bewildered question as they hastened to the phone.

It was Father who took down the receiver. "A telegram? For Mr. Seth Marshall! Yes, I'm listening! Write it down, Mother! A telegram!"

"Mercy! Perhaps she wasn't well enough to start!" gasped Mother, putting her pencil in place.

Miss Brentwood left tonight at nine-fifteen on express number ten, car Alicia lower berth number eight. Please let me know if she arrives safely.

PAUL COURTLAND

"Now isn't that thoughtful of him!" he said, as he hung up

the receiver. "He must have sensed we wanted to send her word, and now we can do it!"

"Send her word!" said Mother, bewildered.

"Why, surely! Haven't you read in the papers how they send messages to trains that are moving? It's great, isn't it, Mother? To think this little dinky telephone puts you and me out here on this farm in touch with all the world."

"Do you mean you can send a telegram to her on board the train, Seth?" asked Mother, in astonishment.

"Sure!" said Father. "We've got all the numbers of everything. Just send to that express train that left tonight. What was it—Express number ten, and so on, and it'll be sent along and get to her."

"Well, I think I'd ask her to answer then, to make sure she got it. I think that's a mighty uncertain way to send messages to people flying along on an express train. If you don't get any word from her you'll never know whether she got it or not, and then you won't know whether to meet her at Sloan's or Maitland," said Mother, with a worried pucker on her forehead.

"Sure!" said Father, taking down the receiver. "I can do that."

"It's just wonderful, Seth, how much you know about little important things like that!" sighed Mother, when the telegram was sent. "Now, I think we better go right to bed, for I've got to get to baking early in the morning. I want to have bread and pies and doughnuts fresh when she comes."

It was while they were eating breakfast that the answer came:

> Telegram received. Will come to Sloan's Station. Having comfortable journey.
>
> R. B. B.

"Now isn't that just wonderful!" said Mother, sitting back weakly behind the coffeepot and wiping away an excited tear with the corner of her apron. "To think that can be done! Now, wouldn't it be just beautiful if we had telephones to heaven! Think if we could get word from Stephen today, how happy we'd be!"

"Why, we have!" said Father. "Wait!" and he reached over to the little stand by the window and grasped the worn old Bible. "Here! Listen to this!

> "For this we say unto you by the word of the Lord, that we which are alive and remain unto the coming of the Lord shall not prevent them which are asleep. For the Lord himself shall descend from heaven with a shout, with the voice of the archangel, and with the trump of God: and the dead in Christ shall rise first: Then we which are alive and remain shall be caught up together with them in the clouds, to meet the Lord in the air: and so shall we ever be with the Lord. Wherefore comfort one another with these words.

"There, Mother! Ain't that just as good as any telegram from a moving train? And it's signed with His own seal and signature! It means He's heard our sorrow about Stephen's leaving us, and he heard it ages before we felt it ourselves, and wrote this down for us! Sent us a telegram this morning, just to comfort us! I reckon that meeting with Stephen and the Lord in the air is going to knock the spots clean out of this little old meeting tomorrow morning down at Sloan's Station. We won't need our ottymobeel any more after that. We'll have *wings*, Mother! How'll you like to fly?"

Mother gave a little gasp of joy and smiled at Father like a rainbow through her tears. "That's so, Father! We don't need telephones to heaven, do we? I guess His words cover all our needs if we'd only remember to look for them. Now, Father, I must get at those doughnuts! Was you going to take the machine and run down to town and see if those books have come yet? They surely ought to be here by this time. Then don't forget to fix that fire up in the bedroom so it'll be all ready to light when she gets here. Isn't it funny, Father, we don't know how she looks! Not in the least. And if two girls should get off the train at Sloan's Station we wouldn't know which was the right one!"

"Well *I should*!" declared Father. "I'm dead certain there ain't two girls in the whole universe could have written that letter, and if you'd put any other one down with her, and I saw them side by side, I could tell first off which she was!"

So they helped each other through that last exciting day, finding something to do up to the very last minute the next morning before it was time to start to Sloan's Station to meet the train.

Mother would go along, of course. She pictured herself standing for hours beside that kitchen window with her cheek against the old hat, waiting, and wondering what had happened that they hadn't come, and she couldn't see it that way. So she left the dinner in such stages of getting ready that it could be soon brought to completion, and wrapped herself in her big gray cloak.

Father went faster than he had ever been known to go since he got the car, and Mother never even noticed. He got a panic lest his watch might be running slow and the train arrive before they got there. So they arrived at the station almost an hour ahead of the train.

"Oh, I'm so glad it's a pretty day!" said Mother Marshall, slipping her gloved hands in her sleeves to keep from shivering with excitement.

Mother Marshall sat quite decorously in the automobile till the train drew up to the platform and people began to get out. But when Bonnie stepped down from the car she forgot all about her doubts as to how they would know her, and jumped right out on the platform without waiting to be helped. She rushed up to Bonnie, saying, "This is our Bonnie, isn't it?" and folded her arms about the girl, forgetting entirely that she hadn't meant to use the name until the girl gave her permission; that she had no right to know the name even, wasn't supposed to have heard of it, and was sort of giving the young man away as it were.

But it didn't matter! Bonnie was so glad to hear her own name called in that endearing tone that she just put her face down in Mother Marshall's comfortable neck and cried. She couldn't help it, right there while the train was still at the station and the other travelers were peering curiously out of the sleeper at the beautiful pale girl in black who was being met by that nice old couple with the automobile. Somehow it made them all feel glad, she had looked so sad and alone all the journey.

What a ride that was home again to the farm, with Mother Marshall cuddling and crooning to her: "Oh, my dear pretty child! To think you've really come all this long way to comfort us!" and Father running the old machine at an unheard of rate of speed, slamming along over the road as if he had been sent for in great haste, and reaching his big fur glove back now and then to pat the old buffalo robe that was tucked snugly over Bonnie's lap.

Bonnie herself was fairly overcome and couldn't get her equilibrium at all. She had thought these must be wonderful people to be inviting a stranger and doing all they were doing, but such a reception as this she had never dreamed of.

"Oh, you are so good to me!" sobbed Bonnie, with a smile through her tears. "I know I'm acting like a baby, but I can't seem to help it. I've had nobody so long, and now to be treated like this, I just can't stand it! It seems as if I'd got home!"

"Why, sure! That's what you have!" said Father in his big, hearty voice.

"Put your head right down on my shoulder and cry if you want to, my pretty!" said Mother Marshall, pulling her softly over toward her. "You can't think how good it is to have you here! Father and I were so afraid you wouldn't come! We thought you mightn't be willing to come so far to utter strangers!"

So it went on all the way, all of them so happy they didn't quite know what they were saying.

Then, when they got to the house even Father was so far gone that he couldn't let them go upstairs alone. He just had to leave the machine standing by the kitchen door and carry that little handbag up as an excuse to see how she would like the room.

Bonnie, pulling off her gloves, entered the room when Mother opened the door. She looked around bewildered a moment, as if she had stepped from the middle of winter into a summer orchard. Then she cried out with delight:

"Oh! How perfectly beautiful! You don't mean me to have this lovely room? It isn't right! A stranger and a pauper!"

"Nothing of the kind!" growled Father, patting her on the shoulder. "Just a daughter come home!"

Then he beat a hasty retreat to the fireplace and touched a match to the fire already laid, while Mother, purring like a contented old pussy, pushed the bewildered girl into the big flowered chair in front of the fire and began unfastening her coat and taking off her hat, reverently, half in awe, for she was not used to girl's fixings, and they held almost as much mystery for her as if she had been a man.

In the midst of it all Mother remembered that dinner ought to be eaten at once, and that Bonnie must have a chance to wash her face and straighten her hair before dinner.

So Father and Mother, with many a reluctant lingering and last word, as if they were not going to see her for a month, finally bustled off together. In just no time at all Bonnie was down there, too, begging to be allowed to help, and declaring herself perfectly able, although her white face and the dark rings under her eyes belied her. Mother Marshall was not sure, after all, but she ought to have put Bonnie to bed and fed her with chicken broth and toast instead of letting her come downstairs to eat stewed chicken, little fat biscuits with gravy, and the most succulent apple pie in the world, with a creamy glass of milk to make it go down.

Father had just finished trying to make Bonnie take a second helping of everything, when he suddenly dropped the carving knife and fork with a clatter and sprang up from his chair:

"I declare to goodness, Mother, if I didn't forget!" he said, and rushed over to the telephone.

"Why, that's so!" cried Mother. "Don't forget to tell him how much we love her!"

Bonnie looked from one to the other of them in astonishment.

"It's that young man!" explained Mother. "He wanted we should telegraph if you got here all safe. You know he sent us a message after he put you on the train."

"How very thoughtful of him!" said Bonnie, earnestly. "He is the most wonderful young man! I can't begin to tell you all he did for me, a mere stranger! And so that explains how you knew where to send your message. I puzzled a good deal over that."

Four hours later Courtland, coming up to his room after basketball practice, a hot shower, and a swim in the pool, found the telegram:

> Traveler arrived safely. Bore the journey well. Many thanks for the introduction. Everybody happy; if you don't believe it come and see for yourself.
>
> FATHER AND MOTHER MARSHALL

Courtland read it and looked dreamily out of the window, trying to fancy Bonnie in her new home. Then he said aloud, with conviction, "Sometime I shall go out there and see!"

Just then someone knocked at his door and handed in a note from Gila.

> DEAR PAUL—Come over this evening. I want to see you about something very special.
>
> Hastily,
>
> GILA

# Chapter 24

*

Gila's note came to Courtland as a happy surprise. He had not expected to see her until the next evening. Not that he had brooded much over the matter. He was too busy and too sanely healthy to do that. Besides, he was only as yet questioning within himself whether he was going to fall in love. The sensation so far was exceedingly pleasurable, and he was ready for the whole thing when it should arrive and prove itself; but at present he was just in that quiescent stage when everything seemed significant and delightfully interesting.

He had firmly resolved that the next time he saw Gila he would tell her of his own heart experience with regard to the Presence. He realized that he must go carefully, and not shock her, for he had begun to see that all her prejudices would be against taking any stock in such an experience. He had only so shortly himself come from a like position that he could well understand her extreme views; her what amounted almost to repugnance, toward hearing anything about it. But he would make her see the whole thing, just as he had seen it.

Now Gila had no notion of allowing any such recital as Courtland was planning. She had her stage all set for entirely another scene, and she had on her most charming mood. She was wearing a little frock of pale blue wool, so simple that a child of ten might have worn it under a white ruffled apron. The neck was decorated with a soft kerchieflike collar. Not even a pin marred the simplicity of her costume. Her hair, too, was simpler than usual, almost carrying out the childish idea with its soft looping away from the face. Little heelless black satin slippers were tied with narrow black ribbons quaintly crossed and recrossed over the slim, blue silk ankles, carrying out the charming idea of a modest, simple maiden. Nothing could be more coy and charming than the way she swept her long black lashes down upon her pearly cheeks. Her great eyes when they were lifted were clear and limpid as a baby's. Courtland was fairly carried off his feet at sight of her, and felt his heart bound in reassurance. This must be love! He had fallen in love at last! He who had scorned the idea so long and laughed at the other fellows, until he had really begun to have doubts in his own heart whether the delightful illusion would ever come to him! The glamour was about Gila to-night and no mistake! He looked at her with his heart in his eyes, and she drooped her lashes to hide a glint of triumph, knowing she had chosen her setting aright at last. Softly, dreamily, pleasantly, in the back of her mind floated the Capitol of the nation, and herself standing amid admiring throngs receiving homage. She was going to succeed. She had achieved her first triumph with the look in Courtland's eyes. She would be able to carry out Mr. Ramsey Thomas's commission and win Courtland to anything that would forward ambitious hopes for him! She was sure of it!

The very important business about which she had wished to see Courtland was to ask him if he would be her partner in a bazaar and pageant that was shortly to be given for some charitable purpose by the society folks with whom she companioned. She wanted Courtland to march with her, and to consult him about the characters they should choose and the costumes they should wear.

As if she had been a child desiring him to play with her, he yielded to her mood, watching her all the time with delighted eyes, that anything so exquisite and lovely should stoop to sue for his favor. Of course he would be her partner! He entered into the arrangements with a zest, though he let her do all the planning, and heeded little what character she had chosen for him, or what costume, so she was pleased. Indeed, his part in the matter seemed of little moment so he might go with her—his sweet, shy, lovely maiden! For so she seemed to him that night! A perfect Solveig!

The reason for the little slippers became apparent later, when she insisted upon teaching him the dancing steps that were to be used in a final splendid assembly after the pageant. There was intoxication in the delight of moving with her through the dreamy steps to the music of the expensive Victrola she set going. Just to watch her little feet like fairies for lightness and grace; to touch her small, warm hand; to be so near those down-drooping lashes; to feel her breath on his hand; to think of her as trusting her lovely little self to him—made him almost deliriously happy. And she, with her drooping lashes, her delicate way of barely touching his arm, her utter seeming unconsciousness of his presence, was so exquisite and pure and lovely tonight! She did not dream, of course, of how she made his pulses thrill and how he was longing to gather her into his arms and tell her how lovely she was. Afterward he was never quite sure what kept him from doing it. He thought at the time it was herself, a sort of wall of purity and loveliness that surrounded her and made her sacred, so that he felt he must go slowly, must not startle her nor make her afraid of him. It never occurred to him that the wall might be surrounding himself. He had entirely forgotten the first visit to Gila in the Mephistophelian garments, with the red light filling all the unholy atmosphere. There had never been so much as a hint of red light in the room since he said he did not like it. The lampshade seemed to have disappeared. In its place was a great wrought metal thing of old silver jeweled with opalescent medallions.

But it was part of the deliberate intention of Gila to lead him on and yet hold him at a distance. She had read him aright. He was a man with an old-fashioned ideal of woman, and the citadel of his heart was only to be taken by such a woman. Therefore, she would be such a woman until she had won. After that? What mattered it? Let time plan the issue! She would have attained her desire!

But the down-drooping lashes hid no unconscious sweetness. There was sinister gleam in those eyes as she looked at herself over his shoulder when they passed the great mirror set in a cabinet door. There was deliberate intention in the way the little hand lay lightly in the strong one. There was not a movement of the dreamy dance she was teaching him, not a touch of the little satin slipper, that did not have its nicely calculated intention to draw him on. The sooner she could make him yield and crush her to him, the sooner he declared his passion for her, that much nearer would her ambitions be to their fulfillment. Yet she must be very sure that she had him close in her trap before she discovered to him her purpose.

So the little blue puritanlike spider threw her silver gossamer web about him, tangling more and more his big, fine manly heart, and flinging diamond dust and powder made of charms and incantations, in his eyes to blind him. But as yet she knew not of the Presence that was now his constant companion.

They had danced for some time, floating about in the pure delight of the motion together, and the nearness of each other, when it seemed to Courtland as if of a sudden a cooling hand was laid on his feverish brow and a calm came to his spirit like a beloved voice calling his name with the accent that is sure of quick response.

It was so he remembered what he had come to tell Gila. Looking down at that exquisite bit of humanity almost within his embrace, a great tenderness for her, and longing, came over him, to make her know now all that the Presence was becoming to him.

"Gila," he whispered, and his voice was full of thrill. "Let's sit down awhile! There is something I want to tell you!"

Instantly she responded, lifting great innocent eyes, with one quick sweep, to his face, so moved and tender; and gliding toward the couch where they might sit together, settling down on it, almost nestling to him, then remembering and drawing away shyly to more perfectly play her part. She thought she knew what he was going to say. She thought she saw the love-light in his eyes, and it was so dazzling it almost blinded her. It frightened her a little, too, like the light in no lover's eyes that had ever drawn her down to whisper love to her before. She wondered if it was because she really cared herself so much now that it seemed so different.

But he did not take her in his arms as she had expected he would do, though he sat quite near, and spoke in a low, privileged tone, as one would do who had the right. His arm was across the back of the couch behind her; he sat sideways, turned toward her, and he still touched reverently the little hand he had been holding as they danced together.

"Gila, I have a story to tell you," he said. "Until you know it you can never understand me fully, and I want with all my heart to have you understand me. It is something that has become a part of me."

She sat quivering, wondering, half-fearful. A gleam of jealousy came into her averted face. Was he going to tell her about another girl? A fierce, unreasoning anger shot across her face. She would not tolerate the thought that anyone had had him before her. Was it—It couldn't be that baby-face pauper in the hospital? She drew her slim little body up tensely and waited for the story.

Courtland told the story of Stephen; told it well and briefly. He pictured Stephen so that the girl must needs admire. No woman could have heard that description of a man such as Stephen had been and not bow her woman's heart and wish that she might have known him.

Gila listened, fascinated, even up to the moment of the fire and the tragedy when Stephen fell into the flames. She shuddered visibly several times, but sat tense and still and listened. She even was unmoved when Courtland went on to tell of finding himself on a ledge above the burning mass, creeping somehow into a small haven, shut in by a wall of smoke, and feeling that this was the end. But when he began to tell of the Presence, the Light, the Voice, the girl gave a sudden start and gripped her cold hands together. Almost imperceptibly she drew her tense little body away from him, and turned slowly till she faced him, horror and consternation in her eyes, utter unbelief and scorn on her lips. But still she did not speak, still held her gaze on him and listened, while he told of coming back to life, the hospital walls, the strange emptiness, and the Presence; the recovery, and the Presence still with him; the going here and there and finding the Presence always before him and yet with him!

"He is here in this room with us, Gila!" he said, simply, as if he had been telling her that he had brought her some flowers and he hoped she would like them.

Then suddenly Gila gave a spring away from him to her feet, uttered a wild scream of terror, and burst into angry tears!

Courtland sprang to his feet in dismay and instant contrition. He had made the horror of the fire too dramatic. He had not realized how dreadful it would be to a woman's delicate sensibilities. This gentle, loving girl had felt it all to her soul and her nerves had given way before the reality of it. He had been an idiot to tell the story in that bald way. He should have gone about it more gently. He was not used to women. He must learn better. Would she forgive him?

And now indeed he had her in his arms, although he was utterly unaware of it. He was trying to comfort and soothe her, as he would soothe a little child who had been frightened. Not only his handkerchief but his hands were called into requisition to charm away those tears and comfort the pitiful little face that looked so streaked and pink and helpless there against his shoulder. He wanted to stoop and lay his lips on those trembling ones. Perhaps Gila thought he would. But he would not take advantage of her moment of helplessness. Not until she was herself and could give him permission would he avail himself of that sacred privilege. Now it was the part of a man to comfort her without any element of self in the matter.

When he had drawn her down upon the couch again, with the sobs still shaking her soft blue and white frilly breast, her blue-black hair all damp and tossed upon her temples, and tried to tell her how sorry he was that he had put her through the horrors of that fire, she put in a quivering protest. It was *not* the fire. She shivered. It was not the horror and the smoke! It was *not* Stephen's death, nor the danger to himself! It was not *any* of those that had unnerved her! It was that other awful thing he had said: that ghostly, ghastly, uncanny, dreadful story of a Presence! She almost shrieked again as she said it, and she shivered away from him, as if still there were something cold and clammy in his touch that gave her the horrors.

A cold disappointment settled down upon him. She had not understood. He looked at her, troubled, disappointed, baffled. It was not possible, then, for him to bring her this knowledge that he wished so much for her to have. It was a thing that one could tell about to one's friends, but could not give to them. It was something they must take for themselves, must feel and see by themselves! With new illumination he turned to her and said in a voice wonderfully tender for a man so young:

"Listen, Gila! I have been clumsy in telling you! You cannot see it just from my poor story. But He will come to *you* and you shall see Him for yourself! I will ask Him to come to you as He has to me!"

Again that piercing scream, and with a quick, little movement, almost like a serpent, she slid from his side and stood quivering in the middle of the room, her eyes flashing, her body shrinking, both little hands clenched to her throat.

"Stop!" she cried. "Stop!" and screamed again, stamping her foot. "I won't hear such horrible things! I *won't have* any spirits coming around me! I *won't see* them! Do you understand? I *hate* that Presence, and *I hate you* when you talk like that!"

She had worked herself into a fine tantrum, but there was behind it all a horrible fear and shrinking from the Christ he had described, the shrinking of the naked soul in the garden from its God. The drooping, childlike eyes were wide with horror now; the sweet, innocent mouth was trembling with emotion. She was anything but Solveiglike. If Courtland caught a glimpse of the real Gila through it all he laid it to his own clumsy way of handling the delicate mystery of a girl's shy nature. He saw she was wrought up beyond her own control, and he was so far under the illusion that he blamed himself only, and set himself to calm her.

He coaxed her to sit down again, put his strong hand on her quivering one, marveling in tenderness at its smallness and softness. He talked to her in quiet, soothing tones, grave and reassuring. He promised he would talk no more about the Presence till she was ready to hear. He was leaning toward her in his strength, his arm behind her, his hand on her shoulder, with a sheltering, comforting touch when he told her this, as one would treat a little child in trouble, and, suddenly, like the sun flashing out from behind the clouds, she lifted up her teary face and smiled, nestling toward him, her head falling down on his shoulder with a sigh like a tired, satisfied child, her face lifted temptingly so close, so very close to his.

It was then that he did the thing that bound him to what followed. He stooped and laid his lips upon her warm little trembling ones and kissed her. The thrill that shot through him was like the click of shackles snapping shut about one's wrist; like the turning of the key in a prison house; the shooting of the bolt to one's dark cell. He held her there and touched her soft hair with his fingertips; touched her cool little forehead with his lips; touched her warm, soft lips again and felt the thrill; but something was the matter. He felt the surging forces within him rise and batter at the gate of his self-control. He wanted to say, "Gila, I love you!" but the words stuck in his throat.

What had he done? Whence came this sense of defeat and loss? The Presence! Where was the Presence? Yes—there—but withdrawn, standing apart in sadness, while he sat comforting and caressing one who had just said she hated Him! But that was because she had not seen Him yet! She was frightened because she did not understand! He would yet be able to make her see! He would implore the Presence to come to her; to break down her prejudice; to let her have the vision also!

So he sat and comforted her, yet longed to get away and think it out. This sense of depression and bitter disappointment hung about him like a burden; now, of all times, when he should be happy if ever he was to be!

But Gila was nestling close, patting his sleeve, talking little, sweet nonsensical words as if she had really been the little child she seemed. He looked down at her and smiled. How small she was, and childlike. He must remember that she was very young, and probably had never had much bringing-up. Serious things frightened her! He must go gently and lead her! It made him feel old and responsible to look at her—tender, beautiful girl!—enveloped as she was in the garment of his ideal of womanhood.

Yet there was something about it all that drove him from her. He must think it out and come to some clear understanding with himself. As it was, it seemed to him as if he were trying to take peace within himself while before him lay a lot of his own broken vows. He had vowed to himself to bring her to the Christ and he had not accomplished it. Instead she had declared she hated him and the Presence both; yet here he sat making love to her and ignoring it all! He felt a distinct weakness in himself, but did not know how to remedy it.

When he finally got away from Gila and walked feverishly toward the university, he felt as if his soul was crying out within him for a solution of the perplexities in which he was involved. By his side walked a Friend, but there seemed to be a veil between them. Ever mingling with his thoughts came the sweet, tear-wet face of Gila, with its Solveig-look, pleading up at him from the mist of the evening, luring him as it were to forget the Christ. He passed his hand wearily over his eyes, told himself that he had been through a good deal that evening and his nerves were not as strong as they used to be since the fire.

He was surprised to find that it was still early when he got back to his room, barely half past nine. Yet it had seemed as if it must be near midnight, so much had happened.

What he would have thought if he could have known that at that very minute Tennelly was seated in the chair in the library that he had so lately vacated, and Gila, posing bewitchingly in the firelight, merrily talking him over, is hard to say.

Not that they were saying anything against him—of course not! Tennelly would never have stood for that, and Gila knew better. But Gila had no intention of giving Tennelly any idea how far matters had gone between herself and Courtland. As for Tennelly, he would have been the most amazed of the three if he could have known all. He had been Courtland's intimate friend for so many years—

years count like ages when one is in college—that he thought he knew him perfectly. He would have sworn to it that Courtland's friendship with Gila had not progressed further than a mere first stage of friendship. He admitted that Gila had an influence over his friend, but that it had really gone heart-deep seemed impossible. Courtland was a man of too much force, even young as he was, and too much maturity of thought, to be permanently entangled with a girl like Gila. That was what Tennelly thought before Gila had turned her eyes toward him and flung a few of her silver gossamer threads about his soul. For always in those first days of his visits to Gila it had been in Courtland's behalf; first, to see if she was good enough for a friend of his friend, and next to get her partnership in the scheme of turning Courtland's thoughts away from "morbid" things.

But that night for the first time Tennelly saw the Solveig in Gila, and was stirred on his own account. The childish blue frock and the simple frilled kerchief did their work with his high soul as well; and he sat, charmed, and watched her. After all, there was more to her than he had thought, or else she was a consummate actress! So Tennelly sat late before the fire, till Gila knew that he would turn aside again often to see her for himself, and then she let him go.

# Chapter 25

*

Gila took herself off to a house party the very next day, with only a tinted, perfumed note, like a flutter of painted wings, to explain that the butterfly had melted into the pleasant sunshine to taste honey in other flowers for a time.

In a way her going was a relief to Courtland. He didn't understand himself. There was something wrong, and he wanted to find out what before he saw her again.

It was while he was in this troubled state that he stumbled upon the Bible as something that might possibly bring light.

He had studied it before in his biblical literature classes, and found it much like other books, a literary classic, a wonderful gem of beauty in its way, a rare collection of legends, proverbs, allegories, and the like. But looking at it now, with the possible hypothesis that it was the Word of God, all was changed.

He remembered once seeing a tray of gems in an exhibit, and among them one that looked like a common pebble. The man who had charge of the exhibit took the little pebble and held it in the palm of his hand for a moment, when it suddenly began to glow and sparkle with all the colors of the rainbow and rival all the other gems. The man explained that only the warmth of the human hand could cause this marvelous change. You might lay the stone under the direct rays of a summer sun, yet it would have no effect until you took it in your hand, when it would give forth its beauty once more.

It was like this when he began to read the Bible with the

idea that it was the Word of God. Things flashed out at him that fairly dazzled his thoughts; living, palpitating things, as if they were hidden of a purpose to be discovered only by him who cared to search. Hidden truths came to light that filled his soul with wonder. Gradually he understood that belief was the touchstone by which all these treasures were to be revealed. Everywhere he found it, that belief in Christ was a condition to all the blessings promised. He read of hearts hardened and eyes blinded because of unbelief, and came to see that unbelief was something a man was responsible for, not a condition which settled down upon him, and he could not help. Belief was a deliberate act of the will. It was not a theory, nor an intellectual affirmation; it was a position taken, which necessarily must pass into action of some kind. He began to see that without this deliberate belief it was impossible for man to know the things which are purely spiritual. It was the condition necessary for revelation. He was fascinated with the pursuit of this new study.

Wittemore came to his room one evening, his face grayer, more strained and horselike than ever. Wittemore's mother had made another partial recovery and insisted on his return to college. He was plodding patiently, breathlessly along in his classes, trying to catch up again. He had paid Courtland back part of the money he borrowed, and was gradually paying the rest in small installments. Courtland hated to take it, but saw that it would hurt him to refuse it; so he had fallen into a habit of stopping now and then to talk about his settlement work, just to show a little friendly interest in him. Wittemore had responded with a quiet wistfulness and a patient hovering in the background that touched the other man's heart deeply.

"I've just come from my rounds," said Wittemore, sitting down, apologetically, on the edge of a chair. "That old lady you carried the medicine to—she's been telling me how you made tea and toast!" He paused and looked embarrassed.

"Yes," smiled Courtland. "How's she getting on? Any better?"

"No," said Wittemore, the hopeless gray look settling

about his sensitive mouth. "She'll never be any better. She's dying!"

"Well," said Courtland, "that'll be a pleasant change for her, I guess."

Wittemore winced. Death had no pleasant associations for him. "She told me you prayed for her! She wants you to do it again!"

It was plain he thought the praying had been a sort of joke with Courtland.

Courtland looked up, the color rising slowly in his face. He saw the accusation in Wittemore's sad eyes.

"Of course I know what you think of such things. I've heard you in the class. I don't believe in them anymore myself, either, now." Wittemore's voice had a trail of hopelessness in it. "But somehow I couldn't quite bring myself to make a mockery of prayer, even to please that old woman. You see *my mother still believes in prayer*!" He spoke apologetically, as of a dear one who had lacked advantages.

"But *I do* believe in prayer!" said Courtland, earnestly. "What you heard me say in class was before I understood."

"Before you understood?" Wittemore looked puzzled.

"Listen, Wittemore. Things are all different now. I've met Jesus Christ and I've got my eyes open. I was blind before, but since I've felt the Presence everything has been different."

And then he told the story of his experience. He did not make a long story out of it. He gave brief facts, and when it was finished Wittemore dropped his face into his hands and groaned:

"I'd give anything if I could believe all that again," came from between his long bony fingers. "It's breaking my mother's heart to have me leave the faith!"

The slick haylike hair fell in wisps over his hands, his high, bony shoulders were hunched despairingly over Courtland's study table. He was a great, pitiful object.

"Why don't you, then?" said Courtland, getting up and going to the closet for his overcoat. "It's up to you, you know. You *can*! God can't do it for you, and of course there's nothing doing till you've taken that step. I found that out!"

"But how do you reconcile things, calamities, disasters,

war, suffering, that poor old woman lying on her attic bed alone? How do you reconcile that with the goodness of God?"

"I don't reconcile it. It isn't my business. I leave that to God. If I understood all the whys and wherefores of how this universe is run I'd be great enough to be a God myself."

"But if God is omniscient I can't see how He can let some things go on! He must be limited in power or He'd never let some things happen if He's a good God!" Wittemore's voice had a plaintive sound.

"Well, how do you know that? In the first place, how can you be sure what is a calamity? And say, did it ever strike you that some of the things we blame on God are really up to us? He's handed over His power for us to do things, and we haven't seen it that way; so the things go undone and God is charged with the consequences."

"I wish I could believe that!" said Wittemore.

"You can! When you really want to, enough, you will! Come on, let's get that prayer down to the old lady! I'm sort of an amateur yet, but I'll do my best."

They went out into the mist and murk of a spring thaw. Wittemore never forgot that night's experience—the prayer, and the walk home again through the fog. The old woman died at dawning.

Courtland spent much time thinking about Gila these days. His whole soul was wrapped up in the desire that she might understand. He was longing for her; idealizing her; thinking of her in her innocent beauty, her charming ways; wondering how she would meet him the next time, what he would say to her; living upon her brief, alluring notes that came to him from time to time like fitful rose petals blown from a garden where he longed to be; but yet in a way it was a relief to have her gone until he could settle the great perplexity that was in his mind concerning her.

Gila prolonged her absence by a trip south with her father, and so it was several weeks before Courtland saw her again.

There seemed to be a settled sadness over his soul when he prayed about her, and when at last she returned and summoned him to her he was no nearer a solution of his difficulty than when he had last left her.

The hour before he went to her he spent in Stephen's room, turning over the leaves of Stephen's Bible. When he rose at last to go he turned again to this verse which had caught his eye among the marked verses that were always so interesting to him because they seemed to have been landmarks in Stephen's life:

> My presence shall go with thee, and I will give thee rest.

It almost startled him, so well did it seem to suit his need. He read on a few verses:

> And he said unto him, If thy presence go not with me, carry us not up hence. For wherein shall it be known here that I and my people have found grace in thy sight? Is it not in that thou goest with us? So shall we be separated, I and thy people, from all the people that are upon the face of the earth.

Wonderful words those, implying a close relationship that shut out to a certain extent all others who were not one with that Presence. He wished he knew what it all meant! And in that moment was born within him a desire to understand the Bible and know how believing scholars explained everything.

But as he went from the room and on his way, he felt that to some extent he had a solution of his trouble. He was to be under the personal conduct of the Presence of God wherever he went, whatever he did! This was to make life less complex, and in some mysterious way the power of the Christ with him was to be made manifest to others. Surely he might trust this in the case of Gila, and feel sure that he would be guided aright; that she would come to see for herself how there was with him always this guiding power. Surely she would come to know it and love it also.

Gila met him with fluttering delight, poutingly reproaching him for not writing oftener, calling him to order for looking solemn, adoringly pretty herself in a little frilly pink frock that gave her the look of a pale anemone, windblown and sweet and wild.

She talked a good deal about the "dandy times" she had had and the "perfectly peachy" men and girls she had met; flattered him by saying she had seen none handsomer or more distinguished than he was. She accepted as a matter of course the loverlike attitude he adopted, let him tell her of his love as long as he was not too solemn about it, teased and played with him, charmed him with every art she knew, dancing from one mood to another like a sprite, winding her gossamer chains about him more and more, until, when he went from her again, he was fairly intoxicated with her beauty.

He had lulled his anxiety with the thought that he must wait and be patient until Gila saw. But more and more was it growing hard to approach her about the things that were of most moment to him. Sometimes when he was wearily trying to find a way back from the froth of her conversation to the real things he hoped she would enjoy with him someday, she would call him an old crab, and summon to her side other willing youths to stimulate his jealousy; youths of sometimes unsavory reputation whose presence gave him deep anxiety for her. Then he would tell himself he must be more patient, that she was young and must learn to understand little by little.

Gila developed a great interest in Courtland's future, his plans for a career, of which she chattered to him much and often, suggesting ways in which her father might perhaps help him into a position of prominence and power in the political world. But Courtland, with a shadow of trouble in his eyes, always put her off. He admitted that he had thought of politics, but was not ready yet to say what he would do.

So spring came on, with its final examinations, and commencement drawing nearer every day.

Through it all Courtland found much time to be with Gila; often in company, or flashing through a crowded thoroughfare by her side; following her fancy; excusing her follies; laying her mistakes and indiscretions to her youth and innocence; always trying to lead up to his great desire, that she might see his Christ.

Tennelly watched the whole performance anxiously. He wanted Courtland to be drawn out of what he considered his "morbid" state, but not at the price of his peace of mind. He was very sure that Courtland ought not to marry Gila. He was equally sure that she meant nothing serious in her present relation to Courtland. He felt himself responsible in a way because he had agreed in the plot with his uncle to start her on this campaign. But if Courtland should come out of it with a broken heart, what then?

It was just a week before commencement that the crisis came.

Gila had summoned Courtland to her.

Gila, in her most imperial mood, wearing a bewildering imported frock whose simple intricacies and daring contrasts were well calculated to upbear a determined spirit in a supreme combat, awaited his coming impatiently. She knew that he had that day received another offer from Ramsey Thomas, tempting in the extreme, and baited with alluring possibilities that certainly were dazzling to her if they were not to her friend. She meant to make him tell her of the offer, and she meant to make him accept it that very afternoon and clinch the contract by telephoning the acceptance to the telegraph office before he left her home.

Courtland was tired. He had been through a hard week of examinations, he had been on several committees, and had a number of important class meetings, and the like. There had been functions galore to attend, and late hours that were unavoidable. He had come to her hoping for a rest and the joy of her society. Just to watch her dainty grace as she moved about a room, handling the tea things and giving him a delicate sandwich or a crisp cake, filled him with joy and soothed his troubled spirit; it was so like his ideal of what a woman should be.

But Gila was not handing out tea that afternoon. She had other fish to fry, and she went at her business with a determination that very soon showed there was no rest to be had there.

Very prettily, but quite efficiently, she bored him for information about his plans. Had he no plans whatever about what he was going to do as soon as he had finished college? Of course she knew he had money of his own (he had never told her how much, and there hadn't really been any way of asking a man like Courtland when he didn't choose to tell a thing like that), but nowadays that was nothing. Even rich men all did *something*. One wasn't anything unless one was in something big! Hadn't he ever had any offers at all? It was queer, such a brilliant man as he was. She knew lots of young fellows who had no end of chances to get into big things as soon as they were done with their education. Didn't his father know of something, or have something in mind for him? Hadn't he ever been approached?

Goaded at last by her delicate but determined insinuations, Courtland told her. Yes, he had had offers; one in particular that was a fine thing from a worldly point of view, but he didn't intend to take it. It did not fit with his ideal of life. There were things about it that were not square. He wasn't quite sure how his own plans were going to work out yet. He must have a talk with his father first. Possibly he would study awhile longer somewhere.

Gila frowned. She had no idea of letting him do that. She wanted him to get into something big right away, so that she might begin her career. So that was what had been standing in his way! Study! How stupid! No, indeed! She wanted no scholar for a husband, who would bore her with horrid old dull books and lectures and never want to go anywhere with her! She must switch him away from this idea at once! She returned to the rejected business proposition with zeal and avidity. What was it? What did it involve? What were its future possibilities? Great! What on earth could he find in that to object to? How ridiculous! How long ago had that been offered to him? Was it too late to accept? What? He had had the offer repeated even more flatteringly that very day? Where was the letter? Would he let her see it?

She bent over Uncle Ramsey's brusque sentences with a hidden smile of triumph and pretended to be surprised.

"How perfectly wonderful! All that responsibility and all those chances to get to the top! Even a hint of Washington!"

She dimpled and opened her great eyes imploringly at

him. She pictured herself in glowing terms going with him and holding court among the great of the land! She wheedled and coaxed and all but commanded, while he sat and watched her sadly, realizing how well fitted she was for the things she was describing and how she loved them all!

> So shall we be separated, I and my people, from all the people that are upon the face of the earth!

He started upright! It was as if a voice had spoken the words, those strange words from the Bible! Was this then what they meant? Separation! But Gila was "his people" now. Was she not one day to be his wife? He must explain it all to her. He must let her know that he had chosen a way of separation that forbade the paths wherein she was longing to wander. Would she shrink and wish to turn back? Nevertheless, he must make it plain to her.

Gently, quietly, he tried to make her understand. He told her of the visit of Ramsey Thomas and his own decision in the winter. He told her of the factory that was built to blind the eyes of those who were trying to uplift and help men. He tried to make conditions plain where girls as young as she, and with just such hopes and fears and ambitions, perhaps in some cases just as much sweetness and native beauty as she had, were obliged to spend long hours of toil amid surroundings that must crush the life out of any pure soul, and turn all the sweetness to bitterness, the beauty to a peril! He hinted at things she did not know nor dream of; dreadful things from which her life had always been safely guarded; and how he could not, for the sake of those crushed souls, accept a position that would close his mouth and tie his hands forever from doing anything about it. He told her he could not accept honor that was founded upon dishonor; that he had taken Christ for his pattern and guide; that he could do nothing that would drive God's Presence from him.

She had been sitting with her face averted, her clasped hands dropped straight down at the side of her lap, the fingers interlaced and tense in excitement; her bosom heaving with agitation under the Paris gown; but when he reached this point in his argument she sprang to her feet and away from him, standing with her shoulders drawn back, her head thrown up, her chin out, her whole lithe body stiff and imperious.

"It is time this stopped!" she said, and her voice was cold like a frozen dagger and went straight through his heart. "It is time you put away forever this ridiculous idea of a Presence, and of setting yourself up to be better than anyone else! This isn't religion, it is fanaticism! And it has got to stop now and *forever*, or I will have nothing whatever to do with you. Either you give up this idea of a ghost following you around all the time and accept Mr. Ramsey Thomas's offer this afternoon, or you and I part! You can choose, *now*, between me and your Presence!"

# Chapter 26

*

Gila had never been more beautiful than when she stood and uttered her terrible ultimatum to Courtland. Her little imperial head sat on her lovely shoulders royally, her attitude was perfect grace. Her spirited face with its dark eyes and lashes, its setting of blue-black hair, was fascinating in its exquisite modeling. She looked like a proud young cameo standing for her portrait. But her words shot through Courtland's heart like icy swords dividing his soul from his body.

He rose to his feet, gone suddenly white and stern, and stood looking at her as if his own heart had turned traitor and slain him. A moment they stood in battle array, two forces representing the two great powers of the universe. Looking straight into each other's souls they stood, plumbing the depths, seeing as in a revelation what each really was!

To Courtland it was suddenly made plain that this girl had no part or lot in the things that had become vital to him. She had not seen, she *would* not see! Her love was not great enough to carry her over the bridge that separated them, and back over which he might not go after her!

Gila in her fierce haughtiness looked into Courtland's eyes and saw, as she had never seen before, the mighty strength of his character! Saw that here was a man such as she would not likely meet again upon her way, and she was about to lose him forever. Saw that he would never give in about a matter of principle, and that his love was worth all the more to any woman because he would not; knew which way he would choose, from the first word of her challenge; yet the little fury within her would not let her withdraw. She stood with haughty mien and cold, flashing eyes, watching him suffer the blow she had dealt him; knew that it was more than his love for her she was killing with that blow, yet did not withdraw it while she might.

"Gila! Do you mean that?"

She looked him straight in the eye and thrust her sword in the deeper with a steady hand. "I do!"

He stood for a moment looking steadily at her with that cold, observant glance, as if he would have this last picture of her this way to cut away all tender memories that might cause pain in the future. Then he turned as if to One who stood by his side. Not looking back again, he said, clearly and distinctly:

"I choose!"

And with erect bearing he passed out of the door.

Gila stood, white and furious, her little clenched fists down at her sides, the sharp little teeth biting into the red underlip until the blood came. She heard the front door shut in the distance, and her soul cried out within her, yet she stood still and held her ground. She turned her face toward the library window. Between the curtains she could presently see his tall form walking down the street. He was not drooping, nor disheartened. He held his head up and walked as if in company with One whom he was proud to own. There was nothing dejected about the determined young back. Fine, noble, handsome as a man could be! She saw that one glimpse of his figure for a moment, then he passed beyond her sight and she knew in her heart he would come to her no more! She had sent him from her forever!

She dashed up to her room in a fury and locked herself in. She wept and stormed and denied herself to everyone; she watched and waited for the telephone to ring, yet she knew he would not call her up!

Courtland never knew where he was walking as he went forth that day to meet his sorrow and face it like a man. He passed some of his professors, but did not see them. Pat

McCluny came up and he looked him in the eye with an unseeing stare, and walked on!

Pat stood still and looked after him, puzzled!

"Holy Mackinaw! What's eating the poor stew now!" he ejaculated. He stood a moment looking back after Courtland as he walked straight ahead, passing several more university fellows without so much as a nod of recognition. Then he turned and slowly followed, on through the city streets, out into the quieter suburbs, out farther into the real country, mile after mile; out a bypath where grass grew thick and wild flowers straggled underfoot, where presently a stream wound soft and deep between steep banks, and rocks loomed high on either hand; under a railroad bridge, and up among the rocks, climbing and puffing till at last they stood upon a great rock, McCluny just a little way behind and out of sight.

It was there in a sort of crevice, where the natural fall of the crumbling rocks had formed a shelter, that Courtland dropped upon his knees. Not as a spot he had been seeking for, but as a haven to which he had been led. He knelt, and all that Pat, standing, awed and uncovered, a few feet below, heard was:

"O God! O *God!*"

He knelt there a long time, while Pat waited below, trying to think what to do. The sun was beginning to sink, and a soft, pink summer light was glinting over the brown rocks and bits of moss and grasses. The young leaves waved lightly overhead like children dancing in the morning, and something of the sweetness and beauty of the scene crept into Pat McCluny's soul as he stood and waited before this Gethsemane gate for a man he loved to come forth.

At last he stepped up the rocks quietly and came and stood by Courtland, laying a gentle hand upon his shoulder. "Come on, old man, it's getting late. About time we were getting back!"

Courtland got up and looked at him in a dazed way, as if his soul had been bruised and he was only just recovering consciousness. Without a word he turned and followed Pat back again to the city. They did not talk on the way back. Pat whistled a little, that was all.

When they reached the gates of the university Courtland turned and put out his hand, speaking in his own natural tone: "Thanks awfully, old chap! Sorry to have made you all this trouble!"

"That's all right, pard," said Pat, huskily, grasping the hand in his big fist. "I saw you were up against it and I stuck around, that's all!"

"I shan't forget it!"

They parted to their rooms. It was long past suppertime. Pat went away by himself to think.

Over and over to himself Courtland was saying, as he came to himself and began to realize what had come to him: "It isn't so much that I have lost her. It is that *she should have done it*!"

Pat said nothing even to Tennelly about his walk with Courtland. He figured that Courtland would rather they did not know. He simply hovered near like a faithful dog, ready for whatever might turn up. He was relieved to see that his friend came down to breakfast next morning, with a white, resolute face, and went about the order of the day quietly, as if everything was as usual.

Tennelly and Bill Ward were on the alert. They had missed Courtland from the festivities the night before, but were so thoroughly occupied with their own part in the busy week that they had little time to question him. Later in the day Tennelly began to wonder why Courtland had not brought Gila, as he intended, for the class play, but a note from Gila informed him that she was done with Paul Courtland forever, and that he would have to get someone else to further his uncle's schemes, for she would not. She intimated that she might explain further if he chose to call, and Tennelly made a point of calling in between things, and found Gila inscrutable. All he could gather was that she was very, very angry with Courtland, hopelessly so, and that she considered him worth no more effort on her part. She was languidly interested in Tennelly and accepted his invitation to the dance that evening most graciously. She had expected to go in Courtland's company, but now if he repented and came to claim his right she would ignore it.

But Courtland had taken Gila at her word. He had no

idea of claiming any former engagement with her. She had cut him off forever, and he must abide by it. Courtland had spent the night upon his knees in the little sacred room at the end of the hall. He was much stronger to face things than he had been when he left her. So when he met Gila walking with Tennelly he lifted his hat courteously and passed on, his face grave and stern as when she had last seen him, but in no way showing other sign that he had suffered or repented his choice. Pat, walking by his side, looked furtively at Gila then keenly at his companion, and winked to his inner consciousness.

"She's the poor simp that did the business! And she looks her part, *b'leeve me*!" he told himself. "But he'll get over that! He's too big to miss *her* long!"

Although there was pain in these days that followed Courtland's choice, there was also great peace in his heart. He seemed to have grown older, counting days as years, and to have a wider vision on life. Love of woman was gone out of his life, he thought, forever! Love wasn't an illusion quite as he had thought. No! But Gila had not loved him, or she never would have made him choose as she did! That was plain. If she had not loved, then it was better he should go out of her life! He was glad that the university days were over, and he might begin a new environment somewhere. He felt something strong within his soul pushing him on to a decision. Was it the voice calling him again, leading up to what he was to do?

This thought was uppermost in his mind during the commencement, which beforehand had meant so much to him; which all the four years had been the goal to which he had been urging forward. Now that it was here he seemed to have gone beyond it, somehow, and found it to be but a little detail by the way, a very small matter not worth stopping and making so much fuss about. Of course, if Gila had loved him; if she had been going to be there watching for him when he came forward to take his diploma; if she were to be listening when he delivered that oration upon which he had spent so much time and for which he received so much commendation, that would have meant everything to him a few brief days ago—of course, then it would have been different! But as it was he wondered that everybody seemed so much interested in things and took so much trouble for a lot of nonsense.

Courtland was surprised to see his father come into the great hall just as he went up on the platform with his class. He hadn't expected his father. He was a busy man who did not get away from his office often.

It touched him that his father cared to come. He changed his plans and made it possible to take the train home with him after the exercises, instead of waiting a day or two to pack up, as he had expected to do. The packing could wait awhile. So he went home with his father.

They had a long talk on the way, one of the most intimate that they had ever had. It appeared during the course of conversation that Mr. Courtland had heard of the offer made to his son by Ramsey Thomas, and that he was not unfavorable to its acceptance.

"Of course, you don't really need to do anything of the sort, you know, Paul," he said, affably. "You've got what your mother left you now, and on your twenty-fifth birthday there will be two hundred and fifty thousand coming to you from your Grandfather Courtland's estate. You could spend your life in travel and study if you cared to, but I fancy, with your temperament, you wouldn't be quite satisfied with an idle life like that. What's your objection to this job?"

Courtland told the whole story carefully, omitting no detail of the matter concerning conditions at the factory, and the matters at which he was not only expected to wink, but also sometimes to help along by his influence. He realized, as he told it, that his father would look at the thing fairly, but very differently.

"Well, after all," said the father, comfortably settling himself to another cigar, "that's all a matter of sentiment. It doesn't do to be too squeamish, you know, if you have ambitions. Besides, with your income you would have been able to help out and do a lot of good. You ought to have thought of that."

"In other words, earn my salary by squeezing the life out of them and then toss them a penny to buy medicine. I don't see it that way! No, Dad, if I can't work at something clean I'll go out and work in the ground, or do *nothing*, but I *won't* oppress the poor."

"Oh, well, Paul, that's all right if you feel that way about it, of course. Ramsey Thomas wanted me to talk it over with you; promised to do the square thing by you and all that; and he's a pretty good man to get in with. Of course I won't urge you against your will. But what are you going to do, son? Haven't you thought of anything?"

"Yes," said Courtland, leaning back and looking steadily at his father. "I've decided that I'd like to study theology."

"Theology!" The father started and knocked an ash delicately from the end of his cigar. "H'm! Well, that's not a bad idea! Rather odd, perhaps, but still there's always dignity and distinction in it. Your great-grandfather on your mother's side was a clergyman in the Church of England. Of course it's rather a surprise, but it's always respectable, and with your money you would be independent. You wouldn't have any trouble in getting a wealthy and influential church, either. I could manage that, I think."

"I'm not sure that I want to be a clergyman, Father. I said *study* theology. I want to know what scholarly Christians think of the Bible. I've studied it with a lot of scholarly heathen who couldn't see anything in it but literary merit. Now I want to see what it is that has made it a living power all through the ages. I've got to know what saints and martyrs have founded their faith upon."

"Well, Paul, I'm afraid you're something of an idealist and a dreamer like your mother. Of course it's all right with your income, but, generally speaking, it's as well to have an object in view when you take up study. If I were you I would look into the matter most carefully before I made any decisions. If you really think the ministry is what you want, why, I'll just put a word in at our church for you. Our old Doctor Bates is getting a little out of date and he'll be about ready to be put on the retired list by the time you are done your theological course. Let's see, how long is it, three years? Had you thought where you will go? What seminary? Better make a careful selection; it has so much to do with getting a good church afterward!"

"Father! You don't *understand*!" said Courtland, desperately, and then sat back and wondered how he should begin. His father had been a prominent member of the board of trustees in his own church for years, but had he ever felt the Presence? In the days when Courtland used to sit and kick his heels in the old family pew and be reproved for it by his aunt, he never remembered any Presence. Doctor Bates's admirable sermons had droned on over his head like the dreamy humming of bees in a summer day. He couldn't remember a single thought that ever entered his mind from that source. Was that all that came of studying theology? Well, he would find out, and if it was, he would *quit* it!

They were all comfortably glad to see him at home. His stepmother beamed graciously upon him in between her social engagements, and his young brothers swarmed over him, demanding all the athletic news. The house was big, ornate, perfect in its way. It was good to eat such superior cooking—that is, if he had been caring to eat anything just then; and there was a certain freedom in life out of college that he knew he ought to enjoy; but somehow he was restless. The girls he used to know reminded him of Gila, or else had grown old and fat. The country club didn't interest him in the least, nor did the family's plans for the summer. It suited him not at all to be lionized on account of his brilliant career at college. It bored him to go into society.

Sometimes, when he was alone in his room, he would think of the situation and try to puzzle it out. It seemed as if he and the Presence were there on a visit which neither of them enjoyed very much, and which they were enduring for the sake of his father, who seemed gratified to have his eldest son at home once more. But all the time Courtland was chafing at the delay. He felt there was something he ought to be about. There wasn't anything here. Not even the young brothers presented a very hopeful field, or perhaps he didn't know how to go about it. He tried telling them stories one day when he wheedled them off in the car with him, and they listened eagerly when he told them of the fire in the theater, Stephen Marshall's wonderful part in the rescue of many, and his death. But when he went on and tried to tell them in boy language of his own experience he could see them look strangely, critically at him, and finally the oldest one said: "Aw rats! What kinda rot are you giving us, Paul? You were nutty then, o' course!" and he saw that, young as they were, their eyes were holden like the rest.

In the second week Courtland made his decision. He would go back to the university and pack up. Gila would be away from the city by that time; there would be no chance of meeting her and having his wound opened afresh. The fellows would be all gone and he could go about as he pleased.

It was the second day after he went back that he met Pat on the street, and it was from Pat that he learned that Tennelly and Bill Ward had gone down to the shore to a house party given by "that fluffy-ruffles cousin of Bill's."

Pat drew his own conclusions from the white look on Courtland's face when he told him. He would heartily have enjoyed throttling the girl if he had had a chance just then, when he saw the look of suffering in Courtland's eyes.

Pat clung to Courtland all that week, helped him pack, and dogged his steps. Except when he visited the little sacred room at the end of the hall in the dormitory, Courtland was never sure of freedom from him. He was always on hand to propose a hike or a trip to the movies when he saw Courtland was tired. Courtland was grateful, and there was something so loyal about him that he couldn't give him the slip. So when he went down after Burns and whirled him away in his big gray car to the seashore Friday morning to stay until Saturday evening, Pat went along.

# Chapter 27

*

They certainly were a queer trio, the little Scotch preacher, the big Irish athlete, and the cultured aristocrat! Yet they managed to have a mighty good time of it those two days at the shore, and came back the warmest of friends. Pat proved his devotion to Burns by attending church the next day with Courtland, and listening attentively to every word that was said. It is true he did it much in the same way the fellows used to share one another's stunts in college, sticking by and helping out when one of the gang had a hard task to perform. But it pleased both Courtland and Burns that he came. Courtland wondered, as he shared the hymnbook with him and heard him growl out a few bass notes to old "Rock of Ages," why it was that it seemed to fill him with a kind of exaltation to hear Pat sing. He hadn't yet recognized the call to go fishing for men, nor knew that it was the divine angler's deep delight in his employment that was filling him. It was while they were singing that hymn that he stole a look at Pat, and felt a sudden wonder whether he would understand about the Presence or not, a burning desire to tell him about it sometime if the right opportunity offered.

The days down at the shore had done a lot for Courtland. He had taken care that the spot he selected was many miles removed from the popular resort where Mr. Dare had a magnificent cottage; and there had been absolutely nothing in the whole two days to remind him of Gila. It was a quiet place, with a far, smooth beach, and no boardwalks nor crowds to shut out the vision of the sea. He leaped along the sand and dived into the water with his old enthusiasm.

He played like a fish in the ocean. He taught Burns several things about swimming, and played pranks like a schoolboy. He basked in the sun and told jokes, laughing at Pat's brilliant wit and Burns's dry humor. At night they took long walks upon the sand and talked of deep things that Pat could scarcely understand. He was satisfied to stride between them, listening to the vigorous ring of Courtland's old natural voice again. He heard their converse high above where he lived, and loved them for the way they searched into things too deep for him.

It was out in the wildest, loneliest part of the beach that night that he heard the first hint of what had come to the soul of Courtland. Pat had come of Catholic ancestry. He had an inheritance of reverence for the unseen. He had let religion go by and shed it like a shower, but he respected it.

Courtland spent much time in the vicinity of the factory and of John Burns's church during the next few weeks. He helped Burns a good deal, for the man had heavily taxed himself with the burdens of the poor about him. Courtland found ways to privately relieve necessity and put a poor soul now and then on his feet and able to face the world again by the loan of a few cents or dollars. It took so pitifully little to open the gate of heaven to some lives! Courtland with his keen intellect and fine perceptions was able sometimes to help the older man in his perplexities; and once, when Burns was greatly worried over a bill that was hanging fire during a prolonged session of Congress, Courtland went down to Washington for a weekend and hunted up some of his father's congressional friends. He told them a few facts concerning factories in general, and a certain model, white marble, much bevined factory in particular, that at least opened their eyes if it did not make much difference in the general outcome. But though the bill failed to pass that session, being skillfully sidetracked, Courtland had managed to stir up a bit of trouble for Uncle Ramsey Thomas that made him storm about the office wrathfully and wonder who that "darned little rat of a preacher" had helping him now!

It was late in September that Pat, with a manner of studied indifference, told Courtland of a rumor that Tennelly was engaged to Gila Dare.

It was the very next Sunday night that Tennelly turned up at Courtland's apartment after he and Pat had gone to the evening service, and followed them to the church. He dropped into a seat beside Pat, amazed to find him there.

"You here!" he whispered, grasping Pat's hand with the old friendly grip. "Where's Court?"

Pat grinned and nodded up toward the pulpit.

Tennelly looked forward and for a minute did not comprehend. Then he saw Courtland sitting gravely in a pulpit chair by the little red-headed Scotch preacher.

"What in thunder?" he growled, almost out loud. "What's the joke?"

Pat's face was on the defensive at once, though it was plain he was enjoying Tennelly's perplexity. "Court's going to speak tonight!" It is probable Pat never enjoyed giving any information so much as that sentence in his life.

"The deuce he is!" said Tennelly, out loud. "You're lying, man!" which, considering that the Scotchman was praying, was slightly out of place.

Pat frowned. "Shut up, Nelly. Can't you see the game's called? I'm telling you straight. If you don't believe it wait and see."

Tennelly looked again. That surely was Courtland sitting there. What could be the meaning of it all? Had Courtland taken to itinerary preaching? Consternation filled his soul. He loved Courtland as his own brother. He would have done anything to save his brilliant career for him.

He hadn't intended staying to service. His plan had been to slip in, get Courtland to come away with him, have a talk, and go back to the shore on the late train. But the present situation altered his plans. There was nothing for it now but to stay and see this thing through. Pat was a whole lot deeper than the rest had ever given him credit for being. Pat was enjoying the psychological effect of the service on Tennelly. He had never been much of a student in the psychology class, but when it came right down to plain looking into another man's soul and telling what he was thinking about, and what he was going to do next, Pat was all there.

That was what made him such an excellent football player. When he met his opponent he could always size him up and tell just about what kind of plays he was going to make, and know how to prepare for them. Pat was no fool.

That was a most unusual service. The minister read the story of the martyr Stephen, and the conversion of Saul of Tarsus, taken from the sixth, seventh, eighth, and ninth chapters of Acts. It was brief and dramatic in the reading. Even Tennelly was caught and held as Burns read in his clear, direct way that made Scripture seem to live again in modern times.

"I have asked my friend Mr. Courtland to tell you the story of how he met Jesus one day on the Damascus road," said Burns, as he closed the Bible and turned to Courtland, sitting still with bowed head just behind him.

Courtland had made many speeches during his college days. He had been the prince among his class for debate. He had been proud of his ability as a speaker, and had delighted in being able to hold and sway an audience. He had never known stage fright, nor dreaded appearing before people. But ever since Burns had asked him if he would be willing to tell the story of the Presence to his people in the church before he left for his theological studies, Courtland had been just plain frightened. He had consented. Somehow he couldn't do anything else, it was so obviously to his mind a "call"; but if he had been a coward in any sense he would have run away that Saturday afternoon and got out of it all. Only his horror of being "yellow" had kept him to his promise.

Since ascending to the platform he had been overcome by the audacity of the idea that he, a mere babe in knowledge, a recent scorner, should attempt to get up and tell a roomful of people, who knew far more about the Bible than he did, how he found Christ. There were no words in which to tell anything! They had all fled from his mind and it was a blank!

He dropped his head upon his hand in his weakness to pray for strength, and a great calm came to his soul. The prayer and Bible reading had steadied him, and he had been able to get hold of what he had to say as the story of the young man Saul progressed. But when he heard himself being introduced so simply, and knew his time had come, he seemed to hear the words he had read that afternoon:

> Fear thou not, for I am with thee: be not dismayed; for I am thy God: I will strengthen thee; yea, I will help thee; yea, I will uphold thee with the right hand of my righteousness.

Courtland lifted up his head and arose. He faced the sea of faces that a few moments before had swum before his gaze as if they had been a million. Then all at once Tennelly's face stood out from all the rest, intent, curious, wondering, and Courtland knew that his opportunity had come to tell Tennelly about the Presence!

Tennelly, the man whom he loved above all other men! Tennelly, the man who perhaps loved Gila and was to be close to her through life! His fears vanished. His soul burned within him.

Fixing his eyes on the fine, vivid face, Courtland began his story; and truly the words that he used must have been drawn red-hot from his heart, for he spoke as one inspired. Simply, as if he were alone in the room with Tennelly, he looked into his friend's eyes and told his story, forgetting all others present, intent only on making Tennelly see what Christ had been to him, what He was willing to be to Tennelly—and Gila! If they would!

Tennelly did not take his eyes from the speaker. It was curious to see him so absorbed, Tennelly, who was so conventional, so careful what people thought, so always conscious of all elements in his environment. It was as if his soul were sitting frankly in his eyes for the first time in his life, and things unsuspected, perhaps, even by himself, came out and showed themselves: traits, weaknesses, possibilities, longings, too, and pride.

When Courtland had finished and sat down he did not drop his head upon his hands again. He had spoken in the strength of the Lord. He had nothing of which to be ashamed. He was looking now at the audience, no longer at Tennelly. He began to realize that it had been given to him to bear the message to all these other people also. He was filled with humble exaltation that to him had been intrusted this great opportunity.

The people, too, were hushed and filled with awe. They showed by the quiet way they reached for the hymnbooks, the reverent bowing of their heads for the final prayer, that they had all felt the power of Christ with the speaker. They lingered, many of them, and came up, pressing about him, just to touch his hand and make mute appeal with their troubled eyes. Some to ask him eagerly for reassurance of what he had been saying; others to thank him for the story. They were so humble, so sincere, so eager, these common people, like the ones of old who crowded around the Master and heard him gladly. Paul Courtland was filled with humility. He stood there half-embarrassed as they pressed about him. He took their hands and smiled his brotherhood, but scarcely knew what to say to them. He felt an awkward boy who had made a grěat discovery about which he was too shy to talk.

Pat and Tennelly stood back against the wall and waited, saying not a word. Tennelly watched the people curiously as they went out: humble, common people, subdued, wistful, even tearful; some of them with illlumined faces as if they had seen a great light in their darkness.

When at last Courtland drifted down to the back of the church and reached Tennelly the two met with a look straight into each other's soul, while their hands gripped in the old brotherhood clasp. Not a smile nor a commonplace expression crossed either face—just that strong, steady look of recognition and understanding. It was Tennelly looking at Courtland, the new man in Christ Jesus; Courtland looking at Tennelly after he had heard the story.

They walked back to Courtland's apartment almost in silence, a kind of holy embarrassment upon them all. Pat whistled "Rock of Ages" softly under his breath most of the way.

They sat for a time, talking, stiffly, as if they hardly knew one another, telling the news. Bill Ward had gone to California to look into a big land deal in which his father was interested. Wittemore's mother had died and he wasn't coming back next year for his senior year. It was all surface talk. Pat put in a little about football. He discussed which of last year's scrubs were most hopeful candidates for the varsity team this year. Not one of the three at that moment cared a rap whether the university had any football team or not. Their thoughts were upon deeper things.

But the recent service was not mentioned, nor the extraordinary fact of Courtland's having taken part in it. By common consent they shunned the subject. It was too near the heart of each.

Finally Pat discreetly took himself off, professedly in search of ice water, as the cooler in the hall had for some reason run dry. He was gone some time.

When he had left the room Tennelly sat up alertly. He had something to say to Courtland alone. It must be said now before Pat returned.

Courtland got up, crossed the room, and stood looking out of the window on the myriad lights of the city. There was in his face a far yearning, and something too deep for words. It was as if he were waiting for a blow to fall.

Tennelly looked at Courtland's back and gathered up his courage: "Court," he said, hoarsely, trying to summon the nomenclature of the dear old days; "there's something I wanted to ask you. Was there anything—is there—between you and Gila Dare that makes it disloyal for your friend to try and win her if he can?"

It was very still in the room. The whir of the trolleys could be heard below as if they were out in the hall. They grated harshly on the silence. Courtland stood as if carved out of marble. It seemed ages to Tennelly before he answered, with the sadness of the grave in his tone:

"No, Nelly! It's all right! Gila and I didn't hit it off! It's all over between us forever. Go ahead! I wish you luck!"

There was an attempt at the old loving understanding in the answer, but somehow the last words had almost the sound of a sob in them. Tennelly had a feeling that he was wringing his own happiness out of his friend's soul:

"Thanks, awfully, Court! I didn't know," he said, awkwardly. "I think she likes me a lot, but I couldn't do anything if you had the right of way."

When Pat came back with a tray of glasses clinking with ice, and the smell of crushed lemons, they were talking of the new English professor and the chances that he would be better than the last, who was "punk." But Pat was not deceived. He looked from one to the other and knew the blow had fallen. He might have prevented it, but what was the use? It had to come sooner or later. They talked late. Finally, Tennelly rose and came toward Courtland, with his hand outstretched, and they all knew that the real moment of the evening had come at last:

"That was a great old talk you gave us this evening, Court!" Tennelly's voice was husky with feeling. One felt that he had been keeping the feeling out of sight all the evening. He was holding Courtland's hand in a painful grip, and looking again into his eyes as if he would search his soul to the depths: "You sure have got hold of something there that's worth looking into! You had a great hold on your audience, too! Why, you almost persuaded me there was something in it!"

Tennelly tried to finish his sentence in lighter vein, but the feeling was in his voice yet.

Courtland gripped his hand and revealed his eagerness with a sudden light of joy and hope: "If you only would, Nelly! It's been the thing I've longed for—!"

"Not yet!" said Tennelly, almost pulling his hand away from the detaining grasp. "Sometime, perhaps, but not now! I've too much else on hand! I must beat it now! Man alive! Do you know what time it is? See you soon again!" Tennelly was off in a whirl of words.

"Almost thou persuadest me!" Had someone whispered the words behind him as he went?

Courtland stood looking after him till the door closed, then he turned and stepped to the window again. He was so long standing there, motionless, that Pat went at last and touched him on the shoulder.

"Say, pard," he said, in a low, gruff voice. "I'm nothing but a roughneck, I know, and not worth much at that, but if it's any satisfaction to you to know you've bowled a bum like me over to His side, why *I'm with you*!"

Courtland turned and grasped his hand, throwing the

other arm about Pat's shoulder. "It sure is, Pat, old boy," he said, eagerly. "It's the greatest thing ever! Thanks! I needed that just now! I'm all in!"

They stood so for some minutes with their arms across each other's shoulders, looking out of the window to the city, lying sorrowful, forgetful, sinful, before them; down to the street below, where Tennelly hastened on to win his Gila; up to the quiet, wise old stars above.

# Chapter 28

*

Tennelly did not come back as he had promised. Instead he wrote a gay little note to tell of his engagement to Gila. He said it was not to be announced publicly yet, as Gila was so young. They would wait a year perhaps before announcing it to the world, but he wanted Courtland to know. In an added line at the bottom he said: "That was a great old speech you made the other night, Court. I haven't forgotten it yet. Your reference to Marshall was a crackerjack! The faculty ought to have heard it."

Courtland read it wearily, closed his eyes for a minute, passed his hand over his brow, then he handed the note over to Pat. The understanding between the two was very deep and tender now.

Pat read without comment, but the frown on his brow matched the set of his big jaw. When he spoke again it was to tell Courtland of the job he had been offered as athletic coach in a preparatory school in the same neighborhood with the theological seminary where Courtland had decided to study. Courtland listened without hearing and smiled wearily. He was entering his Gethsemane. Neither one of them slept much that night.

In the early dawning Courtland arose, dressed, and silently stole out of the room, down through the sleeping city, out to the country, where he had gone once before when trouble struck him. It seemed to him he must get away to breathe, he must go where he and God could be alone.

Pat understood. He only waited till Courtland was gone to fling on his clothes in a hurry and be after him. He had noted from the window the direction taken, and guessed where he would be.

On and on walked Courtland with the burning sorrow in his soul; out through the heated city, over the miles of dusty road, his feet finding their way without apparent direction from his mind; out to the stream, and the path where wild flowers and grasses had strewn the ground in springtime; gay now with white and purple asters. The rocks wore vines of crimson, and goldenrod was full of bees and yellow butterflies. Gnarled roots bore little creeping tufts of squawberry with bright, red berries dotting thick between. But Courtland passed on and saw it not.

Above, the sky was deepest blue and flecked with summer clouds. Loud-voiced birds called gaily of the summer's ending, talked of travel in a glad, gay lilt. The bees droned on; the bullfrogs gave forth a deep wise thought or two; while softly, deeply, brownly, flowed the stream beside the path, with only a far, still fisherman here and there who noticed not. But Courtland heard nothing, saw nothing but the dark of his Gethsemane. For every nodding goldenrod and saucy purple aster was but a bright-winged thought to him to bring back the saucy, lovely face of Gila. She belonged now to another. He had not realized before how fully he had chosen, how lost she was to him, until another, and that his best friend, had taken her for his own. Not that he repented his decision or drew back. Oh no! He could not have chosen otherwise. Yet now, face to face with the truth, he realized that he had always hoped, even when he walked away from her, that she would find the Christ and one day they would come together again. Now that hope was gone forever. She might find the Christ, he hoped—yes, hoped and prayed she would!—it was a wish apart from his personal loss, but she could never summon him now, for she had given herself to another!

He gained at last the rock-bound refuge where he knelt once before. Pat, coming later from afar, saw his old panama lying down on the moss and knew that he was there. Creeping softly up, he assured himself that all was well, then crept away to wait. Pat had brought a basket of grapes and a great bag of luscious pears against the time when Courtland should have fought his battle and come forth. What those hours of waiting meant to Pat might perhaps be found written in the lives of some of the boys in that school where he coached athletics the next winter. But what they meant to Courtland will only be found written in the records on high.

Sometime a little after noon there came a peace to Courtland's troubled soul.

> When thou passest through the waters I will be with thee, and through the rivers they shall not overflow thee!

It was as near to him as whispers in his ear, and peace was all about him.

He stood up, looked abroad, saw the beauty of the day, heard the dreaminess of the afternoon coming on, heard louder God's call to his heart, and knew that there was strength for all his need. It was then Pat came with his refreshment like a ministering angel.

When they got back to the city that evening there was a note from Bonnie, the first Courtland had received since the formal announcement of her arrival and her gratitude to him for being the means of bringing her to that dear home.

This letter was almost as brief as the first, but it breathed a spirit of peace and content. She enclosed a check on the funeral account. Bonnie was well and happy. She was teaching in the grammar school where Stephen Marshall used to study when he was a little boy, and giving music lessons in the afternoons. She would soon be able to pay back everything she owed and to do a daughter's share in the home where she was treated like an own child. She closed by saying that the kindness he had shown her would never be forgotten; that he had seemed to her, and always would, like the messenger of the Lord sent to help her in her despair.

There was a ring so fresh and strong and true in this little letter, that he could but recognize it. He sighed and thought how strange it was that he should almost resent it, coming as it did in contrast with Gila's falseness. Gila who had professed to love him so deeply, and then had so easily laid that love aside and put on another. Perhaps all girls were the same. Perhaps this Bonnie, too, would do the same if a man turned out not to have her ideals.

He answered Bonnie's note in a day or two with a cordial one, returning her check, assuring her that everything was fully paid, and expressing his pleasure that she had found a real home and congenial work. Then he dismissed her from his mind.

A week later he went to the seminary, and Pat accompanied him as far as the preparatory school where he was to enter upon his duties as athletic coach.

Courtland found the atmosphere of the seminary quite different from college. The men were older. They had chosen definitely their work in the world. Their talk was of things ecclesiastical. The happenings of the day were spoken of with reference to the religious world. It was a new viewpoint in every sense of the word. And yet he was disappointed that he did not find a more spiritual atmosphere among the young men who were studying for the ministry. If anywhere in the world the Presence might be expected to be moving and apparent it should be here, he reasoned, where men had definitely given themselves to the study of the Gospel of Christ, and where all were supposed to believe in Him and to have acknowledged Him before the world. He found himself the only man in the place who was not a member of any church, and yet there were but three or four that he had the feeling he could speak to about the Presence and not be looked upon as strange. There was much worldly talk. There was a great deal of church gossip about churches and ministers; what this one was paid and what that one got; the chances of a man being called to a city church when he was just out of the seminary. It was the way his father had talked when he told him he wanted to study theology. It turned him sick at heart to hear them. It seemed so far from the attitude a servant of the Lord should have. He was in a fair way to lose his ideal of ministers as well as of women. He mentioned it one day bitterly to Pat when he came over to spend a spare evening, as he frequently did.

"I think you're wrong," said Pat, in his queer abrupt way. "From what I can figure there was only a few of those guys got around Christ and knew what He really was! You didn't suppose it would be any different now, did you? Guess you'll find it that way everywhere, only a few *real* folks in *any* gang!"

Courtland looked at Pat in wonder. He was a constant surprise to his friend, in that he grew so fast in the Christian life. He had a little Bible that he had bought before he left the city. It was small and fine and expensive, utterly unlike Pat, and he carried it with him always, apparently read it much. He hadn't been given to reading anything more than was required at college, so it was the more surprising. He told Courtland he wanted to know the rules of the game if he was going to get in it. His sturdy common sense often gave Courtland something to think about. Pat was bringing his new religion to bear upon his work. He already had a devoted bunch of boys to whom he was dealing out wholesome truths beginning a new era in the school. The headmaster looked on in amazement, for morality hadn't been one of the chief recommendations that the faculty of the university had given Pat. They had, in fact, privately cautioned the school that they would have to watch out for such things themselves. Instead, however, of finding a somewhat lawless man in their new coach, the headmaster was surprised to discover a purity campaign on foot, a ban on swearing and cigarette smoking such as they had never been able to establish before. It came to their ears that Pat had personally conducted an offender along these lines out to the boundaries of the school grounds, well behind the gymnasium, where there was utmost privacy, and administered a good thrashing on his own account. The faculty watched anxiously to see the effect of such summary treatment on the student body, but were relieved to find that the new coach's following was in no wise diminished, and that better conduct began presently to be the order of the day.

Pat and Courtland were much together these days, and one Sunday afternoon in late October, while the sun was still warm, they took the athletic teams a long hike over the country. When they sat down to rest Pat asked Courtland to tell the boys about Stephen, and the Presence.

That was the real beginning of Courtland's ministry, those

unexpected, spontaneous talks with the boys, where he could speak his heart and not be afraid of being misunderstood.

There were two or three professors in the seminary who struck Courtland as being profoundly spiritual and sincere in their lives. They were old men, noted for their scholarship and their strong faith the world over. They taught as Courtland imagined a prophet might have taught in the days of the Old Testament, with their ears ever open to see what the Lord would have them speak to the children of men. At their feet he sat and drank in great draughts of knowledge, going away satisfied. There were other professors, some of them brilliant in the extreme, whose whole attitude toward the Bible and Christ seemed to have an undertone of flippancy, and who fairly delighted to find an unauthentic portion over which they might haggle away the precious hours of the classroom. They lacked the reverent attitude toward their subject which only could save the higher criticism from being destructive rather than constructive.

As the year went by he came to know his fellow students better, and to find among them a few earnest, thoroughly consecrated fellows, most of them plain men like Burns, who had turned aside from the world's allurements to prepare themselves to carry the gospel to those who were in need. Most of them were poor men also, and of humble birth, with a rare one now and then of brains and family and wealth, like Courtland, to whom God had come in some peculiar way. These were a group apart from others, whom the rest respected and admired, yet laughed at in a gentle, humoring sort of way, as if they wasted more energy on their calling than there was any real need to do. Some of them were going to foreign lands when they were through, had already been assigned to their mission stations, and were planning with a special view to the needs of the locality. Courtland felt an idler and drone among them that he did not yet know what he was to do.

The men, as they came to know him better, predicted great things for him: wealthy churches falling at his feet, brilliant openings at his disposal; but Courtland took no part in any such discussions. He had the attitude of heart that he was to be guided, when he was through his studies, into the place where he was most needed; it mattered not where so it was the place God would have him to be.

In February Burns had a farewell service in his church. He had resigned his pastorate and was going to China. Pat and Courtland went down to the city to attend the service; and Monday saw him off to San Francisco for his sea voyage to China.

Courtland, as he stood on the platform watching the train move away with his friend, wished he could be on that train going with Burns to China. He was to take up Burns's work around the settlement and in the factory section; to see some of his friend's plans through to completion. He was almost sorry he had promised. He felt utterly inadequate to the necessity!

Spring came, and with it the formal announcement of Tennelly's and Gila's engagement. Courtland and Pat each read it in the papers, but said nothing of it to each other. Courtland worked the harder these days.

He tried to plunge into the work and forget self, and to a certain extent was successful. He found plenty of distress and sorrow to stand in contrast with his own; and his hands and heart were presently full to overflowing.

Like the faithful fellow worker that he was, Pat stuck by him. Both looked forward to the week that Tennelly had promised to spend with them. But instead of Tennelly came a letter. Gila's plans interfered and he could not come. He wrote joyously that he was sorry, but he couldn't possibly make it. It shone between every line that Tennelly was overwhelmingly happy.

"Good old Nelly!" said Courtland, with a sigh, handing the letter over to Pat, for these two shared everything these days.

Courtland stood staring out the window at the vista of roofs and tall chimneys. The blistering summer sun simmered hot and sickening over the city. Red brick and dust and grime were all around him. His soul was weary of the sight and faltered in its way. What was the use of living? What?

Then suddenly he straightened up and leaned from the window alertly! The fire alarm was sounding. Its sinister wheeze shrilled through the hot air tauntingly! It sounded again. One! two! One! two! three! It was in the neighborhood.

Without waiting for a word, both men sprang out the door and down the stairs.

# Chapter 29

❋

"The Whited Sepulcher," as some of the bitterest of her poorly paid slaves called the model factory, stood coolly, insolently, among her dirty, redbrick, grime-stained neighbors; like some dainty lady appareled in sheer muslins and jewels appearing on the threshold of the hot kitchen where her servitors were sweating and toiling to prepare her a feast.

The luxuriant vines were green and abundant, creeping coolly about the white walls, befringing the windows charmingly, laying delicate clinging fingers even up to the very eaves, and straying out over the roof. No matter how parched the ground in the little parks of the district, no matter how yellow the leaves on the few stunted trees nearby, no matter how low the city's supply of water, nor how many public fountains had to be temporarily shut off, that vine was always well watered. Its root lay deep in soft, moist earth well fertilized and cared for; its leaves were washed anew each evening with refreshing spray from the hose that played over it. "Seems like I'd just like to lie down there and sleep with my face clost up to it, all wet and coollike, all night!" sighed one poor little bony victim of a girl, scarcely more than a child, as the throng pressed out the wide door at six o'clock and caught the moist fragrance of the damp earth and growing vine.

"You look all in, Susie!" said her neighbor, pausing in her interminable gum-chewing to eye her friend keenly. "Say, you better go with me to the movies tonight! I know a nice cool one fer a nickel!"

"Can't!" sighed Susie. "Ain't got ther nickel, and besides, I gotta stay with gran'mom while Ma goes up with some vests she's been makin'. Oh, I'm all right! I jus' was thinkin' about the vine; it looks so cool and purty. Say, Katie, it's somepin' to b'long to a vine like that, even if we do have it rotten sometimes! Don't you always feel kinda proudlike when you come in the door, 'most as if it was a palace? I like to pertend it's all a great house where I live, and there's carpets and lace curtings to the winders, and a real gold sofy with pink-velvet cushings! And when I come down and see one of the company's ottymobiles standin' by the curb waitin', I like to pertend it's mine, only I don't ride 'cause I've been ridin' so much I'd *ruther* walk! Don't you ever do that, Katie?"

"Not on yer *life*, I don't!" said Katie, with an ugly frown. "I hate the old dump! I hate every stone in the whole pile! I could tear that nasty green vine down an' stamp on it. I'd like to strip its leaves off an' leave it bare. I'd like to turn the hose off and see it dry up an' be all brown, an' ugly, an' dead. It's stealin' the water they oughtta have over there in the fountain. It's stealin' the money they oughtta pay us fer our work! It's creepin' round the winders an' eatin' up the air. Didn't you never take notice to how they let it grow acrost the winders to hide folks from lookin' in from the visitor's windows there on the east side? They don't care how it shuts away the draught and makes it hotter 'n a furnace where we work! No, you silly! I never was proud to come in that old marble door! I was always mad, away down inside, that I had to work here. I had to go crawlin' and askin' fer a job, an' take all their insults, an' be locked in a trap. Take it from me, there's goin' to be some awful accident happen here someday! If a fire should break out how many d'you s'pose could get out before they was burned to a crisp? Did you know them winders was nailed so they wouldn't go up any higher 'n a foot? Did you know they 'ain't got 'nouf fire escapes to get half of us out ef anythin' happened? Did you never take notice to the floor roun' them three biggest old machines they've got up on the sixth? I stepped acrost there this mornin'—Mr. Brace sent me up on a message to the forewoman—an' that floor shook under my feet like a earthquake! Sam Warner says the building ain't half strong enough fer them machines anyway. He says they'd oughtta put 'em down on the first floor; but they didn't want to 'cause they don't show off good to visitors, so they stuck 'em up on the sixth, where they don't many see 'em. But Sam says someday they're goin' to bust right through the floor, an' ef they do, they ain't gonta stop till they get clear down to the cellar, an' they'll wipe out everythin' in their way when they go! B'leeve me! I don't wanta be workin' here when that happens!"

"*Good night*!" said Susie, turning pale. "Them big machines on the sixth is right over where I work on the fifth! Say, Katie, le's ast Mr. Brace to put us on the other side of the room! Aw, gee! Katie! What's the use o' livin'? I'd 'most be willin' to be dead just to get cool! Seems zif it's allus either awful hot er awful cold!"

They went to their stifling tenements and their unattractive suppers. They dragged their weary feet over the hot, dark pavements, laughing and talking boisterously with their comrades, or crowded into places of amusement to forget for a little while, then to creep back to toss the night out on a hard cot in breathless air or to creep to fire escape or flat roof for a few brief hours of relief, til it was time to return to the vine-clad factory and its hot, noisy slavery for another day.

Three girls fainted on the fifth floor and two on the sixth next morning. They were not carried to the cool and shaded rest rooms to revive, but lay on the floor with their heads huddled on a pile of waste, and had a little warmish water from the rusty "cooler" in the back stairway poured upon them as they lay. No white-clad nurse with palm leaf and cooling drinks attended their unconscious state, although there was one in attendance in the rest room whose duty it was to look after the comfort of any chance visitors. When any stooped to succor here, she fanned her neighbor with her apron, casting an anxious eye on her own silent machine and knowing she was losing "time."

Susie fainted three times that morning, and Katie lost an hour in all, bringing water and making a fan out of a newspaper. Also she had an angry altercation with the foreman.

He said if Susie "played up" this way she'd have to quit; there were plenty of girls waiting to take her place, and he hadn't time to fool with kids that wanted to lie around and be fanned. It was his last few words as she was reviving that stung Susie to life again and put her back at her machine for the last time in nervous panic, with the thought of what would happen at home if she lost her job. Up above her the great heavy machines thrashed on and the floor trembled with their movement. Black and thick and hot was the air around Susie and she scarcely could see, for dizziness, the machinery which she worked from habit, as she stood swaying in her place, and wondering if she could hold out till the noon whistle blew.

Down in the basement, near one of the elevator shafts, a pile of waste lay smoldering, out of sight. One of the boys from the lumberyard down the next block had stopped to light his cigarette as he passed out into the street after bringing a bill to the head manager. He tossed his match away, not seeing where it fell. The big factory thundered on in full swing of a busy, driving morning, and the little match lay nursing its flame and smoldering.

How long it crept and smoldered no one knew. It seemed to come from every floor at once, the smell of smoke and cry of fire! More smoke in volumes pouring up suddenly through cracks and bursting from the elevator shaft; a lick of flame darting out like a serpent ready to strike, menacing against the heat of the big rooms.

Panic and smoke and fire! Cries and clashing machinery thundering on like a storm above an angry sea!

The girls rushed together in fear, or, screaming, ran desperately to windows which they knew they could not raise! They pounded at the locked doors and crowded in the narrow passages, frantically surging this way and that. There was no one to quiet them or tell them what to do. If someone would only stop that awful machinery! Was the engineer dead?

Mockingly the little cool vines crept in about the windowsills and over the imprisoning panes, as if to taunt the victims who were caught in the death trap.

"At any rate, if we die you'll die too!" cried Katie Craigin, shaking her fist at the long green tendrils that swept across the window nearest her machine. "Oh, you! You'll burn to a crisp at the roots! You'll wither up an' die. You'll be dead an' brown an' ugly! An' I'm glad! *Glad!* For I hate you, *I hate you!* Do you hear?" And she grasped a handful of leaves that edged the windowsill, spat upon them, and stamped them under her foot, then turned to look for Susie.

But Susie had fallen once more by her machine leaving it unguarded while it thrashed on uselessly. Her little pinched face looked up from the dirty floor in pitiful unconsciousness amid the wild rush and whirl of the fear-maddened company. If terror drove them they would pass over her without knowing it. They were blind with desperation.

The room seemed about to burst with the heat. Timbers were cracking. All the stories they had heard of the frailty of the building came now to goad them as they hurtled from one end of their pen to the other, while intermittent clouds of smoke and darting flames conspired to bewilder their senses.

Katie sprang to seize her friend and drew her out of the path of the stampede. As she lifted her a cry arose, like the wail of a lost world facing the judgment. The floor swayed, the machines about seemed to totter, and the floor above seemed bending down with some great weight. There was a cracking, wrenching, twisting, as of the whole great building in mortal pain, and just as Katie drew her unconscious friend away to the window the floor above gave way and down crashed three awful machines, like great devouring juggernauts, to crush and bear away whatever came in their way.

After that, hell itself could scarcely have presented a more terrible spectacle of writhing, tortured souls, pinned anguishing amid the flames; of white faces below looking up to ghastly ones above that gazed down with horror into the awful cavern, closed their eyes, clung to walls and windows, and knew not what to do!

The fearful noise of machinery had suddenly ceased and been succeeded by a calm in which the soft sound of rushing flames, the babble of the crowd outside, the gong of fire engines, and the cry of firemen seemed balm of music in the ears. Water hissed on hot machinery and burning walls. It splashed inside the window and on the white face of Susie. It touched the hot hands of Katie as she lifted her friend nearer to the blessed spray. A shadow of a ladder somewhere crossed the window. Splintered glass fell all about her, and a hand reached in and crushed the window frame.

It was Pat who lifted out the limp Susie and handed her down to Courtland, who was just below, while Katie turned and looked back at the fearful pit of fire beneath her, knowing that in but a few more seconds, if help came not, she, too, would be a part of that writhing, awful heap! She saw the white face and staring eyes of the gray-haired woman who ran the machine next to hers lying beneath a pile of dead. She reeled and felt her senses going. Her hot hands clung to the hotter window ledge. The flames were leaping nearer! She could not hold out—

Then a strong hand grasped her and drew her out into the blessed air, and she felt herself being carried down, down, safely, wondering, as she went, if the vine was roasted yet, or if it still smirked greenly outside this holocaust; wished she had strength to shake a mocking finger at it; and then she knew no more.

For three long hours Courtland and Pat worked side by side, bringing out the living, searching for the dead and dying, carrying them to an improvised hospital in an old warehouse in the next block. Grim and soiled and gray, with singed hair, blistered hands and faces, and sickened hearts, they toiled on.

To Courtland the experience was like walking with God and being shown the way he might have gone, and how he had been saved. If he had accepted Ramsey Thomas's proposition he would have been a sharer in the sin that caused this catastrophe. He would have been a murderer, almost as much responsible for that charred body lying at his feet, for all those dead and dying, as if he had owned the place.

The whited sepulcher lay a heap of blackened ruins. Only one small corner rose, of blackened marble, to which clung a fragment of brave green to show what had been but a few short hours before. The morning's sun would see it, too, withered and black like the rest. The model factory was gone! But the money that had built it, the money that it had made, was still in existence to build it over again, a perpetual blind to the lawmakers who might have otherwise put a stop to its abuses! It would undoubtedly be built again, more whited, more sepulchral than before.

As he looked upon the ruin a great resolve came to him. He would give his life to fight the power that was setting its heel upon humanity and putting a price upon its blood. He would devote all his powers to the uplifting of people who had been downtrodden and oppressed in the simple act of earning their daily bread!

Ramsey Thomas, happening to be in a nearby city, and answering a summons by telegraph, arrived at the scene in an automobile as Courtland stood there, grimed and tattered from his fight with death.

Ramsey Thomas, baffled, angry, distressed, wriggled out of his car to the sidewalk and faced Courtland, curiously conspicuous and recognizable with all his disarray. Courtland towered above the great man with righteous wrath in his eyes. Ramsey Thomas cringed and looked embarrassed. He had come to look over the ground to see how much trouble they were going to have getting the insurance, and he hadn't expected to be met by a giant Nemesis with blackened face and singed eyebrows.

"Oh, why—I," he began nervously. "It's Mr. Courtland, isn't it? They tell me you've been very helpful during the fire! I'm sure we're much obliged. We'll not forget this, I assure you—"

"Mr. Thomas," broke in Courtland, in a clear, decisive voice, "you wanted to know a year ago why I wouldn't accept your proposition, and you couldn't understand my reason for refusing. There it is!"

He pointed eloquently to the heap of ruins.

"Go over to that warehouse and see the rows of charred bodies! Look at the agonized faces of the dead, and hear the groans of the dying. See the living who are scarred or crippled for life. You are responsible for all that! If I had accepted your proposal I would have been responsible, too.

And now I mean to spend the rest of my life fighting the conditions that make such a catastrophe as this possible!"

Courtland turned, and in spite of his tatters and soil walked majestically away from him down the street.

Ramsey Thomas stood rooted to the ground, watching him, a strange mingling of emotions chasing one another over his rugged old countenance: astonishment, admiration, and fury in quick succession.

"Drat him!" he said, under his breath. "Drat him! Now he'll be a worse pest than that little rat of a preacher, for he's got twice as much brains and education!"

# Chapter 30

*

The summer passed in hard, earnest work.

Courtland had been back at his studies four weeks when there came another letter from Tennelly. Gila had gone to her aunt's, down at Beechwood, for a two weeks' stay. She was worn out with the various functions of the summer and needed a complete rest. They were to be married soon, perhaps in December, and there would be a lot to do to prepare for that. She was going to rest absolutely, and had forbidden him to follow her, so he had some leisure on his hands. Would Courtland like to spend a weekend somewhere along the coast halfway between? They could each take their own cars and meet wherever Courtland said.

It was Saturday morning when Courtland received the letter. Pat had gone down to the city for over Sunday. An inexpressible longing filled him to see Tennelly again, before his marriage completed the wall that was between them. He wanted to have a real old-fashioned talk; to look into the soul of his friend and see the old loyalty shining there. He wanted more than all to come close to him once more, and, it might be, tell him about the Christ.

He took down his road book, turned to the map, and let his finger fall on the coastline about midway between the city and the seminary. Looking it up in the book, he found Shadow Beach described as a quiet and exclusive resort with a good inn, excellent service, and fine sea bathing. Well, that would do as well as anywhere. He telegraphed Tennelly:

Meet me at Shadow Beach, Howland's Inlet, Elm Tree Inn, this evening.

COURT

It was dark when he reached Elm Tree Inn. The ocean rolled, a long black line flecked with faint foam, along the shore, and luminous with a coming moon. Two dim figures, like moving shadows, went down the sand picked out against the path of the moon. Save for those all was lonely, up and down. Courtland shivered slightly and almost wished he had selected some more cheerful spot for the meeting. He had not realized how desolate a sea can be when it is growing cold. Nevertheless, it was majestic. It seemed like eternity in its limitless stretch. The lights in far harbors glinted out in the distance down the coast. Somehow the vast emptiness filled him with sadness. He felt as if he were entering upon anything but a pleasant reunion and half-wished he had not come.

Courtland ran his car up to the entrance and sprang out. He was glad to get inside, where a log fire was crackling. The warmth and the light dispelled his sadness. Things began to take on a cheerful aspect again.

"I suppose you haven't many guests left," he said, pleasantly, as he registered.

"Only him, sir!" said the clerk, pointing to the entry just above Courtland's.

"James T. Aquilar and wife, Seattle, Washington," Courtland read, idly, and turned away.

"They been here two days. Come in a nerroplane!" went on the clerk, communicatively.

"Fly all the way from Seattle?" asked Courtland idly. He was looking at his watch and wondering if he should order supper or wait until Tennelly arrived.

"Well, I can't say for sure. He's mighty uncommunicative, but he's given out he flies 'most anywhere the notion takes him. He's got his machine out in the lot back o' the inn. You oughtta see it. It's a bird!"

"H'm!" said Courtland. "I must have a look at it in daylight. I'm looking for a friend up from the city pretty soon. Guess it would be more convenient for you if we dined together. I'll wait a bit. Meanwhile, let me see what rooms you have."

When Courtland came back to the office and sat down before the fire to wait, the spell of sadness seemed to have vanished.

He sat for half an hour, with his head thrown back in the easy chair, watching the flames, thinking back over old college memories that the thought of Tennelly made vivid again. In the midst of it he heard steps on the veranda. Someone from outside unlatched the door and flung it open. A wild, careless laugh floated in on the cold breath of the sea. Courtland came to his feet as if he had been called! That laugh had gone through his heart like a knife, with its heartless babylike mirth. It was Gila! Had Tennelly played him false, after all, and brought her along? Was this some kind of a ruse to get them together? For he knew that Tennelly was distressed over their alienation, and that he understood to some extent that it was on account of Gila that he always avoided accepting the many invitations which were continually pressed upon him to come down to the city and be with his friends once more.

The door swung wide on its hinges and Gila entered, trig and chic as usual, in a stylish little coat-suit of homespun, leather-trimmed and short-skirted, high boots, leather leggins, and a jaunty little leather cap with a bridle under her chin. Only her petite figure and her baby face saved her from being taken for a tough young sport. She swaggered in, chewing gum, her gauntleted hands in her pockets, her young voice flung almost coarsely into the room by the wind; the innocent look gone from her face; the eyes wide and bold; the exquisite mouth in a sensuous curve.

Behind her lounged a man older than herself by many years, with silver at his temples, daredevil eyes, and a handsome, voluptuous face. He kicked the door shut behind him and lolled against it while he lit a cigarette.

Gila's laugh rang harshly in the room again, following some low-toned remark, and the man laughed coarsely in reply. Then, suddenly, she looked up and saw Courtland standing sternly there with folded arms, regarding her steadily, and her eyes grew wide with horror.

It was Courtland's great disillusionment.

Never had he seen such fear in human face.

Gila's skin grew gray beneath its pearly tint, her whole body shrank and cringed, her eyes were fixed upon him with terror in their gaze.

"Papers haven't come in yet, Mr. Aquilar," called the clerk, affably. "Train's late tonight. Be in pretty soon, I reckon!"

The man growled out an imprecation on a place where the papers didn't come till that hour in the evening, and lounged on toward the elevator. Gila slid along by his side, her eyes on Courtland, with the air of hiding behind her companion. Her face was drooped, and when she turned toward the elevator she drooped her eyes also, and a wave of shame rolled up and covered her face and neck and ears with a dull red beneath the pearl. Her last glance at Courtland was the look that Eve must have had as she walked past the flaming swords, with Adam, out of Eden. Her eyes, as she stood waiting for the boy to come to the elevator, seemed fairly to grovel on the floor.

Was this the sweet, wild, innocent flower that had held him in its thrall all the sorrowful months, and separated him from his dearest friend?

Tennelly! Courtland had forgotten until that instant that Tennelly would be there in a few minutes! Perhaps was even then at the door!

He strode forward, and Gila quivered as she saw him coming; quivered and looked up in terror, putting out a fearful hand to the arm of her companion.

The elevator boy had arrived and was slamming back the steel grating. The man stood back to let Gila enter, and she slunk past him, her gaze still held in horror on Courtland.

"Will you do me the favor to step into the little reception room to the right for a moment?" said Courtland, addressing the man, but looking at Gila.

"The devil we will!" said the man, glaring at him. "What right have you to ask a favor like that?"

But Courtland was looking at Gila, and there was command in his eyes. As if she dared not disobey she stepped forth again from the elevator, her eyes still upon him, her face gray with apprehension. Without further word from him she walked before him, slowly, into the little room at the right that he indicated.

"You're a fool!" said Aquilar, regarding her contemptuously, but she went as if she did not hear him. She entered the room, walked halfway across, and turned about, facing the two who had followed. Courtland was within the room, Aquilar lounging idly in the door, as if the matter were of little moment to him. He had a smile of contempt still on his handsome lips.

Courtland's manner was grave and sad. He had the commanding presence and beauty of an avenging angel.

"Gila, are you married to this man?" he asked, looking sternly at her, as though he would search her very soul.

Gila kept her dark, horrified gaze on his face. She was beyond trying to deceive now. She slowly gave one shake to her head, and her white lips formed the syllable, "No!" though it was almost inaudible.

"And yet you are registered here in this hotel as his wife?"

Her eyes suddenly flamed with shame. She drooped them before his gaze and seemed to try to assent, but her head was drooped too low to bow. She lifted miserable pleading looks to his face twice, but could not stand the clear rebuke of his gaze. It was like the whiteness of the reproach of God, and her little sinful soul could not bear it. She lifted a handkerchief and uttered something like a sob. It was as one might think would be the sound of a lost soul looking back at what might have been.

"What the devil have you got to say about it? Who the devil *are* you, anyway?" roared the man from the doorway.

The elevator boy and clerk were all agog. The latter had come out of his pen and was standing behind the boy, on tiptoe, where they could get a good view of the scene. The room was tense with stillness.

Aquilar's voice was not one to pass unnoticed when he spoke in anger, but Courtland did not even lift an eyelid toward him.

Perhaps Aquilar's words had given Gila courage, for she suddenly lifted her eyes to Courtland's face again, a flash of vengeance in them:

"I suppose you are going to tell Lew all about it?" she flung out, bitterly. "I suppose you will make up a great story to go and tell Lew. But you don't suppose he will believe *you* against *me*, do you?"

Her eyes were flashing fire now. Her old imperious manner was upon her. She had driven him from her once! She would defeat him again!

He watched her without a change of countenance. "No, I shall not tell him," he said, quietly; "but *you will*!"

"I?" Gila turned a glance of contemptuous amusement upon him. "Some chance! And I warn you that if you attempt to tattle anything about it I will turn the tables against you in a way you little suspect."

"Gila, you will tell Lew Tennelly *everything*, or you will never marry him! It is his right to know! And now, sir"—Courtland turned to Aquilar, lounging amusedly against the doorway—"if you will step outside I will *settle with you*!"

But suddenly Gila gave a scream and covered her face with her hands, for there, just behind Aquilar, stood Tennelly, looking like a ghost. He had heard it all!

# Chapter 31

*

Tennelly stepped within the room, gave one keen, questioning look at Aquilar as he passed him, searching straight into the depths of his startled, shifty eyes, and came and stood before the crouching girl. She had dropped into a chair and was sobbing as if her heart would break.

"What does this mean, Gila?"

Tennelly's voice was cold and stern.

Courtland looked at his shocked face and turned away from the pain of it. But when he looked for the man who had wrought this havoc he had suddenly melted from the room! The front door was blowing back and forth in the wind, and the clerk and bell boy stood, open-mouthed, staring. Courtland closed the door of the reception room and hurried out on the veranda, but saw no sign of anyone in the wind-swept darkness. The moon had risen enough to make a bright path over the sea, but the earth as yet was wrapped in shadow.

Down in the field, beyond the outbuildings, he heard a whirring sound, and as he looked a dark thing rose like a great bird high above his head. The bird had flown while the flying was good. The lady might face her difficulties alone!

Courtland stood below in the courtyard, while the moon arose and shed its light through the sky, and the great black bird executed an evolution or two and whirred off to the north, doubtless headed for Seattle or some equally inaccessible point. A great helpless wrath was upon him. Dolt that he had been to let this human leper escape from him into the world again! A kind of divine frenzy seized him to capture him yet and put him where he could work no further harm to other willing victims. Yes, he thought of Gila as a willing victim! An hour before he would have called her just plain innocent victim. Now something in her face, her attitude, as she saw him and walked away with her guilty partner, had made him know her at last for a sinful woman. The shackles had burst from his heart and he was free from her allurements for evermore! He understood now why she had bade him choose between herself and Christ. She had no part nor lot in things pure and holy. She hated holiness because she herself was sinful.

It was midnight before Gila and Tennelly came forth, Tennelly grave and sad, Gila tear-stained and subdued.

Courtland was sitting in the big chair before the fireplace, though the fire was smoldering low, and the elevator boy had long ago retired to slumbers on a bench in a hidden alcove.

Tennelly came straight to Courtland, as though he had known he would be waiting there for him. "I am going to take Gila down to Beechwood. You will come with us?" There was entreaty in the tone, though it was very quiet.

"Shall I take my car?"

"No. You will ride with me on the front seat. Is there a maid here that I can hire to go with us? We can bring her back in the morning."

"I'll find out."

That was a silent ride through the late moonlight. The men spoke only when it was necessary to keep the right road. Gila, huddled sullenly in the backseat beside a dozing, gray-haired chambermaid, spoke not at all. And who shall say what were her thoughts as hour after hour she sat in her humiliation and watched the two men whom she had wronged so deeply? Perhaps her spirit seethed the more violently within her silent, angry body because she was not yet sure of Tennelly. Her tears and explanations, her pleading little story of deceit and innocence, had not wrought the charm upon him that they might had not Aquilar been known to him for the past two weeks, a stranger who had been hanging about Gila, and who had been encouraged against her lover's oft-repeated warnings. A certain mysterious story of an unfaithful wife put an air of romance about him that Tennelly had not liked. Gila had never seen him so serious and hard to coax as he had been tonight. He had spoken to her as if she were a naughty child; had commanded her to go at once to her aunt in Beechwood and remain there the allotted time. She simply *had* to obey or lose him. There were things about Tennelly's fortune and prospects that made him most desirable as a husband. Moreover, she felt that through marrying Tennelly she could the better hurt Courtland, the man whom she now hated with all her heart.

They reached Beechwood at not too unearthly an hour. The aunt was surprised, but not unduly so, for Gila was a girl of many whims, and that she came at all to quiet Beechwood to rest was shock enough for one day. She asked no troublesome questions.

Tennelly would not remain for breakfast, even, but started on the return trip at once, with only a brief stop at a wayside inn for something to eat. The elderly attendant in the back seat was disappointed. She had no chance to get a bit of gossip by the way with anyone, but she got good pay for the night's ride, and made up some thrilling stories to tell when she got back that were really better than the truth might have turned out to be, so there was nothing lost, after all.

It was Tennelly who broke the silence between them when he and Courtland were at last alone together. "She only went for a ride in his aeroplane," he said, sadly. "She had no idea of staying more than an afternoon. He had promised to set her down at the next station in Beechwood, where her aunt was to meet her. She was filled with horror and consternation when she found she must be away overnight. But even then she had no idea of his purpose. She says that nobody ever told her about such things, she was ignorant as a little child! She is full of repentance, and feels that this will be a lesson for her. She says she intends to devote her life to me if I will only forgive her."

So that was what she had told Tennelly behind the closed doors!

Before Courtland's eyes there floated a vision of Gila as she first caught sight of him in the office of the inn. If ever soul was guilty in full knowledge of her sin she had been! Again she passed before his vision with shamed head down-drooped and all her proud, imperial manner gone. The mask had fallen from Gila forever so far as Courtland was concerned. Not even her little, pitiful, teary face that morning, when she crept from the car at her aunt's door, could deceive him again.

"And you *believe* all that?" asked Courtland. He could not help it. His dearest frind was in peril. What else could he do?

"I—don't know!" said Tennelly, helplessly.

There was silence in the room. Then Tennelly did realize a little! Perhaps Tennelly had known all along, better than he!

"And—you will forgive her?"

"I *must!*" said Tennelly, in desperation. "Court, my life is bound up in her!"

"So I once thought!" Courtland was only musing out loud.

Tennelly looked at him sadly.

"She almost wrecked my soul!" went on Courtland.

"I know," said Tennelly, in profound sorrow. "She told me."

"She *told you?*"

"Yes, before we were engaged. She told me that she had asked you to give up preaching, that she could never bear to be a minister's wife. I had begun to realize what that would mean to you then. I respected your choice. It was great of you, Court! But you never really loved her, man, or you could not have given her up!"

Courtland was silent for a moment, then he burst out: "Nelly! It was not that! You *shall* know the truth! She asked me to give up *my God* for her!"

"*I have no God*," said Tennelly, dully.

A great yearning for his friend filled the heart of Courtland. "Listen, old man, you *mustn't* marry her!" he burst out again. "I believe she's rotten all the way through. You didn't see and hear all last night. She *can't* be true! She hasn't it in her! She will be false to you whenever she takes the whim! She will lead you through hell!"

"You don't understand. I would *go* through hell to be with her!"

Tennelly's words rang through the room like a knell, and Courtland could say no more. There was silence in the room. Courtland watched his friend's haggard face anxiously. There were deep lines of agony about his mouth and dark circles under his eyes.

Suddenly Tennelly lifted his hand and laid it on his friend's. "Thanks, Court. Thanks a lot. I appreciate it all more than you know. But this is my job. I guess I've got to undertake it! And, *man!* can't you see I've *got* to believe her?"

"I suppose you have, Nelly. God help you!"

When Courtland got back to the seminary he found a letter from Mother Marshall.

# Chapter 32

*

Courtland opened Mother Marshall's letter with a feeling of relief and anticipation. Here at least would be a fresh, pure breath of sweetness. His soul was worn and troubled with the experience of the past two days. A great loneliness possessed him when he thought of Tennelly, or when he looked forward to his future, for he truly was convinced that he never should turn to the love of woman again; and so the dreams of home and love and little children that had had their normal part in his thoughts of the future were cut out, and the days stretched forward in one long round of duty.

DEAR PAUL [it began, familiarly]:

This is Stephen Marshall's mother and I'm calling you by your first name because it seems to bring my boy back again to be writing so familiarlike to one of his comrades.

We've been wondering, Father and I, since you said you didn't have any real mother of your own, whether you mightn't like to come home Christmas to us for a little while and borrow Stephen's mother. I've got a wonderful hungering in my heart to hear a little more about my boy's death. I couldn't have borne it just at first, because it was all so hard to give him up, and he just beginning to live his earthly life. But now since I can realize him over by the Father, I would like to know it all. Bonnie says that you saw Stephen go, and I thought perhaps you could spare a little time to run out West and tell me.

Of course, if you are busy and have other places you mustn't let this bother you. I can wait till sometime when you are coming West and can stop over for a day. But if you care to come home to Mother Marshall and let her play you are her boy for a little while, you will make us all very happy.

When Courtland had finished reading the letter he put his head down on his desk and shed the first tears his eyes had known since he was a little boy. To have a home and mother-heart open to him like that in the midst of all his sorrow and perplexity fairly unmanned him. By and by he lifted up his head and wrote a hearty acceptance of the invitation.

That was in November.

In the middle of December Tennelly and Gila were married.

It was not any of Courtland's choosing that he was best man. He shrank inexpressibly from even attending that wedding. He tried to arrange for his western trip so early as to avoid it. Not that he had any more personal feeling about Gila, but because he dreaded to see his friend tied up to such a future. It seemed as if the wedding was Tennelly's funeral.

But Tennelly had driven up to the seminary on three successive weeks and begged that Courtland would stand by him.

"You're the only one in the wide world who knows all about it, and understands, Court," he pleaded, and Courtland, looking at his friend's wistful face, feeling, as he did, that Tennelly was entering a living purgatory, could not refuse him.

It did not please Gila to have him take that place in the wedding party. He knew her shame, and she could not trail her wedding robes as guilelessly before him now, nor lift her imperious little head, with its crown of costly blossoms, before the envious world, without realizing that she was but a whited sepulcher, her little rotten heart all death beneath the spotless robes. For she was keen enough to know that she was defiled forever in Courtland's eyes. She might fool

Tennelly by pleading innocence and deceit, but never Courtland. For his eyes had pried into her very soul that night he had discovered her in sin. She had a feeling that he and his God were in league against her. No, Gila did not want Courtland to be Tennelly's best man. But Tennelly had insisted. He had given in about almost every other thing under heaven, and Gila had had her way, but he would have Courtland for best man.

She drooped her long lashes over her lovely cheeks, and trailed her white robes up a long aisle of white lilies to the steps of the altar; but when she lifted her miserable eyes in front of the altar she could not help seeing the face of the man who had discovered her shame. It was a case of her little naked, sinful soul walking in the Garden again, with the Voice and the eyes of a God upon it.

Lovely! Composed! Charming! Exquisite! All these and more they said she was as she stood before the white-robed priest and went through the ceremony, repeating, parrotlike, the words: "I, Gila, take thee, Llewellyn—" But in her heart was wrath and hate, and no more repentance than a fallen angel feels.

When at last the agony was over and the bride and groom turned to walk down the aisle, Gila lifted her pretty lips charmingly to Tennelly for his kiss, and leaned lovingly upon his arm, smiling saucily at this one and that as she pranced airily out into her future. Courtland, coming just behind with the maid of honor, one of Gila's feather-brained friends, lolling on his arm, felt that he ought to be inexpressibly thankful to God that he was only best man in this procession, and not bridegroom.

When at last the bride and groom were departed, and Courtland had shaken off the kind but curious attentions of Bill Ward, who persisted in thinking that Tennelly had cut him out with Gila, he turned to Pat and whispered, softly:

"For the love of Mike, Pat, let's beat it before they start anything else!"

Pat, anxious and troubled, heaved a sigh of relief, and hustled his old friend out under the stars with almost a shout of joy. Nelly was caught and bound for a reason. Poor old Nelly! But Court was free! Thank the Lord!

Courtland was almost glad that he went immediately back to hard work again and should have little time to think. The past few days had wearied him inexpressibly. He had come to look on life as a passing show, and to feel almost too utterly left out of any pleasure in it.

It was a cold, snowy night that Courtland came down to the city and took the western express for his holiday.

There was snow, deep, vast, glistening, when he arrived at Sloan's Station on the second morning, but the sun was out, and nothing could be more dazzling than the scene that stretched on every side. They had come through a blizzard and left it traveling eastward at a rapid rate.

Courtland was surprised to find Father Marshall waiting for him on the platform, in a great buffalo-skin overcoat, beaver cap, and gloves. He carried a duplicate coat which he offered to Courtland as soon as the greetings were over.

"Here, put this on; you'll need it," he said, heartily, holding out the coat. "It was Steve's. I guess it'll fit you. Mother and Bonnie's over here, waiting. They couldn't stand it without coming along. I guess you won't mind the ride, will you, after them stuffy cars? It's a beauty day!"

And there were Mother Marshall and Bonnie, swathed to the chin in rugs and shawls and furs, looking like two red-cheeked cherubs!

Bonnie was wearing a soft wool cap and scarf of knitted gray and white. Her cheeks glowed like roses; her eyes were two stars of brightness. Her gold hair rippled out beneath the cap and caught the sunshine all around her face.

Courtland stood still and gazed at her in wonder and admiration. Was this the sad, pale girl he had sent West to save her life? Why, she was a beauty, and she looked as if she had never been ill in her life! He could scarcely bear to take his eyes from her face long enough to get into the front seat with Father Marshall.

As for Mother Marshall, nothing could be more satisfactory than the way she looked like her picture, with those calm, peaceful eyes and that tendency to a dimple in her cheek where a smile would naturally come. Apple-cheeked, silver-haired, and plump. She was just ideal!

That was a gay ride they had, all talking and laughing

excitedly in their happiness at being together. It was so good to Mother Marshall to see another pair of strong young shoulders there beside Father on the front seat again!

It was Mother Marshall who took him up to Stephen's room herself when they reached the nice old ramblng farmhouse set in the wide, white, snowy landscape. Father Marshall had taken the car to the barn, and Bonnie was hurrying the dinner on the table.

Courtland entered the room as if it had been a sacred place, and looked around on the plain comfort: the homemade rugs, the fat, worsted pincushion, the quaint old pictures on the walls, the bookcase with its rows of books; the big white bed with its quilted counterpane of delicate needlework, the neat marble-topped washstand with its speckless appointments and its wealth of large old-fashioned towels.

"It isn't very fancy," said Mother Marshall, apologetically. "We fixed up Bonnie's room as modern as we could when we knew she was coming"—she waved an indicating hand toward the open door across the hall, where the rosy glow of pink curtains and cherry-blossomed wall gave forth a pleasant sense of light and joy—"and we had meant to fix this all over for Steve the first Christmas when he came home, as a surprise; but now that he has gone we sort of wanted to keep it just as he left it."

"It is great!" said Courtland, simply. "I like it just like this. Don't you? It is fine of you to put me in it. I feel as if it was almost a desecration, because, you see, I didn't know him very well; I wasn't the friend to him I might have been. I thought I ought to tell you that right at the start. Perhaps you wouldn't want me if you knew all about it."

"You would have been his friend if you had had a chance to know him," beamed the brave little mother. "He was a real brave boy always!"

"He sure was!" said Courtland, deeply stirred. "But I did get to know what a man he was. I saw him die, you know! But it was too late then!"

"It is never too late!" said Mother Marshall, brushing away a bright tear. "There is heaven, you know!"

"Why, surely there is heaven! I hadn't thought of that!

Won't that be great?" Courtland spoke the words reverently. It came to him gladly that he might make up in heaven for many things lost down here. He had never thought of that before.

"I wonder if you would mind," said Mother Marshall, wistfully, "if I was to kiss you, the way I used to do Steve when he'd been away?"

"I wouldn't mind a bit," said Courtland, setting his suitcase down suddenly and taking the plump little mother reverently into his big arms. "It would be *great*, Mother Marshall," and he kissed her twice.

Mother Marshall reached her short little arms up around his neck and laid her gray head for just a minute on the tall shoulder, while a tear hurried down and fitted itself invisibly into her dimple; then she ran her fingers through his thick brown hair and patted his cheek.

"Dear boy!" she breathed, contentedly, but suddenly roused herself. "Here I'm keeping you, and that dinner'll spoil! Wash your hands and come down quick! Bonnie will have everything ready!"

Courtland first realized the deep, happy, spiritual life of the home when he came down to the dining room and Father Marshall bowed his head to ask a blessing. Strange as it may seem, it was the first time in his life that he had ever sat at a home table where a blessing was asked upon the food. They had the custom in the seminary, of course, but it was observed perfunctorily, the men taking it by turns. It had never seemed the holy recognition of the Presence of the Master, as Father Marshall made it seem.

There was Bonnie, like a daughter of the house, getting up for a second pitcher of cream, running to the kitchen for more gravy. It was so ideal that Courtland felt like throwing his napkin up in the air and cheering.

It was all arranged by Mother Marshall that Bonnie and he should go to the woods after dinner for greens and a Christmas tree. Bonnie looked at Courtland almost apologetically, wondering if he were too tired for a strenuous expedition like that.

No. Courtland was not tired. He had never been so rested in his life. He felt like hugging Mother Marshall for getting up the plan, for he could see Bonnie never would have proposed it, she was too shy. He donned a pair of Stephen's old leather leggings and a sweater, shouldered the ax quite as if he had ever carried one before, and they started.

He thought he never had seen anything quite so lovely as Bonnie in that fuzzy little woolen cap, with the sunshine of her hair straying out and the fine glow in her beautiful face. He knew he had never heard music half so sweet as Bonnie's laugh as it rang through the woods when she saw a squirrel sitting on a high limb scolding at their intrusion. He never thought of Gila once the whole afternoon, nor even brought to mind his lost ideals of womanhood.

They found a tree just to their liking. Bonnie had it all picked out weeks beforehand, but she did not tell him so, and he thought he had discovered it for himself. They cut masses of laurel, and ground pine, and strung them on twine. They dragged the tree and greens home through the snow, laughing and struggling with their fragrant burden, getting wonderfully well-acquainted, so that at the very doorstep they had to lay down their greens and have a snow fight, with Father and Mother Marshall standing delightedly at the kitchen window, watching them. Mother's cheek was pressed softly against the old gray hat. She was thinking how Stephen would have liked to be here with them; how glad he would be if he could hear the happy shouts of young people ringing around the lonely old house again!

They set the tree up in the big parlor, and made a great log fire on the hearth to give good cheer—for the house was warm as a pocket without it. They colored and strung popcorn, gilded walnuts, cut silver-paper stars and chains for the tree, and hung strings of cranberries, bright red apples, and oranges between. They trimmed the house from top to bottom, even twining ground pine on the stair rail.

Those were the speediest two weeks that Courtland ever spent in his life. He had thought to remain with the Marshalls perhaps three or four days, but instead of that he delayed till the very last train that would get him back to the seminary in time for work, and missed two classes at that. For he had never had a comrade like Bonnie; and he knew, from the first day almost, that he had never known a love like the love that flamed up in his soul for this sweet, strong-spirited girl. The old house rang with their laughter from morning to night as they chased each other upstairs and down, like two children. Hours they spent taking long tramps through the woods or over the country roads; more hours they spent reading aloud to each other, or rather, most of the time Bonnie reading and Courtland devouring her lovely face with his eyes from behind a sheltering hand, watching every varying expression, noting the straight, delicate brows, the beautiful eyes filled with holy things as they lifted now and then in the reading; marveling over the sweetness of the voice.

The second day of his visit Courtland had made an errand with Bonnie to town to send off several telegrams. As a result a lot of things arrived for him the day before Christmas, marked "Rush!" They were smuggled into the parlor, behind the Christmas tree, with great secrecy after dark by Bonnie and Courtland, and covered with the buffalo robes from the car till morning. There was a big leather chair with air cushions for Father Marshall; its mate in lady's size for Mother; a set of encyclopedias that he had heard Father say he wished he had; a lot of silver forks and spoons for Mother, who had apologized for the silver being rubbed off of some of hers. There were two sets of books in wonderful leather bindings that he had heard Bonnie say she longed to read, and there was the tiniest little gold watch, about which he had been in terrible doubt ever since he had sent for it. Suppose Bonnie should think it wrong to accept it when she had known him so short a time! How was he going to make her see that it was all right? He wouldn't tell her she was a sort of a sister of his, for he didn't want her for a sister. He puzzled over that question whenever he had time, which wasn't often, because he was so busy and so happy every minute.

Then there were great five-pound boxes of chocolates, glacéd nuts and bonbons, and a crate of foreign fruits, with nuts, raisins, figs, and dates. There was a long, deep box from the nearest city filled with the most wonderful hothouse blossoms: roses, lilies, sweet peas, violets, gardenias, and even orchids. Courtland had never enjoyed spending money so much in all his life. He only wished he could get back to the city for a couple of hours and buy a lot more things.

To paint the picture of Mother Marshall when she sat on her new air cushions and counted her spoons and forks—real silver forks beyond all her dreamings!—to show Father Marshall, as he wiped his spectacles and bent, beaming, over the encyclopedias or rested his gray head back against the cushions! Ah! That would be the work of an artist who could catch the glory that shines deeper than faces and reaches souls! As for Courtland, he was too much taken up watching Bonnie's face when she opened her books, looking deep into her eyes as she looked up from the little velvet case where the watch ticked softly into her wondering ears; seeing the breathlessness with which she lifted the flowers from their bed among the ferns and placed them reverently in jars and pitchers around the room.

It was a wonderful Christmas! The first real Christmas Courtland had ever known. Sitting in the dim firelight between dusk and darkness, watching Bonnie at the piano, listening to the tender Christmas music she was playing, joining his sweet tenor in with her clear soprano now and then, Courtland suddenly thought of Tennelly, off at Palm Beach, doing the correct thing in wedding trips with Gila. Poor Tennelly! How little he would be getting of the real joy of Christmas! How little he would understand the wonderful peace that settled down in the heart of his friend when, later, they all knelt in the firelight, and Father Marshall prayed, as if he were talking to One who stood there close beside him, whose companionship had been a life experience.

There were so many pictures that Courtland had to carry back with him to the seminary. Bonnie in the kitchen, with a long-sleeved, high-necked gingham apron on, frying doughnuts or baking waffles. Bonnie at the organ on Sunday in the little church in town, or sitting in a corner of the Sunday-school room surrounded by her seventeen boys, with her Bible open on her lap and in her face the light of heaven while the boys watched and listened, too intent to know that they were doing it. Bonnie throwing snowballs from behind the snow fort he built her. Bonnie with the wonderful mystery upon her when they talked about the little watch and whether she might keep it. Bonnie in her window seat with one of the books he had given her, the morning he started to go out with Father Marshall and see what was the matter with the automobile, and then came back to his room unexpectedly after his knife and caught a glimpse of her through the open door.

And that last one on the platform of Sloan's Station, waving him a smiling good-bye!

Courtland had torn himself away at last, with a promise that he would return the minute his work was over, and with the consolation that Bonnie was going to write to him. They had arranged to pursue a course of study together. The future opened up rosily before him. How was it that skies had ever looked dark, that he had thought his ideals vanished, and womanhood a lost art when the world held this one pearl of a girl? Bonnie! Rose Bonnie!

# Chapter 33

✲

The rest of the winter sped away quickly. Courtland was very happy. Pat looked at him enviously sometimes, yet he was content to have it so. His old friend had not quite so much time to spend with him, but when he came for a walk and a talk it was with a heartiness that satisfied. Pat had long ago discovered that there was a girl at Stephen Marshall's old home, and he sat wisely quiet and rejoiced. What kind of a girl he could only imagine from Courtland's rapt look when he received a letter, and from the exquisite photograph that presently took its place on Courtland's desk. He hoped to have opportunity to judge more accurately when the summer came, for Mother Marshall had invited Pat to come out with Courtland in the spring and spend a week, and Pat was going. Pat had something to confess to Mother Marshall.

Courtland went out twice that summer, once for a week as soon as his classes were over. It was then that Bonnie promised to marry him.

Mother Marshall had a lot of sense and took a great liking to Pat. One day she took him up to Stephen's room and told him all about Stephen's boyhood. Pat, great big, baby giant that he was knelt down beside her chair, put his face in her lap, and blurted out the tale of how he had led the mob against Stephen and been indirectly the cause of his death.

Mother Marshall heard him through with tears of compassion running down her cheeks. It was not quite news to her, for Courtland had told her something of the tale, without any names, when he had confessed that he held the garments of those who did the persecuting.

"There, there!" said Mother Marshall, patting the big fellow's dark head. "You never knew what you were doing, laddie! My Steve always wanted a chance to prove that he was brave. When he was just a little fellow and read about the martyrs, he used to say: 'Would I have that much nerve, Mother? A fellow never can *tell* till he's been *tested!*' And so I'm not sorry he had his chance to stand up before you all for what he thought was right. Did you see my boy's face, too, when he died?"

"Yes," said Pat, lifting his head earnestly. "I'd just picked up a little kid he sent up to the fire escape, and saw his face all lit up by the fire. It looked like the face of an angel! Then I saw him lift up his hands and look up like he saw somebody above, and he called out something with a sort of smile, as if he was saying he'd be up there pretty soon! And then—he fell!"

The tears were raining down Mother Marshall's cheeks by now, but there was a smile of triumph in her eyes.

"He wanted to be a missionary, my Stephen did, only he was afraid he wouldn't be able to preach. He always was shy before folks. But I guess he preached his sermon!" she sighed contentedly.

"He sure did!" said Pat. "I never forgot that look on his face, nor the way he took our roughneck insults. None of the fellows did. It made a big impression on us all. And when Court began to change, came out straight and said he believed in Christ, and all that, it knocked the tar out of us all. Stephen hasn't got done preaching yet. You ought to hear Court tell the story of his death. It bowled me over when I heard it, and everywhere he tells it men believe! Wherever Paul Courtland tells that story Stephen Marshall will be preaching."

Mother Marshall stooped over and kissed Pat's astonished forehead. "You have made me a proud and happy mother today, laddie! I'm glad you came."

Pat, suddenly conscious of himself, stumbled, blushing to his feet. "Thanks, Mother! It's been great! Believe me, I shan't ever forget it. It's been like looking into heaven for this poor bum. If I'd had a home like this I might have stood some chance of being like your Steve, instead of just a roughneck athlete."

"Yes, I know," smiled Mother Marshall. "A dear splendid roughneck, doing a big work with the boys! Paul has told me all about it. You're preaching a lot of sermons yourself, you know, and going to preach some more. Now shall we go down? It's time for evening prayers."

So Pat put his strong arm around Mother Marshall's plump waist, drew one of her hands in his, and together they walked down to the parlor, where Bonnie was already playing "Rock of Ages." It seemed to Pat the kingdom of heaven could be no sweeter, for this was the kingdom come on earth. When he and Courtland were upstairs in their room, and all the house quiet for the night, Pat spoke:

"I've sized it up this way, Court. There ain't any dying! There's only an imaginary line like the equator on the map. It's heaven or hell, both now and hereafter! We can begin heaven right now if we want to, and live it on through; and that's what these folks have done. You don't hear them sitting here fighting like the professors used to do, about whether there's a heaven or a hell! They know there's both. They're living in one and pulling folks out of the other, hard as they can; and they're too blamed busy, following out the Bible and seeing it prove itself, to listen to all the twaddle to prove that it ain't so! I sure am darned glad you gave me the tip and I got a chance to get in on this little old game, for it's the best game I know, and the best part about it is it lasts forever!"

Tennelly was away all that summer, doing the fashionable summer resorts and taking a California trip. The next winter he spent in Washington. Uncle Ramsey had him at work, and Courtland ran on him in his office once, when he took a hurried trip down to see what he could do for the eight-hour bill. Tennelly looked grave and sad. He was touchingly glad to see Courtland. They did not speak of Gila once, but when Courtland lay in his sleepless sleeper on the return trip that night Tennelly's face haunted him, the wistfulness in it.

A few months later Tennelly wrote a brief note announcing the birth of a daughter, named Doris Ramsey after his grandmother. The tone of his letter seemed more cheerful.

Courtland was so happy that winter he could scarcely contain himself. Pat had great times kidding him about the western mail. Courtland was supplying a vacant church down in the old factory district in the city, and Pat often went along. On one of these Sunday afternoons late in the spring they were walking down a street they did not often take, and suddenly Courtland stopped with an exclamation of dismay and looked up at a great blaring sign wired on a big old-fashioned church:

CHURCH OF GOD
FOR SALE

was the startling statement.

Pat looked up at the sign and then at Courtland's face, figuring out, as he usually could, what was the matter with Court.

"Gosh! That's darned tough luck!" he said, sympathetically.

"It's terrible!" said Courtland.

"H'm!" said Pat, again. "Whose fault do you s'pose it is? Not God's. Somebody fell down on his job, I reckon! Congregation gone to the devil, very likely!"

"Wait!" said Courtland, gravely. "I must find out."

He stepped into a little cigar store and asked some questions. "You were right, Pat," he said, when he came out. "The congregation has gone to the devil. They have moved up into the more fashionable part of town, and the church is for sale. There's only one member of the old church left down here. I'm going around to see him. Pat, that sign mustn't stay up there! It's a disgrace to God."

"What could you do about it?" Pat was puzzled.

"Do about it? Why, man, I can buy it if there isn't any other way!"

They went to see the church member, who proved to be a good old soul, but deaf and old and very poor. He said they had to give the church up; they couldn't make it pay. All the rich people had moved away. He shook his head sadly and told how he and his wife were married there. He hobbled over and showed them how to get in a side door.

The yellow afternoon sun was sifting through windows of cheap stained glass, and fell in mellow quiet upon the faded cushions and musty ingrain carpet. The place had that deserted look of having been abandoned, yet Courtland, as he stood in the shadow under the old balcony, seemed to see the Presence of the eternal God standing up there behind the pulpit, seemed to feel the hallowed memories of long ago, and scent the lingering incense of all the prayers that had gone up from all the souls who had worshiped there in the years that were past.

"They think an iron foundry's going to buy it, or else someone may make a munition factory out of it," the old man contributed. "This war's bringing a big change over things."

"Their plowshares into swords, their pruning hooks into spears," chanted an unseen voice, sadly, behind Courtland. His face set sternly. He turned to Pat:

"I can't let that happen, old man!" he said. "I'm going to buy it if I can. Come, we'll go and look it up!"

Pat looked at his companion with awe. He had always known he was rich, but—to purchase a church as if it were a jack-knife! That sure was going some!

Courtland did not return to the seminary until Tuesday morning. By that time he had bought his church. It didn't take him long to come to an agreement. The Church of God was in a bad way and was willing to take up with almost any offer that would cover their liabilities.

"Well," said Pat, "that sure was some hustle! There's one thing, Court. You don't have to candidate for any church like those other guys in your little seminary. You just went out and bought one; though I surmise you and I'll have to do some scrubbing if you calculate to hold services there very soon."

"H'm!" said Courtland. "I hadn't thought of that, Pat! Maybe that would be a good idea!"

"Holy Mackinaw, man! What did you buy it for, then, if you didn't intend to use it? Do it just to have the right to tear down that blooming sign, did you?"

"That's about the size of it," smiled Courtland as he halted in front of his newly acquired church and looked up at it with interest. "But now I've got it I might as well use it. Suppose we start a mission here, Pat, you and I? Let's cut the sign down first, and then, Pat, I'm going to hunt up a stonecutter. This church has got to have a new name. 'Church of God for sale' has killed this one! A church that used to belong to God and doesn't anymore is what that means. They have sold the Church of God, but His Presence is still here!"

A few weeks later, when the two came down to look things over, the granite arch over the old front doors bore the inscription in letters of stone:

CHURCH OF THE PRESENCE OF GOD

Courtland stood looking for a moment, and then he turned to Pat eagerly. "I'm going to get possession of the whole block if I can; maybe the opposite one, too, for a park, and you've got to be physical director! I'll turn the kids and the older boys over to you, old man!"

Pat's eyes were full of tears. He had to turn away to hide them. "You're a darned old dreamer!" he said, in a choking voice.

So the rejuvenation of the old church went on from week to week. The men at the seminary grew curious as to what took Pat and Courtland to the city so much. Was it a girl? It finally got around that Courtland had a rich and aristocratic church in view, and was soon to be married to the daughter of one of its prominent members. But when they began to congratulate him, Courtland grinned.

"When I preach my first sermon you may all come down and see," he replied, and that was all they could get out of him.

Courtland found that a lot had to be done to that church. Plaster was falling off in places, the pews were getting rickety. The pulpit needed doing over, and the floor had to be recarpeted. But it was wonderful what a difference it all made when it was done. Soft greens and browns replaced the faded red. The carpet was thick and soft, the cushions matched. Bonnie had given careful suggestions about it all.

"You could have got along without cushions, you know," said Pat, frugally, as he seated himself in appreciative comfort.

"I know," said Courtland, "but I want this to look like a *church!* Someday when we get the rest of the block and can tear down the buildings and have a little sunlight and air, we'll have some *real windows* with wonderful gospel stories on them, but these will do for now. There's got to be a pipe organ some day, and Bonnie will play it!"

Pat always glowed when Courtland spoke of Bonnie. He never had ceased to be thankful that Courtland escaped from Gila's machinations. But that very afternoon, as Courtland was preparing to hurry to the train, there came a note from Pat, who had gone ahead on an errand:

> DEAR COURT—Tennelly's in trouble. He's up at his old rooms. He wants you. I'll wait for you down in the office.
>
> PAT

# Chapter 34

*

Tennelly was pacing up and down the room. His face was white, his eyes were wild. He had the haggard look of one who has come through a long series of harrowing experiences up to the supreme torture where there is nothing worse that can happen.

Courtland's knock brought him at once to the door. With both hands they gave the fellowship grip that had meant so much to each in college.

A moment they stood so, looking into each other's eyes, Courtland, wondering, startled, questioning. It was Gila, of course! Nothing else could reach the man's soul and make him look like that! But what had happened? Not death! No, not even death could bring that look of shame and degradation to his high-minded friend's eyes.

As if Tennelly had read his question he spoke in a voice so husky with emotion that his words were scarcely audible: "Didn't Pat tell you?"

Courtland shook his head.

Tennelly's head went down, as if he were waiting for courage to speak. Then, huskily: "She's gone, Court!"

"Gone?"

"Left me, Court! She sailed at daybreak for Italy with another man."

Tennelly fumbled in his pocket and brought out a crumpled note, blistered with tears. "Read it!" he muttered, and turned away to the window.

Courtland read:

DEAR LEW—I'm sure when you come to your senses and get over some of your narrow ideas you'll be as much relieved as I am over what I've decided to do. You and I never were fitted for each other, and I can't stand this life another day. I'm simply perishing! It's up to me to do something, for I know, with your strait-laced notions, you never will! So when you read this I shall be out of reach, on my way to Italy with Count von Bremen. They say there's going to be war in this country, anyway, and I hate such things, so I had to get out of it. You won't have any trouble in getting a divorce, and you'll soon be glad I did it.

As for the kid, if she lives she's much better off with you than with me, for you know I never could stand children; they get on my nerves. And, anyhow, I never could be all the things you tried to make me, and it's better in the end this way. So good-bye, and don't try to come after me. I won't come back, no matter what you do, for I'm bored to death with the last two years and I've got to see some life!

GILA

Courtland read the flippant little note twice before he trusted himself to speak, and then he walked over to the window, slowly smoothing and folding the crumpled paper. A baby's cry in the next room pierced the air, and the father gripped the window seat and quivered as if a bullet had struck him.

Courtland put his hand lovingly within his friend's arm: "Nelly, old fellow," he said, "you know that I feel with you—"

"I know, Court!" he said with a weary sigh. "That's why I sent for you. I had to have you, somehow!"

"Nelly! There aren't any words made delicate enough to handle this thing without hurting. It's raw flesh and full of nerves. There's just One can do anything here! I wish you believed in God!"

"I do!" said Tennelly, in a dreary tone.

"He can come near you and give you strength to bear it. I know, for He did it for me once!"

Courtland felt as if his words were falling on deaf ears, but Tennelly, after a pause, asked, bitterly:

"Why did He do this to me, if He's what you say He is?"

"I'm not sure that He did, old man! I think perhaps you and I had a hand in it!"

Tennelly looked at him keenly for an instant and turned away, silent. "I know what you mean," he said. "You told me I'd go through hell, and I have. I knew it in a way myself, but I'm afraid I'd do it again! I loved her! God! I'm afraid—I *love her yet!* Man! You don't know what an ache such love is."

"Yes, I do," said Courtland, with a sudden light in his face, but Tennelly was not heeding him.

"It isn't entirely that I've lost her; that I've got to give up hoping that she'll sometime care and settle down to knowing she is gone forever! It's the way she went! The—the—the *disgrace!* The humiliation! The awfulness of the way she went! We've never had anything like that in our family. And to think my baby has got to grow up to know that shame! To know that her mother was a disgraceful woman! That I gave her a mother like that!"

"Now, look here, Tennelly! You didn't know! You thought she would be all right when you were married!"

"But I *did know!*" wailed Tennelly. "I knew in my soul! I think I knew when I first saw her, and that was why I worried about you when you used to go and see her. I knew she wasn't the woman for you. But, blamed fool that I was! I thought I was more of a man of the world, and would be able to hold her! No, I didn't, either, for I knew it was like trying to enjoy a sound sleep in a powder-magazine with a pocketful of matches, to trust my love to her! But I did it, anyway! I dared trouble! And my little child has got to suffer for it!"

"Your little child will perhaps be better for it!"

"I can't see it that way!"

"You don't have to. If God does, isn't that enough?"

"I don't know! I can't see God now; it's too dark." Tennelly put his forehead against the windowpane and groaned.

"But you have your little child," said Courtland, hesitating. "Isn't that something to help?"

"She breaks my heart," said the father. "To think of her worse than motherless! That little bit of a helpless thing! And it's my fault that she's here with a future of shame!"

"Nothing of the sort! It'll be your fault if she has a future of shame, but it's up to you. Her mother's shame can't hurt her if you bring her up right. It's your job, and you can get a lot of comfort out of it if you try!"

"I don't see how," dully.

"Listen, Tennelly. Does she look like her mother?"

Tennelly's sensitive face quivered with pain. "Yes," he said, huskily. "I'll send for her and you can see." He rang a bell. "I brought her and the nurse up to town with me this morning."

An elderly, kind-faced woman brought the baby in, laid her in a big chair where they could see her, and then withdrew.

Courtland drew near, half-shyly, and looked in startled wonder. The baby was strikingly like Gila, with all her grace, delicate features, wide innocent eyes. The sweep of the long lashes on the little white cheeks, that were all too white for baby flesh, seemed old and weird in the tiny face. Yet when the baby looked up and recognized its father it crowed and smiled, and the smile was wide and frank and lovable, like Tennelly's. There was nothing artificial about it, Courtland drew a long sigh of relief. For a moment he had been looking at the baby as if it were Gila grown small again; now he suddenly realized it was a new little soul with a life and a spirit of its own.

"She will be a blessing to you, Nelly," he said, looking up hopefully.

"I don't see it that way!" said the hopeless father, shaking his head.

"Would you rather have her—taken away—as her mother suggested?" he hazarded, suddenly.

Tennelly gave him one quick, startled look. "God! No!" he said, and staggered back into a chair. "Do you think she looks so sick as that? I know she's not well. I know she's lost flesh! But she's been neglected. Gila never cared for her and wouldn't be bothered looking after things. She was angry because the baby came at all. She resented motherhood because it put a limitation on her pleasures. My poor little girl!"

Tennelly dropped upon his knees beside the baby and buried his face in its soft little neck.

The baby swept its dark lashes down with the old Gila trick, and looked with a puzzled frown at the dark head so close to her face. Then she put up her little hand and moved it over her father's hair with an awkward attempt at comfort. The great big being with his head in her neck was in trouble, and she was vaguely sympathetic.

A wave of pity swept over Courtland. He dropped upon his knees beside his friend and spoke aloud:

"O Lord God, come near and let my friend feel Thy Presence now in his terrible distress. Somehow speak peace to his soul and help him to know Thee, for Thou art the only One that can help him. Help him to tell Thee all his heart's bitterness now, alone with Thee and his little child, and find relief."

Softly Courtland arose and slipped from the room, leaving them alone with the Presence.

Gila had been gone two months when the day was finally set for Bonnie's wedding.

There had been consultations long and many over what to do about telling Tennelly, for even Bonnie saw that the event could not but be painful to him, coming as it did on the heels of his own deep trouble. And Tennelly had long been Courtland's best friend; at least until Pat grew so close as to share that privilege with him. It was finally decided that Courtland should tell Tennelly about the approaching wedding at his first opportunity.

Bonnie had long ago heard all about Gila, been through the bitter throes of jealousy, and come out clear and trusting, with the whole thing sanely and happily relegated to that place where all such troubles go from the hearts of those who truly love each other and know there never could be anyone else in the universe who could take the place of the beloved.

Courtland had been preaching in the Church of the Presence of God for four sabbaths now, and the congregation had been growing steadily. There had not been much advertising. He had told a few friends in the factories near by that there was to be service. He had put up a notice on the door saying that the church would be open for worship regularly and everyone was welcome. He did not wish to force anything. He was following the leading of the Spirit. If God really meant this work for him, He would show him.

Courtland's preaching was not of the usual cut-and-dried order of the young theologue. His theology had been studied to help him to understand his God and his Bible, not to give him a set of rules for preaching. So when he stood up in the pulpit it was not to follow any conventional order of service, or to try to imitate the great preachers he had heard, but to give the people who came something that would help them to live during the week and enable them to realize the Presence of Christ in their daily lives.

The men at the seminary got wind of it somehow, and came down by twos and threes, and finally dozens, as they could get away from their own preaching to see what the dickens that closemouthed Courtland was doing, and went away thoughtful. It was not what they had expected of their brilliant classmate, ministering to these common working people right in the neighborhood where they lived and worked.

At first they did not understand how he came to be in that church, and asked what denomination it was, anyway. Courtland said he really didn't know what it had been, but that he hoped it was the denomination of Jesus Christ now.

"But whose church is it?" they asked.

"Mine," he said, simply.

Then they turned to Pat for explanation.

"That's straight," said Pat. "He bought it."

"*Bought* it! Oh!" They were silenced. Not one of them could have bought a church, and wouldn't have if they could. They would have bought a good mansion for themselves against their retiring day. Few of them understood it. Only the man who was going to darkest Africa to work in the jungles, and a couple who were bound, one for the leper country, and another for China, had a light of understanding in their eyes, and gripped Courtland's hand with reverence and ecstatic awe.

"But, man alive!" lingered one, unwilling to leave his brilliant friend in such a hopeless hole. "Don't you realize if you don't hitch onto some denomination, or board of trustees, or something, your work won't count in the long run? Who's to carry on your work and keep up your name and what you have done, after you are gone? You're foolish!" He had just received a flattering call to a city church himself, and he knew he was not half as well fitted for it as Courtland.

But Courtland flung up his hat in a boyish way and smiled. "I should worry about my name after I am gone?" he said. "And as for the work, it's for me to do, isn't it? Not for me to arrange for after I'm dead. If my heavenly Father wants it to keep up after I'm gone He'll manage to find a way, won't He? My job is to look after it while I'm here. Perhaps it won't be needed any longer after I'm gone. God sent me here to buy His church when it was for sale, didn't He? Well, then, if it is for sale again He'll find somebody else to buy it, unless He is done with it. The New Jerusalem may be here by that time and we won't have to have any churches. God Himself shall be the tabernacle! So you see I'm just going on running my own little old church the best I can with what God gives me, and I won't trouble any boards at present, not so long as I have money enough to keep the wheels moving."

They went away then with doubtful looks, and Courtland heard one say to another, shaking his head in a dubious way:

"I don't like it. It's all very irregular!"

And the other replied: "Yes! It's a pity about him! He might have done something big if he hadn't been so impractical!"

"The poor stews!" said Pat, dryly, looking after them. "They haven't got religion enough to carry them over till next week, the most of them, and what they'll do when they really see what kind the Lord is I can't guess! I wonder what they think that rich young man that Jesus loved would have been like, anyway, if he hadn't gone away sorrowful and kept his vast possessions. Cut it out, Pat! You're letting the devil in again and getting censorious! Just shut your mouth and saw wood! They'll find out some little old day in the morning, I guess."

Courtland wrote it all to Bonnie, all the happenings at seminary and church, what the theologues had said about his being impractical and irregular, and Bonnie, with a tender smile, leaned down and kissed the words in the letter, and murmured, "Dear impractical beloved!" all softly to herself.

For Bonnie was very happy. The possession of great wealth that would have to be spent in the usual way, surrounded by social distinction, attended by functions and society duties, would have been an inexpressible burden to her. But money to be used without limit in helping other people was a miracle of joy. To think that it should have come to her!

Yet there was something greater than the money and the new interests that were opening up before her, and that was the wonder of the man who had chosen her to be his wife. That such a prince among men, such a friend of God, should have passed by others of rank, of beauty and attainments far greater than hers, and come away out West to take her, fairly overwhelmed her with wonder when she had time to think about it. For she was as busy as she was happy in these days. There was her school work, her music, the little home duties, all she could make Mother Marshall leave for her; the beautiful sewing she was doing on her simple bridal garments; and stealing time from all to write the most wonderful letters to the insatiable lover in the East.

Softly Bonnie went through these days, tender, happy, blithe as a bird; a song on her lips whenever she went about the house; a caress in her very touch for the dear old people who had been Father and Mother to her in her loneliness; realizing only vaguely what it was going to be to them when she was gone and they were all alone again. For her heart was so full of her own joy she could not think a sad thought.

But one afternoon she came home from school a little earlier than usual. Opening the door very softly that she might come on Mother Marshall and surprise her, she heard voices in the dining room, and paused to see if there was company.

"It's going to be mighty hard to have Bonnie leave us," said Father Marshall, with a wistful quaver.

There was a soft sigh over by the window, then Mother Marshall: "Yes, Father, but we mustn't think about it, or the next thing we know we'll let her see it. She's the kind of girl that would turn around and say she couldn't get married, perhaps, if she got it in her head we needed her. She's got a grand man, and I'm just as glad as I can be about it"—there was a gulp like a sob over by the window—"I wouldn't spoil her happiness for anything in the world!" The voice took on a forced cheerfulness.

"Sure! We wouldn't want to do that!"

"It's 'most as bad as when Stephen was going away, though. I have to just shut my eyes when I go by her bedroom door and think about how we fixed it up for her and counted on how she'd look, and all. I just couldn't stand it. I had to shut the door and hurry downstairs."

"Well, now, Mother, you mustn't feel that way. You know the Lord sent her first. Maybe He has some other plan."

"Oh, I know!" said Mother, briskly. "I guess we can leave that to Him; only seems like I can't bear to think of anybody else coming to be in her room."

"Oh no! no! We couldn't stand for that!" said Father, quickly. "We'd have to keep it for her—for them—when they come home to visit! If any other party comes along I reckon we'll just build out a bay window on the kitchen chamber, and fix that up. Now don't you worry, Mother. You know he promised to bring her home a lot, and it ain't as if he hadn't got money enough to travel, let alone an ottymobeel. I shouldn't wonder maybe if we could go see them, even, sometime. We could get to see the university then, too, and go look at Steve's room. You'd like that, wouldn't you, Mother?"

Bonnie did not go into the dining room to surprise them. Instead, she stole away down in the orchard to hide her tears.

A little later she saw the postman ride up to the letterbox

on the gatepost and drop in a letter, and all else was forgotten.

Yes, from Paul! A lovely, big, thick letter!

Mother and Father Marshall and their sadness suddenly vanished from her thoughts, and she hurried back to a big stump in the orchard, where she often read her letters.

# Chapter 35

*

DEAR BONNIE ROSE [she read, and smiled tenderly. He was always getting her a new name]:

I've been to see Tennelly at last, and he's great! What do you think? He's not only coming to the wedding, but he's asked if I will let him be best man, unless I'd rather have Pat! I told Pat, and you ought to have heard him roar. "Fat chance! Me best man, with you two fellows around!" he said.

Father and my stepmother will come; but please tell Mother Marshall she needn't worry because they will only stay for the ceremony. I know she was a little troubled about my stepmother, lest things would seem plain to her; bless her dear heart! But she needn't at all, for she's a kindly soul, according to her lights. She's not to blame that they're only candlelights instead of sunlight. They will come in their private car, which will be dropped off from the morning train and picked up by the night express at the junction, so you see they'll have to leave for Sloan's Station early in the afternoon.

But the greatest news of all I heard tonight! Pat brought it, as usual. It beats all how he finds out pleasant things. You remember how we wished that Burns hadn't gone to China yet, so he could marry us? Well, he's coming back. He's been sent on some errand or other for the government, in company with a Chinaman or two, and he's due in San Francisco a week before the wedding. I've sent a wireless to ask him to stop over and take part in the ceremony. I was sure this would meet with your approval. Of course, we'll ask your minister out there to assist. You don't know how this pleases me. There's only one of the professors I'd have cared to ask, and he's with his wife, who is very ill at a sanitarium. It seems somehow as if Burns belonged to us, doesn't it, dear?

I stood tonight on the steps of the church and looked at a ray of the setting sun that was slanting between buildings and laying a finger of gold on the old dirty windows across the street till they blazed into sudden glory. As I looked the houses faded away, as they do in a moving picture, and gradually melted into a great open space that stretched a whole big block, all clear and green with thick velvety grass. There were trees in the space—a lot of them—and hammocks under some of them, with little children playing about. At the farthest end there were tennis courts and a baseball diamond; and who do you think I saw teaching some boys to pitch, but Pat! On the other side of the street a big, old warehouse had been converted into a gymnasium with a swimming pool.

All around the block there were model tenements, with thousands of windows; and light and air and cheerfulness. There were flowers in little beds between the curbing and the pavement, that the children could water and cultivate and pick. There was a fountain of filtered water in the center of the green, and a drinking fountain at each corner of the block, but there wasn't a saloon in sight!

I looked around to my right, and the old stone house with its grimy face that belonged there had changed into a beautiful home with vines and flowers. There were windows everywhere jutting out with delightful unexpectedness, and just lovely green grass and more trees all the way to the corner! On the left, the old foundry had been cleansed and transformed and had become a hospital belonging to the church. I couldn't help thinking right then and there what a grand doctor Tennelly would have made if he only hadn't been an aristocrat. The hospital was all white, and there was an ambulance belonging to it, and nurses who worked not only for money, but for the love of Christ. There wasn't a doctor in it who didn't know what the Presence of God meant, or couldn't point the way to be saved to a dying sinner.

Back of the church block, in place of the old shackly factories, there was one great model factory with the best modern equipment, and the eight-hour system in full swing. No little children working for a scanty living! No tired girls and women standing all day long! No foremen that did not have a love for humanity in his soul and some kind of an idea what it was to have the Presence of the living God in the factory!

I went back to the big stone house and discovered there was a great big living room with a grand piano at one end, and a stone fireplace large enough for logs. A wide staircase led up to a gallery where many rooms opened off, rooms enough for everyone we wanted, and a big special one for Father and Mother Marshall, winters, opening off in a suite, so that they could be to themselves when they got tired of us all. Of course, in summers they might want to go home sometimes and take us all with them; or maybe run down to the shore with us in an off year now and then. Break the news to them gently, darling, for I've set my heart on that house just as I saw it, and I hope they won't object.

There were other rooms, but they were vague, because I saw that you must have the key to them all yet, and I must wait till you come, to look into them.

Then I heard sweet sounds from the church, and turning, I went in. Someone was playing the organ, high up in the dusky shadows of the gallery, and I knew it was you, Bonnie Rose, my darling! So I knelt in a pew and listened, with the Presence standing there between us. And as I knelt another vision came to me, a vision of the past! I remembered the days when I did not know God; when I sneered and argued and did all I could in my young and conceited way against Him. I remember, too, the time He came to me in my illness and I began to believe; and the day I read that verse marked in Stephen's Bible, "He that believeth on the Son of God hath the witness in himself." I suddenly realized that that had been made true to me. I have the witness in my own heart that Christ is the Son of God, my Saviour! That His Presence is on earth and manifest to me at many times. No seeming variance of science, no quibble of the intellect, can ever disturb this faith on which my soul rests. It is more than a conviction; it is a perfect satisfaction! I KNOW! I may not be able to explain all mysteries, but I can never doubt again, because I know. The more I meet with modern skepticism, the more I am convinced that that is the only answer to it all: "He that doeth His will shall know the doctrine," and that promise is fulfilled to all who have the will to believe.

All that came to me quite clearly as I knelt in the church in the sunset, while you were playing—was it "Rock of Ages"?—and a ray of the setting sun stole through the old yellow glass of the window in the organ loft and lay on your hair like a crown, my Bonnie darling! My heart overflowed with gratitude at the great way life has opened up to me. That I, the least of His servants, should be honored by the love of this pearl of women!—

There was more of that letter, and Bonnie sat long on the stump reading and rereading, with her face a glow of wonder and joy. But at last she got up and went to the house, bounding into the dining room where Mother and Father Marshall were pretending to be busy about a lamp that didn't work right.

Down she sat with her letter and read it—at least as much as we have read—to the two sad old dears who were trying so hard to get ready for loneliness. But after that there was no more sadness in that house! No more tears nor wistful looks. Father whistled everywhere he went, till Mother told him he was like a boy again. Mother sang about her work whenever she was alone. For why should they be sad anymore? There were good times still going in the world, and *they were in them*!

"Father!" whispered Mother, softly, that night, when she was supposed to be well on her way toward slumber. "Do you suppose the Lord heard us grumbling this afternoon, and sent that letter to make us ashamed of ourselves?"

"No," said Father, tenderly. "I think He just smiled to think what a big surprise He had ready for us. It doesn't pay to doubt God; it really doesn't!"

# Chapter 36

*

Pat was out with the ambulance. He had been taking a convalescent from the hospital down to the station and shipping him home to his good old mother in the country, to be nursed back to health. Pat often did little things like that that were utterly out of his province, just because he liked to do them.

Pat had seen his patient off and was threading his way through a crowded thoroughfare, with eyes alert for everything, when a little bright red racer passed him at a furious rate, driven by a woman with a reckless hand. She shot by the ambulance like a rocket, and at the next corner came face to face with a great motortruck that was thundering around the corner at a tremendous speed. From the first glance there was no chance for the racer. It crumpled like a thing of paper and lay in bright splinters on the street, the lady tossed aside and motionless, with her head against the curbing.

The crowd closed in about her, and someone sent a call for the police. The crowd opened again as an officer signed to the ambulance to stand by, and kindly hands put the lady inside. Pat put on all speed to the home hospital, which was not far away, and was soon within its gates with the house doctor and a nurse rushing out in answer to his signal.

There was a light in the church close at hand, although it was not yet dark. Bonnie was playing softly on the organ. Pat knew the hymn she was playing:

At evening, ere the sun was set,
The sick, O Lord! around Thee lay;
Oh, with what divers ills they met,
Oh, with what joy they went away!

Once more 'tis eventide, and we,
Oppressed with various ills, draw near—

Pat was following the melody in his mind with the words that were so often sung in the Church of the Presence of God at evening service. He jumped down from his driver's seat and went around to the back of the ambulance, where they were preparing to carry the patient into the building. He was wondering what sort it was this time that he had brought to the House of Healing. Then suddenly he saw her face and stopped short, with a suppressed exclamation.

There, huddled on the stretcher, in her costly sporting garments, with her long, dark lashes sweeping over her hard, little painted face, and a pinched look of suffering about her loose-hung baby mouth, lay Gila!

He knew her at once and drew back in horror. What had he done! Brought her here, this viper of evil that had crept into the garden of his friends and despoiled them of their joy! Why had he not looked at her before they started? Fool that he was! He might easily have taken her to another hospital instead of this one. He could do so yet.

But Courtland was standing on the steps, looking down at the huddled figure on the stretcher, with a strange expression of pity and tenderness in his face.

"I did not know! I did not see her before, Court!" stammered Pat. "I will take her somewhere else now before she has been disturbed."

"No, Pat, it's all right! It is fitting that she should come to us. I'm glad you found her. You must have been led! Call Bonnie, please. And, Pat, watch for Nelly and take him into my study. He was coming down on the Boston express. Let me know as soon as he gets here."

Courtland went swiftly into the hospital. Pat looked after him for a moment with a great light of love in his eyes, and realized for the first time what was meant by the expulsive power of a new affection. Court hadn't minded seeing Gila in the least on his own account. He was only thinking of Tennelly. Poor Nelly! What would he do?

There was no hope for Gila from the first. There had been an injury to the spine, and it was only a question of hours how long she had to stay.

It was Bonnie's face upon which the great dark eyes first opened in consciousness again. Bonnie in soft, white garments sitting beside the bed, watching. A strange contraction of fear and hate passed over her face as she looked, and she spoke in an insolent, sharp little voice, weak as a sick bird's chirp.

"Who sent you here?" she demanded.

"God," said Bonnie, gently, without an instant's hesitation.

A startled look came into Gila's eyes. "God! What does He want with me? Has He sent you here to torment me? I know you, who you are! You are that poor girl that Paul picked up in the street. You are come to pay me back!"

Bonnie's face was full of tenderness. "No, dear! That is all passed. I've just come to bring you a message from God."

"God! What have I to do with God?" A quiver of anguish passed over the weird little face. "I hate God! He hates me! Am I dead, then, that He sends me messages?"

"No, you are not dead. And God does not hate you. Listen! He says, 'I have loved you with an everlasting love.' That's the message that He sends. He is here now. He wants you to give attention to Him!"

The little blanched face on the pillow tightened and hardened in fear once more. "That's that awful Presence again! The Presence! The Presence! I've been trying to get away from it for three years, and it's pursued me everywhere! Now I'm caught like a rat in a trap and can't get away! If I'm not dead, then I must be dying, or you wouldn't dare talk to me this awful way! *I am dying!* And *you* think *I'm going to hell!*" Her shrill voice rose almost to a scream.

Above the sound, Bonnie's calm, clear voice dominated with a sudden quieting hush. Courtland, standing with the doctor and Tennelly just outside the partly open door, was thrilled with the sweetness of it, as if some supernatural power were given to her at this trying time.

"Listen, Gila! This is what He says: 'God sent not his Son into the world to condemn the world; but that the world through him might be saved. . . . God so loved the world that he gave his only begotten Son, that whosoever believeth in him should not perish, but have everlasting life.' He wants you to *believe now* that He loves you and wants to save you."

"But He couldn't!" said Gila, with the old petulant tone. "I've hated Him all my life! I *hate Him now*! And I've never been good! I couldn't be good! I don't *want* to be good! I want to do just what I *please*! And I *will*! I won't hear you talk this way! I want to get up! Why does my body feel so queer and numb, as if it wasn't there? Am I dying now? Answer me quick! Am I dying? *I know I am.* I'm dying and you won't tell me! I'm dying and I'm afraid! I'M AFRAID!"

One piercing scream after another rang out through the corridors. In vain did Bonnie and the nurse seek to soothe her. The high, excited voice raved on:

"I'm afraid to die! I'm afraid of that Presence! Send for Paul Courtland! He tried to tell me once, and I wouldn't hear! I made him choose between me and God! And *now I'm going to be punished*!"

"Listen, dear!" went on Bonnie's steady, tender voice. "God doesn't want to punish. He wants to save. He is waiting to forgive you if you will let Him!"

Something in her low-spoken words caught and held the attention of the soul in mortal anguish. Gila fixed her great, anguishing eyes on Bonnie.

"Forgive! Forgive! How could anybody forgive all I've done! You don't know anything about such things"—half-contemptuously. "You've always been goody-good! I can see it in your look. You don't know what it is to have men making fools of themselves over you! You don't know all I've done! I've been what they call a sinner! I sent away the only man I ever loved because I was *jealous of God*! I broke the heart of the man who loved me because I got tired of him and his everlasting perfection! I hated the idea of being a mother, and when my child came I deserted her! I would have killed her if I had dared! I went away with a bad man! And when I got tired of him I took the first way that opened to get away from him! God doesn't forgive things like that! I didn't expect He would when I did them. But it wasn't fair not to let me live out my life! I'm too young to die! And I'm afraid! I'm AFRAID!"

"Yes. God forgives all those things! There was a woman once who had been like that, and Jesus forgave her. He will forgive you if you ask Him. But He can't forgive you unless you are sorry and really want Him to. He says, 'Though your sins be as scarlet they shall be as white as snow; and though they be red like crimson, they shall be as wool,' but you have to be sorry first that you sinned. He can't forgive you if you aren't sorry."

"Sorry! *Sorry!*" Gila's laugh rang out mirthlessly and echoed in the high, white room. "Oh, I'm *sorry*, all right! What do you think I am? Do you think I've been *happy*? Don't you know that I've suffered torments? Everything has turned to ashes that I've touched! I've gone everywhere and done everything to try to forget myself, but always there was that awful Presence chasing me! Standing in my way everywhere I turned! Driving me! Always driving me toward hell! I've tried drowning my thoughts with cocktails and dope, but always when it wore off there would be the Presence of God pursuing me! Do you mean to tell me there is forgiveness for me with Him?"

Her breath was coming in painful gasps as she screamed out the words as the nurse leaned over and gave her a quieting draught.

Bonnie, in a low, clear voice, began to repeat Bible verses:

> "'The blood of Jesus Christ his Son cleanseth us from *all* sin!
>
> "As far as the east is from the west, so far hath he removed our transgressions from us.
>
> "I, even I, am he that blotteth out thy transgressions for mine own sake, and will not remember thy sins.
>
> "If we confess our sins he is faithful and just to for-

give us our sins and to cleanse us from all unrighteousness."

Gila listened with wondering, incredulous eyes, like the eyes of a frightened, naughty child who scarcely understood what was being said and was in a frenzy of fear.

"Oh, if Paul Courtland were here he would tell me if this is true!" Gila cried at last.

Instantly, from out of the shadow of the doorway, stepped Courtland, and stood at the foot of the bed where she could see him, looking steadily at the dying girl for a moment, and then lifting his eyes, as if to One who stood just beside her:

"O Jesus Christ! who came to save, come close to this poor little wandering child of Thine and show her that she is forgiven! Take her gently by the hand and help her to see Thee, how loving Thou art! Help her to understand how Thou didst come to earth and die to take her place of punishment so that she might be forgiven! Open her eyes to comprehend what love like that can be!"

Gila turned startled eyes on Courtland as she heard his voice, strong, beseeching, tender, intimate with God! She lay listening, watching his illumined face as he prayed. Watched and listened as one who suddenly sees a ray of light where all was darkness; till gradually the tenseness and pain faded from her face and a surprised calm came to take its place.

The strong voice went on, talking with the Saviour about what He had done for this poor erring one, till with a sigh, like a tired child, the eyelids dropped over her frightened eyes and a look of peace began to dawn.

While the prayer had been going on, Tennelly, with his little girl in his arms, had slipped into the room and stood with bowed head looking with anguished eyes at the wreck of the beautiful girl who was once his wife.

Suddenly, as if alive to subtle influences, Gila opened her great eyes again and looked straight at Tennelly and the baby! A dart of consciousness came into her gaze and something like a wave of anguish passed over her face. She made a piteous, helpless movement with the little jeweled hands that lay limply on the coverlet, and murmured one word, with pleading in her eyes:

"Forgive!"

Courtland had ceased praying and the room was very still till Bonnie, just outside the door, began to sing, softly:

Rock of Ages, cleft for me,
Let me hide myself in Thee!
Let the water and the blood
From Thy riven side which flowed
Be of sin the double cure,
Save me from its guilt and power!

Suddenly little Doris, who had been looking down with wondering baby solemnity on the strange scene, leaned forward and pointed to the bed.

"Pitty mamma dawn as'eep!" she said, softly; and with a groan Tennelly sank with her to his knees beside the bed. Courtland, kneeling a little way off, spoke out once more:

"Lord Jesus, the Saviour of the world, we leave her with Thy tender mercy!"

As if a visible sign of assent had been asked, the setting sun suddenly dropped lower, touching into blazing glory the golden cross on the church, and threw its reflection upon the wall at the head of the bed just over the white face of the dead.

The baby saw and pointed once again. "Pitty! Pitty! Papa, see!"

The sorrowing father lifted his eyes to the golden symbol of salvation, and Courtland, standing at the foot of the bed, said, softly:

"I am the resurrection, and the life; he that believeth in me, though he were dead, yet shall he live."